Also available from Charish Reid

Hearts on Hold
Mickey Chambers Shakes It Up

T0014786

THE WRITE ESCAPE

CHARISH REID

carina
press

carina press®

Recycling programs for this product may not exist in your area.

ISBN-13: 978-1-335-14689-2

The Write Escape

First published in 2019. This edition published in 2024.

Carina Press
22 Adelaide St. West, 41st Floor
Toronto, Ontario M5H 4E3, Canada
www.CarinaPress.com

Printed in U.S.A.

To the Black girls who vow to get away,
to find themselves in the great
wide world...keep plotting.

Chapter One

BOOM!

A nearby explosion sent a tremor beneath Augusta's feet, causing her to stumble on the sidewalk. She was uncomfortably close to her story. Perhaps it would have been smarter to follow the more skittish journalists back to the press hotel. There, she could sit at the bar and piece together the Sidi Bouzid story through the passionate Twitter accounts of young activists. But something big would happen in Tunisia that winter, something that could change the Middle East forever. Augusta ignored how her hands shook and pushed onward as an anxious crowd swelled around her. When her phone vibrated against her breast, she fumbled for it in a vest pocket.

Bryon. She sighed before answering.

Antonia bit down on her ink pen and stared at the screen. She was disconnected from the words she typed. "But *does* she really want to talk to him?"

"Talk to who?" asked the voice in her ear. "What are you talking about?

Antonia jumped in her seat, forgetting she was still

on the phone with her mother. Another mom phone call during work hours. Luckily things were moving slowly at Wild Hare Publishing. So slowly, that she was arrogant enough to break out her own novel and talk to her meddling mother at the same time. "Nothing, Mom." Her hands fell away from her keyboard as she sank against her chair. Antonia closed her eyes. "What were you saying?"

"I'm just telling you the truth, baby." Whenever Diane Harper started any sentence with *I'm just telling you the truth*, it usually ended with something she was proud to be honest about. And Diane's truth usually hurt Antonia's feelings. "Did you ever think this whole affair is running a little too fast?"

The pit in Antonia's stomach sank lower as her mother continued. The "affair" Diane referred to was Antonia's wedding. An event happening in four days. Her mother loved to dabble in dramatic flair and her poor timing didn't make a wit of difference. Antonia slumped deeper into her office chair and stared at the floor. "Mama, what are you talking about?"

Diane let out a tired sigh. "You've been dating this boy for less than a year, Antonia. What do you really know about him?"

"His name is Derek; you've met him several times," Antonia said. "And we've been dating for a little over a year. I mean, you married Charlie after he changed your tire." It was a low blow, but her mother always took her there. When Diane Harper sent a flaming arrow into the battlefield, Antonia returned with several cannons.

"Tuh! Things are different when you're my age, Toni. After your daddy died, I didn't know if I'd ever get married again. And girl, I knew Charlie from back in the day."

Antonia shook her head. She didn't want to delve into the particulars of how her mother, who was in her sixties, "got her groove back." She and her sister, Octavia, lost their father when Antonia was twelve-years-old. When their mother announced her hurried courthouse nuptials, they were adults who were shocked, but ultimately supportive. Charlie was an easygoing stepdad who stayed out of the way when Diane went on a warpath with either daughter. Even during her phone call, Antonia pictured Charlie somewhere in the background quietly reading the morning paper. "Your problem with Derek is…what? Why don't you like him?"

"Well if you want the honest answer, I'll just say this: I don't like how you act when you're with him. When you brought his bougie-ass down here, you worried over him like he was the King of Saudi Arabia."

Antonia straightened in her chair. Her mother was opening the full armory for this argument. "Now wait a minute—"

"—I saw you fix that boy a plate," Diane continued. "Now I didn't teach you girls to fix *any* man's plate like some sad housewife."

"I fixed him a plate to make him comfortable, Mom. It's called being nice."

"Was he *that* uncomfortable in my home? Was Florida too country for his delicate self?"

"Mom, we're from Chicago. Anyone would be wary of going to the Panhandle. I don't even know why *you* live there."

Her mother brushed off her comment and delivered the final blow. "The point is I don't like the little stuck-up brat who thinks he's too good for your family. He looks down his nose at me like I didn't break my back raising two successful daughters. I didn't raise you and Octavia to take any wooden nickels, and honey, you're about to marry one."

Antonia held her tongue and her breath. If she said exactly what was on her mind, the damage would be irreparable. But then every life-altering decision she made came with unsolicited advice from Diane. Whether it was jobs, boyfriends, or haircuts, her mother made certain to throw her two cents into any situation. For some reason, Diane's lectures only made Antonia anxious. Her sister, more self-possessed than she, usually shrugged these arguments off and continued doing what she pleased. Sensitive Antonia did her best to hold her own against Overbearing Diane. Nevertheless, she gripped her editing pen so tightly, her brown knuckles turned white. After a long beat and a deep breath, Antonia started again. "Mother, our wedding is in four days. Will you be here...or not?"

"I'm trying to tell you *not* to have the wedding, Toni. Aren't you listening to me?"

Antonia rubbed the space between her eyes, a stress headache was approaching. "You're being unreasonable and you know it," she said in a low voice. "Derek and I are happy together. Sure, he's a little bougie or whatever, but that's because he grew up with money. You can't hold wealth against him. He's been nothing but nice to you and you're just finding any little thing to criticize him for."

Diane heaved another sigh. "Toni, can we talk about this later? Charlie and I are already late for dinner."

Shoving Antonia off the phone with a flimsy excuse? Classic Diane Harper move. "I'll call you tonight."

Antonia rolled her eyes upward, catching a glimpse of her friend and fellow editor, Eddie, standing in her doorway. He made a cautious gesture and Antonia waved him inside. As soon as he closed the door behind him, Antonia returned to her mother. "I can't talk tonight, Mom. Derek and I are meeting with the wedding planner and then we're having dinner with his parents."

She hoped her sneaky maneuver would pressure her mother into making a decision on the phone. Instead, Diane took the opportunity to start on Derek's parents. "Oh! Where is the judge and his siddity wife taking y'all tonight?"

"I don't know," Antonia said as she tapped her pen on her desk in irritation. Eddie glanced down at her nervous hand and arched a brow.

"I can come back," he whispered.

Antonia shot him a glare and shook her head.

"Well, you let his mother cut his steak, baby."

"Mom, don't you kick me off the phone without an answer. Are you and Charles coming or not? Because this wedding is definitely happening." Eddie appeared uncomfortable, like he'd much rather be anywhere than Antonia's office. She couldn't blame him. Antonia didn't want to argue with her mother either.

Diane paused, for effect, before saying: "If you're really going to do this, I should be there…" Antonia released the breath she held and pumped her fist in the air. "…to talk you out of it in person."

It was still a small victory. "Please book your tickets for god's sake. I'll add you and Charles to the block of hotel rooms we've reserved."

"Fine, baby…but we really do need to go."

"I love you, Mom."

"Love you too, baby."

She hung up and she rested her forehead against the cool surface of her desk. No matter how heated their arguments got, they always managed to end them on a civil note. The war wasn't over, but this battle went in her favor.

"Mom issues?" Eddie asked.

Antonia's mouth curled slightly as she exhaled a mirthless laugh. "She's the only one who can get under my skin."

"Today's disagreement?"

"She hates Derek."

The pause, followed by a nervous throat clearing, made Antonia lift her head. Eddie's gaze had shifted to the wall hanging behind her head.

"Ed?"

"Mmh?"

"Is there something you'd like to say?" she asked, propping her chin on her knuckles.

"Megan and I will certainly be at your wedding," he said. "You don't have to worry about that."

Antonia shook off her uneasiness as she swept a loose curl behind her ear. "I know you didn't come in here to talk wedding plans," she said, taking the conversation to safer grounds. Since their stressful days in graduate school, Antonia could always pick up on Eddie's pensive expressions. "What's going on, Ed?"

He ran his slender fingers over his sandy beard and sighed. Eddie leaned forward and lowered his voice. "I've been hearing a lot of stuff about our finances,

Toni. Like we might not have enough to last the year. People are talking about layoffs."

She frowned. "I don't know about all of that, Ed. I mean, we still have Peterson's book release. From what I was able to read, I think it's got a *DaVinci Code* vibe that readers will enjoy. Plus, acquisitions was lucky enough to snatch him from Sixpence Publishing after his debut mystery. William Peterson is the ticket."

"I heard he wants to pull his book," Eddie said. "It's been six months and we haven't received a finalized proof from him. Antonia, he's getting cold feet about sending it to print."

She shook her head, wanting to dismiss her friend's gossip. "Richard is working on his manuscript and he hasn't said anything that would worry me. As far as I know, Peterson contacts Richard often enough." Antonia was thinking out loud, trying to make sense of what she hoped was ridiculous. But Eddie wasn't a dummy and if he felt like something was off, something was probably off. "He already signed the contract for *Hallowed Ground* and two follow-ups. I'm sure legal would advise him against breaking contract."

Eddie shook his head. "Yeah, but we may not have the money to back up legal. I think Peterson knows what kind of slump the company is in."

Antonia sat for a moment to take in Eddie's theory. Wild Hare employees had doubted Richard's judgement when he signed his own nephew, Greg Dobbs, for a sci-fi thriller set on Mars. Editing the novel had been a struggle that left her anxious and exhausted. Each time she'd emailed Greg with new edits, Antonia had girded her loins for a fresh wave of disappointing work.

"Come on, Toni, think about the last batch of titles

we released," Eddie continued. "They had a shit reception and now they're idling at the bottom of Amazon."

Eddie was right: reception was still shit. Plus, the cost to market *Starman* had been excessive, surpassing the normal budget for a boutique operation like Wild Hare Publishing. Greg Dobbs hadn't even had an author's blog or a social media following when they first signed him. He'd also insisted the book be called *Starman* despite Antonia's repeated warnings that the title sounded too much like a David Bowie interstellar romp.

She had the sneaking suspicion Richard was keeping her out of the loop when it came to these important decisions. Several months ago, he gushed over Antonia's "untapped potential" for leadership and promised to mentor her. But that was after she slaved over his nephew's project and before he decided to keep Peterson's *Hallowed Ground* series for himself. Antonia sat back in her chair and stared at her own incomplete manuscript, all two chapters shining bright on her desktop. Since her projects had decreased noticeably, she had been able to turn her attention back to those two chapters. But instead of pushing the plot forward, Antonia obsessed over piecemeal edits here and there. She'd change her protagonist's name six times before forcing herself to move on to something equally trivial.

"What else have you heard?" she asked wearily.

"Brenda told me that she's fielding a lot of skittish phone calls from the board. They've had about four conference calls in the last month," Eddie said. "She claims he's fending off accusations regarding the company's budgets."

Antonia was nervous. Brenda, Richard's secretary, was like Eddie. She kept her head down, worked hard, and didn't participate in idle gossip. If she was concerned about Richard's behavior, they should all be concerned. If Richard was grooming her for a leadership role, Antonia should have been privy to those conference calls. She wondered how she had managed not to keep her ear to the ground like Eddie. What else had she missed, while planning her wedding, these past months? "Do you think they're looking for a way to fire him?" Antonia asked in a hushed voice.

Eddie shrugged. "That, or maybe they shut down operations."

Layoffs.

Antonia still had a wedding to plan and pay for. The list of expenses slithered around her like a python, threatening to strangle her. Catering, the DJ, a reception at Shedd Aquarium, the rings, her dress... Most of the things on her list were not her idea, but Derek's mother's. While Antonia did insist on having the wedding at Shedd Aquarium, it now seemed like an expensive petty swipe at Mrs. Rogers. Vivian was aghast when Antonia suggested her favorite childhood location for the wedding reception. Derek insisted he didn't care, so long as the place was large enough to host all of his business associates and former frat buddies. She remembered how embarrassing it was to tell Vivian Rogers, "I love the ocean. It's a vast area of exploration we've forgotten." *Jesus*... She also recalled her fiancé's silence when she said it.

"You look tired," Eddie said, interrupting her thoughts.

"Do I?"

"Yeah, you look like you haven't slept for days."

Antonia checked herself in the mirror that hung in

her office. Eddie was right. Her skin, which usually shone in a healthy nutmeg brown, was dull and ashen. The dark circles under her eyes started to show beneath the hurried concealer job she did that morning. She'd make certain to do a quick touch-up when she met with Derek. She smoothed down the wild black curls that escaped her librarian bun and made a mental note to get her hair relaxed before the wedding. Vivian Rogers didn't approve of her natural hair and often noted back in her day, "black women kept their hair pressed and professional at the office."

"I don't think I like my in-laws."

"Duh," Eddie said with a grin. "No one likes their in-laws."

Her gaze flew to his before she chuckled. "No, I suppose that isn't unusual."

The tension of Wild Hare Publishing disappeared for a moment as she and her friend shared a laugh. "But you're not marrying his parents; you're marrying Derek."

Antonia gave her friend a weak smile. She'd love to believe that, but Derek's imposing father and harpy mother were a package deal. It was hard to argue with her mother about those two because Diane's observations were correct: they were the old money Talented Tenth who expected the best. Antonia often wondered if she had what it took to impress them with her common education and regular literary job. "Please, Eddie, tell me everything is going to be okay."

Eddie stood up and walked around her desk, his arms outstretched. "Toni, everything is going to be okay." She accepted his white lie as she stood and hugged him tightly.

"I'm doing the right thing?"

He returned her hug before pulling back to peer down at her. "Getting cold feet?"

Antonia shrugged. "You like Derek, right?"

Eddie gave a strained smile before replying. "Derek…is cool. We don't exactly run in the same circles, but that won't stop me from supporting you guys."

"I do love him."

"I know you do," Eddie said quickly. "You two are great together. It's just the wedding that's stressing you out. And I'm sure I haven't made it any better with my speculation and conspiracy theories."

She nodded. Wild Hare business bothered her, but this wedding, which took only four months to plan, bothered her more. She loved Derek, but something about the whole "affair" nagged at her. Antonia let her mother's words settle in her brain.

"It's just a whole bunch of extraneous shit that's coming at you," Eddie assured her. "You're due for another drinking night with me and Meg anyway. She's the wedding expert who can talk you off the ledge."

He was right. His girlfriend had supplied Antonia with boxed wine and coaxed her into relaying all of the wedding plans in excruciating detail. Megan loved all the stuff that Antonia didn't want to think about. *Why don't I want to think about the details?*

She released Eddie and glanced down at her watch. "I've got to get going," she said in a tremulous voice. "I have a meeting with Derek and the wedding planner." As she gathered up her things, her hands shook. Antonia closed her eyes and inhaled through her nose. *Get a grip, Toni.*

"Make sure you save your document," Eddie said, gesturing to her computer screen.

"Oh! Yes, thank you." She quickly saved and closed the browser.

"By the way, when are you going to let me look at that?"

Antonia shook her head as she stuffed her files in her satchel. "It's really nothing."

"If you don't share it with anyone, it won't be. You're an excellent writer, Toni. At least you were in college."

She scoffed as she flung her bag over her shoulder. "That was a long time ago, Ed."

He wasn't swayed. "The stuff you write is far better than the stuff we've been publishing. I wish you believed that."

Antonia didn't have time to think about her story. Her brain was already full of things that she couldn't keep track of. One day, the storm in a teacup that was her life would settle long enough for her to breathe. *If* that day came, then she would give the manuscript more attention. Until then, she'd keep staring at the same miserable two chapters that had remained unchanged since Derek proposed to her. *Later. I'll work on it later.*

Chapter Two

Aiden was late for his last class of the semester and tried not to look like he was speed walking the crowded hallways to get to his office. He had only ten minutes to get his teaching materials straight before he performed for the department chair. His mentor and the resident Medieval scholar, Robert Lewison, thought the last day of classes was an appropriate time to observe Aiden's American Literature class. Of course, it wasn't, but he wasn't going to argue with the old man about bad timing. It wasn't Robert's fault that Aiden didn't go to bed until 4 a.m. after completing rushed edits on a revise and resubmit journal article. Nor was it Robert's fault that the traffic between Claddagh and the National University of Ireland, Galway was heavy with the early onslaught of tourists.

As he mentally catalogued the key points of his last lecture on *Invisible Man*'s race issues and the review of the final take-home exam, Aiden mistook the young woman who stood at his office door for a student. "I can't do office hours right now," he said.

When the woman turned around, he froze. With a glossy red smirk on her face, she cocked her head to the side. "Not even for an old colleague?" she asked.

Pulling an all-nighter and sitting in terrible traffic were playful irritations compared to the kick in the balls of seeing his ex-girlfriend, Lisa Brennan, outside his office. Her empty office was across the hall. Was she here to take a stroll down memory lane? "Lisa," he breathed. Anxiety and anger coursed through his body as he fished his keys out of his pocket to unlock his door. "What are you doing here?"

When he opened his door, he fully expected her to stay on her side of the threshold, but she followed and took a seat in one of his chairs. "I'm visiting my Irish roots. Paris is lovely, but I do miss home."

Aiden tried not to look at her as he moved around his desk. He needed a safe barrier between them so he could keep his shit together. He wasn't the one who bailed on the university and a relationship for sunnier pastures. After accusing him of not taking his career seriously and going on the job market in secret, Aiden had an entire year to get over her. And when he felt he was safely over the Lisa Hump, she came blowing back into town glowing with Sorbonne prestige.

From the look of her, she was still the stiff professional who dumped him during an end of the year faculty banquet. She still wore her famous all-black skirt suit and her black bobbed haircut stayed in place, just like the rest of her. When they first met, he enjoyed how put-together she was. So sure and calculating in her mannerisms and speech. Lisa was the human manifestation of everything in its right place. Her stiffness was something he got used to over their two-year relationship. Now, as they faced each other in his office, she was foreign to him. She was more severe than ever. "It's nice to know that humble old Galway still has a soft spot in your heart," he muttered while gathering his textbook and handouts for the students.

Lisa sighed. "I didn't come here to make waves, Aiden."

He stopped and looked at her. "Then why are you here?"

"We've got the Western Ireland Humanities Conference in a week and I'm staying with friends. You're still presenting, right?"

Aiden's heart sank. He didn't have time to think about the conference. The call for papers was a lifetime ago, back when he promised Lisa that he would try to pick up the pace on his scholarship. Now that he was struggling with his tenure checklist, a circlewank event was just another distraction from his writing. "Yes, I'll be there."

Lisa leaned forward in her seat, her fingers steepled at her pointed chin. Condescension threaded her voice as she chose her words carefully. "I simply wanted to meet with you with the hope that things were cordial between us."

Aiden checked his watch. Six minutes until class. "I can be cordial," he said through gritted teeth.

"It's important that we not let our past relationship shadow the important work we're to present to the university," she said in a voice just as haughty as the Victorian literature she obsessed over. Since leaving Ireland, Lisa had buried her Dubliner accent in favor of something more continental.

The corner of his lips curled. "You won't have to worry about that, Dr. Brennan," he said mocking her professionalism.

Lisa sat back and clapped her hands. "Wonderful. I'm glad we could get that unpleasantness out of the way."

Collecting everything he needed for his class, Aiden stood up straight, slinging his bag over his chest. "Anything else you need?" he asked, smoothing down his neck tie. "I've got to get to class."

She quickly stood. "I wanted to say sorry."

Aiden swallowed and dropped his gaze to the floor. He didn't have time to deal with this either. "Lisa…"

"I should have apologized for the way I left things last year. I should have done it sooner," she said in a hurried voice. "All of the things I told you about yourself were true. But I realize that I didn't speak to you in a tactful way. We were just growing apart and I don't know if either one of us knew how to address it. So I decided to look for another job without telling you."

He rolled his eyes to the ceiling of his small office, wanting to be anywhere else but there in front of his ex-girlfriend. A year ago, she'd told him his laziness was holding her back. They may have been hired together, but she wasn't going to toil her life away with him. "You don't have to do this," he said.

"I do," she said. A pleading expression in her eyes, made Aiden take pause. "When we stopped talking about our future, I needed to leave Galway and see what I could accomplish. Deep down, I wanted you to come with me, wherever we might end up, but I never saw the drive in you or your work. I felt like you were content drifting around here and wasting your potential. I'm sure you're coming up on tenure review, right?"

"Next year."

Lisa's brows raised. "How's it going?"

"Not well," he admitted. "I frittered away the last feckin' year getting over you."

She winced. "I'm sorry."

Aiden shook his head. "No, no, don't apologize for that. You're not responsible for what I muck up. I'm just trying…" He trailed off and his shoulders slumped. "I've got a lot of things to publish. A journal made me change nearly everything in an article I sent them, so I stayed up all last night to make that deadline. I've got to get a book proposal ready by the end of the summer and I almost forgot about the conference."

She nodded. "So you're doing the work."

"I am. It's just hard," he said. "But look, I appreciate your apology." He was mature enough to know that adults came together and talked these awkward moments out. Anger slowly flowed from his body as he gazed at her. She was the same Lisa who he thought he loved, but he now felt nothing for her. When he had helped move her things out of his Claddagh house, he'd bitten down his anger while they worked in silence. Later that evening, when all traces of her had been wiped away, he remembered drinking away his pain in a local pub. He barely made it home afterward, but when he woke up the following morning in an empty bed, loneliness plagued him for several months.

The woman who stood in his office made his heart pound. Not out of arousal or love, but as a reminder of his past mistakes. In his desperation to build a relationship that wasn't there, he'd let the rest of his life slide into a comfortable numbness. He didn't challenge himself, push himself, or hold himself accountable. Aiden was now fearful of the woman who reminded him of the time he skated through his tenure-track job on charm.

Lisa Brennan was the ant and he was the grasshopper. Autumn was coming and if he didn't get his shit together, Aiden was in for a world of trouble.

"You can do it," she said in a sincere voice, no malice or sarcasm in her expression. "You just have to have a plan. I know that's not your nature, but you're capable."

"Thanks, I needed to hear that." He glanced at his watch again.

"I won't keep you," Lisa said moving toward his door. "I'll see you at the conference."

"You will," Aiden said as she left his office. He gave a feeble wave and listened to the sturdy clack of her heels travel down the hallway. The tension of their conversation forced him to lean against his desk and close his eyes. She didn't say anything vague like 'see you later' or 'do you want to grab a drink?' and he was glad of that. While he no longer wished her ill-will, Aiden didn't want to pretend to be her friend. As far as he was concerned, their conversation, no matter how late it was, made for the closure he needed.

He took a long slow breath through his nose and exhaled from his mouth before standing and exiting his office. For the next hour and a half, teaching had to be his priority. Getting his students prepared for a final exam and out the door with enough confidence wouldn't have been a challenge last year. Not while his only job was being a fun literature professor who reveled in making his students laugh and didn't slave over lesson prep. Now that he was hard-nosed Dr. Aiden Byrnes, pushing the importance of Walt Whitman, he felt the pressure mounting in his aching shoulders. They were often tense when he taught, when he attended departmental meetings, even when he lay in bed at night. Regardless of how productive he was, the school year was killing him. *One way or another, this goddamn semester needs to end.* If he had the summer to decompress from the arduous semester, Aiden might summon the strength to tackle another year of teaching.

Chapter Three

Derek sat across from Antonia on the train, thoroughly engrossed in the blue light of his iPhone screen. The soft glow shined against his handsome face, making his gray eyes dull and vacant. After leaving the aquarium, a quiet distance had grown between the two. Truth be told, he'd been distant throughout the entire walking tour of the facilities. He'd nodded occasionally, murmured how lovely the space was, but ultimately returned to his phone. The incessant buzzing had embarrassed Antonia. While Derek was distracted, she was nailing down plans with their wedding planner.

Now, as they sat opposite from one another on the "L," Derek remained silent about what was supposed to be the happiest day of their lives. "Derek?"

"Yes, babe?"

"Is everything okay?"

"Mm-hmm."

His eyes never left his phone. "Where are you right now?"

"Mm?"

"Derek," Antonia said louder.

His head snapped up. "Yeah?"

Antonia's face warmed with embarrassment. "I'm trying to talk to you."

Derek flashed her the smile that attracted her a year ago in a sports bar. His dimples creased at both cheeks, extinguishing her flare of anger. It was difficult to stay frustrated at him when he gave her that smile. She suspected he knew that. "And I'm listening, Toni." He put on a show of slipping his phone in his suit jacket and holding up his empty hands. "See? It's gone."

"Who have you been texting all evening?"

His smile was stuck in place. "Kevin sent me some files for a new account and I wanted to look them over."

Antonia nodded. Her frustration eventually faded, but her loneliness remained. She needed this train to go faster. The small window of time she had alone with him, before dinner, made her desire something more meaningful. She missed being intimate with him. Antonia flashed him her own smile. "We've got about an hour before we see your folks."

"Yep," he said checking his large gold-faced watch. "That gives me enough time to shower and change."

Antonia frowned. That wasn't what she had in mind. *What would Augusta do?* It was the question she asked whenever she found herself in a pickle. Augusta was the intrepid young heroine of her novel, who always kept her shit together. Augusta would know why she hadn't slept with *her* boyfriend in a month. *Oh lord, has it been a month?* Antonia quickly did the math in her head. *You don't slow-down in sex a month before your wedding, do you?* "I was thinking we could make a little time for us," she blurted out just as the train slowed to a stop.

Derek gathered his briefcase and stood, offering her his hand. "What was that?"

"Some time for us," she said again in a whisper. She could have sworn that his body tensed as they stepped off the train.

"Oh, babe, we'll see," he said. "I need to get ready for Mom and Dad."

Antonia squeezed his hand. "I'm not asking for a long passionate night," she said forcing a chuckle. "You know, a quickie or something?"

"Is something wrong?" he asked, guiding her from the platform. She walked fast to keep up with his long stride. Derek was nearly a foot taller than her and much more active. Every time she walked with him, it was like she was chasing him to stay underfoot. The symbolism didn't escape her notice. Augusta would not chase her boyfriend down Roosevelt St. Her gutsy heroine wouldn't go straight from work in her rumpled business attire to meet with her boyfriend's parents at an incredibly fancy restaurant. Antonia never got the chance to touch up her makeup or smooth out her curls. She was running; trotting behind Derek as he led them back to his apartment. Never mind Augusta, if Antonia's mother were watching this scene, she'd say: "I told you so."

"I don't know."

Derek's home was a stylish and modern two-bedroom apartment on the fourteenth floor of a high-rise. Every time Antonia walked across the threshold, an uneasiness settled in her stomach.

She would have to live here.

Not that she didn't love the clean Scandinavian decor or its location on the South Loop; not too far from everything that was popular in Chicago. If she wanted to, she could walk only five minutes to Grant Park from

Derek's apartment. She enjoyed shuffling around in her socks on his wooden floors and running her hand over the exposed brick walls. His furniture was lovely and modern, arranged with extreme care. Everything was perfect in Derek's apartment. But he assumed that when they got married, she would just move here. The apartment, after all, was closer to both of their jobs...

She wondered what, in her eclectic apartment, she could make fit into Derek's orderly life. Would she bring her favorite old reading chair, the one with the sunken cushion and worn spots on the arms? Where would she put all of her books? Derek didn't exactly have the bookshelf space for her immense library. As Derek set his briefcase on the same vestibule bench, she was reminded of the phrase: *everything in its right place*. Antonia stepped out of her high heels and let the cool wood floor relax her aching feet. *My god, I have to say something.*

"Derek, we need to talk."

He had already disappeared around the corner and into the master bedroom, leaving her in the living room. "What's that?" he called out.

She waited a moment, thinking of what to say, before following his trail. When she found him, he was already in his bedroom undressing. He was down to his boxer briefs. Antonia inhaled sharply and made the effort to engage him in a conversation. His body was always a distraction. Derek's skin shone like amber in the low light of his bedroom. He was what her mother would call "high-yella," a term Antonia disliked. It smacked of an older time in her mother's life. But Derek's golden skin made him a black Adonis. The constant trips to the gym also kept his tall frame lean and fit. Dark brown hair peppered his bare chest, trailing down to his waistband.

Her throat went dry.

Words that were ready to tumble forth, were now stuck in her mouth. Antonia shook her head. "I just wanted…"

"Hold that thought, babe," Derek said sliding his black briefs down. He kicked them off his feet and stood legs astride, pleased with himself. Antonia's mouth snapped shut. She noted how his stride to the bathroom was a confident one. Even while he was entirely nude, he walked taller than most. She was a wilted plant compared to his lion-like display. "Let me get some hot water on me," he said from the bathroom. The shower's spray blasted the silence of the apartment, effectively drowning her out.

Antonia resigned to flopping herself against his plush California king bed. As her head hit the goose-down pillows, she closed her eyes and used the moment to rest her weary body. The last thing that she wanted to do was leave the haven of Derek's bed. The high thread-count alone was enough to "Netflix and chill" the night away. But his parents were still on her mind. Antonia probably looked as tired as she felt. Had she planned accordingly, she could have brought a change of clothes and her makeup bag to the office. Derek couldn't account for these things like she did. When they first started dating, she'd managed his calendar like it was hers. Antonia had reminded him to attend company sponsored events and parties, arranged thoughtful gifts for the hosts, and always came prepared with something clever to say about finance or sports. The third had been especially difficult because she cared nothing for either subject. But wherever they went, Antonia made certain that they appeared perfect and orderly. *Everything in its right place.*

Buzz.

Antonia's eyes popped open. She shifted her head to the side and searched for the vibration that startled her. The blue flash of Derek's phone lit his crumpled jacket that he usually took care to drape over a chair. The phone continued to vibrate against the bed, reminding Antonia of her frustration with him. This damned device took his focus away from her. Antonia stared at the blue light that taunted her. *Should I?*

No. That's an invasion of his privacy.

There wasn't anything for her to check on anyway. He already told her he was concerned about work. He usually grew more tense when he was assigned a new project. Derek kept saying he was closer to making partner at the firm and a large part of that had to do with their wedding. Apparently his bosses needed to see some stability from him before making that final step. He was ecstatic when Antonia said yes. She thought they were sharing the same feelings of happiness, and Derek assured her that he was excited about marriage, but he had to add the comment about his career. She'd chosen to ignore her initial deflated feelings, instead focusing on their future.

But today, of all days, he was even more distant than usual. Regardless of the stress from his job, he seemed more muted. When the phone's buzzing stopped, Antonia forcefully turned her head away to face the ceiling. *Of all days.* Derek was still showering. Antonia figured that she had plenty of time to sneak her hand in his jacket, slide the home-screen, and take a peek.

Sneak, slide, and peek. *Nothing to it.* Antonia sat up on her elbows and stared at his jacket. She didn't know what she expected to find. She certainly didn't know what she would do if she found something suspicious. *What would Augusta do?*

"Fuck it," she muttered, reaching for his phone. Before she knew it, his sleek iPhone was in her hand. The weight of it, and her actions, sat solidly in her palm as she quickly took her next step. Derek had no password, which made her strangely relieved. It wasn't a good idea for his general security, but perhaps it meant that he wasn't hiding something.

The alert on his home-screen read: Missed Call.

She slid the screen, revealing the notification. Naomi.

Antonia's lips went numb. She licked them to make sure they were still attached to her face as her thumb paused above the screen. *Who...* She needed to dig deeper. Her mind was a flurry of beautiful models with hourglass figures and hair down to there. The name, Naomi, played on repeat in Antonia's brain while she searched the call-log. An involuntary groan escaped her parched throat. The number of calls between the two were astounding. Most of them were missed, but they were plentiful. Before she could stop and think, Antonia pressed the text icon.

Naomi: I miss you

Derek: I miss being between your thighs

Naomi: When will you be alone?

Derek: N a min

Naomi: Is she still there?

There were more text messages, but Antonia's vision blurred with unshed tears. She was terrified to blink because it would break the dam. Her hands trembled as she scrolled onward. And there was so much to scroll through. The most damning messages had been sent while Antonia wandered through the tour behind the wedding planner. She remembered passing through the underwater exhibit where friendly gray seals smiled through the glass. Antonia had turned to point them out to Derek, who had been focused on his phone. The blue shimmer of the tank had competed with the blue light of his screen, and failed. He'd glanced over at the gliding giants and nodded. *This was what he was typing? This is who he was talking to?*

Antonia's face grew warm and she became dizzy. She choked back a sob and buried the phone facedown into Derek's duvet. She couldn't bear to see anymore. *What now?* Her mind raced. She was frozen, stuck in a moment of indecision. Dealing with this horrific discovery was infinitely harder than sneak, slide and peek. She did the deed and found out the worst. Antonia searched her memory for moments that could have revealed truth and turned up nothing. She'd been had. Derek successfully pulled the wool over her eyes while she planned their wedding. *When had this started?*

Antonia turned the phone over and continued scrolling. *Too many text messages!* Her face contorted as she scrolled past Derek making plans with Naomi; her sending him hearts and xoxo's. Finally, she stopped at an image. Her own hand clapped over her mouth before she could let out a scream.

Oh god, no. May 10th, 11:23 p.m.

Nearly a month ago, a text was sent from Derek.

A crude photo of his dick was posed in the soft lights of his bedroom. From where she was sitting, Antonia glanced at her reflection in the mirror that hung in front of his bed. She glanced back at the photo. It was indeed his dick. His narrow hips were thrust forward so that Naomi couldn't miss the subject of his amateur photography. Behind him was the same bedside table and lamp that Antonia currently sat next to. She'd bought the lamp from Pottery Barn to impress him.

The stream of the shower stopped; the curtain rustled as Derek stepped out. Antonia's gaze flew to the now foggy bathroom. She had to leave. Her throat was tight with dread. His normally spacious bedroom with its fancy bachelor trappings quickly became a tomb.

What would Augusta do?

Antonia's mind went blank from the fright and fury that bubbled within her.

"What did you want to talk about, babe?" Derek asked, wrapping a plush white towel around his waist.

Antonia looked up, phone still in hand, and stared at him. She was too shocked to speak. Derek gazed back at her, his expression was unreadable as he glanced from her to his phone.

"What…" Her voice was strangled and foreign to her own ears. "…what have you done, Derek?"

He heaved a tired sigh and hung his head. "Okay, so what do you want to do?"

Antonia frowned as she wiped tears from her face. "What?"

Derek raised his gaze to hers, his brow arched. "I'm saying, what do you want to do, Toni?" He tightened the towel at his waist and leaned against the door-frame, staring her down with an expression that Antonia didn't recognize. Complete apathy? "Do you want to talk about how you feel and then have dinner or do you want to have dinner and talk about it when we're home?"

Her mouth fell open. "You still expect us to go to dinner?"

"Mom made the reservations last week."

His indifference was bewildering. "You're cheating on me, Derek. We're getting married in *four days* and you're talking about dinner? What is wrong with you?" Her voice grew shrill. "Who is Naomi? How long has this been going on?"

Derek straightened up and sauntered to where she stood. In an eerily calm manner, he took her by the shoulders and peered down at her. Antonia was horrified by the ease he took in approaching her. With his thumbs, he lightly kneaded the muscles of her arms, pulling her close to his damp body. "Babe, you don't have to worry about her. That's over."

Antonia's blouse was getting wet against his chest. Her hands were clenched in fists at either side of her body, as she shook violently. She was terrified of what she might do in that moment. A quiet rage boiled in her chest, threatening to spill out and destroy something or someone. "Get. Your. Hands. Off of me," she said through clenched teeth.

Derek stepped back slightly, holding his hands up. "Okay, so you want to talk now. Naomi was a temp who used to work at the office. She came on to me. The whole thing was just physical, just meaningless sex. I don't love her at all. In fact," he added, "I was trying

to break it off with her. I told her that I was really serious about you. You're going to be my wife, after all."

As Antonia stood and listened to Derek list every
excuse in the book, her mind returned to her phone call
with her mother. *Don't take any wooden nickels.* Her
face finally crumpled into a sob, hot tears spilled down
her cheeks as she stared at the man she loved. In the
blink of an eye, her world had taken a hard left turn.

"Toni, if you start crying, your face is going to get
all puffy," he said reaching out to wipe her face.

She slapped his hand away and threw his phone on
the bed. "Don't," she snapped. "Don't do any of that
slimy shit you do with your clients. You're not going
to talk your way out of this and I'm not going to have
dinner with your horrible parents. The wedding is off,
Derek."

His brow furrowed slightly. "Okay, we don't have to
have dinner tonight, but we're not calling off the wedding." His tone was incredulous as though he was rea-
soning with a toddler. "Toni, we have a hundred guests
coming from all over the country. Do you know how
much money my parents have spent on this? Don't be
crazy."

Crazy?

If she didn't get out of his apartment, Antonia was
going to show him what crazy *really* looked like. "Who
are you?"

He heaved another sigh. "I'm a man who's going to
make mistakes. I'm sorry. It won't happen again." His
words were like a tired recitation of something he'd
memorized.

Antonia couldn't listen to it any longer. "I'm leaving," she murmured as she backed out of the room. "The fucking wedding is definitely off."

He followed her, giving half-hearted attempts to apologize, but the growing buzz in her head drowned out most of his words. As she gathered her bag and jacket, she marched to the vestibule to find her shoes. Derek was still droning on, but Antonia only caught snippets like "needs" and "pressure to be the best" and "I don't think you understand." As her hand rested on the doorknob, she turned to look at him once more.

"Don't go, Toni," he said. There was a small measure of shame on his face, but not nearly enough. "Babe, what would I do without you?"

Antonia opened her mouth to say something, but clamped it shut.

"Hell," he continued. "What would you do without *me*? You don't want to waste away at that pitiful publishing place, in your thirties, alone with your mountain of books, do you?"

The final blow of his callous words made her flinch. "I think I'll manage somehow."

In the hallway of the fourteenth floor, she fought the urge to pass out. Every step in her high heels was as wobbly as a newborn giraffe. She quickly stumbled toward the elevator, casting a glance over her shoulder. In her mind she prayed, to whoever was listening, for Derek not to follow her. She couldn't bear to look him in the face without slapping that beautiful smile. Images of his X-rated text message and his hurtful words mingled with those of their past. A walk in Grant Park, him surprising her at work, him going down on one knee. She kept seeing his dick and that lamp. She pressed the

Down button at the elevator. The orange light slowly ticked from the lobby.

"Goddammit," Antonia yelled, mashing the button. In the time the elevator would reach her, she was sure she would faint or Derek would try to reason with her. Neither were an option. Slapping the button wouldn't make the elevator pulley go any faster, but she couldn't think of anything else to do.

A door opened down the hallway. She turned to see Derek's face poking from his door. "Toni, just come back and we'll talk about it as long as you want."

"Fuck you!" she shouted. The goddamn numbers rolled onward in an agonizingly slow pace.

"What else do you want me to do?" He edged closer to the threshold, revealing his damp torso. She hoped his wealthy neighbors were getting an eyeful.

12… 13…

"You don't have to do anything else," Antonia called out in a shaky voice. She kept her eyes planted on the numbers. 14. When the doors slid back, she squeezed herself past them as fast as she could. "Cheating on me is good enough, thank you!"

"Toni…" That was the last thing she heard him say before the elevator doors slowly closed. Antonia decided that was a perfect opportunity to fall against the wall and sob. She wept for fourteen floors. Her phone vibrated in her bag, accompanied by a personalized jingle she'd set for Derek's calls. She ignored it and continued to weep. Antonia couldn't pick which part to be most devastated about. There were the lies, the wedding she needed to call off, and the intimate messages that she read. *I miss being between your thighs.*

As the elevator descended to the third, then second

floor, Antonia wiped her face on her jacket. The rest of the day's makeup was rubbed away to reveal her red and puffy face. She caught herself in the shining reflection of the elevator wall and fought the urge to release another sob. She looked beat up. Her mascara smudged her under eye, her already full lips were swollen. Before hitting the lobby, she tried wiping her eyes again, desperate to move the stubborn black rings. She couldn't face Derek's doorman looking like a complete mess.

The doors slid open and she hesitated to leave the elevator. She could go back upstairs. She could talk to him. There could have been a misunderstanding. Maybe she misunderstood everything. Derek had a way of explaining things, maybe this was another thing he could explain away. *Am I overreacting?*

The doors tried to close during her inner debate. She waved her arm through the opening, sliding them back. *What would Augusta do?* Her ball-busting heroine, Augusta Sinclair, would have slapped, no, punched, Derek in the face. Antonia had certainly missed that opportunity. But one thing Augusta would never do is return to the scene of the crime. She'd never return to let a man talk his way out of a dick pic. Antonia set her jaw and straightened herself up. Hitching her satchel on her slumped shoulder, she pushed her way forward.

There was no going back.

Chapter Four

"People were bound to have mixed feelings regarding the protagonist of Invisible Man," Aiden said, turning to the next slide. "And sure, when your main character's been through the wringer and comes out the other side claiming that he still has possibilities, a segment of your audience is going to call you a liar."

He tried not to look at Robert, who was sitting in the back of his darkened classroom, as he pressed the clicker. Instead, he focused on the students, some of which he'd lost around the fifth slide of his PowerPoint. The connections he tried to make between Ralph Ellison's novel and Irish history was lost on many of them, but Aiden continued with the hope that he could articulate ideas for his own scholarship. "But that's the beauty of hope, isn't it?" he asked those who were still awake. "It's the very foundation of an oppressed people, trapped in a system that doesn't acknowledge them. It's how you keep going when the man has his boot on your neck."

Of the students who were still alive, a hand flew up in the darkness. It was his star pupil, Abby, who always sat in the front row taking feverish notes as he spoke. "Professor Byrnes?"

"Yes?"

"Could you make a connection with Irish oppression and African American oppression?"

He nodded, pleased that she followed his line of thinking. "Yes, you could, but you'd have to be careful not to conflate the Irish experience with the systematic oppression of the black diaspora. While the parallels are fascinating, we need to remember these are two different issues." The old, fun Professor Byrnes would have stopped what he was doing, deviated from the path in an effort to make new discoveries. Hard-nosed Byrnes had to keep it moving because he only had ten minutes left before the class ended. "Good question, Abby."

She scribbled in her notebook as he returned to the PowerPoint lecture. "As I was saying, the response to Ellison's work was mixed, but I'd like to think any critic of their time could spot the parallels and jabs he took at the Transcendentalists. Emerson, Hawthorne, Melville, to name a few. These were the forefather authors of the American experience. What black writer of the 1950s wouldn't want to take those early ideas and skewer them?"

Abby's hand popped up again.

Aiden rubbed his hand over his mouth. "Yes."

"Could you make a connection between Ellison and Melville's writing styles?" she asked.

He was afraid to venture into this rabbit hole with Abby. She was a smart girl, but she was often scatterbrained with her thoughts, forcing ideas to fit where they couldn't. Aiden saw poorly connected thoughts in her papers, but he appreciated the creativity that came with those thoughts. Right now, however, he simply didn't have time. "Which Melville text are you refer-ring to?"

"*Moby Dick*, of course."

Aiden drew a deep breath. "Sure, both texts are deal-ing with an unreliable narrator's epic journey grappling with forces beyond his control..." He found himself dis-tracted by the boy next to Abby. Despite being in the front row, the young man was in a deep slumber and close to falling out of his chair. "The secondary charac-ters are basically controlling the fate of Ishmael and our invisible narrator. And yes, you could say that the reader reaction to these two texts was wildly inconsistent..."

Abby was in midscribble by the time Aiden trailed off. She looked up with questioning eyes, waiting for him to continue. "Yes?"

Aiden blinked. "Huh?"

"You said 'wildly inconsistent' and then you stopped," the girl said, reading from her paper.

"Billy, wake up," Aiden said in a sharp voice.

The boy jumped in his seat as his eyes sprang open. "What?"

Without thought, Aiden marched over to the door and flipped the lights on. "Jaysus, Mary, and Joseph, everyone wake up," he shouted. Students sat up in their seats with confused expressions. "I've paid my dues and gotten my degrees, so I don't need a review for a take-home exam. What's your excuse?"

He was met with silence as his students didn't know how to react to his sudden outburst. His perfect child, Abby, had long stopped taking notes and stared down at her desktop. Upon seeing her flushed face, Aiden sud-denly felt embarrassed. He'd broken his own teaching rule that dictated he never punish an entire class for a few bad apples. He heard the cadence of his own voice and was reminded of his father. It was a brusque tone that told him and his brothers to hop to it. Another rule broken: Never sound like Liam Byrnes, hard-ass sailor who couldn't hack it at being a father.

"Look," he said in a softer tone. "I know it's the end of the semester. We're all a little knackered, yeah? I need you to last for just ten more minutes so I can get you prepared for the final exam."

Abby met his gaze. All was forgiven.

"I'll hand out the study guide and if you have questions, just let me know in an email."

In the awkwardly quiet classroom, Aiden moved around the rows of students, handing out the carefully crafted study guide he'd created when he should have slept. Students stuffed the papers into their folders or backpacks and waited for him to dismiss them. This was not how he wanted the last class to end. He was hoping he'd get to do his traditional 'it was wonderful to be a part of your lives for the semester' speech before releasing them into the world, but today, the moment was ruined. He wanted to be done with them as much as they were done with him. Aiden regretted having an enthusiastic student like Abby think he was an ogre who didn't care about her ideas. But he was even ready to let her go if it meant getting a break.

"What exactly happened there?" Robert asked after the students left. He closed his portfolio and sat back in his chair with a ghostly smile on his face.

Aiden stood at his lectern, barely making eye contact with his mentor. "Have you ever caught yourself sounding like your father?"

Robert chuckled. "It usually doesn't happen until you've had your own children, but yes."

"I saw that jack-arse sleeping in the front row and I snapped," he admitted. "Any other day, I would have ignored it, made a joke about it, but today I just snapped."

Robert pulled himself from his seat and slowly ambled up to the front of the room. He was getting up in age, close to retirement, but Robert Lewison carried out the duties of a department chair with the mental agility of a young professor. As he adjusted his rumpled corduroy jacket, he cleared his throat. "I'll say this, your PowerPoint was a tad long for my taste," he said. "And with the lights off for that long, you can't expect the whole class to stay awake."

"But it was the last class," Aiden objected.

"That's true, but your little outburst wasn't really about the sleeping boy, was it?"

Aiden sucked in his cheeks and gripped his lectern. "I guess not." Leave it to Robert to dig at the heart of most issues concerning his young ingénue. Ever since Aiden had accepted the Assistant Professor position at the NUI Galway, Robert was there to take him under his wing and show him the ropes. It was his first grown-up job after getting his PhD at University College Cork and most of what he learned about teaching was impractical and too rigid for his personality. Lewison, an old veteran, had a different approach to pedagogy that he appreciated; he made historical literature come alive in his lectures. Aiden desperately wanted to be like him.

Robert's wife, Penelope, also took to Aiden. She would stop by his tiny flat with a lamp or a rug in an effort to spruce things up. Sometimes she'd bring over a stew or a pie to feed him. After some time, Aiden realized their affection may have stemmed from the two being a childless couple. Their son had died in a tragic car accident, leaving them bereft and empty. Aiden was a delightful distraction for the both of them. Which was fine for him as he had to grow up making most of his important decisions without a father. With Liam Byrnes nowhere to be found, Aiden clung to the elderly man with all his might. And now, while his head was swimming with worries, Aiden needed Robert to be his anchor.

"I'm guessing you saw Professor Brennan?" Robert said as he leaned against the front row desk. "You haven't spoken since…"

Aiden ran his hand over his eyes. Robert was the only faculty member who knew about his relationship with Lisa. It was one of the demands that she'd made when they started sleeping together. In hindsight, he could see why she wanted secrecy. As a young woman in academia, her reputation could have taken a downward turn. And of course, if their relationship soured, there was no need for the whole department to know about it. But as the months slid away, Aiden found himself resentful that he couldn't express his affection for her in public. Their quiet relationship at work eventually became their quiet relationship in his home, until it felt like they were only roommates. "No, this was the first time in a year," Aiden finished. "It was an amicable conversation though."

"Was it?" Robert's owlish brows furrowed in confusion. Behind his round spectacles, his expression was one of skepticism.

"Aye, it was," Aiden said. "But she reminded me that

I have so much to do before tenure review. I don't want to hit forty and still be an assistant professor, Robert."

The old man scoffed. "You're in your thirties and not on anyone else's timeline, my boy."

As much as he wanted to believe that, Aiden was thirty-eight and working without proper job security. Trying to get tenure was like being on a four-year probation. Sure, he signed the teaching contract and made good with administration, but the work was far from over. If he didn't pass this one test, he would be out on his ass and forced to look for another job. "I can get it done, right?"

"Of course you can, Aiden. I'll write a glowing recommendation letter, but you'll have to gather the materials," he laughed. "Aside from today's lesson, you're a fine teacher. You challenge your students and they seem to like it. I've looked at all your evaluations and the kids sing your praises. Now why don't *you* believe it?"

Aiden pursed his lips before answering. "Entertaining students is the easy part. I blow into class telling a few jokes and stories, but I never know if they're learning anything."

"But they are," Robert said with insistence. "And you know as well as I, entertaining is not the easy part. It takes a certain kind of charm to light up a room. I didn't see it today, but that's usually what you're known for."

"Charm?" Aiden frowned. The word struck him as vain and hollow. Charming is what his father tried to be when he came home with a half a paycheck after trawling at sea. "That's not going to keep my job."

"You're thinking about this too hard," Lewison decided. "There's a healthy balance you're unable to strike and it's making you doubt yourself. Yes, Professor Brennan is right, you must take this next step seriously. But in the process of proving yourself, you cannot *lose* yourself."

Aiden walked around the lectern and shut down his computer station. "You're right," he said in a tired voice.

"Perhaps you need rest," Lewison said, peering at him. "A young lad should have a bit of merriment every once in a while."

"Rest and merriment will come when I've completed a conference paper and book proposal."

Robert laughed. "A conference paper can be finished in a day. Go somewhere and get some rest, Aiden. Hell, go to the country like you used to. What's that place you like?"

"Tully Cross?" Aiden said as he stuffed books in his bag. "I haven't been there in a year, not since Lisa…"

"Go there and get some fresh air. Go to the water where you belong."

He straightened up and looked at his mentor. "I don't know, Robert. I don't think I have time."

"You have the entire summer to get your head on straight. The end of the spring semester is the hardest. If you don't take time to cut loose now, you're not going to be any use to the students in the fall." Robert was fully invested in this plan now. "That's right, escape before grades are due and the conference starts."

Go to the water where you belong. Try as he might, he couldn't deny the powerful lure of the water, the peace he felt when he was near it. It was why he bought his Claddagh house right on the River Corrib. He awoke, each morning, with a natural source of pleasure and serenity that the middle of Galway couldn't give him. The small village of Tully Cross, out on Renvyle Peninsula, afforded him the same peace. He'd made the trip annually since his years in the PhD program. "Maybe I could go for a week…"

Robert sprang on his sentiment. "That's right! Get out there and take your mind off the bustle of Galway."

Aiden nodded. "Yeah, maybe that will help."

"And while you're out there," Robert said as he stood. "Trim those whiskers down. I've noticed that you tend to forget shaving when you're depressed."

Aiden laughed and absently scratched the side of his bearded face. "Fine, I'll shave."

"And you'll get rest?" Robert said. "As your superior, I must insist on it."

"If it's an order from my boss, then I suppose I must."

As they exited the classroom, Robert clapped Aiden's back. "You'll see. When you get to the water, you'll find what you're looking for."

Aiden looked down at the old man and managed a smile. He didn't know what he was looking for, but he trusted Robert's judgement. If Tully Cross had the answers, he'd make the pilgrimage.

Chapter Five

Antonia woke up with cottonmouth.

As she cracked her swollen eyes against the harsh light of her living room window, she groaned from the shooting pain in her head. She shifted her stiff body against sunken couch cushions and hissed from the pain in her neck. On her coffee table sat an empty bottle of red blend wine and no wineglass. "Of course."

Most of last night's memories came back in a miserable flood: the long painful train ride back to her apartment on Devon Avenue, fleeing Derek's apartment, Derek's text messages... Reality slammed into her all over again. Today was just a new, worse day for her to handle. Antonia lifted her wristwatch close to her face to check the time. "Shit."

It was already noon.

She darted up from the couch and instantly wove from a wash of dizziness. She sat back down and searched the living room for her bag. It was lying on the floor near the kitchen. Afraid to test her legs, Antonia slid off the couch onto the carpeted floor. Her head was pounding, an awful reminder of her indulgence. She didn't quite indulge, that would suggest that she *enjoyed* drinking an entire bottle of wine on her own.

It wasn't even good wine. It was the cheap stuff she purchased from Mr. Spivak at the corner mart. On an unsteady crawl, she finally reached her bag and found her phone.

11 Missed Calls.

23 New Messages.

Some of them were from Derek, but as she scrolled Antonia grew worried. Her mother, her sister, and Eddie had all called this morning. Derek called five times last night. Did Derek have the guts to call her family after she'd left him? What had he told them? She checked the text messages from Eddie first.

OMG WHERE ARE YOU?? Richard called a meeting. People are losing it

SHIT. Are you ok? Octavia just called me. What happened with Derek?

Shit shit shit. We're fucked.

Are you awake? Can you call?? Richard has lost his FUCKING MIND!

The more Antonia read, the more confused she became. She had hoped to get her shit together and tell her loved ones herself. She checked the messages from her sister and found just as much alarm from her.

Are you okay?

Derek just called me. He sounds terrible.

Can you call me back?

He sounds like a babbling mess. What did he do?

Toni, call me.

Toni, Eddie sounds frantic.

Why aren't you at work right now?

I'm coming over.

Antonia sank to the floor and lay still. She didn't want to worry everyone with her antics. She just wanted to curl up and die alone and in peace. Her phone buzzed, interrupting her thoughts. Eddie.

"Yes."

"Jesus-fucking-Christ, Toni, I thought you were dead. Hold on, I'm texting Octavia. I'm pretty sure she's on her way to your apartment."

She sighed. "I'm sorry, Ed. I had a very shitty night."

"I heard," he said. His voice sounded distant, like he was talking to her on speaker. "I don't know the details, but I heard."

"Derek is cheating on me."

There was silence on the other end. She waited.

"You still there, Ed?"

"I'm here too, honey," said a woman's voice, Eddie's girlfriend, Megan. "Eddie told me what happened."

Antonia cringed. She loved Megan and her bubbly spirit, but she didn't want to talk to her at the moment. "Hey, Meg."

"Shit..." Eddie trailed off.

A sharp knock at Antonia's door announced her sister. "Give me a second, my sister is here to yell at me." She climbed from the floor and carried her conversation to the front door. Octavia stood on the other side, arms crossed and mouth fixed for a tongue-lashing. Antonia stepped aside and let her in.

"...Toni, I hate to give you more bad news," Eddie said. "But Richard sent us all home today."

"Why did he do that?" she asked, closing the door and following her sister. Octavia stood in the living room and cast a judgmental eye on the mess. Without being asked, she started the annoying spot-cleaning Antonia hated so much. She even made a show of picking up the empty bottle and swirling the remaining liquid around. Octavia, who was forty, glided around her apartment with a grace that came from her past dance training. She wore black leggings that showed off her toned calves and a long gray tunic that hung elegantly off one shoulder. Octavia's recently braided hair sat atop her head in a large bun, giving her the appearance of being almost as tall as Antonia.

"Wild Hare is closing shop, Toni," Eddie said, bringing her back to the present. "He laid everyone off."

She stumbled. "We've lost our jobs?"

Octavia paused in midwipe of the coffee table. "Can you believe that?" Megan cried in the background.

"No," Antonia said in a dazed voice. Only yesterday, did she and Eddie vocalize their suspicions and now they were jobless. Why were there so many things that she failed to spot in time?

"I'm sorry," Eddie said. "I wish there was a better way to tell you, but I tried to call. God, we're going to have to contact all of our published authors. I've never handled a shutdown before."

"Right."

"Are you okay?"

"Can I call you back?"

He paused before asking, "Octavia's there?"

"Yes, I'll get back to you later."

"Hang in there, Toni!" Megan called out.

She hung up and stared into space.

"Go ahead and sit down," said Octavia, from the kitchen. The hollow thump of an empty bottle hit her trash can. Antonia obeyed her sister and returned to the couch. "Now lie down."

She lay back. "I'm not your patient."

Octavia returned to the living room and flung open the curtains. "No, you're not. I had to cancel an appointment with an OCD mama's boy to come over here."

"I'm sorry."

"You're like Mom, still believing black folks don't need therapy."

She rolled her eyes. "Go ahead and fix me then, Dr. Freud."

"No, that's your job. I'm just here to listen." Octavia sat down in Antonia's favorite reading chair and crossed her legs. She put on her therapist hat, her face becoming a blank mask that Antonia struggled to interpret. Octavia looked more like their father. Her skin was deep cocoa and virtually unflawed despite her years. Her dark almond-shaped eyes were inscrutable as they were mysterious. When they were children, Antonia remembered her older sister as the one who observed more than she spoke. Octavia's quiet strength was a deep well which carefully tended to Antonia's constant anxiety.

"Where the hell do I start?" Antonia asked, her voice climbing. Tears threatened to return. "I've just lost my fiancé and apparently my job."

"Start from the beginning with Derek," Octavia said in a soothing voice. "I can tell you that when he called me, he was almost hysterical."

Antonia frowned. "What did he say happened last night?"

Her sister shook her head and shrugged. "I couldn't get a clear picture; he didn't make much sense. He was going on and on about you canceling the wedding, the money it was going to cost him, that sort of thing. I tried to ask him for details, but he was evasive."

"He left out a huge chunk of last night's events," she said through a clenched jaw. Antonia hugged her arms around her body and slowly relayed everything that she remembered from last night. She managed to get through the story without breaking down, which she considered her first win of the day. *Progress*. All throughout, Octavia remained quiet, nodding only once in a while. Had she her notepad, she probably would have been writing notes. When Antonia finished, she looked over at her sister. "What do I do?"

Octavia drew a deep breath and asked, "What would you like to do?"

"I'd like to kill Derek."

Her sister nodded with a smile. "That's fair," she said before adding, "It's good that you're being honest about your anger. I was worried that your first impulse was to turn inward."

"I did drink an entire bottle of wine."

"Yes, but you won't do that again." Octavia leaned

forward in her seat. "Are you sure you didn't know about Derek and his... Naomi?"

"I had no idea. But the weird thing was how he handled the situation. He didn't even bother to deny what he did and he barely apologized. It was like he turned into a completely different person." She remembered being startled by the cool detachment in his voice. The easiness in his suggestion to continue as though nothing were wrong. He told her she would be a lonely woman in her thirties without him. Where did that chilling arrogance come from?

"Was there *anything* about this relationship that made you suspect that Derek was unfaithful?"

Antonia took a moment to think. She did wonder why they hadn't been intimate in the last few weeks, but she figured that they were both tired. But how many times had she tried to initiate? He seemed more tired than she. "We haven't had sex in about a month."

Her sister's eyes flickered with discomfort. "Mmh."

"I'm just being honest."

"Yes, that was probably a sign, but I was talking about something more subtle."

"What do you mean?"

Her sister hesitated for an instant, her dark eyes full of regret. "Maybe I should have said something much earlier, Toni. Speaking as your sister and not a therapist, Derek is an asshole. I've thought so from the start. His cheating on you doesn't surprise me in the least."

Antonia stared. "What?"

"Oh honey..." Octavia said leaving her seat. She quickly knelt next to Antonia and clasped her face between her hands. "Please don't give me those frightened bunny eyes. They're hard to face."

"You've always hated him?"

Her sister nodded. "Well, I hated him as a partner for you, but now I just hate him."

Antonia said nothing as she slid her arms around Octavia. They hugged tightly, Antonia's tears and sniffles were the only sounds in the silent apartment. When they pulled apart, Octavia used the sleeve of her tunic to wipe Antonia's eyes. "Mom gave me a lecture just yesterday. We fought about Derek on the phone and I defended him like an idiot. How could I not see it?"

"Don't feel too bad about a fight with Mom. When it comes to her, it's easy to get defensive. She doesn't always give her opinion with kid gloves…" Octavia trailed off, possibly remembering arguments she'd had with their mother. "As far as Derek is concerned, I think we see what we want to see. Things are always different when you're on the inside actually living it."

"How did it look from the outside?"

Octavia sat back on her heels and pursed her lips. "Remember that night I met up with you two and you announced your engagement?"

"Yeah?"

"You were so excited, showing off the ring. We all drank champagne. But he looked so vacant. Very handsome, very charming, but he just didn't seem to have any real feelings."

Antonia stared at the engagement ring on her finger. She tugged it from her finger and set it on the coffee table.

"I'd like to think I'm pretty good at spotting robotic people," Octavia continued. "I remember congratulating the both of you and watching him hold your hand, but he held it like a stone. When I asked if you two were going to find a place together, he naturally assumed that you'd just move into his apartment. When I asked about your book project—"

"—He laughed," Antonia finished. Her face flushed as she evoked the memory of Derek's chuckling. "He called it a 'cute idea.'"

"He said that if everything worked out at his firm, you wouldn't have to work at all," Octavia reminded her. "His mother didn't have to work, why should you?"

She'd been thoroughly embarrassed by his remark. Antonia came from a family of hard-working women. After their father died, Diane had worked three jobs so that Antonia and her sister could continue attending a private Catholic school. When Octavia graduated from high school, she'd been determined to get into the University of Chicago. She'd worked as a waitress and depended on her scholarships while commuting from their old Southside neighborhood. Even Antonia had worked as a bartender throughout her graduate degree. The Harper women knew how to hustle.

"I think I ignored more than that," Antonia said.

"I think you might be right. The struggle with his mother over these wedding plans may have been another sign. Did you really want a wedding at Shedd Aquarium or were you just being stubborn?"

Antonia detected laughter in her sister's eyes. Her heart lifted as she let out a startled laugh. "What are you talking about? I love the ocean."

"The underexplored bastion of our world?"

Antonia wiped tears from her face while she giggled. "I didn't say it like that."

"Yeah, well, I saw Vivian Rogers's face when you said it. I thought she would fall off her chair."

"I was serious about the aquarium, though," Antonia said. "It would have been a nice ceremony."

"And were you serious about your honeymoon?" Octavia asked, arching a brow. "Where on earth were you guys going?"

Antonia tried to stifle her disappointment. "Derek wanted to go to Bali or something. I wanted us to go to Ireland."

"What's in Ireland?"

"I don't know," Antonia admitted. "I've always wanted to go there. I booked a place on the west coast, right on the ocean. Oh my god, you should see the pictures." She scooted off the couch to retrieve her laptop. "I found this little town called Clifden. It's got these beautiful green grass hills dotted white with sheep. Craggy gray cliffs that kind of tumble into the Atlantic. There, look at that B&B, isn't it adorable?"

Octavia peered at the screen. "Are those three pubs sitting right next to one another?"

"Romantic, huh?"

"This is the whitest thing I've ever heard of."

Antonia frowned. "I thought it would be nice. Not that it matters…"

Octavia went quiet, her eyes darting between the computer screen and her sister. "Mmh."

"What?" She knew the wheels were turning rapidly in her sister's brain.

"It's just that…well, what if you could still kiss your Blarney Stone?"

"What do you mean?"

"How much money have you saved?"

Antonia shook her head. "Octavia, I just lost my job.

I have a million wedding things I need to cancel. Even then, I'll have to pay for the cancellations."

"Yes, but how much have you saved? Enough for a rainy day?"

Antonia knew what she meant. The sisters took after their mother when it came to preparing for emergencies. For Diane, a rainy day meant your husband could up-and-die, leaving you with two growing daughters. They grew up learning how to be incredibly shrewd with money. Everything in Antonia's apartment was bought secondhand or given to her from her mother. She accumulated her work wardrobe during well-timed, end of the season sales. Even Derek was excited to learn that she would come to the marriage with a significant savings and no student loan debt. Was this disaster her rainy day?

She met her sister's gaze with a tremulous smile. "Should I just go?"

"What would your girl-character, Augusta, do?"

Maybe there is a chance. Antonia was buoyant with hope. Perhaps this was the time she needed to become reacquainted with the characters of her book. She could get Augusta through the next chapter of her life. If she was lucky, she could figure out how to get through the next chapter of her own life. But reality quickly crept back in. How could she leave with so many loose ends? There was a huge guest list waiting on a wedding that would never happen. She had to find another job. So many things needed to be handled.

"Look, if the answer is, yes, Augusta would go to Ireland by herself and write a book, then I will personally make sure that things here are in order."

"It feels like I'm just running away from my problems."

"Running away is different from running toward," Octavia explained. "If you're finally willing to make yourself happy, I would call this running toward something. Let's face it, Wild Hare was on shaky ground for a while. Eddie was upset when I spoke to him this morning, but he wasn't terribly shocked."

"No, I suppose you're right."

"There's nothing wrong with licking your wounds, Toni."

"What about Mom? I don't think I can talk to her right now."

Octavia scoffed. "I'll take care of her."

She rolled her eyes before giving a small smile. Hope was inching its way back into her heart. "Are you sure you can handle the wedding stuff? Derek's mom, all of it?"

"I've treated women like Derek's mother for years. She suffers from narcissism just like her son," Octavia said with a grin. "And if it makes you feel better, I'll employ Eddie's girlfriend. She's got a type A personality that's good for planning *and* dismantling weddings."

"Yeah? You'll do it?"

Octavia gave her a solemn stare. "I'll only give you this non-wedding gift on two conditions."

"What?"

"First, I need you to figure out what drew you to someone like Derek. You can give me the short answer, but you need to think about what you believe you're lacking."

Antonia groaned. There *was* a short answer and a long one, but she didn't want to dig too deep so quickly after the destruction of her relationship. "I guess... I just thought I was punching above my weight. Derek was the kind of guy who would never look at me when I was in college and now that I'm thirty-three." She rolled her eyes. "I thought someone like him wouldn't wait for me much longer."

Octavia let her mask slip and grimaced. "What the hell does that even mean?"

"I don't know, I just thought that I was a homely nerd."

"Jesus Christ, Toni. You need to seriously work on this self-image business. You're young, brilliant, and beautiful. Derek is just a pretty face with no real substance. Why would you want to fit yourself into his tiny box?"

Antonia gave a tired shrug. She didn't have an answer for that.

"Well I need you to figure that shit out," her sister said in a stern tone that reminded Antonia of their mother. "My second condition is that you have to take your book with you. Whatever it was, it seemed like the one thing that made you happy. Can you do those two things?"

Antonia missed her writing terribly. The thrill she got when she sorted out the puzzles of her plot was euphoric. But she'd put it on the backburner for so long that she wondered if she could possibly return to it. There was a chance that she could. If she took advantage of this rainy day in her life, she could write her next chapter. She could also put in the hard work of understanding how she lost herself for a full year. Maybe she could find Augusta and herself in Ireland.

"I can do it," she said with resolve. "I'll go."

Chapter Six

"I read an article saying people can't drive and talk on the phone at the same time, did you know that?" Aiden's mother said, her concerned face filling the screen of his phone. "It just can't be done."

It was a cloudy Thursday afternoon when he decided to take off for Tully Cross, but made the mistake of answering his mother's phone call. Clare Hannigan, who was still figuring out the intricacies of her new iPhone, had discovered FaceTime. "I've heard that, Mam."

"People think they can multitask and it just can't be done," she repeated. Her phone was tilted upward, showing more of her neck and chin than her eyes.

"Mam, go ahead and hold the phone up. At your face."

"M'dear, what do you think I'm doing? Anyway, how are you feeling?"

"Well, I'm on my way to Tully Cross," he said, leaning against the steering wheel. "And I don't want to talk and drive."

"You can talk to your poor mother for just a moment, can't you?" She moved the phone to her jade green eyes and peered at him. "It's not too far to the peninsula anyway. Also you didn't answer my question: How are you feeling?"

Aiden rubbed his temples. "I feel fine, Mam."

"You're a worse liar than your da, you know that? And you look an awful mess, Aiden. Have y'even shaved?"

He glanced at his rearview mirror before answering her. No, he had not followed Robert's orders and shaved his beard. In the past semester, the black stubble he usually sported had grown much fuller. He tilted his face slightly and frowned. The small patch of gray near his jaw was becoming more noticeable. "I'll shave when I get to the cottage," he promised.

The phone dipped back to her pursed lips. "Please do, you look like a wild man. Have you gotten any sleep? Your eyes are a bit dark."

"I've slept."

"Out of all of my boys, you're the chattiest one, you know that? I could always tell when you were worn-out. You'd close right up like a little clam. When you were small, you were so loud and boisterous, performing for the family. Dancing and singin' in your tap shoes. But as soon as you got tired, you stuck out your lip and furrowed your black brow until I made you take a nap."

Her rambling made Aiden smile in spite of himself. "I didn't perform…"

"You did," his mother insisted. "You're the theatrical one."

He was reminded of his talk with Robert last week. He liked entertaining and charming people. Though it didn't work on everyone, he tried nonetheless. Aiden's mind drifted back to Lisa and their last interaction. Looking back on it, he felt his performance with her was less than stellar. "I saw Lisa last week," he told his mother. He didn't know what he wanted Clare to say, but he needed to tell her. "She came back to town because of that damn Western Ireland Humanities Conference and it threw me off my game."

"Mmh." Clare raised a brow. "Why do you think that is?"

"Because I was trying my best to forget her," he finally told his mother.

Clare took him into her kitchen where she pulled the kettle off the stove. "Dear, do you mind if I put you on the counter while I make tea? We can't multi-task, you know."

Aiden chuckled. His mother always had a way of cheering him up. She'd even managed to maintain a jovial spirit during the tougher times. Being a school teacher and a single mother of four sons was no easy feat, but Clare had pulled it off. Aiden now looked at his mother's ceiling, listening to her clatter dishes. "You certainly don't need to forget the girl. You remember her so you don't make the same mistake again," she said over the noise.

"I want to forget her for this week," he said. "Is that an appropriate amount of time?"

"Don't sass, Aiden. You do what you want for a week, but you must see her again before she leaves, right?"

"Yeah."

"Well then," she said, pouring her tea. "Spend this time getting some rest and working on your paper. You'll feel better when you've finished it."

Her advice sounded vague, like she couldn't remember which son she was talking to. Whenever one of her children had a problem, she offered sage advice that could have applied to any of them. "I suppose you're right."

"Of course I'm right," his mother said. The phone was back at her face. "When you're there you can work in peace and quiet; nothing but the sheep to keep you company. You'll come back a different man."

A different man. "I'm sure I'll be the same. Morose and irritable."

Clare ignored that. "Well, you'll at least have a visitor next Friday," she said in a bright tone. "Soircha is coming to Galway."

Aiden's head fell back against his headrest. He couldn't handle a visit from his twelve-year-old niece. "Oh god, I forgot about that."

"I'm thinking of taking the trip with her. It would be nice to see you."

"Oh Mam…" His brother Sean was still sending his daughter to the Irish-language immersion program, about twenty minutes from Galway. Aiden's place made for a good pit-stop for the girl. While he now remembered the conversation, he did not recall his mother wanting to come along for the ride. Aiden suspected she wanted to baby him.

"She loves her uncle Aiden. You're her favorite, you know that?"

And he loved his niece dearly. Soircha was a smart girl who shared his interest in reading and writing. She was definitely more interesting than his older brother's sons, Freddie and Donnie, who were growing up to become a couple of hooligans. "Just know that I'll be busy with the conference on Thursday, but I should be available after that. Any idea on how long you two need to stay with me?"

"Just a night or two. But you'd know that, if you and your brothers didn't communicate through smoke signals."

He needed to get on the road. "Yes, fine. I'll call Sean as soon as possible."

"And do be patient with Soircha," Clare said after a sip of her tea. "Sean and Mary have complained about her moody behavior lately. Maybe you two can commiserate on how awful it is to be bookish."

He rolled his eyes. "Jayus…"

"I'm telling you this—" his mother lowered her voice and knelt closer to her screen "—because she might be starting her *curse*. She's at the age, y'know."

Aiden laughed. "Mam, why in the hell are you whispering?" There was nothing like his mother's Catholic prudishness. "Also, I don't think they call it a *curse* anymore."

"Well, if you had 'em, you'd think it were a curse too. Thank the saints, I haven't got that to worry about."

"Alright then. So when you and Soircha show up on Friday, I'll need to have a box of tampons at the house?"

"Dear me, please don't tell the child you know!"

"We'll cross that bridge when we get to it, mother. But for now, I do have to go."

"Fine, but remember this: Lisa was a snob and you're better off without her. Everyone thought so."

"Who's 'everyone'?"

"All of your brothers. No one liked her," Claire replied. "What do you expect from a rich Dublin girl? The whole lot of 'em are lace curtains, you know that?"

"It would have been nice if 'everyone' were more honest about my girlfriends."

"It was hard to tell if you were truly serious about her. You both seemed like roommates."

"I had the same realization," he said. "I'm worried about my judgement."

"We have to learn from our mistakes, Aiden. But you'll soon find someone who suits you. And when you do, you can have your own little Soircha."

A smile cracked his face. He did want a family. When he looked at his brothers, he felt like he was missing something in his own life. He wanted a wife and children to fill his world. Aiden worried that he was the one son who was turning into his wandering father, a man who couldn't handle commitment. "I'm not too much like Da, am I?" he asked his mother.

Her expression softened. "Oh Aiden, you're the lovely parts of Liam. You got his handsome looks, his charm and craic. But the rest, you got from the Hannigan side."

Aiden didn't know why he needed to hear her affirmations so badly. At thirty-eight, he wondered if he was getting too set in his ways, not making any concessions for another person in his life. He had to take his mother at her word since she was the most honest person he knew. But the nagging thought still lingered. "Thanks, Mam."

Clare gave a quick nod. "Well, you take care on the road, will you?"

He put his phone in its hands-free holder. "Of course, I'm just making a quick stop in Clifden for groceries before I get to Tully Cross. No more than a couple of hours."

"Fine then," she said. "Call me when you get there."

Aiden glanced at the dashboard clock. "How about I send you a text instead?"

She arched a brow. "My stubborn little clam."

He rolled his eyes. "Goodbye, Mam." He gave a quick wave before switching her off and turning his GPS on. If he was going to collect his keys before nightfall, he needed to haul-ass immediately. A week of rest in the country awaited him.

Chapter Seven

"No, no, please don't tell me this," Antonia pleaded with the hotel receptionist. She was exhausted after a six-hour flight to Shannon Airport and a long, confusing drive to Clifden. The rental car was a manual-shift that stalled out every time she came to a stop. The only reason she'd reserved it was because it was cheaper and she had assumed Derek would drive the entire trip. And now this young bright-eyed brunette was telling her she had no room. Ireland was quickly feeling like a mistake. "I checked on this reservation last night. No, not last night, I was on a plane. What day is it?"

The receptionist, her name tag read "Breda," gave a pitying smile. "It's Thursday and I'm truly very sorry, Mrs. Rogers—"

"—No, not Mrs. Rogers," Antonia interrupted. "I didn't marry, I mean, I know I made the reservation under that. But…" She knew what she must have sounded like. A single woman showing up to a hotel suite meant for a newlywed couple. The young woman, who couldn't have been more than twenty-five, simply nodded her head.

"Of course, Ms. Harper?" she said checking her credit card once more. "Your reservation was canceled yesterday evening. Mr. Rogers called and said your stay wouldn't be necessary."

"He called?" Antonia bit back her anger as she clenched the counter. "You mean he actually *called* you and canceled our—my reservation?"

Breda nodded. "I'm afraid that is the case. Your room is now gone."

Antonia was seething. *How could he do something so low-down and dirty like that?* The last conversation she had with him was a stressful one, but he gave no indication that he would pull this kind of stunt. After news of the canceled wedding had circulated to all their guests, Derek had called her on the night before her trip, making a last attempt to keep her in the country so they could talk. She told him she would still take their honeymoon trip, by herself, and didn't want to hear anymore. She'd even done the polite thing of mailing his engagement ring back to him. Did he want to get back at her by throwing a wrench in her plans? Antonia closed her eyes and took a deep breath. *Do not let this asshole thwart you again.* When she opened her eyes, she struggled to smile. "None of this is your fault, Breda. But could you please, pretty please, just help me out? This is my first day in Ireland, my car is an absolute piece of shit, and I'm so tired."

Breda's eyebrows furrowed. "I understand, Ms. Harper. But my hands are tied. The Renvyle Oyster Festival is this weekend, that's why everything is so busy." She paused, taking pity on Antonia's ragged appearance. "I can check with surrounding hotels for something."

Antonia was grateful for the courtesy. "You don't know how helpful that is. I would really appreciate it."

Breda gave her the same sympathetic smile as she returned to her computer and started making phone calls. Antonia found a seat in the small lobby and lamented the thought of going anywhere else. She had specifically picked this quaint little hotel because it was centrally located within Clifden. She had planned to walk down the street to a café that sold fresh-baked scones, for coffee and people watching. As she sank into the lobby couch, her spirits followed. This was supposed to be her romantic and rustic Irish honeymoon with her future husband. Her second best chance of enjoying this trip was pretending that she could do it all by herself. Derek managed to fuck that up too.

As she began to lose all confidence in herself, Antonia was reminded that she had never gone abroad by herself. The last time she'd left the country was when she was in college. She did a summer program in Rome and thoroughly enjoyed herself, but she had been with a large group of students and a couple of professors. Ireland was more daunting than she imagined. She'd stumbled her way through airport customs before she presented her passport to an elderly agent. Antonia had been the only black person in line and wondered if that was somehow suspicious. The man had waved her on after she eventually made up her mind on if her trip was business or pleasure. "It's a mixture of pleasure and novel writing," she'd told him with a nervous laugh. "So it's kind of business?" She'd stopped short of telling him that she was also trying to find herself.

Antonia glanced around at the empty lobby with its warm fireplace and plush furniture and wondered how many black people she'd actually meet in Ireland. *Probably not too many.* She forgot to do that kind of research when she planned the trip. Derek had his reservations about going, citing that they should just go to Dublin where there was more to do. And when they got tired of that, they could just go to London. Shedd Aquarium and Western Ireland were her only real wedding decisions. *Did I make a mistake?*

"Ms. Harper?" called a voice behind her. Antonia was jerked out of her thoughts and promptly stood.

"Yes. Could you find anything?"

"I did," Breda said pulling out a map. "I just didn't find anything in Clifden."

"Oh no," she breathed. "How far away?"

"It's only thirty minutes away," the young woman said, proud of her discovery. "There's a small village named Tully Cross that has beautiful rental cottages. It appears only one of the six have been booked, so you're in luck. The price is comparable to your stay here and you'll have more amenities, like a full kitchen."

Antonia studied the map labeled *Renvyle Peninsula* and sighed. "Tully Cross? A village?"

"Yes, and it's only thirty minutes away. I'm afraid it was the only thing available. Again, this area gets very busy with the Renvyle Oyster Festival."

"Right, that's why I picked these dates," Antonia said, trying her best to keep the irritation from her voice.

"It's a very exciting festival," Breda said with a bright smile.

Antonia returned to the map. "Could you talk me through this drive?"

"Of course," Breda said, snaking her ink pen around the curvy coastline. "You will take N59 to a town called Letterfrack, a town where I used to live! Oh, and just so you know, Letterfrack is where the nearest grocery store is located. Unfortunately, it's nearly 5 p.m. and they're known to close early. I think you might want to get your food here."

Antonia was inching closer to a panic attack. "Okay."

"So anyway, when you get to Letterfrack, you'll take a right to get on the Connemara Loop. It will take you directly to Tully Cross. Now if you've gone to Tully, then you've gone too far."

Antonia rubbed the space between her eyes. "There's a village called Tully Cross and there's a town called Tully?"

"It's also a small village," Breda said. "Tully Cross is very small, but I don't think you'll miss it. The main street has a church, a pub, and a hotel on one side—"

"—And that hotel is all booked up?"

"Yes, it is. It's a very lovely place, but so are the cottages. Anyway, the cottages are on the other side of the main street. They're lined up in a row."

Antonia paused for a think. "Okay, I think I've got it. Go up N59 until I hit Letterfrack and take a right on to the…what kind of loop?"

"The Connemara Loop," Breda said. "I've marked it all on this map."

This was the moment where Antonia would have to test her resolve. If she could do this, perhaps the rest of the trip wouldn't be a complete shit-show. "Alright, I can do this."

"Of course you can," Breda said with full support. "I do hope that you have a lovely time in Tully Cross."

The kindness that this young woman exuded startled Antonia. She wasn't used to people in the service industry caring about mix-ups like this. In Chicago, people could be as cold and distant as the wind their city was known for. She smiled back at Breda. Tully Cross may not have been what she had in mind, but she was lucky it was an option. A "thirty-minutes-away" option, but something nonetheless. "Thank you so much for your help, Breda."

"Of course, Ms. Harper. Enjoy your stay in Ireland."

Antonia grabbed her two suitcases and wheeled them out the door, casting another regretful glance at the lobby as she went. She would follow Breda's advice and stop at the SuperValu she'd spotted on her way into town. If she wanted to eat tonight, she had better stock up now. When she found her car on the street, Antonia drew her jacket closer to her. Even in June, western Ireland was still a little chilly from the Atlantic air. *Derek would certainly hate this.* As she loaded her bags in the trunk, Antonia smiled to herself. The weather was as moody and dramatic as she imagined. To her, the clouds forming overhead were a beautiful sign that things might not be so terrible.

Chapter Eight

The goddamn Renvyle Oyster Festival.

Aiden pushed his shopping cart past two rowdy children, who rolled around the floor of the dairy aisle, grabbing butter as he went. He had forgotten all about the festival that made Clifden and the surrounding area fill up with visitors. The masses gathered here every June to partake in fresh seafood offerings. The Super-Valu was a madhouse just as people were getting off from work. He glanced at his watch again to see it was close to 5 p.m. If he wanted to pick up his cottage keys from the front office, he'd have to hurry this shopping excursion along. With his head still down, he rounded the corner and was met with resistance as he crashed carts with another shopper.

"Jaysus, I'm sorry," he said, looking up. His breath caught in his throat. Staring back at him was the most beautiful woman he'd seen in a long time.

"No, I'm sorry," she said quickly. Her large dark eyes widened in embarrassment. A lovely deep blush crept up her neck and settled into her cinnamon brown cheeks. She was tall and slender, but possessed a generous hourglass shape. The black ankle-boots she wore added another inch making her statuesque. She dressed in simple black leggings and a cropped brown leather jacket. It hung open revealing a clingy gray sweater.

Aiden's gaze snapped back to her face. It was rude to stare, and the way he stared was probably downright lascivious. "It's my fault," he admitted. "I wasn't minding my cart. Are you alright?"

Her face broke into a beautiful grin, her lips full and inviting. "I'm fine, but while I have you…"

Yes, you have me.

Aiden drifted back to taking her in. He was mesmerized by her hair. It was huge and flowing with loose black curls that framed her oval face. One of those curls fell carelessly down her forehead, making Aiden grip his cart tighter. He wanted to push that curl aside and kiss her.

"…maybe you can tell me where I could find the yogurt."

"I'm sorry?"

Her dark eyes twinkled with laughter. "Do you know where I could find the yogurt?"

Aiden couldn't remember anything about the layout of the SuperValu; where he'd gone or where he was going, before seeing her face. "Yogurt?"

"Back that way," said the mother of the two rowdy boys. She pulled one of the towheaded children by the jacket while the other hung off the cart.

"Oh, thank you!" The gorgeous woman started off in the direction that Aiden had come from. "Sorry again, for hitting you," she said to him.

"No worries," he said, mentally kicking himself. He knew damn well where the yogurt was. Aiden looked over his shoulder, his eyes following her as she navigated through the crowd of shoppers. Just as he sus-

pected, she was just as sexy from behind. With several
more items on his shopping list, he wondered if he
would run into her again. She'd disappeared around
the corner, minding her own business, just as he should
have done. Aiden pushed forward, mourning his sudden loss of speech.

When he reached the paper towels, he threw paper
plates and plastic cutlery in his basket. No sense in
doing dishes if he didn't have to. He paused in the paper
goods aisle and debated if he needed some salmon or
if he needed to follow the woman he crashed into. The
fish was a given, he'd get that momentarily, but that
woman… She would be easy to spot again. As far as
Aiden could tell, she was the only black woman in the
store. She sounded American too, her voice throaty and
warm with no discernable trace of a European or African accent. There wasn't a point to wondering all of
this if she was staying in Clifden. She was probably
shopping for her and her boyfriend. They would probably enjoy the weekend's festivities, hugged up in an
adorable B&B. *Get a hold of yourself!*

Aiden walked through a fog to get several frozen
shepherd's pies and pizzas, before grabbing a bag of
crisps. The smoked salmon he chucked into his cart
would be the healthiest thing in there. *Where's the
brown bread?*

Aiden didn't see the woman when he made it to the
checkout line. Perhaps that was for the best. Getting
to Tully Cross before dark was more important. The
sooner he could unpack, the sooner he could set up shop
at the local pub and catch up with the villagers. The
lines were alarmingly long and he had the misfortune
to park right behind the oldest woman in the world. He

closed his eyes and asked St. Anthony, patron saint of lost things and the elderly, to help him find his patience for her. Something hard bumped against his ass and he heard a light chuckle. He opened his eyes and turned around. To see *her*.

Thank you, St. Anthony.

"I did *that* on purpose," said the beautiful yogurt woman.

Aiden's breath escaped in laughter. "Fair play," he said.

"I found my yogurt, among other things," she said, putting her items on the line behind his partition. She glanced at his groceries and frowned. "But I forgot the frozen pizza."

Aiden looked at his items. It must have looked bad. Two bottles of whiskey, crisps, and dozens of frozen items. But for all she knew, he was having a party. *A party for one.* "You haven't lived until you've tried Goodfella's thin crust margherita pizza." *For fuck sake...*

She laughed another one of those light breezy chuckles. "I already regret not stopping by the frozen aisle, please don't make it worse."

"You're welcome to one of mine," he offered and immediately cringed at the sound of his own voice. "I mean, if not having frozen pizza might ruin your night, don't let it be on my account."

One brow arched as she looked from him to his many pizzas. "Well, you have talked it up."

Before she could change her mind, Aiden promptly set the boxed pizza on her side of the partition. "You won't regret it."

She leaned on her cart and assessed him thoughtfully. "I heard the Irish were friendly, but I didn't know they just went around giving their pizzas to strangers."

"I don't know how many of us do that, but I can tell you I get my charitable nature from my mother. She'd be disappointed if I hadn't shared a frozen bounty with a beautiful woman." Aiden clamped his mouth shut, shocked he'd let his words get away from him.

Very faintly, her brown cheeks grew pinkish by his remark. "Your mom raised a good boy," she said.

"I'm sorry," he said, holding out his hand. "I'm apparently still learning my manners. My name is Aiden and I speak without thinking."

She laughed again and she reached to shake his hand. "My name is Antonia and I treat grocery stores like my own Thunderdome."

Jesus, she's as funny as she is cute. Aiden held her hand in his, shaking longer than he should have. When he released her, he could still feel her warmth against his skin. He wanted more. "Antonia? That's a class name," he said, nodding in appreciation.

"Oh jeez," she said scrunching up her pert nose. She had a lovely nose too. "You think? Everyone just calls me Toni."

"No, I like Antonia quite a bit," Aiden insisted. "It's real class."

Antonia shrugged. "I think my father was on some neo-classical kick. My older sister's name is Octavia."

"Sounds like a couple of Roman generals," Aiden said. "Real strong."

She gave a half smile. "I think my sister does a better job of living up to her name." There was a small note of sadness in her voice as she glanced down at her empty cart.

"Where are you from, Antonia?" he asked, changing the subject.

"I'm from Chicago," she said, her face lit up again. "In America," she added for clarification.

He laughed. "I'm familiar," he said. "Home of Barack Obama."

"Yep," she said with pride.

"Is this your first time to Ireland?"

"Yes, it is," she said with a grin. She gestured to her face before asking, "I hope I don't stick out too much."

He understood what she meant. She was definitely the first black person he'd seen in Clifden that day. "A bit," he said returning her knowing grin. "But in a good way. How do you like it so far?"

Antonia sighed. There was a far off look that shadowed her dark brown eyes. "I had a stressful time getting here from the airport, but I already love the countryside, it's so...green."

"Aye, that it is," Aiden said. "It's plenty green. How long do you think you'll stay?"

Antonia appeared to think about it. "About two weeks, I think. It was originally going to be just the one, but things changed."

"Good, good," he murmured. After the old woman finally paid and left the checkout, Aiden stepped forward. He was running out of time. As the cashier rang his food items, he turned back to Antonia and made a quick note of her bare ring finger. "So uh, you're going to tour the green countryside with your...boyfriend?"

Her gaze fell back to her empty shopping cart. "I'm traveling solo."

Yes! Aiden ignored his pounding heart, took a deep breath and nodded. "That sounds lovely. You'll be able to see the sights on your own time. Wake up and go to bed whenever you want." The cashier, a shaggy haired teenager, pretended he wasn't listening as he pushed Aiden's third pizza through the scanner. A small smile played on the boy's lips while Aiden rambled on. "I find that travel is more productive when you discover things on your own, you know? James Baldwin, he's an American novelist, he wrote some beautiful essays about his time in France. He really dug in there and understood what Paris was all about. The stuff with the Algerians was a crying shame, though. But it gave him a chance to reflect on what it meant to be an American." *Shut up. Shut up. Shut the fuck up.*

The curious expression on her face was enough to tell him that he was making a fool of himself. "I love James Baldwin," she finally said.

He let out a breath.

"That's eighty euros fifty-three," said the young man, who looked like he was thoroughly enjoying this.

"Yeah," Aiden said, inserting his card into the machine. "Anyway, I hope you enjoy your time here."

"Me too," Antonia said with a nod.

God, I'm out of time. Aiden waited for his card to read and for her to say something else. He couldn't keep babbling at her. "Well, maybe I'll see you around for the festival," he offered. It was unlikely that he'd want to come back to this place once he settled in Tully Cross.

She looked down at her watch. *Is she already bored of me?* "It's hard to say. I don't know if I'll be able to fit it in at this point."

"Right, well, pace yourself during your stay," he said taking his receipt from the cashier. He had to leave. He had to get in his car and drive away from here.

"Thank you, Aiden," she said with a grin. "Maybe I'll *bump* into you again."

Jesus, she's adorable. He laughed a little too loud as he slowly pushed his cart toward the exit. The chance was slipping away, but she hadn't given him any indication that this was an appropriate moment to ask where she was staying. It didn't matter what country she was from, women generally didn't like it when strange men took an intense interest in them.

Before he knew it, Aiden was in the busy parking lot, loading his bags into the boot of his car. It was for the best. Antonia was an American tourist after all. She would go back home just like the rest of them. There was no sense in mourning something he'd ultimately lose to citizenship. In his car, he gave himself another look in the rearview mirror. It didn't help that he probably looked like the wild man his mother described. Chances were, she was being polite to him while waiting on him to leave. He scratched at his beard. It had been awhile since he'd been in a position to flirt with a woman. He worried he'd sounded a little insane as well.

Carefully maneuvering his way out of the parking lot and onto the street, Aiden tried to put the woman out of his mind. It proved to be difficult as he repeatedly checked his mirrors for the SuperValu entrance. He didn't see her exit, but he could still feel the softness of her hand from their brief handshake. Her black mane of wild curls and her laughing eyes taunted him. The glow of her brown skin was imprinted on his memory. *I should have said something.*

Chapter Nine

"Recalculating…recalculating…"

Antonia glanced at the GPS that chastised her wrong turn. Somewhere along N59, she misunderstood the machine and made a poorly-timed exit. She pulled over to the narrow shoulder of the road and surveyed her environment. She was slowly getting used to driving on the left side of the road, but its narrowness was still daunting. All of the rugged beauty that Antonia drove through would have been more enjoyable from the passenger's side. *You're doing this alone.*

"Recalculating…" the mechanical voice of the GPS reminded her.

"I get it, you obnoxious bitch." At the beginning of her drive, the British female voice was pleasant enough for her to name it "Vera." Somewhere close to Clifden, "Vera" had changed to "you dumb bitch." Variations of the phrase were screamed shortly after she departed the city.

Antonia thought, for a moment, to make a quick U-turn. She had only driven a couple miles past her blunder, but the sharp bends around the small mountain made visibility nearly impossible. She doubted her skill with the stick shift, knowing she couldn't do it fast enough. She heaved a sigh and checked her mirrors before merging back onto the road, intending to find someone's driveway to pull into so she could double-back. But the distance between houses was quite far. She had passed plenty of pastures and herds of sheep, but no houses. Antonia grew worried about the length of her mistake. How long would it take to readjust?

"Recalculating…"

"Shut up." The reason that "Vera" couldn't find an alternative route was probably because she drove through an uncharted wasteland. That wasn't entirely true. It wasn't a wasteland, but the scenery was certainly stark and wild. The gray clouds made the black cliffs loom taller and the hills a beautiful verdant green. The curvy roads wound haphazardly into those hills, threatening to tumble into blue-gray fjords. There were startling signs of beauty that caught Antonia by surprise, though. Along the roadside were yellow wildflowers and purple foxgloves that blew against tall grasses. And to her right, abandoned potato mounds were etched into the mountains like an ancient map of past misfortunes… It was breathtaking.

A city girl, Antonia had never seen anything like it. While she tried her best to enjoy it, she fought to ignore her fear of getting lost. She wanted to make it to the village before it got dark and things became more anxiety-provoking. Antonia did not want to accidentally hit one of the sheep who wandered onto the road or fly off a cliff. She was probably not in any danger of the latter, considering how slow she was moving. Shifting gears without grinding the clutch was still very challenging.

She spotted an empty scenic lookout up ahead with enough space to park several cars. *Oh, thank god.* Antonia pulled over again and carefully maneuvered her car for a U-turn. She stalled on the edge of the road and started again. When she successfully returned the car in the right direction, she was able to breathe easier. It took her a few minutes, but she finally found where she made her last exit.

"Continue for 15 kilometers to Letterfrack," Vera recited.

"Thanks, you dumb bitch." Antonia checked the time again. 6:27 p.m. Never mind the impending darkness, she only had thirty minutes to check into her cottage before she was screwed. After purchasing her food, she stopped by the customer service desk to buy a sim card for her cellphone and place a quick call to the cottage rental. Of course, this was all after meeting that interesting guy. *Aiden?* Antonia grinned. He was just as handsome as he was awkward. She laughed, remembering his frozen pizza offering. If that was his idea of flirting, she didn't mind it at all. He was certainly easy to look at. Aiden was about as tall as Derek, but more broad shouldered and barrel chested. She noticed that his arms looked stronger too. She did wonder how old he was, though. The only giveaway was the sparse gray that peppered his beard and the way his bright green eyes crinkled when he smiled. His thick black hair was cut short with a side part and she remembered him smoothing it away from his heavy brow.

She was surprised by herself when she made a point to join his checkout line, even more surprised when she nudged his firm ass with her shopping cart. She hoped it wasn't too forward of her, but the way his dark blue denim hugged his solid thighs made her act on impulse. The way his forest green sweater hugged his chest *defi-*

nitely made her act with urgency. Antonia was amazed that she actually flirted with a man and didn't embarrass herself. She wished their time hadn't been so brief because she could have stood there listening to his melodic Irish accent for hours.

"C'est la vie." He was probably a Clifden local and would return to his life as usual. There was a good chance she'd never see Aiden again, but she'd enjoyed her first genuine interaction with a local. "I can't believe I said Chicago. In America. Of course it's in America, Toni. Where is the other Chicago?"

Judging by the sudden appearance of houses, Antonia reasoned that she might be approaching Letterfrack. It was the little town that Receptionist Breda came from. The streets weren't very busy at all. Antonia slowed down to take a better look, noticing the grocery store on her right. It was closed alright. She was thankful for Breda's little tip.

"Turn right to Connemara loop."

The town looked pretty slow for a Thursday night and it didn't appear to have any hotels. Or any other major businesses, for that matter.

"Turn right."

Antonia turned slowly veered right, thankful that there weren't any cars behind her. Several kilometers back, a few cars had to pass her on the left, but they were good enough to not honk at her. She definitely wouldn't get this polite treatment in Chicago.

"Continue on Connemara Loop for ten kilometers," Vera instructed. Antonia couldn't wait to shut her off and plant her feet on solid ground.

"What if I modeled Augusta's boyfriend after Aiden? He seems like the kind of guy I've been imagining."

Antonia stopped for a herd of sheep, a cute white lamb leading the pack. While she waited, she rolled the idea around in her mind. "Bryon is a sturdy man in his thirties who's been roaming the world with a backpack and camera. He would look a lot like Aiden."

She stalled again as the last ghostly sheep crossed the road. This herd had blue stripes sprayed onto their wool. She wondered if they were in need of a shearing or if it were some kind of identification marker. When she started the ignition again, she pulled off still thinking about Aiden. She cared about her character, Bryon, sure. But she was more concerned about handsome Aiden. Like, what was his last name? What did he do for a living? Was he single?

"Jesus, where did that come from?" Antonia knew that she had no business thinking about another man just after fleeing Derek. She wasn't thinking about Derek's feelings, she was more concerned about her own. If her judgement was so impaired that she almost married a cheater, she had plenty of time before getting back into the saddle. "No, this trip is not for that," she said in a stern voice. "I've got to get my shit together and write a book."

Her singular focus needed to be getting Augusta into the arms of Bryon, the only man who could help her crack the sex trafficking story in Thailand. She was still uncertain about the plot. The months of research she'd done on Bangkok had been interrupted by the Migrant Crisis of 2013. She started reading up on the ethnic Muslim group from Myanmar making their perilous escape from government brutality. Antonia doubted how much she knew about the very real-world tragedy in Southeast Asia, but was compelled to include it in her novel.

Tall trees hung over the road, blocking out a setting sun. Antonia checked the GPS map and grew excited that she was rapidly closing the distance. "You will approach your destination in one kilometer."

"Yes, lord!" Antonia cried, slapping her steering wheel. "I did it! I fucking did it."

When she saw the sign for Tully Cross, a thrill shot through her body. And then she saw the village and realized how accurate the description was. It was indeed a village. The main street that Breda had spoken of was Tully Cross's only street. There was a small white church with a very small parking lot. Up ahead the lights were on at the pub and locals stood outside under plumes of cigarette smoke.

"You destination is on your left," Vera announced. "You have reached your destination."

Antonia spotted the row of white cottages on her left. "Thatched roofs?" She frowned. "Whatever." If she could just stop the car for the night, she'd be elated. If the place had a hot shower, that would be even better. She peered at the simple cottages with their red doors and cute flower boxes in each window. This was her Irish home for the foreseeable future.

Mr. Creely stooped over her door lock, alternating between jamming her key in the door and peering at it over his thick glasses. He looked up at her in amusement, his pale blue eyes magnified like Mr. Magoo. "Dear girl, we'll get you inside somehow," he joked.

Antonia watched his fumbling and wondered when

it would be a good time to intervene. "No worries," she said, shifting her computer bag to the other shoulder.

"These locks, they do as they like."

"Of course."

"Eh, there we go." An ancient *click* against rusted metal indicated progress. "Like a glove."

He swung the door open and Antonia smelled the mustiness of the cottage before anything else. She'd need to open the windows immediately. Mr. Creely allowed her to enter first. He followed behind her, shutting the door as he went.

"Please remember that your front door locks from the outside, even without the key. So don't you go forgetting it when you step out."

She made a mental note of that as she looked around. To her right, there was a small galley kitchen no bigger than her own in Chicago. To her left, a spacious living room with one couch, a dining table with six chairs, and a small television set.

Mr. Creely led the tour, starting with the kitchen. "You've an oven and stove, a refrigerator, and a microwave. This here switch," he gestured to the wall. "Is for your hot water. You don't need to turn it on until you want to do the washing up. Speaking of the washing up, you can clean your clothes here." He pointed to the tiniest washing machine under the cabinet where the microwave sat.

She looked around the small space. "Is there a dryer?"

"Your dryer is the Irish gale," he said with a chuckle. "There's a clothesline for every cottage."

Antonia vaguely remembered her mother talking about doing the family laundry "the old way" when she was a child growing up in the South. Her children were used to going to a coin operated laundromat down the block. Hanging clothes wasn't the end of the world, she decided. It would be…rustic.

"Now these cottages are mostly used for large groups, you know? There are two bedrooms this way." She followed him down the hallway to a master bedroom and a smaller bedroom with two twin-sized beds. "You can fit three people down here and two upstairs."

"There's an upstairs?" Judging from the quick look she had in the living room, the high beamed ceiling seemed to suggest that this was it.

"Oh yes, there are two beds and a toilet in the attic."

It was impressive as it was lonely. She'd only need one room for her stay. "Here's the WC, right here," he said opening the door to the downstairs toilet. "Behind it, here's the shower and sink. Now pay attention to this," he flicked on the light to the actual bathroom. "The shower is controlled by this box."

She watched in confusion as he pulled a string on a box situated beside the shower head. The sound that emitted from the contraption sounded like a small generator. "Why?"

"It controls the hot water," he said above the noise.

"And is that different from the water heater switch in the kitchen?" she asked loudly.

"That's right," Mr. Creely said, switching it off.

Antonia stared at the shower, unable to understand the logic. "Alright."

He exited the bathroom. "Let's get you back to the living room."

As she followed the old man, she took a quick peek out of the kitchen window. She spotted her designated clothesline and sighed. It was a far cry from her hotel in Clifden.

"Here, you've got a fireplace. Fer the love of Mary, do not put paper in the fire. The roof will catch fire quicker than the flight of the *sidhe*."

She didn't know what that meant, but she nodded anyway.

"You've got plenty of peat to burn, but you may want to buy fire starters and logs at the store."

She peered into the bin that he referred to and saw black bricks of some kind of dirt. "Peat?" she asked, pointing at them.

"Irish fuel."

"Is there another heat source for the evenings?"

"Ye got central heating, the control panel is on the wall there," he pointed at the dial beside the fireplace. Antonia went ahead and turned the dial. With the setting sun, the cottage was already a little chilly. "The internet comes from that thing up there," he said craning his head upward.

She followed his gaze and spotted the small Wi-Fi router near the ceiling.

"I had those installed just last year," he said with pride. "Got complaints that people couldn't do their work."

"Great to know."

Mr. Creely shook his head. "All of that beauty out there and people still need to stare at a screen."

"Mm-hmm." Antonia kept her mouth shut.

"I'll leave you to look upstairs," he said, handing her the key. "My knees aren't what they once were."

Antonia slipped the key in her jacket pocket. "Of course, I'll check it out later."

Mr. Creely ambled to the front door, but paused to regard her for one last time. "You'll be staying here alone?" he asked.

"Yes."

"Mm. Your first time to Ireland?"

"Yep."

"How do you like it so far?"

She smiled. "I like it just fine."

"You from America?"

"Yep."

Mr. Creely nodded. "I got a brother who lives in Boston. You ever been to Boston?"

"Sure, once or twice," she said. "I'm from Chicago."

His clouded eyes lit up in recognition. "Obama!" he said with a smile. "He was a fine president."

"Oh yes," Antonia agreed.

"When he came here, several years back, oh was that wonderful."

"I bet."

"And what did you say you do?"

Antonia distinctly remembered not telling Mr. Creely anything about herself. "I publish," she stopped short. "Well, I used to publish books. But now I'm trying to write a novel."

Mr. Creely was impressed. By what, she wasn't entirely sure. "You're a writer? My goodness, how grand."

"I haven't finished anything," she said.

He patted her on the arm. "Ah, but ye will, ye will, dear girl. You'll find inspiration out here." He turned and slowly started for the door. "You'll be a Joyce, yet," he called over his shoulder.

Antonia chuckled. "I don't know if I've got a *Ulysses* in me."

Mr. Creely swatted the notion away. "Ah, start off slow and try fer a *Finnegans Wake*," he joked.

She shook her head with a grin. "Sure, I'll try that."

Once he stepped outside, he turned and said, "You might want to talk to your neighbor about writing."

"My neighbor?"

"There's only one other visitor here and he's right next door. Dr. Byrnes is a professor who comes here every year. Galway man, I believe."

"Oh really?" Antonia asked leaning against her doorway. "Do you know what he teaches?"

"Literature," Creely said with a wink. "Although, tonight you may find him at Coynes."

"Coynes?"

"Paddy Coynes, the pub across the street. Also, the chipper is next door."

"The chipper?"

"Fish and chips, hamburgers and whatnot."

Antonia nodded. "Good to know."

"Well, I'll leave you be," Mr. Creely said. "You have any problems, you just stop by the office."

"I will," Antonia said, relieved to settle down. "Thank you so much for your help, Mr. Creely." She closed the door on him and sank against the other side. A powerful wave of exhaustion swept over her. She still had to retrieve the rest of her bags from the car, get her groceries in the fridge, and email her loved ones before she could consider resting. "But I'm home," she announced to the empty cottage. The silver lining was finally starting to appear before her. Antonia could already feel her shackles lighten. The weight that she left back in Chicago was just that, left in Chicago.

Chapter Ten

Antonia steeled herself against the stares from the smokers outside of the Paddy Coynes Pub. She folded her arms across her chest as she walked through their thick cloud of smoke to gain entrance.

"Evening," one heavy-set man said, flicking his ashes at the sidewalk.

"Evening," she breathed, reaching for the door. *So far so good.*

Inside the small and cozy establishment, things weren't quite as busy as she feared. Most of the clientele must have been outside smoking. A table of young men and women looked up at her as she entered. They gave her a good once-over before returning to their drinks. Antonia had experience with being one of just a few black people in a classroom, a workplace, or at one of Derek's work functions. This, however, was even more alienating. She was the only black person in an *entire village* and imagined that she would be known as "that new black woman," in no time.

Antonia veered straight to the bar. A stiff drink could do her good right about now. She was weary from the road and jet lag was sure to follow. She wedged herself between two, red-faced men—one fat, the other bald—

and flagged down the barman who had his back to her. "Excuse me?" He couldn't hear her voice over the traditional pipe and drums that filtered through the pub's speakers. "Excuse me."

"Danny!" the bald gentleman barked.

The wiry barman turned on his heel, flinging a dish towel over his shoulder.

"There's no need for ye to be shoutin', Steven."

"I ain't shoutin' for my sake," the bald man said hitching a beefy thumb at Antonia. "I'm shoutin' for the church mouse."

"Thank you," Antonia said.

Steven, who already looked bleary-eyed for six o'clock, looked her up and down. "And yer very welcome. Dear me, where'd ya come from?"

"The cottages across the street."

The bald man burst into a loud braying laughter. "I mean, *where* are ya from?"

Antonia's face warmed. This was the second time today she'd flubbed this question. "I'm from America."

"I've got a cousin in Boston," he said. "You ever been to Boston?"

She nodded. "Yep. I'm from Chicago though." How many times would she have to repeat this?

"Steven, leave her be," Danny snapped. "Can't you tell you're drivin' her to drink?"

"Oh, it's fine."

Danny leaned against the bar, adjusting the loose cigarette tucked behind his ear. "Now, what can I get you?"

She didn't want to look like a novice on her first night. "Guinness, please."

"That's a real woman," said the red-faced fat man from the other side of her. He looked fairly tall and wide, perched precariously on his barstool. While he wore an expensive gray three-piece suit, he also appeared to be in his cups.

"Coming up," said the barman, retrieving a glass. She watched as he pulled the Guinness lever, filling a glass with the dark brown beer. A lovely thick creamy foam formed as it hit the top, making her lick her lips. "You're from Chicago, huh?"

"Yep."

"Your first time to Ireland?"

How can everyone tell? "It is."

"How are you liking it so far?"

She pulled her gaze from the beer and looked at Danny. Antonia didn't know if it was the exhaustion or the repetition, but the question sent her into a peal of laughter. "Jesus," she said in between gasps. "I'm sorry."

Danny gave her a curious smile. "Beggin' yer pardon?"

Antonia leaned over the bar and shook her head. "It's not you, it's everyone…"

"I'm pretty sure I asked her the same thing earlier today," said a masculine voice from behind her. It was a very familiar deep and husky voice that she remembered hearing not too long ago. Antonia whirled around to face her frozen pizza friend, Aiden. He was wearing the same snug sweater and gorgeous smile from earlier.

Her mouth must have fallen open because Steven remarked, "She looks like she seen a ghost."

"Aiden," she breathed.

"Antonia," he replied, tipping an empty glass at her.

"Her name's Antonia?" Danny said. "That's a real class name!"

"That's what I told her," Aiden said, leaning past her

to place his glass on the bar. She felt the warmth of his body as he pressed closer to her. His scent was a pleasant mix of soap and citrus. Her belly flopped as his arm brushed against hers.

"What's she do for a living?" Danny asked as if she weren't standing there.

Aiden gazed down at her and pursed lips that were almost shrouded by his black beard. "I'm not sure, Danny. I don't think I got around to asking her that."

She shook herself out of her stupor and answered, "I publish, I mean, I used to publish books."

Aiden gave a nod. "Well, there you are. She used to publish books."

"Any Irish books?" Steven asked.

Antonia frowned. She had no memory of her past life before arriving to this bar. "I don't know," she murmured. She also wondered how the tables had turned so quickly. Only hours before, it was Aiden who was the nervous one. She swore that she'd had the upper hand in their previous interaction. Now, she bumbled like an idiot, a passive viewer of a spectacle that was quickly unfolding. "I'm not sure," she clarified.

"Don't worry boys," Aiden said with a wry grin, his forest green eyes twinkling in the low light of the bar. "One day, an Irishman will make it across the pond. I heard Oscar Wilde did alright for himself."

"He did alright indeed," Danny said. "Your Guinness?"

Antonia was, as her mother called it, "stuck on stupid." She slowly turned to reach for her beer, hesitating to take her eyes off Aiden. She didn't remember being this nervous when she met Derek. That was a walk in the park compared to the flush of embarrassment that currently struck her. "Thank you," she said to Danny.

"I'll have the same as the lady," Aiden spoke up. "And please put it on my tab."

"Oh, you don't need to do that," she insisted.

He smiled. "I don't, but I'd like to."

"First your pizza and now this," Antonia murmured into her glass. "You're a very giving guy."

"You have no idea." His voice was low and directed just to her.

A flash of alarm shot through her body. No, not alarm, something else… Antonia was desperate to extricate herself from the situation. But before she could move past him, she saw a flash of something heavy making a fast descent. The red-faced gentleman in the three-piece suit was taking a dive from his barstool and threatened to take her with him. Antonia moved too slowly to hear Danny's shout from behind the bar and the scrape of wood against the floor.

Before she had time to react to the flurry of movements, Aiden's strong arms scooped her up by the waist and shoved her against the bar. They narrowly missed the man who tumbled like a boulder, but she accidentally sloshed her fresh Guinness all over the front of Aiden's sweater. Antonia gasped from the panic but when she caught Aiden's gaze, she almost swooned within his grasp. He stared down at her as he shielded her body, and in that split second, she saw something in his eyes: A fierce possessiveness. She now understood the feeling that shot through her body. It wasn't alarm, it was arousal. His large hands were planted on her hips, clutching her firmly, a vivid reminder of where a man's hands could trail. While his touch didn't linger for too long, she recognized the sensation that scorched her skin. Unable to speak, Antonia simply watched Aiden push her to safety before assisting the other men rescue the gentleman on the floor.

They certainly had their work cut out for them. The man was unconscious and lying on his back like a giant tortoise. Three grown men struggled with all of their might to pull dead weight from the floor. "Antonia, go 'round 'em and pull up a chair," Danny shouted, the tendons in his neck stretched as he dragged the man by his arm.

Antonia set her beer down and raced behind the group of men for the nearest chair. While they heaved, she tried to fit the chair under the man's hindquarters. "Can you get him to the chair?" she asked.

"Brace yourself!" Danny called out.

"Steady the chair, lass," Aiden said in an authoritative baritone. "Put your back into it."

If the situation weren't so laughable, Antonia would have thought they were hauling a harpooned beast onto a whaling ship. She was slightly shaken, but still alert and strong enough to hold the weight of a drunken patron in a chair. When they got him squarely fitted into a safer seat, they straightened and looked upon their handiwork. Danny took the towel he'd tucked in his waist and wiped the sweat from his brow. "Jaysus, Michael..."

Michael, the drunk man, came to after a couple light slaps on his ruddy cheek.

"Where's me whiskey?" he demanded, oblivious to the sweating men around him.

Aiden chuckled as Danny and Steven swore under their breath. "You've had enough whiskey," the barkeep barked. "Just sit here and settle your hash, will ya?"

"I wanna sing a song," Michael slurred loudly. At this point, Danny threw his hands up and walked back behind the bar. Antonia assumed that this was a good time to release her death grip on Michael's chair.

Aiden reached out and took her arm. "Are you okay?" he asked. His large hand held her still as he appraised her for any injuries. The warmth of his touch made her tremble slightly. His closeness was inviting and dominated the space around them. The energy vibrating around him was almost enough for Antonia to forget where she was.

"Yes," she said with a halting laugh. "I didn't expect this kind of excitement from a sleepy village."

Aiden's face broke into a handsome grin that was just as contagious. She couldn't help but return it and blush profusely. "Sounds like it's your first time in an Irish pub."

"Thanks for the welcome and the drink…that you're currently wearing," Antonia said, pointing to his wet chest. "Sorry about that."

He looked down, as if he hadn't noticed the dark stain on his sweater. "No worries, darling. We'll get you another."

"Already working on it," Danny said from behind the taps. "Can't have the lass's first beer in Ireland spoiled on Michael's account."

After receiving her second beer of the evening, Antonia and Aiden found a quiet seat next to the bar's fireplace. It burned with peat and gave off a pleasant earthy scent that she didn't mind. Antonia looked forward to building a fire in her cottage later on.

"Mesmerizing to stare at, isn't it?" Aiden asked as

he sat beside her. The only thing that separated them was a small table to rest their beers on.

She ignored her pounding heart and focused on the comforting warmth of the crackling fire. "It is," she said. "I don't have a fireplace at home, in Chicago,"

"In America."

Her gaze flew to his and found laughter in the small wrinkles around his eyes. "Yes, in America," she said, stifling a smile.

"What are the odds that you and I would end up in the same tiny village in the middle of nowhere?"

"This wasn't meant to be."

Aiden took a swig of his beer. "No?"

"My original plan was to stay in Clifden, but my hotel reservation fell through."

"And the goddamn oyster festival brought you out here?"

She shrugged. "Go figure."

Aiden leaned back in his seat and contemplated her situation. Antonia snuck a peek at his long, sturdy Viking legs. *What would it feel like to sit on his lap?* Feeling very thirsty, she returned to her beer. The creamy metallic taste would take some getting used to, but it relieved her dry mouth. Yes, she was thirsty, indeed. Her polite sips of Aiden's body became long languid stares. He had ditched his wet sweater and now sat in a black T-shirt, revealing muscular forearms covered with smooth black hair. Her gaze traveled to his sizable biceps and powerful shoulders. *What's under that T-shirt?* "...when we were at SuperValu."

Antonia barely heard him. She blinked and returned to his face. "What's that?"

His smile was teasing. *Lord, he has a wickedly sen-*

suous mouth. His bottom lip was especially plump and kissable. "I said that I should have asked you where you were staying when we were at SuperValu."

Her brow shot upward. "Why would you do that?"

"Because I regretted not asking once I stepped outside. But I already gave you a pizza, so there was no need to be creepy."

"Thank you for that," she said evenly. Why did she sound so defensive? He was being nice and charming enough. She shook her head, the half beer seemed to make her a little foggy. "I'm sorry, I think I'm a little tired."

He leaned forward and peered at her with a concerned expression. "That's understandable," he said. "Are you staying at the hotel next door?"

She sighed. "I couldn't even swing that. I'm staying at the cottages across the street. Apparently, it's just me and a literature professor named Byrnes."

Aiden nodded. "Really?"

"I hope he's a quiet neighbor," Antonia continued. "I'll bet he's an old man who smokes pipes and reads..."

"Oscar Wilde?" Aiden tried.

She took another drink and nodded. "Exactly, Oscar Wilde." She tried to focus her gaze on his beautiful face with his dark green eyes and their secretive humor, but it was becoming increasingly hard to do so.

"He probably teaches in tweed jackets with those elbow patches."

Antonia grinned. "I think that's the only way to teach literature," she joked. "His students probably fall asleep."

Aiden tipped his head and seemed to think about it.

"I imagine you're right. Although, you look like you're about to fall asleep yourself."

She glanced at the remainder of her beer. "I better get going," she said, feeling self-conscious. "It's getting late." As she stood to her feet, the room spun slightly.

Aiden sprang from his seat to catch her by the elbow. "Whoa, nelly," he said in a soothing tone. His hands, long-fingered and strong, held her steady as she swayed. "Let's not have *two* drunken falls tonight."

Antonia fought the urge to relax against his hard body, his heat battling against that of the fireplace. She blushed again. When she looked up, she saw the sharp planes of his face, shadows rising and falling with the flicker of the flames below. With those dark brows and glittery green eyes, he looked positively wicked. *Aiden is a potential mistake.* "I'm fine," she whispered, trying her best not to smell him. *Is that a mixture of bergamot and cedar?*

"Of course you are," he said, his voice husky and thick. "Let me help you across the street."

Antonia straightened up and away from him. "I can manage," she said with a confident smile. She did not want him coming back to her cottage. She didn't want to make a mistake. "Really, I'm fine."

He released her and stepped back. "Fair enough," he said with a smile.

"Thank you for my first...or second Guinness," she said, trying to be friendly. She worried that her brush-off sounded harsh.

"But not your last."

"Nope," Antonia said as she walked away. She left him standing by the fireplace. *Good, that's where he needs to stay.* She drew her jacket close to her neck as she exited the pub. In the chilly night, her breath was visible in the cold damp air. It helped her shake off the warm fog of the pub and kept her vigilant enough to check both ways before she scampered across the road. Antonia walked past the unit where the professor stayed. There wasn't a light on in his cottage and she presumed that he was already asleep. Which was exactly what she needed to be.

Aiden. His name lingered around the edges of her fatigued mind as she set her key on the nearby window sill. Antonia was concerned about her behavior around him and tried ignoring that she may have sounded short with him. It was different when she thought he was just a passing stranger. In the grocery store, his flirtation earlier seemed fleeting and harmless. It was a chance for her to "stretch her legs" away from Derek. There was a small part of her that wondered if she was being irrational. There was a chance that Aiden wasn't flirting with her. Maybe he was just a nice guy and this was what people meant when they spoke of the Irish "gift of gab."

Antonia kicked off her shoes and made her way back to the solitary bedroom, skipping the bathroom altogether. She shrugged out of her clothes and whipping the covers back, the ache between her shoulders eased slightly as she climbed into bed. "He's just a nice guy," she murmured in the dark. Sleep was ready to claim her any moment, but the image of his face burned its way into her memory. His eyes, green as the rolling hills of Connemara. *Aiden...*

Chapter Eleven

Aiden woke up drenched in sweat and hard.

The dream he'd experienced had been so vivid and sexual, he regretted opening his eyes to the morning light filtering through his bedroom window. He looked at the raised tent in his sheets and groaned. "Jaysus."

Aiden reached down and enclosed the aching stiffness, rubbing his length gingerly. Closing his eyes, he tried to return to the hot memories of his sleep. Antonia's soft body stretched beneath him, her full breasts undulating with each stroke he took. Her face was an expression of delirious desire as she gripped the multitude of pillows surrounding her head. Aiden stopped midstroke. *Where did all the pillows come from?* He opened his eyes and stared at the ceiling above him. "What are you doing?" he asked. "Who cares about the feckin' pillows?"

He sat up, cock in hand, and cursed the dream. He still had a hot club between his thighs as he scooted out of bed. He cursed the chance meeting they had in Super-Valu and the second chance meeting at Paddy Coynes. He tried pushing aside the idea of her reappearance acting as a sign. There was no reason to suspect that; it was all chance. Coincidence. Aiden turned the shower box on, switching the water to cold, and proceeded to flagellate himself in the jolting spray. One thing he would not do is pleasure himself with the thought of the woman next door. His journey to Tully Cross was for rest and writing, not to chase after American women.

He hung his head under the freezing water, wetting his hair and waiting for the ache to fade. When he was satisfied that his sexual urge had receded, he rewarded himself with warm water and washed briskly. The shock on her face when she had seen him though... Her mouth had fallen open, luscious lips gaping in genuine surprise. When she'd finally found her voice, it had been halting and breathy. Aiden was surprised she'd lost her wit since their grocery store meeting. He'd began to feel more confident the more she stumbled over her words. Perhaps it was because he was steadier on his home turf. And perhaps the incident with Drunk Michael helped. Rescuing a beautiful damsel from a tumbling fat man never hurts the cause. His heart had sunk when she decided to leave the pub so abruptly. He hoped that he hadn't scared her off. Aiden rinsed the shampoo from his hair while recounting their short conversation. Had he said something untoward?

"She was drinking pretty fast," he murmured. Perhaps she *was* tired and tipsy. He remembered holding her steady; standing so close that he smelled her hair. He caught the scent of coconut and maybe...vanilla? The flash of the memory forced him to turn his shower dial back to cold. He had to write something today. Anything really. *Just start writing.*

As he stepped out to towel off, Aiden reviewed his original paper proposal. Homecoming narratives. He would return to the DuBois biography and reread the passages on his life in Ghana. Aiden padded into his bedroom and searched his suitcase for jeans. Still running hot, he skipped the shirt and started his day. *A couple of eggs and toast should do the trick*. First, he would need a little motivation to accompany his breakfast. He found his phone and scrolled through his music playlist, settling on some Hozier. A nice bluesy Irish boy could set the breakfast tone. Aiden connected his phone to the portable speaker he brought with him and flooded the entire cottage with the mournful death march of "Take Me to Church." He sang loudly to the tune of lost love and regret while searching the kitchen cabinets for a frying pan.

As he fired up the stove, he set his pan on the burner and buttered it liberally. After an entire semester of rushing out the door without eating, he basked in the pleasure of a decadent breakfast. As he cracked two eggs, he lamented forgetting a pack of rashers at SuperValu. He missed cured breakfast pork.

As the next Hozier track began, his own voice rang out, off key and piercing the loneliness of the cottage. He was grateful that Mr. Creely hadn't inquired about Lisa when he checked in. Her previous visit had caused quite a stir. Any new female visitor to Tully Cross usually got people talking. The young women were largely outnumbered in the village because many of them fled to university, leaving the young men to stick around working their fathers' farms. Lisa's appearance, coupled with her aloof attitude, had garnered plenty of attention. She hardly spoke to the locals and barely left the cottage.

From the stove, Aiden caught a flash of black curls

hurry past his kitchen window. He frowned as he shut off the burner and slid his eggs on a plate. *Is that her?*

Seconds later, a sharp rap came from his front door. He wiped his hands on a dishtowel and approached the door. When he pulled it open, he found a fuming Antonia dressed in a T-shirt and sweatpants. Though her hair was disheveled and last night's makeup smudged her eyes black, she still looked sultry. He imagined that he could make her look like that after a good romp in bed. When she saw that it was him behind the door, her lips parted to form a dismayed "O." Aiden was quickly becoming accustomed to this kind of greeting. "Antonia! Good morning on ya."

This was the second time he had her at a disadvantage.

Antonia stepped back to look at his cottage number as if that would tell her who lived there. Her gaze flashed back to the shirtless man standing in the doorway. She blinked away the sight of his jeans dipping slightly off his hips. Black hair sprinkled over his broad and powerful chest with a long line tracing a path down the middle of his well-defined abs. The path disappeared at the waist of his jeans. *Lord, please stop tempting me.*

"You're…you're him?" she asked, reclaiming her voice.

He smoothed his damp hair out of his eyes and peered at her with feigned confusion. "I'm the man you keep meeting," he said over the music that came from his home.

"You're Professor Byrnes?"

"At your service," he said with a grin. That perfect smile with his perfectly straight teeth and that perfect bottom lip. She could not trace the origins of her anger. Was it because she was dead tired and needed more sleep or that he continued to confuse her? He caught her off guard with that perfectly disarming grin.

"Why didn't you tell me he was you? You were him?" She shook her head. "That you were Dr. Stuffy-elbow-patches?"

"Honest mistake," he said. "What can I help you with?"

Her mouth snapped shut. *Honest mistake, my ass.* "Could you please keep your music down?"

Aiden frowned. "You don't like Hozier?"

"I don't know who that is, I'm just trying to—"

"—Oh, he's grand," Aiden interrupted. "You've probably heard something by him. Surely some of Ireland's singers make it to your shores. It's not all Irish Rovers and pipes, you know."

"I don't—"

"We gave you Sinéad, didn't we?" The mirth in his eyes annoyed the hell out of her. "She's a bit gone in the head lately, but she had that one song. What was it?"

"'Nothing Compares 2 U,'" Antonia answered, amazed that she was following his train of thought.

He snapped his fingers. "That's right! Admittedly, Prince wrote it, but the girl still came from Ireland."

"Sure, I get it—"

"And you guys love Van Morrison, right? 'Brown-eyed Girl'?"

"Aiden!"

He paused. "You don't like 'Brown-eyed Girl'?" he asked, peering down at her.

She stewed under his piercing gaze. Yes, she was at a clear disadvantage. There was no way that she could out-talk this man. Antonia also felt foolish standing out there in the cold fog wearing the sleep clothes she'd managed to change into in the middle of the night. She hadn't even washed her face before marching over to Dr. Aiden Byrnes's cottage. She probably looked a frightful mess, with hair sticking out in every direction and tired raccoon eyes.

"I love a brown-eyed girl," he said punctuating each word. His eyes traveled over her body before returning to her face.

His roundabout chatter confused her. "Yes, it's a great song," she said, brushing off his comment. "But I came by to tell the doddering old professor to turn his music down. I'm trying to sleep."

Aiden nodded. "Why didn't you just say so?" He disappeared from the doorway. Soon, the quiet enveloped them. With the music off, she could hear herself think. A low moo from the pastures behind them wafted through the fog. "Have you had breakfast?" he called from inside.

Antonia edged closer to his doorway. Was he inviting her into his home? Offering her more of his food? "No…"

He appeared at the front door with a furrow in his dark brow. "Oh, that won't do. Didn't your mother ever tell you that breakfast was the most important meal of the day?"

Antonia rolled her eyes as she took a step back. "I didn't exactly have time to think about that when I was awoken at the crack of dawn."

"It's ten o'clock."

"I'm jet-lagged."

"Then it's best to stay on a schedule."

"I was told to enjoy Ireland *on my schedule*," she said. "That's the whole point of traveling solo, isn't it?"

One black brow arched. "You got me there. So no breakfast for you? I've got eggs."

Antonia didn't have eggs. The scent of cooked butter from his kitchen made her stomach growl in protest. "I can eat later."

"Why eat later if you can eat now?" His voice was low and conspiratorial, as if they shared this secret. "Life's too short to delay pleasure."

His tone was seemingly innocent. However, the way he rested languidly against his doorframe, muscles taut and ready to spring, she didn't know if she should chance it. Although, it *was* only breakfast. She'd eat quickly and return to her cottage to clean herself up. "Fine."

"Good," Aiden said, stepping aside so she could enter. "Go ahead and take a seat at the table."

She did as she was told and found a seat facing the kitchen. *He's just being a nice guy.* Antonia kept thinking this regardless of how beautiful his body was. He emerged from the kitchen with a plate of eggs and two pieces of toast. He set it on the table and took his own chair opposite of her. "You're not going to have any?"

"I will," he said. "Later. For now, I'd like to talk."

Antonia picked up a fork and cut into the eggs, the runny yolk a deep orange that looked more appealing than the anemic eggs back home. "You seem to do a lot of that," she said.

"That's what my mother told me just yesterday," he said, leaning back in his chair. "I don't believe I talk any more than she does."

Antonia let the rich creaminess settle on her tongue a

moment before she took a bite of toast. An involuntary moan escaped her throat as she closed her eyes. "Why are the eggs better here?" Using the toast to sop up egg, she quickly devoured her meal. When she looked up, she found Aiden sitting forward in his chair, staring at her. Antonia blushed. "Sorry."

"Don't apologize," he said, his eyes wandering over her. "You were hungrier than you thought."

Her eyes returned to her nearly empty plate. "I guess so."

"And are you always this stubborn?"

Antonia scrunched her nose as she dragged her fork across the plate, scooping up the remainder of her egg. "I'm not stubborn," she said, giving her fork an undignified lick.

"Let me make you some more," he offered, taking her plate.

"Oh, I couldn't," she said, shaking her head.

"That's what women have to say," he said, heading off into the kitchen. She heard the pop of the stove as he switched on a burner. A skillet was set back on the gas and two more eggs were cracked. "You lot act as if having a second helping is unseemly."

Antonia wiped her mouth on the napkin he gave her. "It's not unseemly," she called out. "It's just not…cute."

He gave a hearty laugh over the pop and crackle of the eggs. "One man's unseemly is another man's cute." His voice dipped into a mocking English accent.

"You don't get it," she said, remembering how she'd hid the fact that she was always hungry around Derek. She'd barely eaten in front of him when they went out to restaurants. He always ordered fancy dishes that required tweezers to assemble. When she returned home from their nights out, she'd usually tore into a bag of chips she hid away in a cupboard. She frowned at the memory of hiding her junk food when he came around to her place. "It's different for us."

"Perhaps," he said. "But I find it unusual when someone doesn't enjoy the most basic things in life. Humans deserve to enjoy food and drink."

"I guess."

"It's one of the few things that separate us from beasts."

She smiled at his refreshing honesty. She didn't get to listen to many people speak plainly at her job. Aside from Eddie, everyone constantly looked over their shoulders for the stealthy knife in the back. Derek's work colleagues had been even worse. All pleasant smiles to your face, but vicious barbs in your absence.

When he returned with her plate, he brought another fork with him. "What are your plans for today?"

Antonia picked up her fork and cut off a piece of egg. "I might take a walk before I start writing."

He joined her with his fork. "What are you writing?"

"Nothing important," she said after a hard swallow. She didn't want to talk about her book with him. Not after she'd decided to base one of her characters on him.

"I'm also writing something not important," he replied.

She sat up straighter. "Like what?"

"It's a dumb paper."

"An academic article?"

He exhaled harshly. "Not exactly, I just finished rewriting one of those. This is just a conference paper."

Antonia nodded. "It's been a long time since I've had to write anything for school," she admitted. "I like to keep my master's thesis far back in the recesses of my mind."

He shot her a crooked grin. "What was it about?"

"It was fifty-something pages of nonsense," she said recalling the all-nighters she pulled to get it done. "I wrote about Zora Neale Hurston."

"I love her writing," he said. "I usually assign my students her essay, 'How It Feels to Be Colored Me.'"

The fact that he was so well-read was just as attractive as his naked torso sitting at the breakfast table. *Of course he's well-read*, she thought, returning to her side of the plate. *He's a literature professor.* "I wrote about her anthropological work."

Aiden nodded in appreciation. "That sounds very interesting. Was it her field research in the American South or the Caribbean?"

He was actually listening to her. She had a fleeting memory of Derek and his phone. Always with that phone. "Mostly in the South. I found her folklore research exciting."

"Ah yes," he said. "That's right. She was able to incorporate local color in her writing because of her research. I don't think people appreciated it at the time, but it's truly valuable work now."

"Yes!" Antonia agreed. "That was part of my argument."

"Of course," he said, taking another bite. "You can't talk about her fiction without addressing all of the grunt work she did. Reading about her gives me hope for Ireland."

"How do you mean?"

"Well, we have our own language problems, you know. No one spoke Irish for the longest time, but it's making a resurgence," he said with a full mouth. "My little niece is going to a language camp this summer. I certainly didn't have that growing up."

"I didn't know that. I know nothing about the Irish language."

He tilted his fork at her. "And that's what the feckin' Brits wanted. It's not the same as black oppression in the states, but we're still rebounding from a lot of cultural thievery here in Ireland."

Antonia had stopped eating at this point, leaning forward and getting an impromptu history lesson. "Really?"

"Well, if you think about it, there are some interesting parallels between the black experience and that of the Irish people."

"None of that Irish slave nonsense, though?" Antonia asked.

He chuckled as he shook his head. "Oh lord no. Anyone who spins that yarn is trying to wind you up."

"It's a load of shite?"

He looked up at her, a curious smile played on his lips. "Yes, it's a load of feckin' shite."

"Well go on with this idea of parallels," she said.

"I think it's the colonialism that still troubles both groups. In America, black culture and black English isn't valued for itself, but has to be stolen and made a mockery of. And the idea of trying to reclaim something that's been lost isn't foreign to us either. Thousands of us had to leave this land during the famine, never to return to our home." He paused to think, cocking his head to the side. "You could say that in our absence, Irish culture has been snatched and made a mockery of as well. On the other hand, while we know where we come from, there's millions of African Americans who still wonder where in West Africa their lineage starts..." He trailed off, staring into space. "Hmm."

"What?"

He didn't answer her. Instead, he sprang from his seat and ran from the room. "I've just got an idea," he said over his shoulder. The clock that hung above his mantel made her wonder if it was time for her to take her leave. If he actually had work to do, she didn't want to stand in his way. Her mother always said "don't wear out your welcome."

She stood from the table, taking the empty plate with her. She'd at least wash a dish before she left. When Antonia entered the kitchen, she took a quick peek around the corner, to find him sitting on his bed scribbling something in a notebook. Her cottage had the same layout as his, she noticed. Only opposite. She squeezed dish soap on his plate and contemplated. *That means my bedroom is on the other side of his wall.* The thought sent a tingle through her belly. As she scrubbed the plate, she fell into deep thought. *When did he eventually get home last night?*

"Oh, you don't have to do that," Aiden said from behind her. "I don't feed guests only to make them wash up."

Antonia kept her eyes on the plate. His nearness, the whiff of his fresh soap scent, made her hands tremble slightly as she ran a sponge over the flat porcelain. She worried that it might slip from her hands if he didn't move away from her. But Aiden didn't leave her side. Instead, his arms surrounded her body, both hands resting gently on her forearms. He was trying to still her movements. Antonia froze as he took the plate from her hands and set it in the sink.

"I should go," was the first thing she thought to say aloud.

One of Aiden's hands stayed longer than intended. Antonia stared at his long, graceful fingers, at his pale thumb grazing her soft flesh, and fought the urge to rest against his muscular chest. Under the running water, Aiden slowly rinsed the dish soap from her hands, rubbing her fingers between his own. She stood there, hypnotized by the rough calluses of his palms slowly sliding across the back of her hands. Antonia let her eyes fall shut as warm pleasure washed over her body, starting at her fingers and landing squarely in her womb. She released a quiet sigh as a shiver ran up her back and left goosebumps on her arms.

"But we were chatting about literature," he said in a throaty voice. His warm breath brushed the fine hairs at her temple as his arms bracketed her body with delicious restraint.

She sensed his lips were far too close; her breath hitched and she opened her eyes. "I'm sure we can pick this chat up another time," she said in a shaky voice. *Must control yourself.* She willed herself not to appear rattled by this embrace, which may have not been an embrace at all.

He released her and stepped back. "I hope so." She heard a trace of humor in his voice.

Antonia snapped out of her trance, quickly dried her hands off with a nearby dish towel, and moved out of the kitchen. She couldn't bear to look at him at that moment. She was terrified of what she might see. Another man who looked at her with lust; a man who wasn't

Derek. What was she thinking? Her face burned with embarrassment. *Where is Derek now?* He was still in Chicago, unconcerned with her or her feelings. *Why on earth am I afraid of this new man?*

"Antonia," he said.

Her hand was on his front door. She hesitated before turning back to him. "Sorry," she said, meeting his gaze. Aiden cocked his head to the side and regarded her with curiosity. "I hate to eat and run..."

"Have a good writing day," he said, shoving his hands into his pockets, pushing the waist of his already low-slung jeans, even lower.

She had to get out of there. "You too," she said, forcing a smile.

"Yeah, well, talking to you was helpful," he said, moving closer to her. "I might actually start my paper today."

And her character, Bryon, was about to come to life. "Good!" she said a little too loudly. Antonia cleared her throat and opened the door. She needed some air. "I'll see you around." Only when she finally made her escape did Antonia feel relief. The cold morning air hit her in the face and brought her back down to earth. She didn't want to fly higher, closer to the sun that was Aiden. If she wasn't careful, he could burn her up.

Chapter Twelve

This was a surprise that Bryon hadn't counted on. Before him stood a very disheveled and very angry Augusta Sinclair, clutching a briefcase and phone in both hands. After all these years, she was still seething. He couldn't help but smile.

"What brings you to the Windy City, Caesar?"

"Don't call me that!" she snapped at him. She hated that nickname, but it always made him laugh. *Even though it wasn't quite her namesake, she had to admit that sometimes she could be a bit of a dictator.* "What are you doing here? Ugh, never mind." *She turned on her heel and stalked toward the building that he also meant to enter. This is going to be interesting.*

"Where are you headed in such a hurry?"

"Don't follow me," Augusta shouted over her shoulder. "I don't want to talk to you."

He had to jog to catch up with her pace. She was close to stomping holes into the city's pavement with each angry step. He moved ahead of her to grab the door. "Look, honey, I have no idea why our paths would cross after all of these years,

> *but hell…if you're still sore about what happened in 2010——"*

Antonia's hands hovered above her keyboard. Bryon's character appeared before her as an interesting mix of "dick" and "good guy." Brusque and crass, but endearing and great for a laugh. It felt right to her. It seemed like a mix of the men who were currently in her life. Derek was definitely a dick, smooth and sly, a man who could keep his lies packed away in the dark. Aiden was still a bit of a mystery, but from what she saw, he was endearing. His masculinity frightened her and kept her on her toes, but he seemed great for a laugh.

Now seemed like a good time to take a break and talk to someone else about her concerns. Octavia was the only person she knew who was up this early considering the new time difference. She saved her work and wandered back to the bedroom to find her phone. Along the way, she walked through the kitchen, catching the status of the washing machine. On her afternoon hike, Antonia had tripped and fell into what felt like a bog. She'd spent her long, miserable walk back to the cottage in wet, muddy pants. She peered through the circular glass pane at the wet clothes that still spun in clear water. *That's weird.* It was still running after even after her hour-long writing sprint, which seemed well past what her muddy jeans needed.

As she continued to her bedroom, she tried to remember which setting she put the machine on. After she retrieved her phone, she ran back to the kitchen. *Did I put it on the wrong setting?* Antonia panicked, she didn't want to break anything in a cottage rental.

She didn't know how much a washing machine cost in euros. *What if I broke it?*

With her phone in hand, she wondered who she could call. Antonia instinctively dialed her sister. Her sister in another country. When Octavia picked up on the second ring, she yelled, "What do you do about a washing machine that's been running for over an hour?"

"Good morning to you," Octavia's calm voice said.

"Hi, sorry, things are great in Ireland," Antonia said, staring at the still-spinning machine. It didn't even look like it was ready for the spin cycle.

A note of concern threaded her sister's voice. "Are you sure?"

"I mean, apart from my neighbor and this machine, yeah."

"What's wrong with your neighbor? Is he a racist?"

She didn't want to alarm her sister, whose main concern was that she remained safe while visiting another country. "No, no, nothing like that," she assured. "He's uh, very friendly actually."

"Creepy friendly?" Octavia demanded.

"No! It's not like that," she said, trying to pull open the washing machine's door. It was stuck and would be until the machine eventually stopped. Whenever that would be. "He's nice, very nice, I think. And really handsome and it's just a whole thing. Never mind, I was going to call you and talk Irish pleasantries, but I think there's something wrong with my washing machine."

Octavia sighed. "How long has it been running?"

"Close to an hour and a half maybe?"

"What setting do you have it on?"

Antonia checked it again. "Wash, I think. It's got, like, a million settings."

"And how can I help you?"

Of course she didn't know how her sister could help her. She just needed someone to talk to. Antonia was lonely in her five-person cottage, stuck in her writing, and unsure what to do in another country. "I need you to talk me down," she said, hearing the weariness in her own voice.

"Well, I can do that," Octavia said. "But, you're going to have to talk to the rental guy about the machine."

"Thanks."

"I got your long email before I went to bed. It sounds like Derek tried to screw you over."

"He did screw me over," Antonia corrected, as she walked to the door and slipped her sneakers on.

"I said what I said. He tried, but you rebounded."

"Why would he do something like that?" Antonia asked, leaving the house. Outside, it had warmed up enough for her to walk to Mr. Creely's house without a jacket. Aiden's car was gone. It brought her some relief to know that he was away. "Do you think he did it on purpose?"

"You did tell him what your plans were, so yes. Maybe he thought that would be a parting blow," Octavia said. "He knows what makes you anxious and insecure. I imagine abrupt change is at the top of that list?"

Octavia knew her well. Like any reasonable person, Antonia appreciated a good plan. No one *likes* for their world to be turned upside-down. She'd lost her job and her wedding in the same 24-hour period. It was enough to make anyone a little tight. "Still, it was a real dick move," she muttered.

"Oh, of course," her sister replied. "I'm just saying

that even though he threw you a curve ball, you've managed to sidestep it beautifully."

Antonia's face lit up with a smile. "You think so?"

"Definitely. Everything from here is smooth sailing," Octavia said in a tone designated for her toughest patients.

"I don't know about smooth sailing," she said, returning to realism. "I haven't told you about this village."

"Lemme guess," Octavia said with a chuckle. "You're the only black person there?"

"Yes," Antonia said in an exasperated voice. "My god, I don't think I've ever been this *alone*."

"Think of this as your James Baldwin experience," Octavia offered. "He left a terrible America to experience Europe. It gave him some time to reflect on his life back home."

Antonia stopped in her tracks, only a few feet from Mr. Creely's front door. "What made you think of Baldwin?"

"Because you used to study him. He was part of your scholarship in grad school, right?"

Antonia shook her head. "Yes. Right, it's just…" She looked at the handwritten note on Mr. Creely's door: *Gone to Letterfrack. Will return this evening.* "Shit."

"What's up?"

"Shit, shit, shit," Antonia repeated. "The owner, Mr. Creely, isn't here."

"No need to panic," Octavia said. "Just go back to your place and unplug the machine."

"Hey stranger!" said a man's voice from the road. She turned around to see Aiden sticking his head out of his car window. She gave him a reluctant wave. "Creely's not there; he's in Letterfrack."

"That's what the sign says," Antonia called back. She didn't bother hiding the sarcasm from her voice.

"Anything wrong?" Aiden asked.

"My washing machine is acting weird."

"Give me a minute and I'll help you with it," he said, rolling up his window. He didn't bother sticking around for her refusal. He was pushy as hell. Sure, he was helpful, but goddammit, he was pushing himself squarely into her vacation.

"Who was that?" Octavia asked.

"The man from next door," she muttered.

"Oh, well there you are. Saved by a helpful gentleman," her sister teased.

"Should I leave you on the line to hear him mansplain what I did wrong."

"Absolutely not," Octavia said. There was running water on her side. "I'm going to take a shower and head to work."

"But it's your day off."

"I've got some insurance filing to do. But good luck with the wet clothes."

Antonia rolled her eyes as she walked back to her cottage. She knew when she was being pushed off the phone. Like their mother, Octavia had no social graces when it came to ending conversations. "Yeah, thanks." Aiden was waiting on her when she rounded the corner. He was at least wearing a shirt, which was *something* to be thankful for.

"It's been running for a long time."

"How long?"

She was sheepish as she approached him. "I don't know, like an hour or so."

"I don't know if that's too alarming."

"Okay," she admitted. "Close to two hours, I suppose."

His poorly disguised smile widened. "Okay?"

Antonia crossed her arms in front of her chest. "Can you help me or not?"

He laughed in reply. "I'm sorry, but you've used a washing machine before, right?"

"Our machines are a hell of a lot more efficient in America."

"You're in Ireland now, darling," Aiden said with a shrug. "We have a different idea of *efficiency*."

She sucked her teeth and looked away. "Well I'm sure I can just unplug it myself."

"I'm sure you could," he said while wiping his tear-filled eyes. "Let's see what we can do."

"Yeah, well, I'm sure I can manage a plug," she said, turning to open her door. "Thanks for the laughs, Aiden." She knew she was starting to sound childish, but this was the most dissatisfaction she had been able to show toward a man in a long time. She quite liked not being so congenial all the time. Although, Aiden didn't look too turned off by her sharp tongue. If anything, it seemed to have the opposite effect on him.

"Oh don't be on that way," he said. "I'm just winding you up. Takin' the piss, is all."

She barely heard him as she jiggled her door knob. Antonia was met with resistance when she pushed at her door. "Shit."

"You need a key, darlin'," he joked, sounding just like her character, Bryon. The eeriness of his phrasing wasn't lost on her as she tried to turn the knob.

"I left it on my window sill," Antonia said, closing

her eyes. She thought nothing of it when she was talking to her sister on the phone. "Jesus, I'm locked out."

Aiden stepped back to survey the small house. "I bet you've got an open window somewhere."

Antonia thought for a moment before clapping her hands in excitement. "My bedroom!" she cried. "I shut it last night when it got cold, but I don't think I locked it."

He gave her an appraising nod. "Then you've got a break-in to conduct."

"I guess so," she said with a grin.

"There's that smile," he said softly. "I was wondering when I'd see it again."

Her grin fell away as quick as it appeared. "I'll lead you to the back," she said, turning on her heel.

They walked around their connected homes to the grassy area of the backyard, where her bedroom window was located. She prayed that she was correct as she laid her hands on the thin-paned glass. When it slipped open at her tentative push, she beamed at Aiden, who stood off to the side. "Bingo," she said.

"Do you want me to pop in?" he offered.

"I got this," she said with a confident scoff. Antonia hoisted her body up against the opening and awkwardly stuck her head inside. Sure enough, she could still hear the washing machine rinsing her clothes. "Although…"

"Hold yourself there," she heard his voice behind her. "I'll give you a nudge." His hands were on either side of her hips, steadying her balance.

"Hey," she said in a wary tone. "Don't try anything fresh."

"I'm only helping."

With his support, she wedged one knee against the window sill and angled herself halfway in. Aiden held on to her free leg and eased her through. When both feet were on the floor, she gave him a thumbs-up. "I'll let you in on the other side."

Minutes later, Antonia met him at the front door. "It's still running," she said wearily.

He moved past her and went straight to her kitchen. Aiden squatted down before the machine and examined the settings.

"What do you think is wrong with it?" she asked, hoping that she wasn't an idiot.

"It appears you set the machine to intensive wash. That adds quite a bit more time," he said, squinting up at her. "What were you trying to clean?"

"Some muddy clothes," she said. "I fell on my hike today."

"Aww, where'd you go hiking? I could have gone with you."

Antonia gestured to the machine. "The problem at hand, Aiden."

"Right." He nodded as he pressed one of the buttons. The clothes eventually stopped spinning as the water drained from the machine. "There you are."

"How did you do that?" she cried.

He opened the door. "You have an off button, dear."

Antonia shook with fury, cursing herself for panicking in the face of logic. As she reached into the machine and pulled out the garments, she found that all of her clothes were still soaking wet. "Oh my god," she said. "How am I going to dry these before nightfall?"

Aiden took a T-shirt from the pile she cradled away from her body. "We start wringing," he said, twisting the excess water into her kitchen sink. "And then we'll hang them on the line."

Antonia stared at him, his powerful forearm muscles rippling as he wrung her clothes. "You don't have to do that," she said in a tired voice. Her day had started off so productive and now this frustration thwarted her. Watching him help her made her feel foolish. "You're spending the day cooking and cleaning for me."

He smiled to himself. "It's not a big deal, Antonia."

But it was a big deal. A man had never helped her with the little things. His easy confident manner was a stark contrast from her constant anxiety. Between the mess she left in Chicago and this new environment, hypervigilance was threatening to break her down. Right now, this did not feel like a relaxing vacation in the Irish countryside. Antonia's heart began to pound and her face grew warm. Before she could stop herself, her face crumpled and she began ugly crying. "It's just very nice of you," she said, wiping her nose.

Aiden looked up from his wringing in alarm. "It's just a washing machine."

She shook her head. "It's not just the washing machine," she said as the heavy pile of clothes slipped from her tired arms. Antonia stared dumbly at the wet articles that plopped onto the kitchen floor. *Great, I'll have to wash those again.* "I'm making a mess out of this trip."

"But it's only been a couple days."

The dam broke and she didn't know what to do. She was officially crying to the handsome man from next door. She probably looked like an unhinged lunatic. "But it's the start of something shitty," she wailed.

Aiden gathered her in his arms and pulled her head against his muscled chest. "You don't know that," he said, his voice gentle in her ear.

She wanted to stay like this forever, his arms

wrapped like a warm blanket around her body. One damp hand kneaded the middle of her spine, while the other cradled the back of her head. His fingers wove through the tight curls of her nape, massaging the ache away. She sniffed and said in a low voice, "I'm getting your shirt wet."

"Not as wet as your intensive-washed clothes." His voice rumbled deep from his chest.

Antonia couldn't help her laughter. "Shut up," she said through her tears.

He squeezed her closer. "I'm sorry, but the Irish laugh to keep from crying."

"My mother has said something similar," she replied. "I think I need a drink."

"The Irish also do that to keep from crying," he said. "Let's hang these and go to the pub."

Antonia looked up at him. She hadn't noticed, until now, how much he had shaved down his beard. The planes of his face and the angle of his jaw were more defined with less scruff. His aquiline nose and straight forehead fit perfectly with the rest of his features, she realized. At this angle, only inches from his face, Antonia was keenly aware of their embrace. Her hands were still planted on his sturdy chest. Beneath her fingers, she felt his muscles twitch. Antonia was close enough to notice the small flecks of amber set in the backdrop of emerald irises.

She felt his hands move along her body, one sliding to the small of her back, the other tilting her head away. Antonia understood that, in this moment, she could kiss him. She could sink into his body and taste what she was too afraid to try. Judging by his half-hooded lids, the way he teethed at his bottom lip, Aiden would surely return the kiss. "It's not too late?" she breathed. She was half referring to her clothes and half wondering if she could share another man's bed.

"The pub is open until midnight."

Antonia blinked before laughing. "To hang the clothes." The water in her eyes began to recede.

"Of course not," he said, reaching up to wipe a tear from her cheek with his thumb. The gesture was simple and sweet enough for her to lean her cheek into the palm of his hand. "We might not have the sun for too long, but we've got plenty of wind."

Aiden's certainty of everything made her feel better. He assured her of the best when she was constantly expecting the worst. "Alright then, let's get that drink."

Chapter Thirteen

"We're getting a fierce gale tonight," Danny announced
to no one in particular. He was emptying the cash register and clearing down the bar.

Aiden looked up from his laptop to find that he and
Steven were the only patrons left at 4 p.m. "You're not
closing down, are you?"

"Aye, didn't you hear me?"

Aiden glanced out the window. Sure, the clouds
were dark but it didn't look any worse than the seaside
weather he was accustomed to. "But I was actually enjoying my work, Danny."

"Enjoy it at home," the barman said, slamming the
register closed and slinging his dishtowel over his shoulder. "I'm planning to."

Aiden reluctantly closed his laptop and shoved it
into his bag. He was nearly done with his paper, but he
was still mulling over his introduction. Antonia didn't
know it, but she was a large part of why he returned
to his work with enthusiasm. Talking to her yesterday
morning had jogged something within him. Even their
night, right here in the pub, was the shot of energy he
needed. After her sudden crying fit, Aiden sensed that
something, much larger than this trip, weighed heavy

on her mind. Cradling her tear-stained cheek in his hand had stirred something deep within him; Aiden just wanted to make her happy. He had a desperate desire to kiss her tears away. The very thought made him nervous because she wasn't his to make happy. Aiden finished his beer in one last gulp and took his glass to the bar. "Thanks anyway."

"I'll probably open the shutters sometime tomorrow," Danny said. "Say, how's your friend, Antonia? She was a real craic last night."

"I wouldn't be surprised if she had the brown bottle flu," Aiden said.

Danny nodded as he took the empty glass and went back to wiping down the bar. "The girl was bolloxed before she left. Seemed like one of those knackered Americans."

She did seem very stressed out. But once she got a couple drinks in her, she loosened up and started taking the piss with a few patrons. By the time their night came to a close, she was on her way to learning a few seafaring shanties. Unlike Lisa, who had always quietly sipped her white wine in a corner, Antonia had definitely been a hit.

Danny told him as much. "Lot more fun than the *lace curtains* from last year. What's her name?"

Aiden laughed at the expression. Apparently his mother wasn't the only one who used it. "Lisa," he said. "We broke up."

"I'm sorry to hear that," Danny said without much sympathy. "What's the American's story?"

"Honestly, I don't know. She's from Chicago and she published books."

"You might want to find out more," said Steven, who was still hunched over the bar. "I like the lass."

"Yeah, Steven," Aiden said. "You like all the young lasses." Aiden hitched his bag over his shoulder and made his exit. Outside, the air was filled with warm static. A light breeze swept over his face, sending a chill down his spine. Perhaps Danny was right. The clouds coming in from the west were menacing, blowing fast and black. He hurried across the road, whistling an old familiar tune that came to him out of the blue. His father, who was a shadowy presence in his youth, always sang shanties from the boats he worked on. When he was in a fair to middlin' mood, he'd belt out in a thunderous voice, "Oh, a plate of Irish stew wouldn't do us any harm." It signaled that he was ready for his mother to get in the kitchen, Aiden recalled with chagrin. He also remembered his mother rolling her eyes in response, but a sly smile played on her lips. As he approached his cottage, he saw Antonia's car parked outside. Relieved that she wasn't on the road, he unlocked his door and let himself in. Under his breath, he caught himself singing, "So we'll roll the old chariot along, An' we'll roll the old chariot along…"

Aidan sighed, wondering when the bothersome memories of his father would finally fade into the background of his life. He didn't think that his brothers felt this way; they probably moved on long ago. They were now fathers themselves. But there were odd flashes of childhood scenes that still haunted Aiden, the songs were just some of them.

When Liam Byrnes left for the last time, Aiden had been fifteen and convinced that he'd take to the sea like his father. The restless beauty of open oceans and getting his hands rough tying ropes seemed more appealing than taking his school exams. Luckily, his mother had berated the notion from him, citing that he was "too smart to be wasting his time on a fishing boat." Once he was accepted into university, Aiden had let the drifter's career and the idea of his father go by the wayside. Liam wasn't coming back, and he had to catch up with the revelation like his mother and brothers.

Luckily, he didn't have too much time to reflect on his past when he heard his phone ring. He sighed again, this time out of frustration because it was probably his mother, checking up on him. While turning on the television and flipping through all seven channels, he debated even taking the call. In the end, his mother always had him on a tight leash of Catholic guilt.

"Mam," he answered.

"Aiden, I'm glad I caught you," Clare said in a breathless voice. "Have you seen the weather service?"

"Does the pub owner count?"

"I don't know what that means," she replied. "A strong gale is going to hit the peninsula. You're going to get a hearty blow this evening."

"I felt it in the air," Aiden said.

"You've got your father's sailing nose."

Aiden rolled his eyes. As much as she warned him off his father's track, she still recognized he had the calling and chided him about it. "I think anyone could feel a storm coming in from the Atlantic."

"I didn't say it in offense," Clare said in soothing tones. "You're so sensitive sometimes."

"What can I do for you, mother?" Aiden asked settling himself in front of the television.

"Well, have you got provisions?"

"Have I got enough spuds in the root cellar?"

"You're a smart one, you know that?"

"Yes, Mam, I've got plenty of whiskey and crisps."

"And candles?"

"And an actual torch," he said, stretching out on his couch. "With batteries. Creely keeps them in the kitchens for emergencies."

"Very well."

When he successfully reassured his mother, he switched gears. "Hey Mam, do you remember that song Da sang?"

Clare chuckled. "Liam sang so many songs…"

Aiden grinned. "The one about Irish stew."

"Oh lordy me, *that* terrible one."

"It just came back to me," Aiden said. "I hadn't thought about it in years."

There was a long silence on the other line before his mother finally said, "Your old da held the drink better than he could a tune, but I suppose it wasn't his worst song."

"It's got me thinking about the origins though. I might like to write about it."

"I haven't a clue as to where it came from," Clare said absently. "I just assumed it came from those awful boats he worked on."

"It's an African American work song adapted by Irish sailors. I might want to make reference to it in my paper."

"Is it now? I didn't know that. How is your writing doing?"

"Slow and steady," Aiden replied. "I've been struck with inspiration."

"Really, now? What's her name?"

Her knowing tone disturbed him. "I'm sorry?"

"I know you heard me."

He sighed. "She's an American woman. Her name is Antonia."

"Isn't that a lovely name!"

"She's a lovely woman," Aiden admitted. "I can't tell if she's interested in me."

"If I know anything about my Aiden, I'll bet she's curious."

"I'll let you know how it goes." Outside his window Aiden saw the trees sway wildly away from a harsh gust of wind. It shook the cottage's shutters and howled down the chimney. "Until then, pray to the pagan spirits that this gale doesn't blow the sheep to sea." Just as he said it, the television screen went black. He hated it when his mother was right.

Chapter Fourteen

He took her by the hand and brought her close to him. As he nuzzled her neck, inhaling her fragrance, her body relaxed against his. "Let's go back to the guesthouse," he whispered in her ear. Augusta quickly pulled back, staring up at him. "Wow, you think this is going to be easy, don't you?"

Bryon cocked his head in curiosity. "Yeah."

"Tell me that you're willing to work on this story with me."

"Tell me that you're willing to consider the possibility of seduction."

Augusta burst into laughter. The spell was broken. "You're so full of yourself!"

He sure did like seeing her smile, even if she was teasing him. "I can wear you down, darling."

"Give me your word," she said, trying to be as stern as she could.

"I can give you something else."

She shook her head. "Keep 'em coming, Bryon."

"So you're going to make me work at this?"

Augusta appeared to think about it. He wanted

to know where her head was. Was this a possibility? "Yeah." It was like a lightbulb went off in her brain. "Yes, I want you to work at it. If you help me on this story, I will let you try to—" She used exaggerated air quotes for this. "Wear me down. Happy?"

Actually, that did make him happy. If she was open to the chance of picking up where they left off, he would find a way to help her navigate this city. They had five days to either write a Pulitzer Prize-winning piece on Bangkok's sex trafficking culture or they could finally reunite as past lovers.

The first time her bedroom light flickered, Antonia paid no mind. She hadn't heard the howling of the impending storm because she was listening to music with her earbuds. The long writing block she had set aside for herself was finally paying off. She was playing God to her characters and pushing them into situations that could potentially solidify their love for one another. Her intrepid reporter, Augusta, just had an accidental meet up with her old flame, Bryon, after years of not speaking to him. It's just her luck that they must work together for a new magazine. It was her second chance at journalism after Augusta's traumatic accident in Tunisia.

By the time her bedroom light flickered again, Antonia had sent her characters to Bangkok, the setting for her novel. When the lights finally went out, she paused her writing to save what beautiful progress she had made.

"Third day in Ireland and there's a power failure," she said in the darkness.

Only after removing her earbuds, did she fully understand what was going on beyond her bedroom window. *It sounds like a goddamn hurricane.* Antonia flung her covers aside and got out of bed. Her home was dark, but there was still some visibility. She didn't know if there were candles in the house or even a flashlight. In the darkness, the wind sounded more menacing. It screamed like the village banshee, shaking her shutters and rattling her door.

Antonia could remain unnerved by a little storm if she got her bearings and started a fire. She had experienced her fair share of damaging hurricanes while visiting her mother and stepfather in Florida. "Now those were storms," she said as she carefully entered the living room. A packet of matches sat atop the mantel. She groped for them and put them into the pocket of her sweatshirt. She scrunched her nose when she reached into the collection of peat bricks. Some were dried bricks of dirt while others were slightly damp. Using her sense of touch, Antonia tried to separate the dry ones to throw into her fire. She wished that she had the fire-starters that Mr. Creely spoke of, but figured that the Irish had used peat long before modern conveniences.

When she struck a match and tossed it in, she waited for a reaction. When a tiny flame flickered in the darkness she smiled proudly. She tossed in a couple more matches, for good measure and within moments, a soft glow lit her living room. She sat back on her heels and watched the fire. "You've still got a few tricks up your sleeve, old girl."

The fire was a small victory that she was able to pull off without panicking. It symbolized that she was capable of fending for herself. Aside from her meltdown over the washing machine, Antonia was actually doing alright. She got to Tully Cross, Ireland, managed to make friends, and now she was finally making progress with her writing. She was especially excited about the writing. When she was away from her novel, Antonia thought about it, and even missed her characters. Waking up this morning, she had decided to get straight to it. It had been the first thing on her mind as she prepared her coffee and brushed her teeth.

Of course, it hadn't been the only thing on her mind that morning. She replayed her night at the pub with Aiden. She'd absolutely needed a good night out with strangers who were quickly becoming family. As she listened to the patrons' stories and sang their songs, she'd felt like one of the locals. They reminded Antonia of her family from down South, warm folks who wanted to know how you were doing. Sure, they had asked a lot of questions, but they were interested and wanted to share their own perspectives of America with her. Like her family, she was held up several times when she tried to leave the bar. Antonia smiled at the memory. She'd tried to make her exit nearly four times, but paused to exchange social media information with several women whom she'd gotten to know.

Aiden was there too, but in the background. Every once in a while, they would catch one another's eye across the bar. She would smile and he would tip his glass to her. At one point, he saved her from an over-friendly gentleman who was quite drunk. Aiden came over and clapped the man on the back, re-introducing himself. Once they got to talking, Antonia quietly slipped away, thanking him later. Earlier that evening, a man stopped by with his young daughter, a cute blonde

girl who was about six years old. Antonia watched
Aiden hoist the girl onto his knee and jostle her while
she ate her crisps. The girl giggled hysterically as she
struggled to hold on to her snack. Watching that scene
made Antonia's heart melt. *Is there anything wrong
with the man?* Sitting down with the little girl, chatting with her while trying to steal her crisps, was very
touching. Apparently this beautiful man was also very
good with children.

Antonia sighed while staring in the fire. *This man...*
Even though the whole crying incident was embarrassing, she was thankful that he was able to talk her off
the ledge. On one hand, there was something so comforting about his presence. Whenever he was around,
Antonia could be vulnerable and loose. Unlike her time
with Derek, she didn't have to perform with a plastered
smile and memorize her lines. She felt somewhat normal around Aiden. On the other hand, that same presence could be overbearing and far too masculine. Being
close to him made her stomach clench and panic riot
within her. When she looked at him, she found it impossible to steady her erratic pulse. *Oh my god, when was
the last time a man made me feel this way?* She searched
her memory for any eager affection from Derek. Around
a month ago, their lovemaking fell on the side of short
and ineffective. It lacked the necessary foreplay for her
to feel comfortable and the "main event" was anything
but an event. Now that she knew the reason was another
woman, the pieces quickly fell into place.

Antonia's self-esteem also took a steep dive around
that time. She'd started examining herself in mirrors
and had become more critical of her weight. What her
mother would've called "thick," Antonia started to call

"pudgy." When Derek became obsessed with getting her in the gym with him, her alarm bells went off. It would be nice to be around a man who just let her be…her.

As if on cue, she snapped out of her thoughts to the sound of a sharp knock at her door. Antonia scrambled from the floor and ran to the front door. *What on earth is he doing out in the middle of this storm?* The rain was coming down in sheets and Aiden Byrnes was standing on her stoop. A bright flash of lightning lit the black sky behind him, illuminating the wild grin he wore and the green bottle of Jameson he held out to her. "Need a drink?"

"Jesus Christ, get in here," Antonia said, trying to contain her laughter. She stepped back to avoid the downpour and his wet body. The crack of thunder was ear-splitting as she slammed the door shut. She watched in amazement as the fully-drenched man hurried past her, nearly slipping in the kitchen.

"Where are your glasses?" he said.

"What are you doing here?"

"I was concerned about you," Aiden replied, searching her cupboards. When he found two rocks glasses, he shook out his wet hands and proceeded to pour heavy shots in both. "If you haven't noticed, it's storming out there."

"Yes, it is," she said, hiding her smirk. "You look like you went swimming in it."

He took his shot in one gulp and passed her a glass. "I feel like it." Aiden swept his wet black hair from his brow and winked at her.

She took the glass and swirled its contents around before she sipped it gingerly. She didn't usually consume straight shots of anything. "Thank you for your concern, but I'm quite alright," she said, wincing from the sting of alcohol.

"Well I'm not the biggest fan of storms," he admitted. "It looks like a hurricane doesn't it?"

"It's not," she assured him. "Your water is too cold for a decent hurricane."

He poured himself another shot. "You sure about that?"

"I'm pretty sure," she said, gazing at his torso. "You might want to take that off."

Aiden looked down at his soaked T-shirt. The wet fabric clung to his muscles, outlining every line and groove. "You don't mind?"

She absolutely did not. After all, there wasn't any harm in looking at his sculpted abs and firm pecs. Nothing wrong with a little window shopping. "No, I can hang it next to the fire."

Aiden took his sweet time pulling his shirttail up his body and over his head. He wrung it out in her sink and hand it to her. She took it, wondering if that was a subtle attempt to flirt with her. *Any opportunity for this guy to take off his shirt...*

"You can grab a towel from the linen closet and dry off," she said over her shoulder. "And put your wet shoes near the door."

"Yes, ma'am."

As Antonia draped his T-shirt over the rack that swung from her fireplace, she caught that familiar chill again. Her proximity to Aiden sent small jolts of electricity through her body. She quickly gathered her voluminous curls in a hair tie, balancing them on top of her head. She had no way of checking her appearance, but hoped that she looked okay in her favorite slouchy pajama pants and hoodie.

No, stop that. You're fine as you are. Instead of fretting needlessly, she took her place before the fire and continued to sip on her straight whiskey. In that moment, Antonia decided to stop struggling with perfection issues. Where had it gotten her in the past? She was now on vacation; in the midst of trying to find herself. *Augusta would wear her pajama pants.*

"I can't believe you built a fire," Aiden said, appearing in the living room with his glass and the bottle of whiskey. One of her bath towels was wrapped across his broad shoulders, his chest was still damp.

She looked up with a frown. "Why can't you believe that?"

He took a seat beside her and took a sip of his drink. "The washing machine was a major setback for you."

Antonia chuckled. "I'll never live that down?"

"It *was* kinda funny."

She looked down at his blue jeans, which appeared dark with water. "Are your pants really wet?"

He shrugged. "A little damp."

Without thinking, she reached out and laid the back of her hand against his thigh. His leg was rock-solid against her touch, and he jumped slightly. "Sorry," she said, quickly withdrawing her hand, realizing her overstep. "Do you need to dry those too?"

He peered over his glass at her before answering. "Darling, if I come out of these pants, it might be hard to get back into them."

It wasn't the fire or the drink that made Antonia's face flush in embarrassment. "I didn't mean…" She trailed off, watching his lips quirk with humor. He was teasing her. In this darkness, his eyes glinted in shades of gold and green. *Positively wolfish.*

"So what did you get up to today?" he asked, shifting the conversation.

Antonia took a breath. "I did quite a bit of writing. I finished three new chapters today."

He leaned closer to the crackling fire. "Did you really? That's excellent."

"I thought so too." She beamed at him. "I just put my head down and worked until the power went out."

"Good job," Aiden said with an encouraging tone. He appeared to actually be impressed. A university professor commending her efforts made her feel warm. "Now tell me what your book is about."

Antonia's mouth clamped shut. She feared that question. She had been so secretive about her writing that she wouldn't even know how to describe it. "It's nothing really."

"You said that already," Aiden reminded her. "I find that hard to believe. No one escapes to Ireland to write about 'nothing.' It's just not done."

"I didn't escape just to write," she protested and immediately closed her eyes. She didn't mean to say that.

Aiden nodded as he lay back against the rug. He propped himself up on one elbow, his abdomen muscles taut. "I plan on drinking the night away with you, Antonia. You might as well spill it."

As their eyes met, another jolt ran through her. The way he said her name caught her off guard. The sudden vibrancy of his voice and lilt in his accent made her shiver. "Was that your plan?" she breathed.

He nodded again. "A gentleman sits with a lady during a battering storm."

"Does he?"

"At least that's what my mam taught me…"

Antonia's shallow breath turned into a relieved laugh. He lobbed her emotions back and forth between lust and humor so easily. It was confusing and thrilling at the same time. "If I tell you, do you promise not to laugh?"

"I promise," he said.

She waited for a moment, watching his face for any signs of humor. "Okay then. First pour me another drink. I'd like to get slightly more tipsy before I do this."

He obliged her with another heavy pour. "Fair play."

Antonia took a large gulp and coughed, her eyes watering from the sting. "Goddamn!" she cried.

Aiden sat up and clapped her on the back. "If you're not a shooter, don't try to act like one."

"Alright," she said, heaving a breath. "So I'm writing a romance."

"Okay."

She watched his expression before continuing. "My protagonist is a ballsy journalist, who's always after her next big story. She covered the Arab Spring from Tunisia where she got shot from a stray bullet."

"Jaysus, that's a bit intense for a romance."

"I know," she said excitedly. "I want the reader to really get a sense of how important her career is. So anyway, she's laid up in the hospital suffering from PTSD. She doesn't get back on her feet until a few years later, when she's headhunted to work for this cushy travel magazine. She thinks that it might be a good way to get her feet wet again. Only, the thing is…"

"What?" Aiden asked. He was actually interested.

"When she shows up for her interview, she finds her ex-boyfriend, a photojournalist, at the same interview.

She hasn't seen him in years and they broke up because she thought he was cheating on her."

"Was he?"

Antonia took another drink. "No, it was some stupid misunderstanding. She's shocked to see him at this interview after all this time has passed. He's all: 'hey baby, nice to see you.' And she's furious all over again. But it turns out the magazine editor wants the both of them. They have to go to Bangkok and cover a touristy story for middle-American readers. Augusta is pissed."

"That's the main character's name?"

"Yes, and her ex-boyfriend's name is Bryon."

Aiden nodded. "And she's mad that she has to work with him while they still have this giant misunderstanding looming over them."

Antonia grinned. "Exactly."

"And even though she's just getting her feet wet with this new job, I'll bet she'll get bored with a cover story about rice paddies and elephants."

He gets it! "Right."

"What does she do?" Aiden asked.

"She goes to Thailand with Bryon, but she wants to spice this story up if she can. I'm thinking she'll want to investigate sex-trafficking and somehow that might be connected to the Migration Crisis of 2013."

His brows furrowed. "The people from Burma?"

"You've heard about it?"

"I have. It's just… Well, how does Bryon feel about all of this?"

"He's totally against it," Antonia continued. "He just wants to make a paycheck at this point in his freelancing career. Plus, he's already been there, which makes her so angry because it was an old job with National

Geographic that she wanted. Anyway, he was already
there during the Thai "red shirts" protest and saw some
seedy stuff. He doesn't want to experience it again nor
does he want to expose her to it." Talking her plot out
with another person was quite exhilarating, Antonia realized. Whether Aiden understood it or not, she could
hear her own good ideas out loud for the first time.

"So how are you going to get these two to come together and have sex by page one hundred forty-one?"
Aiden asked. His tone was completely serious.

Antonia stared at the bottom of her glass. "Well,
that's where I'm stuck. I read this book that said it's
supposed to be midway through the plot. Which is fine,
except I'm nervous because I've never written anything
smutty. So far, I've got a lot of stolen glances and near-
kisses." She looked up to see him studying the fire,
contemplating her statement.

"I see…"

"I mean, I published capital L literature, the high-
brow shit. Paperback romances never came across my
desk."

"But you obviously like reading them," he said.
"Which are your favorites?"

She paused to regard him warily. "Your promise to
not laugh extends to this as well."

His eyes widened in feigned insult. "I'm not judging you."

"You're a literature professor," she said through her
buzzed laughter. "Everything I'm saying goes against
everything you teach."

He gave her a good-natured smile. "Maybe, maybe
not. I'm not too familiar with the genre. And I'm also

not a creative writer, so you'll have to explain these things to me."

Antonia felt comfortable enough. "Alright then, I love historical romances."

"Bodice-rippers."

"Right, but I'm writing a contemporary romance because I never see myself in what I read."

"Hm, what do you mean?"

Antonia shrugged. "I don't know," she said, choosing her words carefully. "I guess I like reading about Victorian women who sneak off to the gardens to kiss suitors, but they're all white women who have 'pale porcelain skin and flaxen locks of gold.' And the problem with contemporary erotica is that there's fucking every twelfth page."

Aiden exploded with laughter, spraying whiskey into the fireplace. "Jaysus, Mary, and Joseph," he howled. Antonia almost tipped over as she dissolved into giggles.

"I'm sorry," she said, wiping her eyes.

"Dear me," he said in between gasps. "You've a mouth on ya."

"Only sometimes," she said. "But this is my first book and I'm not ready to write the 'in your face' erotica. Maybe later I'll have the courage, but for now...do you get what I mean?"

He took another drink. "Aye, it makes sense," he replied. "You want the sweeping romance of the past, but with a touch more diversity. You also want some global politics and adventure, but without the whole Fifty Shades business."

"That's *exactly* what I want. Is that too much?"

"It's your book, Antonia. You're meant to have whatever you want."

A smile played on her lips as she stared into the fire. "It *is* my book," she murmured. And she'd just shared it with him. He listened to her without judgement and even asked critical questions about it. She didn't feel like her dream was ridiculous when she was around Aiden. "My fiancé didn't think my writing was very important."

He raised a dark brow as he peered over his glass. "Your fiancé?"

While she was revealing intimate details about her life, during a thunderstorm, one more detail couldn't hurt. Antonia smiled sadly. "There was another reason why I 'escaped' to Ireland," she began.

Chapter Fifteen

And the plot thickens.

Aiden sat and listened to Antonia recount what it was like to find out her fiancé was cheating on her. He did his best to contain his anger as she described running away from his apartment. If the prick was arrogant enough to pull something like that off before his own wedding, who knows what life may have been like after two years of marriage. He admired her though. Antonia may have been a little buzzed, but she talked about Derek stoically. She wasn't on the verge of tears this evening. He knew there was something more to yesterday's washing machine panic. This was the pain that lay just below the surface.

"How did you two meet?"

She chuckled. "Oh god, I was at a sports bar for a work colleague's birthday. He was there with his finance buddies and talked me up at the bar."

Aiden stared into the fire, hating this guy the more he heard about him. "Honestly, everything just moved so fast after that. He gave me his phone number, I called, and he wooed me with dinner. Within eight or nine months, he asked me to marry him."

"What made you say yes?"

Antonia shrugged. "I loved him. I thought we were compatible? Looking back on it, I think I ignored a lot of things. At least, that's what my sister says."

Aiden opened his mouth to say something supportive, but closed it. He was unsure of how to regard her. His initial idea of going to her cottage now seemed silly. This woman was still in tremendous pain. He looked at her, sitting cross-legged before the fire. Her beauty shone through her frumpy house clothes. Those wild curls piled on her head were begging to be released so he could bury his face against them. Her large brown eyes followed the flicker of flames with a sadness that Aiden was desperate to kiss away.

"I'm tired of not being listened to," she said after a long pause. She turned toward him, setting her glass on the rug. "Derek didn't hear me that much and when he did, he wasn't listening. My ideas were useless to him. It wasn't just how he disregarded my book, there were other things. When I told him that I was burned out at work, I didn't mean that I was going to quit my job." Antonia stopped and searched for the right words. "I mean, my boss wasn't listening to me there, if you want to be perfectly honest about it. He didn't listen to me when I told him publishing his nephew's novel was a terrible idea. But Derek heard me complain and took that to mean..." She trailed off.

"Mean what?"

"...that when we got married, I'd just quit my job anyway. I think he wanted me to be like his mother. A wealthy woman who sits at home. Someone he could just show off at company Christmas parties." Her long, dark lashes lowered as her gaze dropped to the floor. "When I told him that the wedding was off, I also told him about my layoff. He made it sound like an excuse for us to keep going."

"Like, you'd still need him?"

Antonia nodded. "And for a minute, it was tempting."

"What about now?" Aiden asked. His heart pounded as he waited to hear her answer.

She peeked at him and smiled bashfully. "I don't think I need him," she said. "I was hustling before I met him. I guess I'll continue to hustle."

He released the breath he'd held and nodded. "I'll drink to that," he said, holding his glass aloft.

She picked up her glass and tapped it against his. "*Slainte,*" she said.

"*Slainte.*"

After taking another sip, she asked him, "What about you, Aiden? Have you ever almost been married?"

"Not even close," he said. "The last woman I dated was my colleague and she left me for better career prospects."

"Oh?" By the look on her face, Aiden wondered if she was relieved that she wasn't the only damaged person in the room. "How long ago was that?"

"Nearly a year ago," he said, smiling to himself. "Around this time, actually."

Antonia asked, sitting up straighter. "What was her name?

"Lisa Brennan. She's moved to Paris to teach at the Sorbonne."

"Was there someone else?"

Aiden shook his head. "As far as I know, just Victorian literature and job opportunities."

Antonia sighed. "That's good, at least. I wouldn't wish what happened to me on my worst enemy."

"That's thoughtful of you," Aiden said with a chuckle. "But I'm not blameless in my relationship with Lisa."

Antonia studied him. "How did it end?"

"It's hard to say," he said, carefully choosing his words. "If she had one foot out the door, I'm sure my priorities weren't in order. I didn't know that she was unhappy or that I was moving too slow for her. I thought she liked Galway, that she might want to build a life there with me. But I think she wanted us to be an academic super duo. Perhaps she had it in her mind that we'd get tenure together and I was dragging my feet."

"Are you still trying to get tenure?"

He gave a mirthless laugh. "Aye, I'm trying. I've got a year before they review everything, but it's still nerve-racking. Although she and I were quite different, Lisa was right about one thing: I had my head buried in the sand while this was quickly approaching. I'm paying for it now."

"What happens if you don't get tenure?" Antonia asked, nibbling on her bottom lip.

Aiden stared at her mouth and realized he didn't want to talk about this anymore. He wanted to nibble on her lip instead. "The university is going to have to let me go," he said.

"You'll lose your job?"

"That's how academia works, my dear," he said with a rueful grin. "It's not as liberal as you think. But don't fret, I'm steadily working on it. I've got a conference next week and I'm going to put out a book proposal."

"If you need help with your proposal," Antonia said in a bashful voice. "I'm qualified to assist you."

Aiden paused. "Really?"

She nodded. "Sure, I won't know everything about your subject matter, but I know what makes for a good nonfiction proposal. My first editing job was at my university's press."

It was a generous offer that he had nothing to counter with. The sweet glow in her cheeks touched his heart in a way he didn't think was possible. "That would be lovely. Thank you, Antonia," he said, glancing away from her. Unsure what to do with himself, he went back to his drink.

"So you're steadily working on your career. What about the relationship part of your life?" Antonia asked, tilting her head. "Did you want to marry Lisa?"

"Perhaps," he said. "It took me awhile to realize that I wanted to get married, but just not to her I suppose. When we first started out, I thought she was an efficient woman…" Aiden trailed off when he saw Antonia frown. "That's a terrible way to describe her."

"Yes," she said with a laugh. "No woman wants to be known as *efficient*."

He nodded. "Right. I liked how put-together she was. But after a while, I could see that our differences were getting harder to ignore. I like teaching, but I want to start a family one day. I want to come home from the university and share something with someone. Lisa wasn't interested in that."

"Her career is important," Antonia reminded him.

"Yes, it is. There are a lot of minefields for a woman in this industry, so I can't blame her for choosing her career over me. I just wish…"

"What?"

It was difficult for him to articulate his past, but with Antonia, he found himself easing into her warm embrace. Aiden had not even described his conflicting feelings regarding Lisa with Robert, who knew them both quite well. "I just wish I had convinced her that we could have worked on both *together*. Instead, I just pulled away from her."

The look in Antonia's eyes wasn't one of pity, but sadness. "I think I can understand that."

"While she's in the past, I still needed to learn that lesson," Aiden said, searching her gaze. He wanted her to look at him, but she was staring into the fire. "I needed to recognize my mistakes before the next relationship."

With her eyes fixed on the flames, Antonia nodded. "You're right," she murmured. "We have to fix the mistakes now…for the next relationship."

Aiden wanted to know what she was thinking about as she worried her thumbnail between her teeth. "Antonia," he said in a soft voice.

She finally turned to look at him. "Hm?"

"Thank you for talking."

Antonia nodded and flashed him a beautiful smile. In that moment, Aiden wanted nothing more than to kiss the smart arch of her brow, the bridge of her nose, and the corners of her mouth. She pulled him with an invisible lure that made his body alive with electricity. *Does she feel it too?* "Are you hungry?" she asked. The question ended with her eyes dropping to his naked torso.

"I am," he said with a thick voice. Her tone was innocent, but Aiden was brought back to the SuperValu where they first met. Her smile had the ability to make him lose his words as his blood rushed downward. He sat up and discreetly adjusted his damp jeans.

"Me too," she breathed, met his gaze, and blushed.

"The drink is going to my head." She drew herself from the floor, stood, and stretched.

"Do you need any help in the kitchen?"

Antonia shook her head. "No, you stay there. While you're in my cottage, I'd like to try feeding you."

He watched her walk away, the gentle slope of her hips swayed as she went. Quiet intimacy like this was what Aiden missed most. He and Lisa had stopped talking honestly to one another long before she announced she was leaving him. In the evenings, they'd come home, tired from teaching and settled into watching television. On the weekends, she'd worked on things in her office, while he went out on the boat he kept tethered by the river. Instead of talking to his girlfriend, he'd taken to the water. The irony didn't escape his notice. Aiden had to remember that all of his answers didn't lie at the bottom of the ocean.

Antonia felt her way around the kitchen, listening to the storm batter the village. She hated to imagine what it might look like the next day. She wanted to avoid thinking about tomorrow for a more pressing reason; Aiden would leave her in the morning. Antonia didn't want the storm or the night to end.

"Are you alright in there?" she heard him ask.

With her head in the fridge, searching for a wedge of soft cheese that needed rescuing, she called back, "I'm fine."

She patted things with her hands, feeling for the cheese. When she found it, she put it on the counter and went searching for the crackers. If she remembered correctly, she'd left them on top of the fridge. Blindly, she reached up and swept her hand across the top, knocking over the electric teakettle. It hit the floor with a clatter, making her jump back and yelp. "Shit!"

"What happened?"

"I'm fine," she said. "I just knocked something off the fridge."

In the darkness, she heard his footsteps travel from the living room to the kitchen.

She detected the dark outline of his body against the dim light of the dying fire. She stood in the opposite doorway, watching him take halted steps into the kitchen. "Are you hurt?" His voice was a low and warm vibration that filled the space.

"No," she said, taking a tentative step forward. "It was the teakettle, but it didn't hit me."

"What are you looking for?"

"Crackers," she laughed. "I swear that I'm not usually a klutz in the kitchen. I can find my way around in the light."

"I don't know if I believe that," he said. His voice drew closer. The air became thick and heavy when he closed the distance between them. "This kitchen and its appliances have been giving you problems from day one."

Antonia's voice caught in her chest in response to the warmth of his body right before her. She was between a rock and a hard place, positioned before the refrigerator, facing him. He was still shirtless. She closed her eyes and imagined his rippling muscles from earlier. Her breathing became shallow and fast as he drew closer still. "Aiden," she whispered.

"Antonia," he replied, his voice thick.

He stood so close to her, his hands hovering over her arms until finally they closed around her. He slid one hand up to her shoulder and to her neck. His long and graceful fingers intertwined through tight coils at the back of her head. Aiden's movements were agonizingly slow, as if he could not trust his sense of touch in the darkness. As Antonia tilted her head back against his supporting hand, she waited for his gentle exploration to gain traction. His other hand slid down to her hip before traveling to the small of her back, pulling her hips closer to his. It was like yesterday's washing machine incident. She'd felt the urge then and hoped for release now.

She let out a soft moan as he gently tugged her head back. When his lips pressed against the rioting pulse of her neck, her knees shook in anticipation. Antonia was unsure of what to do with her hands; they hung at her sides helplessly as he kissed her collarbone. Ever so slightly, his chest brushed against her breasts, causing a new warmth to spread throughout her body. Her movements were tentative, as she slowly lifted her hands and placed them on his tight biceps. She held on as her emotions pitched like the restless seas. Her excitement was quickly put on hold when he paused, pulled away from her neck, and whispered, "I'm sorry."

Antonia's eyes flew open. *Sorry?* With her hands still gripping his strong arms, she pulled him closer. "For what?" she breathed.

Aiden dropped his hands to her waist, his thumbs gently caressing her hips, but he did move back a scant. "I truly didn't come over here to liquor you up and have my way with you." There was an edge in his voice, as if he struggled against his desire. His breath was ragged as he continued. "I don't want you to think…"

Antonia was confused. And aching. The excited

shiver that still coursed through her body made her
breasts heavy and full as the juncture between her legs
grew wet. These were all of the feelings she had missed
with Derek. She felt them with a new man, a powerful arousal that needed to be sated. *Why not tonight?*
Her hands traveled up his arms, to the sides of his face,
cupping his lean cheeks. The stubble she ran her fingers against thrilled her all over again. Only seconds
before, that stubble had tickled and scratched her neck.
Why not tonight? He started this and, by god, she would
make some progress. In the darkness, Antonia leaned
forward and pressed her lips against his. She caught his
lower lip by accident, and her hands moved to tilt his
head down to adjust accordingly.

He groaned, relaxing his body as she took her first
tentative kiss. Aiden's arms circled her waist, pulling
her against him. She wanted desperately to take off her
sweatshirt to feel the heat of his bare chest. His body
crowded against hers, pressing his bold arousal to her
softness. He returned her kiss, his mouth covering hers
hungrily. Antonia did her best to keep up with his de-
manding lips, countering with an urgent and explor-
atory tongue. She savored the smoky sweet flavor of
whiskey, as his scent and taste pulled her down, below
the surface, into new depths of pleasure. Antonia was
fully prepared to drown in the wet darkness of her own
lust, as she pushed against his body, helplessly rocking
her hips for more sensation.

Between his devouring kisses, she shrugged out of
her sweatshirt, pulling her arms out of the sleeves and
forcing it over her head. Aiden slipped his hands upward and gently tugged at her loose ponytail until her
curls cascaded around her shoulders. She tossed her

sweatshirt to the floor and returned to his lips. Feverish with want, she was ready to swoon from his careful ministrations. His hands left her tangled curls and
traveled slowly down her neck to her chest, settling on
her pounding heart. Finally, his large hands cupped
her breasts, pushing them up against the neckline of
her tank top. Antonia arched against him, tipping her
head back against the refrigerator. "Please," she begged
as his fingers fanned against each nipple, causing them
to tighten beneath her shirt.

His hands left her swollen breasts and swiftly took
her by the thighs. Antonia yelped in surprise when he
hoisted her against his midsection. She wrapped her
legs around his waist as he spun her around and set
her on the edge of the kitchen sink. His lips returned
to her neck, pressing kisses along her hot skin until his
tongue lathed down to the tops of her breasts. Antonia
balanced herself against the sink, legs still wrapped
around him, pushing her sex against his grinding hips.
As his wet tongue dipped into the valley of her cleavage, she gasped from the pleasure.

Boom, boom, boom!

The pounding at her front door frightened them both.
Aiden straightened up, nearly knocking Antonia off the
counter. She screeched as she pitched forward, but he
managed to catch her before she fell to the floor. "Jaysus, Mary, and fucking Joseph," he shouted. "Who is
it?"

Antonia quickly found her footing in the dark,
breathless from part fright and part arousal. "Goddammit," she muttered, brushing the curls from her face.

Before she had time to gather her thoughts, Aiden
stormed off toward the door. When he swung it open,

a flash of lightning brightened the sky, revealing his heaving bare chest. His face was tense with thin-lipped irritation. "What?"

"Oh! Dr. Byrnes… I'm a, erm, where's the young woman…" Antonia heard a familiar voice stammering from the kitchen. It was old man Creely.

"Mr. Creely," Aiden said in a softer tone. "I'm sorry, please come in."

Antonia searched the dark kitchen with her feet, feeling around for her discarded sweatshirt. She swooped it up and slipped it over her head before running to the front door. Mr. Creely regarded the both of them with a curious stare.

"Mr. Creely," she said, still out of breath and slightly disheveled. "Please get out of the rain, I've got a fire going."

She pulled the elderly man inside and closed the door behind him. He stood in the foyer and shook out his umbrella, his hand still gripping the neck of his raincoat. "I won't be stayin' fer long," he said.

"Would you like a drink?" Aiden suggested. He was shirtless and standing at an awkward angle. Antonia looked down at his groin and guessed why. *Jesus, he's trying to hide an erection.*

"Oh no, I've got something at home," Creely said with a chuckle. "I was just checking on the lady. It's a powerful gale out there and with the lights out, I hoped you weren't too afraid."

She gave a nervous laugh and waved her hand dismissively. "Nothing to be afraid of," she said. "Dr. Byrnes was thoughtful enough to stop by with whiskey."

"Yes, yes, I see…" Creely looked around at their intimate scene. Aiden's shirt draped over the fireplace rack should have been a good reason for his half-naked appearance. "Well if you're okay, I'll see m'self out. The power ought to be back by the morning."

"Yes, well, please be careful out there," Antonia said. She certainly appreciated the thought behind his visit, but was anxious for him to leave. There was plenty of unfinished business between her and her first guest.

"Well," Creely said slowly. "If you're alright…"

"Doing pretty well," she said in a chipper tone.

Aiden walked him to the door and closed it behind him. With both of his hands planted on the door, his head hung in embarrassment. "Jaysus," he muttered.

Antonia sank into the couch and burrowed into the cushions with shame. "What do you suspect he's thinking right now?"

Aiden gave a wry chuckle and made his way back to the living room. "If he likes you, and I reckon he does, he probably thinks I'm a lech."

They looked at each other. There was a clear and apparent line that they had crossed. There was no going back and they probably needed to talk about it. "You're not a lech," she said with a smile. "Could you pass me the whiskey?"

He gathered their glasses and the bottle, taking a seat beside her. As he poured them both another shot, she drew her knees to her chest and snuggled against the arm of the couch. There was a considerable amount of space between the two of them and perhaps that was a relief. Maybe Mr. Creely's interruption was a blessing in disguise. She'd actually been about to have sex with a man in her kitchen during a blackout. *That's how babies are made.*

"What are you grinning about?" he asked, handing her a glass.

Antonia shook her head. "I think we were about to do something rather foolish."

Aiden returned her smile. "You think?"

"Unless you brought something else besides whiskey?" she asked. "Like protection?"

"I'm afraid I didn't," he admitted. "Like I said, it certainly wasn't my intention to, uh, you know." He cleared his throat.

Antonia scooted to his side of the couch and settled against him. He gathered her to him, wrapping an arm around her waist. "To get into my pants?" she offered.

"Right. That."

"It was quite alright," she said, resting her cheek against the soft springy hair of his chest. Antonia didn't want to admit it, but that passionate make out session was what she needed to affirm what she should have thought about herself. She was still sensual and still desirable. Antonia just needed to be herself and let the chips fall where they may. Aiden awakened something in her that she'd ignored out of hurt.

"What would you like to do tomorrow?" Aiden asked.

She stifled a yawn and snuggled closer to him. "I don't know. I think I might write some more."

"Have you found some more inspiration?" he asked. She heard the smile in his voice.

"I have," she replied. "Bryon is going to make out with Augusta."

"Sounds like a right wolf, that one."

Chapter Sixteen

Aiden woke up to the morning light shining through the living room. The clattering in the kitchen reminded him that he was still in Antonia's home. After that magnificent storm from last night, it was now a quiet sunny day. He stretched his legs along her couch and twisted his back to work out the kinks.

"Antonia?"

"I'm making something to eat," she said from the kitchen. "I don't have eggs, but I've got pizza."

He smiled. No doubt, one of his frozen margherita pizzas. "That sounds wonderful."

Aiden was famished and thirsty with all the drinking they'd done on empty stomachs. It'd been fine enough at the time, when it seemed like Antonia would be on the menu. He sat on the couch staring into the now dead fireplace. *My god*. The kiss they had shared in the dark kitchen was far better than any naughty fantasy he could have dreamt. Antonia's body was so right in his hands. He remembered cupping every delicious curve as he picked her up and hugged her close. Everything about her fit perfectly against his mouth and in his hands. While Mr. Creely's poorly timed interruption was infuriating, he was relieved he didn't do anything foolish. Another wave of relief swept through Aiden. One tangled with powerful lust. He was glad they'd been interrupted because he wanted to make love to her during the day. He wanted to see the warm glow of her brown skin bathed in light. He wanted Antonia with an overwhelming intensity that he hadn't known in ages.

"It'll be done in a minute," she said, peeking through the doorway. She was still wearing that baggy sweatshirt that covered her figure, but she looked more refreshed than he felt. "Do you want some tea?"

"I'd love some tea," he said brightly. "And a gallon of water as well."

She laughed. "You'll have to make it," she said. "I don't know how to work the kettle and I think I might have broken it last night."

Aiden retrieved his now-dry T-shirt from the fireplace and walked to the kitchen, ruffling her messy hair as he went. "We'll see what we can manage," he said with a yawn.

In the small kitchen space, he moved around her, examining the kettle and filling it up with tap water. When he plugged it up, she scooted around him to pull the pizza out, setting it on the stove. The well-timed dance between the two of them didn't go unnoticed by Aiden. He swiftly grabbed her in his arms and pulled her close to him. Her reaction was a startled laugh that brightened her eyes. "What are you…"

He raised one of her arms high and wrapped his other arm around her waist, pulling her even closer. "Do you dance?"

She looked up at him, her brown eyes twinkling. "Not without music," she said. "And not waltzing."

"But you've danced with a man?"

"Well, since they invented a dance called the twist, women have had the freedom to dance with partners without intricate steps." *God, she is a keeper.* Aiden noticed Antonia's feisty wit emerged the more she relaxed.

"You mean you don't wear corsets and foxtrot with a chaperone nearby?"

She rolled her eyes. "I do not."

"Then I'm going to teach you a quick two-step," he said. He led her around the kitchen as she tried not to step on his toes. "One and two and one and two..."

"Oh my god, this is silly," she giggled.

"You never know when it might come in handy," Aiden replied. "Least that's what my mam told me when she signed me up for classes."

Antonia kept her face down, staring at their feet as they moved together. "How old were you?"

"I was eight," he said with a rueful smile. He was the only boy in his grade who was dropped off for dance classes while the others were learning how to fight in a boxing ring. Now that he was older, he understood his mother was making an early attempt to lead him from a different path than his father. He smiled at the memory and realized the skill proved to be mighty helpful with women.

"My mom made me take piano lessons when I was eight," she said with a chuckle.

"That is also very helpful," he said, trying to twirl her. She tripped over her own feet and stumbled against him. "You're still drunk, aren't you?"

She glanced over her shoulder with a demure smile. "Yes, that's definitely it."

As he released her to check on the teakettle, his

phone buzzed in his back pocket. "Sorry, hold on," he said. "It's probably my mother."

But his screen displayed a different, more surprising name. It was Robert. "It's my boss," he said.

"You should take that," Antonia said, holding a large butcher knife over the pizza. "It could be mysterious tenure stuff."

Aiden rolled his eyes. "He demanded I go on holiday. Mysterious tenure stuff could wait a little while."

She smiled as she cut herself a slice of pizza. "Still. You have to think about your future."

Antonia's gentle chiding was pleasant to his ears. It was as if they'd been dancing around the kitchen, making breakfast pizza, for years. He let his gaze linger on her smile as he answered the phone. "Hey, Robert."

"Oh, good, Aiden, I'm glad I caught you. How is Tully Cross?"

"It's fine, Robert. We had a good storm last night, but it will dry out soon enough. What can I do for you?"

"I won't take up your time, but Penny and I are leaving for Greece tomorrow and I need to make sure things are in order before we leave. I came across a call for chapters in an American Literature anthology that might be up your alley."

"Oh yeah?" Aiden said absently, keeping his eyes on Antonia as she pulled her slice away from the pan. Cheese stretched with every tug, until she took the strings of mozzarella between her thumb and index finger and dropped them into her mouth. When she licked her fingers, Aiden licked his lips. She tilted her head back and let the corner of the slice rest against her tongue before taking a large bite. *How can anyone make eating pizza look so sexy?* Her eyes closed as a low groan escaped her throat.

"This is so good," she whispered.

He nodded. He was a believer in Goodfella's thin crust pizza, but it couldn't have been better than his current view of her mouth.

"Yes, the ad was calling for an interesting mix of international voices to juxtapose certain themes in American Literature," Robert continued. "Identity and nationality seems quite important to them."

Aiden switched gears and returned to his phone conversation. "How exactly?"

"I've emailed it to you," Robert said. "I think you should take a look at their criteria, but I imagine your conference paper could easily transition into a longer length article."

"And possibly a chapter," Aiden finished. "Yeah, I'll look at that today."

"How is the writing going?" his mentor asked in a cautious tone. "Have you been able to get back to it?"

He chuckled at Robert's concern. He hated that the old man felt he needed to check in, but he appreciated the support nonetheless. "I have."

"You seem a little distracted. Have I called at a bad time?"

As he continued watching Antonia nibble at her pizza, without a plate, he smiled. Her curls balanced precariously atop her head as she leaned over the stove, dropping crumbs over the burners. He wanted nothing more than to get off the phone and join her. And after they finished their meal, he could drive at a breakneck speed to Letterfrack for condoms. "No, not a bad time," he said. "I'm actually at my neighbor's cottage having breakfast."

"Oh, how pleasant. A local?"

"She's from America," Aiden said and paused. "I met her a few days ago."

Robert waited a beat before replying. "I see... Then I *am* interrupting."

Antonia licked her thumb again. Her lush lips circled the saucy digit as her eyes fell shut. It was like watching her eat eggs all over again. Aiden forced his body to relax. "Only slightly. But I will read your email today and let you know if it's something I could do."

"Of course, of course. Don't trouble yourself too much if you're, uh." Robert coughed. "Otherwise occupied."

"Thank you and safe travels to you and Penny."

"Yes, thank you. I'll pass the sentiment along to Penny. I'll see you at the conference, Aiden."

"You will."

When he hung up, he tucked his phone into his back pocket and reached out to Antonia. The back of his fingers grazed her soft cheek while she chewed her breakfast. "I could watch you eat for hours," he whispered.

Her mouth twisted into a frown. "That turns you on?"

"Watching your mouth does," he said, taking another step toward her. "I don't care what it's doing, I just imagine it doing other things."

The crease in her brow relaxed as she gazed up at him. "What other things?"

He took what was left of her pizza and set it on the stove, all while focusing his stare at her lips. "You're the romance writer," he said. "I shouldn't have to tell you."

Antonia's face broke into a wide grin. "Let me get back to you on that."

His fingers traveled to her pointed chin and tilted it upward. "You do that, darling," he said before kissing her. Her body relaxed against his as her arms wrapped around his shoulders. Aiden held her close and kissed her deeply until his erection reminded him that he had to remain responsible.

Antonia broke away from his lips to glance down. "He's back."

"He's persistent," Aiden said with a desperate laugh. "I'm sorry about that."

She glanced up at him, their faces only an inch apart. "I don't think apologies are necessary."

"I'm not always a horny teenager," he said. "I'm usually much better at—"

"Stop," Antonia said through her laughter. "It's not the insult you think it is. Now, are you hungry?"

"Always."

"Let me cut you a slice of this," she said, reaching for the knife.

He took it before she could and kissed her cheek. "My dear, I can always serve myself."

She glanced up at him with a confused expression. "I just…"

"And I can serve you too," he said, separating a slice for himself. "I like to do both."

Antonia shook her head and chuckled to herself.

"What?"

She cast him another glance. "Oh nothing," she said with a bemused grin. "I just thought of something my mother said."

"Men should serve you pizza, in bed, when the occasion calls for it?"

"Something like that."

He ate his slice in a couple bites and watched her expression shift from confusion to amusement. "Would you mind if I used your computer to check my school email? My boss sent me something about an anthology seeking submissions."

"Sure, it's in my bedroom," she said. "Is the tea ready?"

"Yep," Aiden said, walking to her bedroom. Her bed was a mess of books, mostly paperback romances, notebooks and notecards. When he found her laptop, he was careful not to tamper with her story, which was still open. Antonia was already on a page eighty-four. Aiden glanced out the door to see her pour a cup of tea and move to the living room. He knew he shouldn't, but he scrolled through her document and began reading her book from the beginning.

Aiden didn't know any actual writers. Real ones at least. He'd written a dissertation, but instead of publishing it as a monograph, he'd let it fall by the wayside when he started teaching. This, however, would be something that the world could read. A thrill shot through him as his eyes swept over the text. It was obvious that the heroine, Augusta, was based on Antonia. The protagonist may have been brash and mouthy, but some of her mannerisms felt familiar. The way she nibbled on her lip when she needed to think. The way she rubbed the space between her eyes when she was irritated. He'd seen it a few times after interacting with Antonia. As Aiden settled against her bed, he continued reading the harrowing introduction to Augusta's character. The research that Antonia did to accurately describe the Arab Spring held his attention. The actions her heroine took to hunt down her story made him want to read more.

"Holy shit," he muttered. "Shot in the leg?"

Augusta was going to cover this story at all costs and Aiden was right there with her. He scrolled ahead to get to the bit about Bryon and his mouth curled into a smile. Aiden didn't want to think of himself as an arrogant bastard, but the description of the hero was *quite* familiar. Right down to the smiling green eyes and heavy black brow. He glanced at the doorway again. Aiden could never tell Antonia that he had read this much. It was almost akin to reading her diary. His eyes widened when he read the passage regarding the heroine's physical reaction to Bryon's closeness.

Her chest tightened at the sight of him. Their years apart diminished in an instant as a tsunami of heat hit her body. Already wet with her own desire, her nipples constricted into stiff peaks, brushing against her blouse and creating a delicious friction. She wanted to forget how angry she was and climb him like the magnificent tree he was. But Augusta couldn't forget the rage that she'd carefully nursed since their break up. Bryon Donnelly broke her heart and she'd remind him of it as soon as she could quiet the aching throb between her thighs.

Whew... If he wasn't supposed to be checking his email, Aiden would have stayed and read the rest of her first draft. But he *was* supposed to be checking his email. He carefully minimized her document and did so. He read Robert's email, rather distractedly, as it wasn't nearly as interesting as the hot story he'd made himself quit. Sure enough, the call for submissions sounded like something he could participate in. If he tailored his conference paper correctly, he could easily stretch it into something for the anthology. Aiden sighed. He'd tack the anthology chapter onto the long list of things he'd need to work on for the summer.

"Does the internet work okay?" Antonia asked from the doorway.

His gaze shot up. "Yes, yes, it does."

She peered at him. "Everything okay?"

"Everything is perfect," Aiden said. "I'm going to submit something to an American Literature anthology."

"Cool," she said with a nod. "Sorry about the mess. I was writing when the storm got bad."

He closed her laptop. "No worries. I see you've got some inspirational literature for your work," he said, holding up a worn book. On the cover, a woman with a heaving bosom was being held by a shirtless man.

"Oh god," she said, thoroughly embarrassed. "Please ignore those."

Okay then, she definitely wouldn't want to know I've been reading her book. "It's nothing to be worried about," he said. "I'm not going to wind you up over research."

Antonia's face was not relieved. She entered the room, snatched the book from his grasp and gathered the rest of her books from the bed. "Yes, but I don't want you to think I sleep with porn," she said with shaky laughter.

"Admittedly, what I'm imagining is delightful," he said with a chuckle. She carried the books to her suitcase and dropped them inside. "But the books can serve more than one purpose, right?"

She shot him a look. "Aiden."

"If I were to start reading romance, which of those books would you recommend?"

Antonia stood still with her arms crossed over her chest. This wasn't like when they were tipsy. She was dealing with the fact that she'd told him about her book in the cold sober light of the morning. "Why do you want to know?" she asked, narrowing her large brown eyes into suspicious slits.

"Because I might like to read one," he said in an easygoing tone. "I've never read a romance. Frankly, with all of the teaching and writing, I haven't had time to read anything."

She was still suspicious, but she loosened her arms. "Okay…"

"What do you recommend?"

"It depends," she said. "I only brought historical romances with me. Do you prefer the English or French period pieces?"

"Fuck the English," he said bluntly.

"Alright," she said retrieving a book and tossing it to him. "If you don't mind reading about the French Revolution, try this."

He caught it with one hand. The cover was much less conspicuous than the others, no half-nude couples grasping at one another. It was a simple French flag and an unfurled lace fan. "Doesn't look very romantic."

"Trust me, you'll get what you're looking for."

The cover, like all the others, was worn and tattered,

its spine was broken in several places where Antonia had refused to use a bookmark. "Well, then let me make a suggestion for today's activities."

"Yeah?"

Aiden pulled himself off her bed, her book in hand. "Let me take you to Letterfrack for some grocery shopping. Afterwards we can stop at a coffee shop for some writing. You can continue working and I can read."

The look of suspicion eventually melted away to reveal a puzzled grin. "You really want to read that while I write?"

"How can we keep talking about your book when I don't know anything about the genre? I'm a researcher at heart, Antonia."

Her contagious grin soon lit his face as she nodded. "Okay, yeah, let's do that."

"Excellent."

Chapter Seventeen

"This is what you listen to?" she said, flipping through the CD book from under Aiden's passenger seat. It seemed that the man was stuck firmly in the '90s grunge scene and only deviated for Pink Floyd and Led Zeppelin. He chuckled as he easily rounded a curve through the countryside. He drove his stick shift Volvo with an adeptness that made her jealous.

"What's wrong with my music?" he asked, slowing down for passing sheep. Aiden pulled to a complete stop and reached over to take the book from her. "This is classic stuff."

"Yes, it definitely is."

"Please tell me you're not too young to remember Zeppelin."

"You've only got five years on me," she said. "But there are nearly twelve Zeppelin CDs in here."

Aiden plucked one of them from its sleeve and slid it into the player. A very loud, but familiar Jimmy Page riff filled the car. She immediately turned it down. "'Black Dog,'" he cried. "That's a brilliant song."

"I appreciate them as much as the next layman, but twelve CDs?"

"Dear me, what kind of music do you like?"

"I like all kinds of things," she said.

Aiden shifted the gear and started up when the last of the sheep finished crossing. "Spoken like a true fair-weather friend. Lemme guess, you're the biggest Beyoncé fan there ever was?"

Antonia let out an exaggerated gasp. "You can let me out of this car and I'll walk to Letterfrack if you utter one word against Bey."

He laughed uproariously. "Let the record show I've got nothing to say about Queen Bey."

"That's what I thought."

"She's just a tad overrated, is all."

"Boy, if you don't stop…" she warned, giving him a swat on the arm.

"I'm just taking the piss, darling!" he said.

She bit back a smile as she gave him a sidelong glance. "That's what I thought," she repeated. Antonia enjoyed this. She missed laughing and joking with someone like this. She was happy that he suggested this trip to Letterfrack. When he'd asked for one of her books, she was shocked that a man who taught literature would be interested in her hobby. After working for Wild Hare for several years, a place that wouldn't even entertain the idea of genre fiction, she was used to colleagues denigrating romance. But of the few instances romance manuscripts accidentally landed on her work pile, she had read them carefully, and mourned the rejection letters she'd sent the authors. They were good, but they weren't good enough for her publishing house. Richard would have laughed at her if she attempted to acquire a kissing book. Antonia struggled to find fault with happily-ever-after endings that made women believe in true love. What was wrong with reading about a perfect man who could unconditionally love a woman?

And then Antonia glanced at the man next to her. Aiden could be that man. That morning, when she'd woken up in his embrace, she'd seen the sleeping face of a content man. His arms had tightened around her body when she shifted against him. He hadn't wanted to let go. She had especially enjoyed the way his face lit up when she met him by his car. He'd complimented her outfit and gushed over how she styled her hair. *Another thing Derek stopped doing long ago.* Derek had usually regarded her with spot-inspections that made her feel more doll than woman. Her mother once told her that if a man's face didn't brighten when she entered a room, there was something missing.

"What's on your mind?" Aiden asked, interrupting her thoughts.

"Nothing," she lied.

"You're an introspective little lady," he said, glancing over at her. "When you're quiet, I feel like you've gone somewhere deep."

"Oh, I don't know about that," she said.

"I've watched your face when you're not looking. Your eyes get darker and your nose twitches like a rabbit."

Antonia was startled. "That's not true!"

He laughed. "Maybe not like a rabbit."

"I don't know when you've had the time to observe me like that."

"I had more than enough time to observe you," he said.

Antonia blushed. That much *was* true. "I think my sister and I are generally pretty quiet people."

"Then I don't know how you'd feel hanging out with the Byrnes Clan. We're a pretty loud bunch."

"Octavia and I were raised by a theatrical woman who was loud enough for everyone," Antonia said, recalling some particularly embarrassing highlights from her childhood. "But she gives pretty solid advice and she's…protective over her girls."

"You're also very diplomatic," Aiden noted.

"You enjoy telling me about myself, don't you?"

He nodded. "I like learning about you."

Antonia grinned as her gaze drifted toward the scenery. She remembered driving through this a few days earlier and was glad to see it again from a passive position. As they drew closer to the small town of Letterfrack, she grew excited by the change of scenery. Tully Cross was lovely and quaint, but she did want to hang out in a slightly busier area.

"*That* look on your face is quickly becoming my favorite thing in the world," he said, parking the car.

Redness flooded her cheeks as she turned to look at him. His masculine energy suffocated her when she was near him. She had already sampled a small taste of his passion and couldn't imagine what the rest might feel like. "Yeah?"

He saved her from having to reply with anything intelligible by leaning in and giving her a sinful kiss. His lips, pliant and crushing, left fire in their wake as his tongue against her own. She was shocked by her eager response to the touch of his lips as she parted her own and raised herself to meet his kiss. A small moan escaped her throat as she angled her head for more. Before she could drink in the sweetness of it, he pulled away, leaving her aching for more. He sat back, letting her catch her breath, which was quickly getting away from her. Aiden's gaze roved lazily over her body. "I wanted to do that while I was driving. You'll let me know if I'm behaving too impulsively, won't you?" The smoldering flame in his eyes startled her.

Antonia absently touched her swollen lips before answering. "I can try." She spoke in a suffocated whisper that she almost didn't recognize. Were it not for last night's blackout, Antonia wouldn't have recognized the surge of sensations in her body either. But she was convinced that she hadn't felt those sensations with *any* man. *His grin is positively rakish.* It sounded like something she had read in her paperback romances, but she couldn't think of any other way to describe it.

"Right, let's get some vittles," he said, getting out of the car. She watched him walk around the front to get to her side. When he opened her door, she couldn't help but smile.

"You don't have to do that," she said.

"I know, but it makes me look like the gentleman I'm pretending to be," he said with a wink.

Inside Kilian's Grocers, several shoppers milled around the aisles while a smiling checkout boy greeted them. They took a couple of handbaskets and split up. Antonia needed some space from him. If she believed in the power of auras, then Aiden's would be the color of the sun, threatening to knock her off orbit with his energy. She stopped in the bread aisle first, picking out a loaf of the brown bread that she'd grown to love.

"So what do you like to eat?" he asked, sidling up to her.

Once she grabbed the bread, she moved toward the

snack aisle. "Oh, whatever is easy to prepare. I eat at my desk a lot."

"Okay, but what do you like to eat on the weekends?"

She shrugged. "Mostly takeout."

"What do you like to cook?" he pressed. "What's Antonia's favorite home-cooked meal?"

She looked up at him with a grin. "Cook?"

He scrunched his nose. "You don't like to cook?"

"I don't," she said, plucking a bag of cookies that seemed the closest approximation to chocolate chip. She dropped them in her basket and moved on to the chips. "I don't have to cook where I come from."

"People cook in Chicago," he said, giving her a quick and chaste kiss on her forehead. "If you're simply too lazy to cook, don't lay that at the feet of millions of Chicagoans."

Antonia was too distracted by his kiss to mind the jab. She liked this outward show of public affection. She liked how easily it came to him. Her face broke into a goofy smile. "I live in a neighborhood on Devon Avenue that's packed with beautiful Indian and Pakistani restaurants and takeout. My next door neighbor, Mrs. Shah, is a restaurant owner. She regularly feeds me."

She followed him to the condiments aisle, where he shook his head in disappointment. "So I'm not the only poor fool who's keeping you alive," he said. "Here I thought I was special."

Antonia laughed. "I'm not totally hapless."

"You don't even bake?" he asked, selecting a bottle of mustard.

"I especially don't bake," she said, standing beside him. She recognized the brand on a jar of pickles and a wave of homesickness washed over her. Everything in the grocery store looked foreign and off-brand. "I didn't go to school for chemistry, so baking is a bit of a mystery to me."

Aiden laughed at that. "I've never heard it explained that way."

"Maybe we should get some wine?"

"You're not shopping for the week, are you?" Aiden said, turning to face her. His smile was a bemused one. "You're just focused on one meal to the next."

"That's how I eat."

"You seem like a planner though."

Antonia jutted her chin in defiance. "I'm on vacation."

His green eyes twinkled with mischief. "I'm issuing you a challenge, Ms. Harper."

"I don't know if I want to accept it."

"I encourage you to accept."

How could she deny him? How could she look into those smiling eyes and say no?

He could ask her to marry him with those eyes and she'd start planning the next wedding. "Fine."

"I'm going to pick out the ingredients for my favorite cake and we're going to bake it together."

Antonia grimaced. "I hope you're kidding." She followed him through the aisles as he plucked random baking ingredients from the shelves. He completely bypassed the ready-mix cake batters and picked up a bag of white flour.

"I'm not asking you to kill a puppy, darling," he joked. "It's a simple cake."

She sighed. Antonia loved a challenge as much as the next person. *Wait, maybe that isn't the case...* "You don't want to end up sick on your vacation, do you?"

"Confidence is key, my dear. I'll be by your side the entire time and I'll even let you lick the spoon," Aiden said with laughter in his voice. He balanced a carton of eggs on top of his items and turned to face her. With one strong arm, he pulled her close, ducking his head for another kiss. His lips brushing over hers made her knees weak. She leaned against his hard body, clutching her basket. While looking up into his eyes, she saw something that wasn't raw passion. It was a soft loving expression that made his eyes look kind. If he kept kissing her like this, she would agree to climb an Irish mountain and swim the freezing Atlantic.

She breathed shakily before answering. "Yes."

Thoroughly engrossed in the saga of a local vineyard owner in the middle of the French Revolution, Aiden flipped through the pages at lightning speed. Apparently, Claudette's father died and left her to manage the family winery, which serviced the royal family of Versailles. And although she was the daughter of a merchant, she regularly found herself amongst the vile people of Louis XVI's court. Her love interest was the young man who helped her manage the farm, but Claudette was also being pursued by an unscrupulous duke who may have killed his wife.

"Where are you at?" Antonia's voice and the sounds of the coffee place were faraway echoes that Aiden had shut out over an hour ago. "Aiden?"

His eyes snapped up to see her laughing eyes. "Huh?"

"Is it that good?"

Aiden sat up in his seat and looked around him. Letterfrack's only coffee shop, Pooka's Beans, was busy with weekend traffic, but he was in 18th century France waiting for the powder keg of the Bastilles to blow up. "Claudette just had sex with Jean Paul, but she thinks it was a mistake. I don't know how she could think that; Jean Paul is perfect for her. I hate the duke and how he keeps cornering her. And I don't know, can we trust this Pauline woman? Is she selling secrets of the court to the Jacobins? If so, is Claudette going to get caught up in the crossfire?"

Antonia blinked before bursting into a peal of laughter. "Oh my god."

"What?"

She wiped the tears from her eyes. "I can't believe you're enjoying it…"

"I am enjoying it," he said defensively. "Why wouldn't I?"

Antonia was literally crying. "I've never met a man who was enthusiastic about historical romance."

He cleared his throat. "Now that we've established that I'm a different breed of man, will you tell me one thing?"

"Yes?"

"Jean Paul isn't going to die, is he?"

Antonia bit her lip, fighting the urge to laugh. Tears stood out in her eyes as she glanced from him to the book. "Oh god, Aiden."

"Please," he said in a calm voice. "They're perfect for one another, but if the duke tries to eliminate Jean Paul to get to Claudette, I don't know if I can keep going."

"I'm not going to tell you the ending; just know that it's an HEA."

He frowned. "What's an HEA?"

"Happily-ever-after."

Aiden nodded and sighed. "Okay, good. Why are you giving me that look?"

Antonia averted her gaze and went back to her laptop, her grin growing wider as she shook her head. "Nothing, I'm just glad you're enjoying yourself."

Aiden *was* enjoying himself. She had been typing feverishly, only stopping for drinks of coffee or to jot something down in her notebook. Her enthusiasm for her work was a sight to behold. He hadn't felt excitement about his own writing in years, but he remembered the heady moments of victory from the past. Watching someone else create pages of fiction out of thin air was akin to witnessing alchemy. In his short time knowing Antonia, Aiden felt proud to be beside her while she crafted a story. "I do have another question though."

Her eyes cut to his with a smirk. "Hm?"

"I notice the author keeps referring to Claudette's vagina as a quim…"

"Jesus." Antonia sank in her seat.

"Is this a genre-specific thing?" he asked, holding back a grin. "Are you not supposed to say what you mean?"

She covered her face with one hand as she trained her eyes on her screen. "Of course the author can't say… *vagina*," she whispered. "This is historical romance."

He was taking the piss, but he couldn't help himself. The crimson blooming in her cheeks was tantalizing. Aiden leaned forward. "But you're writing contemporary, right? What will you call it?"

"I haven't gotten that far," she said in a curt tone.

"What are you going to call Bryon's, you know… cock?"

Redness settled onto her face as she shot him a glare. "I don't know."

"Well I've read, at length, about Jean Paul's…length. Do you think you might try that?"

"I might?" she squeaked. "I don't know."

"The author also calls it a—" Aiden flipped through the book. "*A generous rod that would not be spared.*"

This made her smile. "I'm trying not to get hung up on the terminology right now."

"I'm sure it will come to you over time." He flashed her a smile and thought about kissing her again. Aiden enjoyed surprising her with kisses. Judging by her reaction, she seemed to enjoy it too. He found it difficult to keep his hands off her. Every glance she gave him, every smile, made him ache with want. Her silent dark eyes dropped back to her screen as she let out a tired sigh. "What are you thinking about?"

"While I'm having a lovely time in Ireland, I wonder how my friend Eddie is doing," she said. A shadow of sadness in her eyes as she spoke.

A twinge of envy shot through Aiden. "Who's Eddie?"

Antonia propped her chin on her fist. "He's my best friend from college. We worked for Wild Hare Publishing until it fell apart."

He nodded, pushing aside his possessive feelings. "You haven't told me much about that job," he said.

"There's not much to tell I'm afraid," she began. "He and I started working there out of school. It started out nice enough I guess, but apparently poor management can tank anything. Eddie warned me that there was something wrong with our boss, Richard, but I think I was too distracted with other things. No matter what kind of editing I did, the books we pushed through were failing in quality. The last straw was probably *Starman*."

Aiden frowned. "*Starman?* Like the Bowie song?"

She rolled her eyes. "Exactly. I told Richard it was a terrible idea. I know there's no copyright on titles, but come on. Who would sign off on that?"

"Gotcha."

"Anyway, Eddie can fall back on his girlfriend's salary for a while, but I worry he might fall into a depression." She paused to stare into space. "He gets like that sometimes. A little somber and in his head."

"Mmh." Aiden nodded. "It's rough, but I'll bet you two will find something new. What do you think you'll do when you get back?" He didn't want to think about her going back home. He didn't want the real world to encroach on what they shared. But real boyfriends asked about these things and Aiden definitely felt like he was in the running for the title of Antonia's potential boyfriend.

"Oh lord," she said with a tired smile. "I don't want to think about that. I'm only a few days into my vacation. The only stress that I want to sort out is baking a cake."

He was relieved to hear that. "That's understandable," he said. But there would come a time where she'd have to think about her life back home, that was only sensible. "Do you think you'll be able to put more work into your book?"

"My book," she said with a grin. "It's hard for me to even call it that. I don't know what I'm doing with my story, if it will even become a book. Things were a lot easier when I didn't have to think about it."

"It was easier to rely on a job that made you unhappy?"

"I don't think working at Wild Hare made me unhappy…it was just stressful."

"How much time did you spend writing while you worked there?" he asked, taking a sip of coffee. "Was it a distraction from what you really wanted to do?"

She paused with a slight frown. "I had to work. I also had to plan a wedding."

He nodded thoughtfully before replying. "I see that." He tried to tread lightly. "It's just that I've been reading the drama of Claudette and her well-hung farm boy, and while it's good, I know you can do better. I think you have genuine talent, Antonia."

"Sure," she said with a confused expression. "I'd love to be that person who could just sit in a country cottage clacking away on a novel, but I have to eat."

She had a point. There was such a thing as a starving artist, but Aiden also knew how easy it was to give up a dream. When Antonia worked or described her book to him, he could tell she got high on her own creativity. It was so simple to dismiss that feeling in favor of practicality. "If you could sit in the country and write, would you really?"

Antonia rolled her eyes. "It's hard to think about it like that when it's still a hobby."

"This can't just be a hobby," he tried. "Your book can't be like building a model airplane."

She sat up straight in her chair. "Okay, it's different, but without a clear idea of what kind of time I can spend on a novel, I'd rather keep it at hobby level."

"Look, as I see it, you've got so many things working in your favor: you were in publishing. You've already got the industry connections, you already understand how the submission process works." He ticked the points off on his fingers. "Plus, I read some of your book. You're a damn good writer, darling."

Her eyes widened as her mouth fell open. "You what?"

Aiden winced. "I'm sorry," he said. "But I couldn't resist a peek."

"This is incredibly personal," she hissed, the redness in her face no longer from his teasing. She appeared genuinely angry with his intrusion. "I haven't even let my best friend read this and you thought you could just sneak a peek?"

Okay, he definitely fucked up. "Would it help if I told you that you were brilliant?"

Antonia's brow knotted. "No, it wouldn't," she said. "You've basically read my diary. A diary where I fumble around in the dark while trying to describe men's cocks. It's not exactly something I'd show a man who I've only known for four days. And please don't think you can tell me what to do with my career after I've just been fired. Derek did enough of that and I wouldn't mind thinking for myself for a change."

She's comparing me to that arse? As far as he was concerned, he'd given her no reason to believe he was a cheater or a liar. "Please don't think I presume to know everything about you, but I know I'm not this idiot Derek. *I'm* actually being supportive" he said, trying to temper his frustration. "I'm only suggesting lessons I've learned over time. Having confidence in your ability is really important for someone in your field."

"I'm not in a field yet, Aiden. I haven't even finished this book." She glared at him again, her eyes narrowed and burning with irritation. "I'm sure the cozy world of academia has its fair share of stressors. Let's see, before the summer is over you need to write an eight-page conference paper and a book proposal? My biggest concern is finding a job when I get back to America."

"I can't believe you want to scrap about this." He swallowed her low blow and a sip of coffee with a grimace before replying. "Shots weren't fired, Antonia. No need to return them."

She straightened her back and stared him down. "I'm not firing shots, Aiden. I'm trying to explain how this book and my career is none of your business."

"You might be a little sensitive about this," he said. "You're still very close to the situation. It just happened."

She nodded, not in agreement, but as if she were gearing up for a good old-fashioned public row in a coffee shop. "So I'm sensitive now?"

"I didn't call you sensitive, I said you might *be* a little sensitive about *this*." He punctuated his words for clarity but she was beyond listening. "I'm saying that the timing of this is part of the issue." He finished his coffee and set his mug down on the tabletop with a loud thud.

"I think we better go home," she said, closing her laptop. *How in the hell did that just happen?* Only moments ago, he'd been enjoying her company with a good book and warm scone. They'd been basking in the final rays of sunshine before the metaphorical clouds blew in. And now he had to drive her back in angry silence. Aiden stood up and dog-eared the page where he'd left off before following her out the door. He sincerely thought he was being helpful when he encouraged her more confidence in her ability. Although he didn't want to think about her going back to America, it was unreasonable not to think about her future in general. After all, she was indeed unemployed at the moment. *My god, I'm not telling her how to run her damn life.*

Chapter Eighteen

Is this man telling me how to run my damn life? Antonia slammed cabinet doors as she put away her groceries. She angrily stuffed bags into the garbage and stalked through her cottage like a mad woman. Antonia was absolutely livid by his suggestion that she was being sensitive. *The fucking nerve of him.* "I didn't even want to talk about it." He was a fucking paper grader for god's sake. Hell, she'd done *that* when she was in graduate school. She taught two freshman composition classes while she took a full course load and wrote her thesis.

"Oh, that's rich," she muttered, returning to the kitchen. She looked at the counter where a pile of baking ingredients sat, taunting her with their uselessness. "Confidence?" she scoffed. "You think confidence is baking a goddamn cake?"

She glanced at the garbage can and thought for a moment how satisfying it would be to toss all this shit in the trash. Antonia instead stomped back to the living room. *The nerve*, she thought as she turned the television on. How could someone be so gorgeous and such a mansplainer at the same time? How could he go from kissing her tenderly in the grocery store to telling her about her business with such…smug confidence?

While flipping through the seven channels offered on her old-fashioned television set, Antonia could hear the growing thud of music from next door. She paused, remote in hand, and listened carefully as the speakers next door boomed. It was a familiar tune that she tried to place while she simmered in anger.

What is that? She drifted back toward her bedroom, where Aiden's cottage connected. The familiar guitar riff was apparent when she stopped at the bathroom. It was The Guess Who... "American Woman." *Christ, what a jerk.*

Two can play this petty game. She plugged in her laptop and scrolled through her own music library. "Ah-hah," she cried triumphantly. She clicked on Beyoncé's *Lemonade*, cranked the volume up as high as it could go, and let the album play on repeat. If war was what he wanted, she could certainly give it to him. No one could outsing Beyoncé and Antonia would prove it.

She closed the bedroom door and strode back to the living room where it was quieter. Sitting at the dinner table, she turned up the volume on the Irish news and waited for victory. When her phone rang, she swore under her breath. She was not in the mood to talk to anyone. But upon closer inspection, she saw that it was Eddie. Antonia sighed and received the call.

"Hi, Ed," she said, turning down the news.

"How's your trip going?" he asked, sounding enthusiastic. "Do you love it there?"

Antonia made herself close her eyes and count to five before answering. "It's fine," she said carefully.

"Try to sound a little more excited."

"I'm more interested in how you're doing?" she said. Eddie was always there when she needed to vent. In the last few weeks, that's all she'd managed to do when they saw one another. She worried that she was quickly becoming one of those friends who only brought bad news to the table. "How are you and Megan doing?"

"Oh, we're good," he said. "She helped me get my CV together and now I've got three interviews next week. She reminded me that I'm ready for something more than editing."

"You are," Antonia said, her mood lightening with his good news. "I've always thought you were ready for management."

"Thanks, Toni. Even though I had a feeling the ship was going down, I guess I just didn't know what else to do. Megan calls it "Chicken Little" syndrome."

Antonia laughed. "How much time has Megan been spending with my sister?" She hadn't realized how much she missed her friend. Talking to him steadied her nerves.

"A fair amount of time actually. I hate to say it, but those two know how to dismantle a wedding. I've never seen Megan shout down a DJ before, but it kind of turned me on."

Antonia couldn't help but laugh. "Oh my god, did she make him cry?"

"Probably?" Eddie said. "I don't ever want to be on the receiving end of that."

"Aww, you just watch out."

"She and Octavia canceled everything without penalty, except for the cake. You're going to have to eat that cost. Excuse the pun."

Antonia was amazed and relieved. There were many frivolous items that Derek's parents paid for, but the cake had definitely been her responsibility. She could take that hit. "I'm just glad that you're doing well," she said honestly.

"Oh, of course. Wild Hare wasn't where I was supposed to be," he said. "I might not have a job yet, but I know that getting laid off was for the best. And it's probably good for you too."

"I don't know about all of that," she said. "You might find a job faster than I do."

"Sure, but you've got a good savings account. I do not. You should be focusing your energy on your novel."

This conversation was veering uncomfortably close to the argument she had with Aiden. "I don't know what will come of the book," she said in a tired voice.

Eddie sighed. "You say that, but I know you, Toni. Out of all of us in grad school, you published more short stories and poetry. You stopped writing because of publishing."

"We had good years there," Antonia said defensively. "We learned a lot at Wild Hare."

He scoffed. "Yep, I learned to always keep my CV updated. Come on, Toni. You have to admit it: the world is no better for the shit we published. Now if you had the confidence to finish *your* book, we'd be cooking with gas. If I get another publishing job, I'll definitely push it to the front of the line."

There was that word again. Confidence. When did everyone think she was just a shrinking violet who avoided all challenging tasks? "Well I had the guts to come out here by myself, didn't I?" she asked.

"Definitely," he agreed. "It was a ballsy move. I'm proud of you."

His comment disarmed her for a second. "Huh?"

"I mean it, I was so proud of you when you told me,"

he said. "Megan was so excited for you to have some space to just write."

"Oh."

"What's wrong with you?" Eddie asked. "You sound edgy."

Antonia rubbed the space between her brows and closed her eyes. "Oh nothing," she said wearily. "I just got into an argument earlier and some of the stuff you're saying sounds familiar."

"Oooh, is it that guy Octavia told me about? Are you already getting into fights with your neighbors?" Eddie asked with a laugh. "That sounds a little too Irish for my taste."

"She told you about my neighbor?" Antonia asked, incredulous. "Why are you two talking so much?"

"We're all friends, Toni," he reminded her. "So who's this neighbor?"

Antonia reluctantly explained the whole thing to her best friend. When she was finished, he gave a thoughtful "mmh," and proceeded to keep it real with her.

"Are you serious?" he asked.

"What do you mean?"

"I mean, it sounds like he was asking you legitimate questions and you flipped out on him."

"I didn't flip out on him," Antonia protested.

"Correct me if I'm wrong, but it sounds like he took an interest in what you do by reading a book you recommended, and you're angry because he made you think about your future?"

When Eddie said it like that, she felt only a tad mortified. "You weren't there," she tried to explain. "He was so sure that I don't know what I'm doing with my life. I'd think that would include almost having sex with him, right? If he doesn't trust my judgement, maybe I shouldn't bother with him."

Eddie laughed. "That's a lot to infer from a conversation about your novel. Are you sure you weren't transferring some of your own baggage?"

Those sounded like Octavia's words. And even though they made sense, she resented them. "This isn't transference," she said.

"I don't know how you'd be so upset if it weren't," Eddie said. "Did it occur to you that he just might be a nice guy who cares? While I agree that he probably doesn't know you well enough to say that you're being sensitive, it sounds like he's just concerned."

Antonia paused to think. "You think I sound stupid."

"No, but…" Eddie trailed off. "What's that noise?"

"What noise?"

"Are you listening to 'Formation' right now?" Eddie's tone was wary. "Is that what's booming in your house?"

"I was angry listening to Beyoncé."

Eddie at least had the decency to hold the phone away from his face before howling in laughter. "God, Toni. Why are you like this?"

"Because Solange was too mellow!"

"You're not being stupid, but I think your Irish dude is right. You're going to have to make a decision while you're out there. Do you want to throw yourself back into a job that didn't make you particularly happy or do you want to chase the thing you're brilliant at?"

"But I don't know if I'll be brilliant at it," she said. "Besides I'm on vacation; I should be resting."

"But you're not just on vacation. You're in another

country trying to find your new purpose. This is your *Eat, Pray, Love* for black girls."

He was right and she knew it. Eddie succeeded in calming her down just enough to make her realize that she was being unreasonable. There was too much on the line for her to be in Ireland for a good time. In the time she was to spend here, she had to get honest with herself. Things would have to change when she got back to Chicago. "Alright," she muttered.

"Alright, what?"

"Alright, I hear you," she snapped. "But I'm not ready to talk to him. I'm still angry."

"That's okay too. But just so you know, he doesn't sound like Derek. If you want to be angry at someone, it is supposed to be the asshole who cheated on you."

Eddie's words were like a sucker punch to her gut. "What else was I supposed to do to Derek?" she asked angrily. "I called off his stupid wedding, didn't I?"

"I'm saying that I'm excited that you're finally angry. I know you well enough to know you hate confrontation, so lashing out at Adrian was probably cathartic, right?"

"*Aiden*, and yes, it did feel good actually."

"Well, being in your feelings is a good first step in the right direction," Eddie said gently. "But don't lash out at the wrong guy. Save it for the next time you see Derek."

She didn't want to see Derek for as long as she lived. The humiliation that he caused her still burned. How could she confront the man who she fell head over heels in love with? Maybe Aiden didn't know how to be as tactful as she wanted him to be, but could he have a point? "I think I'm afraid of Aiden," she admitted.

"How so?"

"He just…he's caught me by surprise. I don't know what it is about him, but he's not what I expected." Antonia struggled to articulate her feelings. "I feel like I'm losing control of the plot."

"Hm."

"It was similar with Derek. Like, I just got caught up in his world and lost my own in the process. The difference is that while I'm still overwhelmed by Aiden, I'm actually enjoying myself. He lets me be myself, even when I'm pissy."

"And he likes you when you're being yourself?"

"I think so?" Antonia said. "Is all of this too soon?"

"I can't be sure," Eddie said. "I hate to sound corny, but you have to follow your heart on that one. I support you in any case."

"I think I'm probably just horny," she sighed.

"Ew," he said. She could picture the scowl on his face. "You're basically my sister; I don't want to hear it."

She smiled. "I had to hear all about it when you and Megan first started dating."

"You heard nothing that could incriminate me later," her friend reminded her. "But yeah, you're probably horny. Go get some."

"Thanks for signing off on that, but I'm going to stew for a while longer."

"Whatever makes you feel better, but remember that Derek still deserves your anger. You have no idea how hard it was not to beat the hell out of that guy when I saw him last."

"When did you see him?"

"When Octavia met with him to discuss dividing the cancellations. I saw them meet up at Murray's Deli on Monday," Eddie swore under his breath. "I stopped inside to see if she needed any help twisting his arm."

"I doubt she needed your help," Antonia said with a chuckle.

"No, she was her usual calm yogi self. Derek was being a dick about the cost of your ring and I wanted to lay that idiot out."

"Well, he's lucky I bothered to send the ring back to him," she said lightly. "I'm sure he'll find a way to pawn it."

"Anyway, Octavia had to push me out of there before I caused a scene."

"But you've been kicked out of much nicer places."

"I know, right?"

"Thanks for talking, Ed," Antonia said as she returned to her bedroom. She turned the music off. Apparently, Aiden was not ready to stop his attempt at drowning her out. He had switched to The Rolling Stones. "I'm glad you're my buddy."

"I'm glad *you're* my buddy. By the way, while I'm sure Beyoncé appreciates your use of her album, I think it should be used as a weapon sparingly."

"Noted."

"I have to get going, Toni. Take care of yourself, okay?"

"I will, Ed. Bye."

When she hung up, she flopped back onto her bed, listening to the steady bass line of "Paint it Black." Had he created a music playlist especially for the women who annoyed him? Antonia thought about her friend's words. Perhaps she still had a rage in her that should have been spent on Derek. The memory of leaving his apartment flashed in her mind. She had been so afraid of what she wanted to say to him, the fight-or-flight response in her brain had pushed her out of the door before she could confront him. She hadn't gotten a chance to ask him why or tell him about the pain he caused her. Even in their last phone call, Derek had tried to talk over her with his excuses while she quietly listened. While Antonia had reiterated that marriage would never happen, there were still so many other things she could have told him. *You damaged my self-worth. You made me think that I was lucky to share your space. I made myself smaller for you.*

"I shrunk myself to fit," she said to her ceiling, her voice trembling. Aiden was right, her self-doubt was endangering her future. Antonia had to get out of this rut before she was stuck for good.

Chapter Nineteen

With the help of Eddie's phone call, Antonia eventually switched on Solange at a lower volume. She pulled herself together and faced the heap of baking ingredients in her kitchen. The grocery bag had sat on the counter, daring her to prove that she had the confidence to assemble its contents into something remotely edible without Aiden's promised help. *I can do this.* With her tablet propped up on the kitchen counter, Antonia followed the recipe she found as best as she could. It was the last few steps that were tripping her up...

"Fucking hell," she whispered as she smeared icing on the side of the cake. The task was like spreading cold peanut butter on fragile bread. A chunk of warm cake broke apart and stuck to her spoon as she dragged along the surface. "Fuck, fuck, fuck."

She licked her chocolate-covered finger and wiped it on the towel hanging from her shoulder. Carefully pushing the chunk of cake back into place, she spackled it with another dollop of icing. She wondered if she should have waited for the damn thing to cool off. No, it was too late to think about that. She'd made her bed and she'd lie in it if it meant she could finish this one stupid task.

Nervous sweat collected under Antonia's arms. *Jesus.* She would need to take a shower before taking the cake next door. She wanted to look her best when she marched over there with a finished cake and a smug smile. When she scooped the last of the icing on top, Antonia was horrified to find the icing she had already applied was now melting. Chocolate began to pool on the platter she'd placed the cake on. She used her spoon to gather the run-off icing and drizzle it over the bald patches, but her attempts were in vain. "Oh my god, this is a mess…"

Straightening up, she stepped back from the cake and stared down at it. *This will not defeat me.* If this was truly her *Eat, Pray, Love* moment, she would pray to her mother's Black Jesus to stop the icing from running. "Black Jesus, this cake is made with love and I—" No, that wasn't entirely true. It was really spite cake. "Fuck it, I did my best," she resigned. "Amen."

Antonia left it where it sat and opened the kitchen window. Perhaps the wind could cool it down while she got herself ready. *Maybe I should have done that earlier?* She shook her head and ran to the bathroom. *No time, just move forward.* As she quickly stripped down and jumped into the power-generated shower, she was excited by the prospect of doing the things that frightened her. She was finally going to take control of the plot, instead of being a bystander to the men in her life.

After her quick shower, she ran to her bedroom to find an outfit. Searching through the closet and in the drawers, she came up with a yellow sundress. Beyoncé *Lemonade* Yellow. She'd bought it on a shopping trip with Megan, who told Antonia that she absolutely needed to have it. When she tried it on the first time,

Megan gasped in that dramatic fashion that Eddie loved so much. "If you don't buy it, you'll regret it for the rest of your life." Everything was do or die with that woman. As Antonia held the dress at arm's length, she wondered if Megan was right. Was this do or die time?

She slipped it over her head and let the soft fabric flutter down to her thighs. Antonia assessed herself in the full-length mirror on the closet door. The dandelion-yellow dress settled comfortably a couple inches above her knees, hugging her hips and bust. She tucked her cleavage inside the bodice, trying her best to contain some of the spillage. Antonia didn't remember being so busty in the dress when she purchased it. She did look hot though.

Running her fingers through her mane, she considered pulling it up in a high bun. "No, that's what Derek liked," she reminded herself. Derek took after his mother; the less intrusive a woman's hair was, the more she could blend in. Antonia couldn't believe that she had almost thought to straighten her hair for the wedding when Octavia would have gladly styled her curls to suit her. Antonia shook her hair down and took a deep breath.

She looked like a sun goddess.

Her brown skin shone like bronze against the bright saffron of her dress. She searched her closet for a pair of high-heeled espadrilles and stepped into them. Perfect. She skipped the makeup and returned to the kitchen. The chocolate icing had stopped running. She let out a victory whoop, as she carefully lifted it from the counter. It wasn't falling apart from movement, so that was a good sign.

Antonia walked to the front door, grabbing her keys

along the way. When she opened the door, her heart dropped. It was starting to rain. "Nooo…" She held the plate with one hand and tried to shield it with her other as she ran from her front door straight to Aiden's.

When she knocked and waited, her stomach flipped. She couldn't hear the thump of his music; he had turned it off around the time she started her baking experiment. She knocked again. The soft patter of rain soon turned into a light drizzle. As she waited, her doubts crept back into her mind. This was easily one of the dumbest things she'd ever attempted. What if he wasn't even in his home? While his car was still parked behind her own, he could have stopped by the pub or the chipper.

Antonia carried the cake around the other side of his cottage, hoping she could knock on his back window. The heels of her sandals sank in the soft ground as she made her way across the grass. She stumbled and it took two quick hands to steady her cake. She and it would get wet, but it certainly would not fall on the ground. When she reached the back window that looked like his bedroom, she tapped against it.

"Ms. Harper, is that you?" said Mr. Creely who stood out in his own yard.

Oh god…

Antonia smiled brightly as she waved at the old man. *I look absolutely insane.* "I'm just delivering a cake to Dr. Byrnes."

Mr. Creely waved and gave a nod, though his bushy eyebrows furrowed in confusion. "Huh, that's nice of you."

Antonia took the cake by both hands again and scampered back to the front of Aiden's cottage. Along the way, she called out, "It's just what neighbors do in America."

"I see."

The rain was now coming down in a deluge. Her dress clung to her thighs as she carefully made her way across the grass patch. The cake's icing was sliding again. She knew that the structural integrity was too dodgy for all of this running around. By the time she reached Aiden's front door, she'd lost all patience. She'd knock again, but if he didn't answer, she would smash this goddamn cake against his front door and let the animals claim it.

She raised her fist to bang just as he swung the door open. Antonia jumped back in fright, nearly tipping her cake to the ground. "Why can't you answer the damn door!" she shouted.

Aiden's frown was mixed with confusion and shock. He stood there wearing only his blue jeans, his hair tousled from sleep. "Antonia? What are you doing, woman?"

She was getting drenched while he asked the dumbest questions. She thrust the cake in his face. "I made a cake," she said through a clenched jaw. "And it's getting wet."

He looked from her, to the cake, and back to her. "You wanna come in?" Aiden stepped aside and waited for her to enter.

She was stuck on his stoop, getting wetter and unable to step forward. "I just wanted to show you that I could do it," she said with a tremulous voice. She was too nervous to move.

"Get inside, Antonia," he said. The steel edge in his voice made her even more nervous.

Antonia gathered herself and escaped the rain. As she edged past him and walked into his living room. She stood beside his dinner table and watched him close the door. When Aiden approached her, she held the cake up like a barrier.

It wasn't enough.

He closed the distance between them, standing over her and her pitiful baking experiment. He ran his eyes over her, stopping to stare at the rise and fall of her chest. She was short of breath as she stood under his steady gaze. "You made this?"

"I did," she said haltingly.

"You made me anger cake?" he asked.

"You don't know if I was angry," she said, finding her voice. "For all you know, I just made a cake for the sake of making a fucking cake."

A dark brow arched as he peered down at her. "You're not angry now?"

She was getting there. "Do you want it or not?"

Antonia watched him take another step forward, his eyes fixed on hers. "It looks pretty waterlogged," he said.

She glared at him. "And I'm pretty wet as well."

Aiden's mouth twitched slightly. "Are you?" he asked. His voice could barely contain the smug arrogance that his expression hid. An unwelcome blush crept into her cheeks as she realized what she'd said. He quietly regarded her before raising one finger to her cake. He swiped the top layer of icing and gave it a quick inspection before licking it off his finger. The simple act made her hands tremble. He gave a curt nod. "It's not bad," he said.

Antonia held her breath and fought to disregard the

tumultuous flip in the pit of her stomach. "Thank you," she breathed.

Aiden then ran his thumb along the top of the cake and held it before her face. He met her gaze, issuing a challenge with forest green eyes that sparkled recklessly. "Would you like a taste?" he asked. His voice dropped to a low vibration that struck a chord between her thighs.

Antonia's eyes went from his face to the chocolate-covered thumb before her. Her mouth fell open as the cake continued to quake in her grasp. Her heart pounded erratically in her ears. *Would she like a taste?* Did the serpent ask Eve the same question? "Yes," she whispered, raising her gaze back to his smoldering eyes. They stayed locked in a feverish stare down as he cradled her face, gently rubbing her bottom lip. Her nervous tongue darted out, licking the icing. Aiden's nostrils flared as he took a breath and waited.

Antonia hesitated before parting her lips. The tip of her tongue was tentative as it grazed his thumb. She tasted the rich chocolate and moved forward to savor more of it. As Antonia closed her lips around him, she watched him fight to keep his breathing under control. He swallowed hard as he stared at her mouth. She was going lightheaded from the thrill of this blatantly sexual action. Her tongue whorled around him, licking the remainder of the chocolate away. When he slowly pulled his thumb out, he ran it along her bottom lip again.

"How is it?" he asked, his voice hoarse.

Antonia leaned into his touch, finding it difficult to keep her eyes open. "Sweet," she breathed.

"I think you should make more cakes in a piss-poor mood," he said. Did she detect a slight shake in *his* voice? Aiden pulled the soggy cake away from her and set it on the table behind her. He wrapped an arm around her wet waist, resting his hand on the small of her back, and slowly backed her against the table. The back of her thighs touched the wooden surface as he eased his own leg between hers.

Her face flushed with heat as she let him lead her body. "Actually, I don't think I should cook in anger anymore…" Aiden's face was only a scant breath from her own.

"Does that mean you're not mad at me anymore?"

His hand slid down her bottom to the hem of her dress. He slipped under the wet fabric, easing it up her thigh. One strong leg parted hers and stepped in between them. Antonia shivered as the hot junction of her thighs rested against his denim.

"I don't know," she said, breathing in quick, shallow gasps. With her dress now hitched to her hips, she couldn't think. She hardly had the strength to stand on her feet. The dizzying pleasure of his fingertips against her feverish skin forced her to sit on the table behind her. Antonia experienced the familiar suffocating haze that Aiden's body emanated. It mesmerized her into babbling incoherence.

"How can I make it up to you, Antonia?" he whispered in her ear.

"I don't know."

He knelt to the floor before her, pushing her knees apart. He glanced up at her as he planted a feathery kiss on the inside of her thigh. The scruff of his beard grazed her skin, leaving goosebumps in its wake. "There's nothing you can think of?"

Antonia shook her head. Her legs hung on either side

of his body, spread scandalously. The exposure made her face burn. But she leaned back against the wood surface, waiting in trepidation as he slid his hands along the backs of her calves.

He turned his head to kiss her other thigh, the bristle of his cheek arousing her senses in the same way. She let out a soft sigh of pleasure when his lips locked to her thigh; his cheeks concaved as he sucked her flesh. When he released her, he looked up. "Do you have anything else I can taste?"

Antonia's eyes widened at the sight of his wolfish smile. She knew what his smile implied and it alarmed her. Derek had only tried that once and had given up when it had done nothing for her. She was convinced that she just didn't get any satisfaction from a man's mouth. When Antonia found her voice, she was apologetic. "I don't think that's ever worked."

"Then he didn't do it right," he said, tracing a lazy trail along her thigh with his finger. His tongue followed the path, sucking the plump flesh closer to her apex. She drew a sharp breath as she watched him. "Talking isn't the only thing an Irishman's mouth is good for."

She couldn't help but smile at his lusty wit. He was talking her right into her own satisfying experience. "Challenge accepted," she said.

"Excellent," Aiden said, raising himself to push her back against the tabletop. He leaned over her while she lay on her back, pushing the hem of her dress up to her chest. He stared into her eyes as he ran his hands down her bare belly and pulled her panties down her thighs. The slickness from her own fluids felt cool against her swollen cleft. She held her breath and closed her eyes when his fingertips grazed her mound. It was the softest

touch, feathery light and quick. She opened her eyes and
saw him appraising her hungrily. "Beautiful," he said
simply and leaned over her to plant another kiss on her
lower belly. She quivered as his lips left her.

Antonia wanted him so badly, she could scarcely
breathe. His kisses went lower, slowly and deliberately,
as though her pleasure hinged on his pace. Perhaps it
did, she didn't know for sure. His hot breath fluttered
against her already sensitive folds, sending a tingling
sensation to her core. When his mouth closed over her,
Antonia gasped. His tongue mimicked her movements
from earlier, but with much more creativity. With his
fingers, he delicately spread open her soft flesh, lapping
along her inner lips, taking care not to touch her clito-
ris just yet. Antonia was wet and desperate, squirming
against his mouth, her breath was ragged as tears came
to her eyes. Aiden wrapped his strong arms around
her thighs and held her firm against the table. She was
locked against his mouth, going delirious with his titillating tongue.

He continued his focused ministrations, methodi-
cally circling her opening before plunging his tongue
inside, in and out, in rapid succession. Antonia's back
arched away from the table as she moaned in ecstasy.
He dragged his flattened tongue up and down, before
circling and diving back into her. She reached down and
raked her fingers through his thick hair, pulling his face
against her. While he licked her, his own hand left her
hips and snaked its way up her belly and to her breast.
He squeezed and fondled her as he finally put her out
of her misery. When he turned his attention to her most
sensitive spot, her body seized. Antonia's head thrashed
side to side and she lifted her hips to meet his tongue.

She released a low, trembling moan as she came. Her walls spasmed and jerked, sending a crashing wave of euphoria over her body. She tightened her thighs around him and rocked her hips until the violent rapture passed. When her body finally fell limp, she sighed contently.

Aiden placed a light feathery kiss on her mound before standing up. With both hands planted on either side of her body, he cocked his head to the side. "Is that proper thanks for the cake?" he asked.

Antonia finally opened her eyes and searched his gaze. "What?" she breathed. She was still shaking from his highly inappropriate use of a dining room table.

His face spread into a wide smile. "Will you forgive the way I badgered you?"

"Of course," she said with a frown. "I should be apologizing too."

"I think that was an apology," he said, gesturing to the cake. "It certainly looks sorry enough." He delicately lowered the hem of her dress back down her legs and offered her his hand to pull her up.

On her feet, Antonia wobbled slightly and grabbed on to Aiden's shoulders for support. "I can't walk," she said bashfully.

He hoisted her up into his arms easily, her bottom resting deliciously against the hard club in his pants. "Let me take you to the bedroom," he said as she wrapped her legs around his waist. He nuzzled his face in her damp cleavage and breathed deeply. "I'm not done with you yet."

Aiden had a naked woman in his bed.

He propped himself up on one elbow and stared down at her sleeping face. The shadows of the room played on her relaxed expression. Aiden gently moved a stray curl from her face and tucked it amongst the others, taking care not to disturb her rest. It was almost painful to be this close to her and not kiss her breasts, which were wrapped and hidden away in his blanket. He ached with the overwhelming desire to be inside of her, to experience what his tongue had felt upon penetrating her.

But he had to wait.

Aiden had forgotten to pick up condoms and he was too old to act irresponsibly. He'd made it all these years without any surprises, there was no need to screw that up. But as he continued to watch the rise and fall of her chest, he wondered what it might be like to be a father. He wondered what kind of mother Antonia would make. Those were thoughts that should have disturbed him, but he couldn't help himself. He'd never looked at Lisa and wondered these things. Understandably, children had been out of the question. Lisa was focused on her career which made sense for any pre-tenured scholar. Aiden hadn't touched the issue with her, but kept it tucked away in the back of his mind. It wasn't until he saw his niece, Soircha, that those feelings came creeping back. They always ended up depressing him.

Antonia began to stir under his intense gaze. When her eyes opened, she looked at him with a puzzled smile. "Are you watching me sleep?" she asked in a groggy voice.

"I couldn't help it," he said softly. "You're too beautiful not to stare at."

She ducked her head away from him and laughed. "You're the damned devil."

Aiden feigned indignation as he pulled her naked

body close to him. Skin to skin contact with her reanimated his senses. "Will ye sign ole Scratch's book?" he said in a menacing voice.

She fended him off through her giggles. "Never," she cried.

"But I'll give you everything you could ever dream of," Aiden promised, kissing her neck. "You've already had a taste of the forbidden fruit."

"You tempted me," she gasped when his hand drifted down her belly and cupped between her legs. "Like you're trying to do now." She was wet again. He took advantage of this, carefully sliding a finger past her folds.

"This is what happens to women who show up on my doorstep in wet clingy dresses," he whispered in her ear. He stretched along her writhing body and watched the deep red settle into her brown cheeks. He loved the way her eyes drifted shut as her mouth fell open. Aiden leaned his head down and ran his tongue across her dusky brown nipple, it puckered like a small pebble under his mouth.

"Aiden," she breathed.

"No, my dear. The devil in me must make a cautionary tale out of you." He then sucked the tight bud while his finger and thumb did their work below the covers. She grabbed his hand, pressing it hard against her and followed his pace, grinding her hips in time with his strokes. Her shallow pants and her curls plastered against her sweating temple were equal parts pleasure and agony for Aiden. His erection pressed uncomfortably against her hip and he didn't know how much more he could take. When she spasmed around his fingers, he remembered why he enjoyed pleasuring her. It was to see her face in that final moment. The crease in her brow and her widened mouth, were almost enough to send him soaring. Antonia's thighs closed around his arm like a vise. He kissed her deeply until she relaxed her body against him. Once his hand was released, he ran it up her belly, to her breast and squeezed.

"Have I done a good job of ruining you, m'lady?" he asked.

"The devil," she repeated with a blissful sigh.

Chapter Twenty

They were going to give this whole "dating" thing another shot. After their misunderstanding in the Letterfrack café, Aiden had suggested they try something that
wasn't work related. As Antonia stood on the floating
docks, she kept her legs relaxed and bent, wondering
if this was his attempt to remain in control. While the
ocean was lovely and inspiring to gaze upon, Antonia
questioned being on it. The small vessel that Aiden
climbed in looked no larger than a canoe with a motor
strapped to the back. Antonia stood on the floating
dock with her arms folded. It would be difficult for her
to throw a fit and leave this particular outing. "Is that
safe?" she asked.

Aiden nudged away the oars that lay at the bottom
of the vessel. "Perfectly safe," he said. "It's a currach,
Ireland's oldest boat."

"How old is this one?" she asked, drawing her raincoat around her neck. The winds were strong enough
to make the gray-blue water choppy.

Aiden looked up at her while wrapping a long length
of rope around his elbow and hand. "Oh, she's only
twenty years old. I brought her up from Galway a few
years back so I could boat around the harbor."

Her brows knotted as she gazed upon the expansive harbor. Tall cliffs surrounded them, but out west lay the open ocean. Seagulls screeched overhead, warning her to turn back to the car and stay where it was safe. "We're not going too far, are we?" she asked. "Can we stay in the harbor?"

Aiden extended his hand, his eyes warm and understanding. "We don't have to go out there," he said. "If we go too far, we might hit Boston."

Antonia took his hand and carefully stepped into the currach. They stood in the middle, she still clung to him with a death-grip. "I love the water," she said, looking around her for somewhere to sit. "I swear I do, I just don't have a lot of experience being in it."

Aiden, who looked like he belonged out on the water in his cream Aran sweater, smiled. "Oh I think you might have a little selkie in you yet."

"What's a selkie?" she asked, taking a seat.

"Here," he said, pulling her up again. "You should sit by the bow, so I can operate the engine."

Antonia slowly moved around his body, gripping his shoulders as she went. Her movements were unsteady and wobbly, as if at any moment, she'd be pitched overboard. "Good idea," she murmured as she watched her footing. "Are there any life jackets?" she asked.

"Under your seat." He gestured behind her. "Slip it over your head and tighten the latches on your chest."

She did exactly as she was told and sat firmly on the bench closest to the front of the boat. "What's a selkie?" she asked again; anything to take her mind off the lapping water that rocked them.

Aiden unhooked them from the float dock. "They're like mermaids, but seals," he said with a grunt as he pushed them away from their last chance of safety. "Fishermen fall in love with these seal maidens and steal their coats. Once he's hidden her coat, she must stay with him as a woman and wife. But really, she longs for the sea."

Antonia was breathless. "I've never heard of that," she said.

Aiden looked out at the horizon behind her as he stuck his oars out. "I think it might be a Scottish tale. The point is, you can't let the selkie find her coat."

"What happens?"

He pulled the oars, propelling them forward. "If she does, she'll leave everything behind and return to the water."

Antonia paused and thought about the folklore. Perhaps she did have a little selkie in her. "It's beautiful out here," she said as she watched the rocky shoreline float away.

Aiden smiled. "I knew it. You're a bewitching seal woman who's tricked me into taking her back to the sea."

She returned his smile with a sneaky grin of her own. "It looks too cold for you to leave me here."

"I'm going to start the engine so we can get to that tree clearing out there." He pointed behind her. Antonia turned in her seat to follow his gaze. Near the harbor's opening lay the ocean, but just before that, she spotted a rocky slope with tall trees.

"Is that a place…uh, where we drop our anchor?" she asked, glancing back him.

His mouth twitched with laughter. "I'm sorry?"

Antonia frowned. "I don't know what it's called."

"She doesn't have an anchor," Aiden laughed. "But

yes, we can disembark over there and walk around if you'd like."

"Sure, that sounds fine."

Aiden pulled the cord and the motor came alive with a growl and then a roar. It pushed them ahead at a slow speed. With his other hand, he gathered up the oars and passed them over to her. "Could you put those below you, port side?"

"Which side?"

"My left," Aiden said, correcting himself. "Keep them together at your feet."

"Gotcha," she said. Feeling a little more confident to move about the vessel, she took the oars and tucked them beside her. "How do you know so much about sailing?" she asked. He looked like a natural, completely unbothered by the choppy waves and brisk wind.

"My father," he replied.

She nodded. "He was a sailor?"

"A fisherman."

His short answers and curt tone made Antonia raise a brow. "Oh, what did he fish for?"

He met her gaze with cool green eyes. "Women, mostly."

She nodded. *Got it.* "Sorry," she said. "I didn't mean to pry."

His expression softened. "You're not prying," he said in a weary voice. "Try as I might, I can't avoid thinking about Liam Byrnes. Especially these days."

Antonia leaned forward. "Why these days?"

He returned his gaze to the horizon before replying, "I've been trying to figure that out. He ran off when I was fifteen and I haven't seen him since. But lately, I've been preoccupied by him."

Anxiety knotted his brow. "He just left your family? He didn't go missing?"

Aiden's smile was rueful. "Between trawling and arguments with my mother, Liam left and came back all the time. The last time was for good though. He was at least good enough to leave a note."

Antonia's heart ached for him and his family. When her father had died, it had taken her years to grieve his absence, but she had been with him for the end. Antonia at least had closure and fond memories of the larger-than-life man who was her father. At the age of twelve, Willy Harper had been her hero and she'd always remember him as such. Aiden, however, had a father out there who just couldn't be bothered. He was as good as dead to his family. The idea of a man who would abandon his family on a whim made her tear up. She blinked her eyes and brushed them against her sleeve. "That's pretty awful," she said.

Aiden glanced back at her, saw her tears, and set his mouth to a firm line. He reached over to pat her on the knee. "Dear me, don't you go crying for that eejit. Liam Byrnes doesn't deserve all of that."

Antonia sniffed. "What's the rest of your family like?"

"Oh they're fine people," he said with a smile. "I come from good, hearty folk. My mother was once a school teacher, so she raised me and my brothers with a good amount of discipline."

"Is she the reason why you went into education?" Antonia asked.

"More or less, I suppose. I had it in my head to do anything but teach, but I turned out to be a good scholar. Clare orchestrated my path with a watchful eye," he said with a chuckle. "If you don't keep an eye on middle children, they drift like a rudderless boat."

His metaphor caused laughter to bubble in her chest. "You were clearly meant for the sea, Aiden. Are you sure you want tenure?"

He nodded. "I do. This past year has made me realize I need to stay on the path. Out here—" he gestured to the open water "—lies wasted potential."

She was unclear on what he meant by that. It seemed less to do with him and more about his father. Antonia decided to change the subject. "And how many brothers do you have?"

"I'm one of four boys. The oldest is Liam Jr., then there's me, my brother Sean, and the youngest is Ryan. Liam is a banker in Dublin, he's married to Mary Catherine, she's a nice girl for him. They've got these twin sons who are absolute assholes."

Antonia gasped. "You can't say that about your nephews."

"I certainly can. If you met them, you'd say the same thing."

She laughed, beside herself. It was a terrible thing to say about children. "Don't say that," she said, trying to stop her laughter.

Aiden grinned. "They're fucking hooligans. Everybody knows it."

"Tell me about your other brothers," she urged.

"Alright, let's see. My brother Sean is a head chef at a gastropub in Limerick, he lives just down the street from our mother. He's married to Mary Agnes and they have a twelve-year-old daughter named Soircha."

"Wait, you have two brothers married to two Marys?"

He nodded. "And my youngest brother just got mar-

ried to a girl named Catherine. Try to keep up with me,"
he said, flashing her that handsome grin. He'd forgotten
to take an electric razor to his beard this morning while
getting ready for this excursion and she was glad. It reminded her of when they first met in Clifden. She liked
seeing the one gray tuft that battled for space among
the black hair. He even looked like a rugged seaman
in his cable-knit sweater. "Now my niece is the sweet-
est girl you'll ever meet," he said with a wistful look
in his eyes. "Soircha would love you. She would spend
hours talking your ear off about books. I can't buy her
enough of them."

This wasn't the first time Aiden had hinted at plans
that extended past their holiday bubble. Despite the cold
air, Antonia warmed to the idea of meeting the people
who were important to him. "She's twelve, you say?"

"Yep, and smart as a whip. She's at the top of her
class and reading Hawthorne for fun," he said with a
proud laugh. "She's going through the change though."

"The change?"

He snuck her a glance. "The curse, as my mom calls
it."

Antonia laughed at his wording. "Oh no, you don't
call it either of those things," she said, gasping for
breath. "The curse is too old-fashioned and *the change*
is reserved for women who are going through meno-
pause. Soircha is starting her period, Aiden."

"I don't know what women are calling it these days."

She shook her head. "So your sweet, angel niece is
going to become a rage-filled monster?"

"That's what my mother imagines. She's still a little
girl to me."

"Of course she is," Antonia said, touched by his sentiment. "But I remember when I first got my period. I was a hell-raising asshole."

"I'll be prepared for that," he laughed. "For now, she's a good kid and the best out of all of them until Ryan has a baby. He and Catherine live in Dingle where they run a B&B."

"That's charming," Antonia said. "Your mother did an excellent job raising you boys. And she got a professor out of one of them."

"She did her best," he said before falling quiet. His emotions hid behind a closed expression.

Antonia watched his face and decided that might be enough pressing him about his family. He loved them, but the issues with his father were still very close to the surface. She did her best to change the subject yet again. "Alright, sailor Aiden," she said, clapping her hands. "If we're sailing the high-seas, you have to sing me a chanty."

His eyes flickered. "You know about chanties, but don't know where port-side is?"

"I've learned the romantic parts of the sea."

"We're technically not on the sea, my dear," he corrected, cracking a smile. "But yeah, I can sing you a chanty, my dad knew a few good ones."

"Well give me your best one."

"I've had one stuck in my head for a while, it was Liam's favorite. It's called 'Roll the Old Chariot Along'?"

Antonia cocked her head slightly, that one actually sounded familiar. "How does it go?"

Aiden made a show of clearing his throat before belting out: "Oh we'd be alright, if the wind were in our sails—"

"I know that one!" she cried.

His look of surprise made her laugh. "And how do you know that one, little lady?"

"My Zora Neale Hurston research. I did some side work in Negro spirituals and work songs. That's a black song."

"It is," he said with a nod. "God, it's funny you mention that. I've been obsessed with it lately and I was thinking about incorporating it in my conference paper."

That was incredible. The more she talked to him, the more alike their interests seemed. If he seemed like a renaissance man, maybe she was too. "Brilliant," she said softly. "I don't remember all of the words, but I think it's a call and response, right?"

"That's right. Start again?"

She nodded.

"Oh we'd be alright, if the wind were in our sails."

"We'd be alright, if the wind were in our sails," she joined in.

"And we'll all hang on behind... And we'll roll the old chariot along..."

"...we'll roll the old chariot along."

They sang in unison taking turns to recite the refrain, until she lost track of the words and giggled along. "Your voice is beautiful," he said, eventually giving up.

"You lie," she said.

Aiden shrugged. "It seemed like a nice thing to say to a woman who was wailing her head off in the middle of the sea."

"Shut up," she said as she reached over the side of the boat. She splashed water on him and laughed as he shook his head.

"Careful, darling. I'll leave you out here with your seal friends." He cut the engine and wiped his face with his sleeve. "Jaysus, who is this?" He shifted in his seat to pull his phone from his back pocket.

"Your boss?"

"Hold on just a second, it's my brother," he said as he swiped his screen. Aiden held his phone in front of his face. "Sean?"

"No, it's your poor old mam."

"She hijacked my phone," said a man's voice in the background. Aiden's eyes darted to Antonia's.

"I'm sorry," he whispered.

"Who are you with, son?"

"I'm with a woman," he said. "Mam, you don't have to use FaceTime for everything."

"I like seeing my children when I talk to them," his mother said. Antonia hid her smile behind her hand as she watched him struggle. "And did you say you're on a date?"

Aiden shook his head while staring at Antonia. "No mother, I didn't say I was on a date."

"You wouldn't call this a date?" Antonia asked.

"You're making a mistake," he said in a low voice.

"I can hear her," Clare said. "Could you swing me over to her?"

Aiden closed his eyes. "Mam…"

Antonia could barely contain her laughter. "I wouldn't mind."

"Mam, I'm actually operating a currach right now. Remember what you said about multitasking?"

"You're hardly going to hit anything out on the water," his mother said. "Just hand me to her while you row."

"Do it, Aiden," said Sean's muffled voice in the

background. "She won't stop until she's thoroughly embarrassed you."

Aiden heaved a sigh and handed the phone to Antonia.

Three people had managed to push their way into the screen. At the front must have been Aiden's mother, a handsome woman with the same brilliant green eyes as her son. Her salt-and-pepper hair was braided into a bun with silver wisps around her forehead. This woman could not have been older than fifty-five. Behind her, a man, close to his early forties, waved at her. Next to him, must have been the young Soircha whose blonde hair was a halo of unruly ringlets threatening to take up most of the screen. Apparently, Antonia was to speak to all three of them at once.

"Hello!" his mother said with a bright smile. "I'm Aiden's mother, Clare Hannigan."

"Hi, Clare," Antonia said, holding the phone upward. "I'm Antonia."

"Oh my, what a fine name! How grand."

"Real class name," Sean intoned. She guessed that he must have taken after their father, Sean's blond hair matched his daughters.

"She's pretty," Soircha murmured not too subtly.

"Are you enjoying Ireland, dear?" Clare asked.

"Oh yes," Antonia said cheerfully. She glanced at Aiden who rolled his eyes. "Your son is showing me a lovely harbor near Clifden."

"Oooh, he took her to the harbor."

"I heard her, Mam," Sean said.

"Is it a date?" Soircha asked, most of her face still out of frame. Antonia could only see her massive hair.

"Uh…" She looked at Aiden for help. He continued

only to roll his eyes in response. "Yes, I think I'd call it a date."

"Oooh, did you hear that? He took her on a date; that's very romantic."

"I heard her, Mam."

"What do you do, Antonia?"

She paused to find Aiden staring at her with new interest. Perhaps he wasn't expecting her to admit to his mother that they were actually on a date. "I'm a writer."

"Oh, a writer!" Clare squealed in delight. "And you know that Aiden teaches literature, right?"

She grinned. "Yes, we talked about that. We've actually been helping one another with our writing this week."

"She looks like a model," Soircha whispered.

Antonia blushed. "Well, I don't know about that."

"Oh, she's right," Clare agreed. "You look like you could be in the magazines."

"I'd like to think I'm too smart for that."

Clare tittered, shaking the phone about. "And she's funny! D'you hear that, Aiden? She's too smart for it."

"I heard her, Mam," Aiden shouted.

"How long are you in Ireland, Antonia?" Sean asked.

"For about a week or so," she answered.

"Ah, you should come to Galway. Aiden is keeping Soircha until she goes to Spiddal. He could show you both the sights," Clare suggested. Aiden's brows shot up as he moved to take back the phone.

His quick movement rocked the boat, causing Antonia to panic. She screamed and lost her grip of the phone in an effort to steady herself. Luckily the phone landed at the bottom of the boat and not in the water. Aiden caught her by the shoulders and held her still before she could overcorrect the rocking. "Stay still," he said. "We're not going to sink."

"That's what they said about the Titanic," she said frantically.

"This isn't the Titanic," he said as he searched for his phone.

"No, it's much smaller," she cried. "It's a bloody canoe."

When he found the phone, he looked into the screen. "See, Mam, this is why I can't always take your calls. And shame on you for using Sean as a shield."

"Please don't capsize the boat with all your carryin' on, Aiden," Clare warned. "That's one quick way to lose a girlfriend."

"Aye," added Sean. "No woman's going to want to swim home from a date, Aiden."

They were teasing him and he clearly didn't like it. "I'm going to hang up now. Soircha, I'll see you soon."

"We love you," Clare said. "Goodbye, Antonia."

Before he hung up, she heard Soircha whisper, "Why would he take her on a boat?"

He slipped the phone back in his pocket and looked down at her. "Are you happy?"

Antonia widen her eyes in feigned surprise. "I didn't know they were going to be that curious. Perhaps I *should* go with you to Galway," she teased. "I can meet the family."

Something flickered in Aiden's eyes as he stared at her. "I'd love to take you back to Galway. Hanging out with my mother and niece is not something to put on the list," he said with a half smile. "Lord, have you never talked to *any* Irish mother? Detectives, they are. When they get to a certain age, their only purpose is to make sure sons are married and grandchildren are produced."

"You're overreacting," Antonia said. "Please sit down, you're making me nervous."

Aiden went back to his bench at the stern. "You don't know my mother," he warned. His accent seemed to thicken as he got riled up. "She pesters all of us like this. But me especially since I'm the last to get married."

"Why has it taken you so long?" she asked innocently. He pulled the motor and got them moving again.

"You really wanna talk about that?" he asked.

She didn't know why she was asking. Part of her wanted to know more about him, even at the risk of prying into their unknown future. "Sure," she said lightly. "I'm the one who almost got married. Do you think you'd like to get married in the future?"

"Of course," he said. "I wish I could have what my brothers have: a good woman to come home to after a long day of work. Instead of playing fun uncle to Soircha, I wouldn't mind being a decent father to my own brood."

"Mmh." Antonia took a moment to watch the water lap at the sides of the currach.

"What about you?" he asked. "You think you could try it again?"

There was a quiet hesitance in his voice that made her look up. "Sure," she said. Her tone was light. "I'd try it again. It would have to be small, no frills, just us." She cringed as the words flew out of her mouth. Antonia immediately regretted how she phrased it.

Aiden's green eyes fastened upon hers. *Oh god, stop*

talking. "That sounds hopeful," he said. He looked away, but she could see his mouth twitch again. "Good luck to the man who tries to take your coat again."

Chapter Twenty-One

After safely docking the currach and returning to dry land, Antonia and Aiden walked through downtown Clifden where the streets were much less busy than when she first landed in West Ireland. Antonia finally felt the buoyancy of a woman on vacation. She hadn't realized she was holding hands with Aiden until she stopped in her tracks before a pharmacy. His grip loosened as he slowed down. "You need to pop in?"

"Yeah," she said releasing him. "I need some...feminine products."

Aiden didn't miss a beat and nodded. "Fair play, I can wait out here if you'd like?"

"Sure. Be right back." Antonia cringed as she left him on the sidewalk. *Why did I say feminine products? I may as well have said sanitary napkins; the kind that come with belts.* She had a mind to grab something personal, but it was definitely more intimate. If things went well with today's date, she wanted to be prepared. She'd gone thirty-three years without an accident and she certainly wasn't going to mess that up now. Even when Derek had assured her that he was "The Pull-out King," she had her doubts and kept buying condoms.

Her mother always stressed, "Only women get left holding a bag more expensive than a Gucci."

Antonia wandered toward the aisle where she thought she would find condoms and came up empty. With her hands on her hips, her eyes scanned over the products. It wasn't a very large pharmacy, they had to be there somewhere. She went from aisle to aisle, cold medicines to vitamin supplements, only to end up back in the same spot.

"You need help?" asked an elderly woman in a white coat. She peered over a pair of half-glasses at a confused Antonia.

Do I really have to ask a woman old enough to be my grandmother? Antonia glanced around the empty store before saying in a low voice. "I'm looking for… contraceptives."

The woman tilted her head and frowned. "What's that, dear?"

"Contraceptives," she replied, slightly louder.

"Condoms, you mean?"

Antonia's face grew hot. "Yes, please."

"Back here, m'dear. I keep the rubber Johnnies behind the counter."

Like a child, she followed the pharmacist to the back counter.

"What's your brand?"

"Regular Trojan should do," Antonia said, staring at the counter. Anything to make the awkward transaction move faster.

"Got a hot date?" the woman asked, taking her sweet time to situate herself behind the partition.

"You could say that."

"Smart girl. Can't trust these fellas to think with the brain the Lord gave 'em. How many packs?"

Antonia glanced at the store's entrance before deciding. Aiden was still standing at the door, checking his phone. "Better make it two."

The pharmacist raised a painted-on brow. "Can't be too careful." She dropped two packages in a small paper sack. "Yes, I remember a time when you couldn't get a rubber Johnny without a marriage license and a prescription. The laws didn't change until the '80s, you know? Cryin' shame, it was."

Her embarrassment turned to amusement as the woman gave a brief history of family planning in Ireland. "You seem like a progressive woman," Antonia said. "Is there a reason you still keep them behind the counter?"

"Aye, and I'm an old woman as well. I'm not quick enough to stop thieving snappers from takin' rubbers without paying. I keep the tests back here too. They're too expensive for a panicky lass who's in the family way."

Antonia held back her laughter as she dug through her purse for spare euros. "That makes good business sense."

The old woman counted her money and slammed it in the register. "Have a good time," she said with a feisty wink.

Antonia chuckled. "Thanks."

She stuffed the paper bag into her purse and walked toward the store entrance when she felt a vibration in her back pocket. Assuming it was either Octavia or Eddie, she waited until she got outside. Aiden stood in the same spot where she'd left him, flashing her that same gorgeous grin as if he hadn't seen her in years. "Got what you needed?"

"I did," she said. "Hold on just a second, someone's trying to call me." When she found her phone and read the contact, it was an unknown Chicago number. *One of the many wedding vendors come to collect?* "Hello?"

"Toni!"

She drew in a sharp hiss and glanced at Aiden. A frown deepened in the wrinkle of his brow as he regarded her. With her heart in her chest and her stomach making a steep dive to her ankles, her jaw fell open to choke out the word: "Derek?"

Realization dawned on Aiden's face as she hung on to his arm for support. She was having a nice time. For the first time in a long time, Antonia was enjoying herself with a man. Of course it was a perfect time for Derek to rain on her parade. "Toni, this has gone on long enough, we need to talk."

"He wants to talk," she whispered to Aiden. "Could you give me a minute?"

He nodded though his mouth was set in a thin line of irritation. "If you don't mind, could you put him on speaker? I wanna hear this jack-arse."

That wasn't what she wanted to hear, since dirty laundry was meant to be hidden from the general public. But because she had a supportive person at her side, Antonia did what was asked of her and held the phone up to both of their faces. "What do you want?" she asked in a shaky voice.

"Are you still in Ireland?"

"I am."

Derek scoffed. "How? I canceled your hotel. I

thought you would have gotten the picture, Toni. You belong back here so we can plan this wedding."

Aiden met her gaze and shook his head. *Fuck. Him.* He mouthed.

"We already discussed this," she said. "The wedding is off. My sister is in the process of canceling things. You know this."

"Those are just *things*, Toni. You and me? We can make this work." Derek's voice began to climb. "Come back here and we can talk about Naomi, we can talk about all of them. Just don't leave me. I need you."

Tears stung Antonia's eyes just as Aiden's hand settled on her back. He had clearly heard what Derek let slip. "All of them?"

"Huh?"

"Derek, you said all of them…" She trailed off into the abyss. The emotions she had experienced in his apartment, that night, came flooding back, filling the vacuum with rage. As her heart rate sped up, sweat prickled her scalp and an icy chill ran down her back. She no longer wanted to have this phone conversation with Derek. No, she would much rather be back in his apartment, on that night, with her fingers wrapped around his throat.

"Is that what you need to hear?" he asked, speaking in a frantic speed. "Yes, there were a couple of other women, but I wasn't thinking. I wasn't in the right frame of mind to settle down yet. I don't know, Toni, I think I might have an addiction? That's why I need you. You're so stable and…and organized. You know how to take care of me."

"Christ, would you listen to him?" She'd almost forgot where she was and that Aiden was standing beside her. His face was a mask of anger that he couldn't hide.

"And when I make partner," Derek continued, "you can have a baby. We'll be fine then, Toni. Please just consider it. None of us are perfect, right? We've all got something to work on. I've got demons like any other man. Hell, you've got things to work on. It's called compromise and I do it all the time at work. A marriage is just like any agreement, if you think about it. Compromises and negotiations all over the place."

Much like his rambling.

Antonia had never heard him sound this desperate, but then she'd never heard him sound so cold as when she'd uncovered his lies. *Who the hell is this man?*

"Antonia." Aiden's eyes read: Stop this man's word vomit before I fly to Chicago, in America, and beat him into the pavement. He held his hand out as if to take control of the phone.

She shook her head and moved away. "I have to do it."

"Who's there?" Derek demanded. "Is someone else there?"

"I'm here with my friend, Aiden, and we're listening to you lose your ever-loving mind," Antonia said with an eerie calmness.

"Hello, Derek," Aiden said.

"Who the fuck is *Aiden*?"

"He's a lovely professor who's showing me a good time in Ireland," she said. "Whatever you think that means, multiply it by ten, and that's how good a time I'm having. I'm tired of listening to your inane bullshit, the excuses, and your 'solution-based' lectures. You can do that to your financial firm clients, but that shit won't fly with me."

"Are you fucking him?"

Since they were starting to draw looks from passing tourists. Antonia turned the speaker function off. "If you'll excuse me," she told Aiden.

He grinned. "That's my girl. Have at it."

Her heart bloomed at the sight of his beautiful smile. Confidence was the key. That, and properly placed rage. Aiden's gift to her was the space to cuss out her ex-fiancé in the middle of a tourist town without hesitation or judgement. When she returned to her conversation, her smile was ear to ear as she proceeded to tell Derek about himself. "If I choose to fuck any man, that's my prerogative, isn't it? I'll tell you whose business it isn't: Derek M. Rogers. You lost that business when you stuck it to every unsuspecting woman on Miracle Mile. For all of your grand negotiation skills, you've fucked up the biggest deal in your life. A marriage contract will not happen between us because your terms are bullshit. If you think that I'll come crawling back to your triflin' ass in the hopes of having your baby, you're sicker than I thought. You of all people should know that a baby solves nothing. Look. At. Your. Parents."

Aiden gave her a thoughtful nod. "Oh, that's good."

She winked at him and continued. "Between the father who doesn't talk to you and the neurotic mother who's trying to act out some Oedipal fantasy, you were fucked from the jump. How I couldn't see it is disturbing, and admittedly something I should work on. But you don't need me, Derek. You need a therapist. You need Jesus. You need to get popped in the mouth. But you can't have me anymore."

Antonia finished with a heaving chest while Aiden pumped a fist in the air. A random woman, who couldn't mind her own business, gave a low whistle. "Goddamn," she said in a Southern drawl.

Aiden gave a throaty laugh. "I know," he said. "It was beautiful."

The pause on Derek's end was plenty of time for her to catch her breath. Antonia had never told anyone off with that kind of conviction. She usually shrank from conflict, took the high road, or refused to rock the boat. But this boat was officially rocking and she was ready to sink it. "So this is it?" Derek said. "You just want to throw it away?"

Antonia took a deep breath. "*You* threw it away."

"Mom was right about you." His voice was a defeated and tired. "Book smart but no real breeding."

Any other time, Vivian Rogers's sentiments would have crushed her. Today they made her burst into laughter. "Yeah, your stuck up mom is probably right about that. I'm smart enough to know this about our relationship: you can't make a silk purse out of a sow's ear, you dick."

And with that, she hung up.

The random tourist woman, who had hung on to the conversation, applauded with vigor. "You go, girl!" she said before moving on.

Antonia blushed. "Holy shit, that felt good," she breathed.

"Yeah?" Aiden said as he grabbed her by the arms and shook the nerves from them. "You wanna go for round two? I'm sure Clifden has a boxing club around here."

Actually, she felt shaken by the amount of adrenaline flowing through her. She hadn't realized how tense her shoulders were until Aiden massaged the space between her neck and shoulders. "I'll pass," she said with a chuckle. "I'd like to sit somewhere."

He quickly led her to the nearest sidewalk bench and sat her down. "Are you okay?"

"I'm good," she said, and truly believed it. "I needed that."

Aiden took her chin in his hand and pulled her gaze to his. "I know," he said with a smile. "Where did that come from?"

"My mother," she said in a daze. "I hate to say it, but I think I channeled my mother for some of that."

"I can't wait to meet her..."

"I feel so...light," she murmured, shaking out her arms. "Like some huge weight is off my shoulders and I can just live." Antonia blinked, as if she were seeing him for the first time. His eyes were brimming with the pride and amazement that she was slowly beginning to feel. "Thank you for being there."

Aiden gathered her into his arms and hugged her tight. "Of course, darling. But you were the one who stood up for yourself."

"You're right."

"The past is in the past," he said intently searching her for gaze. "You don't have to carry the baggage anymore."

Antonia shook her head. "No, I don't."

"'Can't make a silk purse out of a sow's ear,'" Aiden said with a laugh. "I've never heard that before, but I'm liable to add that to my vernacular."

Chapter Twenty-Two

"Finally getting the chance to tell someone off, is like... getting the chance to take off your bra after a really long day."

Dinner with Antonia was certainly entertaining.

Aiden snuck a quick glance at her chest. "Is that so?"

The Clifden seafood restaurant was busy that evening with tourists who were still milling around after the oyster festival. In the warm glow of the candles at their table for two, Aiden listened to Antonia chatter away with a new vigor in her voice. By the time their dessert had arrived, she was giddier than a school girl, giggling and waving her fork around. "I've never felt that powerful in my life."

"Who's next on your list?" he asked, taking a bite of bread pudding. "An old boss, maybe?"

Antonia ran her fingers through her curls and sat back in her seat. "Don't tempt me," she said. "But we're not here to talk about Derek. The past is in the past."

"What would you like to talk about, darling?"

"Something fun and potentially embarrassing."

He narrowed his eyes as he ran his tongue over his teeth. "This seems like a potential mistake, but I like being impulsive."

"Excellent. Tell me about your first girlfriend," she said, licking the sticky toffee from her fingers. "What was she like?"

Aiden could watch her lick sticky things off her fingers all night, but he was a little puzzled by her sudden interest in his past love life. He thought he had succeeded in keeping the conversation light and pleasant. "Why on earth do you need to know that?"

"Pretend we're playing truth or dare," she said with a smirk.

He nodded in recognition. "Okay then I should probably pretend to be a sixteen-year-old girl too?"

"If it helps." She was teasing him.

"Well I can't play truth or dare by myself, Antonia," he reminded her. "I need a willing partner."

She sat back against her seat and regarded him suspiciously. "Fine, but…"

"But what?" he asked. "A dessert game sounds like fun."

"But the dares should be within reason."

He shook his head as he helped himself to ice cream. "I'm not too old to remember the rules of truth or dare. I don't think there's anything that can be considered 'unreasonable.'"

She saw what kind of corner she'd walked herself into. "I think we're old enough to know what reasonable is."

"I suppose that depends on how badly we want the truth from one another?"

Her perfectly shaped brow arched under her curls. "Okay…"

"Eat your ice cream before it melts from your indecision."

Antonia swiped at the bowl. "Well since the stakes have been raised and anything could be acceptable during this game… I'd like to change my question."

"No, no, no," Aiden said waving his spoon. "You know that's not how the game works. You have to ask me if I want truth or dare."

She heaved an exaggerated sigh. "Fine. Truth or dare?"

"Truth."

"Alright." She lowered her voice and leaned close to the table. "How old were you when you lost your virginity?"

Aiden buried his head in his hands. "So, we're playing the sex edition of Truth and Dare? This *is* authentic."

She giggled. "Not necessarily. When I was a kid, we prank called a lot of boys. We didn't have any experiences to report on."

"I was seventeen," Aiden said with a straight face. "She was a girl in my graduating class. We went to the same house party and managed to find ourselves in the same laundry room."

Antonia clapped her hand over her mouth. "Oh my god, that's scandalous."

He shrugged. "It's just the truth," he said. "Now it's my turn."

Before he could think of something, their waitress, Karen, stopped by their table to check up on them. "Is there anything I can get you two?" she asked sweetly, her blonde bob swayed as she looked from Aiden to Antonia, her hands clasped behind her apron in anticipation.

"Oh, I think I'm still working on this delicious bread pudding," Antonia said.

Karen turned to Aiden, "And you, sir?"

Aiden thought it over before replying, "The lady and I are playing a petty game from our youth; truth or dare. Do you know it?"

The young woman grinned. "Yeah," she said. "But I haven't played in ages."

"Of course you haven't," Aiden said with a nod. "Because you're a responsible adult. But we're a little caught up in our own flight of fancy. What kind of whiskey would you recommend for a game of truth or dare?"

Karen and Antonia stared at him.

"Well that depends... Are you driving, sir?" the young blonde asked with a startled laugh.

"That's a good question," Aiden said thoughtfully. "We're both staying in Tully Cross, about 30 minutes away." He glanced at his watch. "It's already 7 p.m."

"Aiden," Antonia said in a concerned voice.

"Antonia, truth or dare."

Their waitress laughed. "Oh, this is fun," she said, folding her arms across her chest.

Antonia shot him a glare from across the table. "Dare."

"Oh no," Karen said with a "tsk." "You picked wrong. You don't let a man like this one dare you."

Antonia cast a glance to their server. "What makes you say that, Karen?"

"Look at him," she said. "Doesn't he look like the kind of man who likes to take the piss?"

"She's right, darling," Aiden conceded. "That's what kind of man I am."

"I'm well aware. I'll stick with dare, thank you."

Aiden smiled broadly. "You heard her, Karen. We'll take two double shots of Jameson."

"That's not my dare, is it?" Antonia asked. "I can take a shot of Jameson."

"No, it's not your dare, but we'll take those shots," he said to Karen. The young woman chuckled as she retreated from their table. He turned back to Antonia who was still very confused.

"Well, spit it out," Antonia said, leaning forward, forgetting about their dessert. "What is it?"

"I dare you to book a hotel in Clifden."

Aiden wasn't surprised by her shocked expression, but he was curious if she'd play along. If she was brave enough, their little outing that had started with a boat ride, could turn into a small getaway from Tully Cross. He hoped he had sized her up correctly.

Her silence was an opportunity for Aiden to playfully goad her. "Now if you're unable to fulfill the obligations of truth or dare, that's perfectly understandable."

"No, I'm not quitting," she said quickly. "I'm just thinking."

Aiden held his breath.

"What if they're all full?" she asked.

"The festival ended yesterday and some of these folks have to go back to work," he said. "I'm sure something has been freed up."

Antonia sighed and rolled her eyes upward. She was thinking hard. The implications of what he asked were obviously not lost on her. "Sure," she finally said. "I'll look something up and…book it?"

Aiden placed his phone on the table top and slid it toward her. "You can use my phone if that's easier," he said with a grin. She regarded the phone with disdain, keeping her hands in her lap.

"You're the devil," she whispered.

"Then you should know better than to accept my dares," he said in a soft voice.

Antonia eyed him with a renewed curiosity. A small smile played on her lips as she picked up the phone. "I suppose you're right," she murmured as she scrolled through his phone. "But this isn't me signing Ole Scratch's book."

"Oh, I've had your name for a while, m'dear."

When Karen returned with drinks in hand, she set them down and placed her hands on her hips. "So is it bad?" she asked Antonia.

Antonia looked up from his phone and smiled. "I have to prank a man named Paddy O'Brien," she said easily. "Ask him if his fridge is running."

Karen looked disappointed. "Aw, that's kind of tame."

Aiden glanced at his date and shook his head. She was quick on her feet when she had to be. "But it's a classic."

"You two let me know if you need anything else," Karen said as she drifted to the next table.

"While I book this," Antonia said. "I'd like to take my turn."

Aiden lifted his drink and took a deep drink. "Do your worst."

"Truth or dare?"

"Truth," he said quickly.

She glanced up from the phone. "Have you dated a black woman before?"

Aiden swallowed. "No."

"Why not?" she said, batting her lashes. "We're quite lovely people."

"I have no doubt," he replied. "But I just haven't had the opportunity."

She nodded. "Do you have any questions for the one ambassador sitting in front of you?"

She knows how to take the piss as well. "I don't know if I'm dating one right now," he said carefully.

"I'm definitely black," Antonia said.

Aiden rolled his eyes in reply.

"As far as your dear mother is concerned, we're on a date," she said. "So technically, you are in fact dating a black woman."

She had him there. Was it this easy to talk to her? Aiden couldn't remember a time where he had a rolling banter with a woman that kept his busy mind captivated. Antonia was, in a word, captivating. "Mmh, well if we're technically dating… How do you get your hair to do that?"

Antonia promptly laughed at him. Loudly. "That's seriously your first question?"

"Sure?"

"What exactly is my hair doing?" she asked, patting the curls near her face.

"It's not *doing* anything, it's very pretty," Aiden tried to sound intelligent about it. "It's just, well I wondered, what do you do to it? What kind of products do you use?"

She shook her head, returning to his phone. "Oh this is telling," she said with a breathy laugh.

"No, no," he said, sitting up. "Not telling. I'm just curious, is all. It's one of my favorite things about you, really."

"I use shampoo and conditioner like everyone else."

"Well it's gorgeous," Aiden said, taking another drink. He now felt mildly embarrassed by his novice question. "Truth or dare?"

"Truth, please."

"Have you ever dated a, erm, white man?"

Antonia handed his phone back to him before taking a gulp of her whiskey. "Of course," she said. "And I don't need to know more about you guys."

While trying to rattle her for the fun of it, she managed to turn his game back on him. In the low lights of the restaurant, her clear brown skin was flawless. The way her white teeth glinted when she smiled at him made Aiden crave her laughter even more. She was beautiful and outwitted him when he least expected. Aiden wondered if he was in love with her. "Nothing more?" he asked.

She gave a low and earthy chuckle as she held her glass to her cheek. "I'm a black woman who learned to play the higher education game before she had to play the business world game. I know white people."

"Fair," Aiden returned. "I think that's fair."

"Sorry," she said. Her smile dipped slightly. "I'm not trying to generalize. It's just that there's a lot of explaining to do when you date a white person. I dated a lecturer from grad school before I took up with Derek. And I had to do a lot of correcting."

"Why would you date a lecturer?" Aiden asked.

"He was cute and he liked my writing."

"That feels like it crosses some kind of boundary," Aiden said. "You were a still a student."

She cocked her head and stared him down. "Oh really? Says the man who was secretly dating his colleague for two years?"

He gave her a dismissive wave. "It's different."

She rolled her eyes in response. "I think we're letting the game get away from us." She took another sip. "Whose turn is it?"

"Yours," he said. "Truth or dare?"

"Truth," she said boldly.

"Have you enjoyed yourself today?"

Antonia stopped. "What? No trick?"

"Honest question. Have you enjoyed yourself today?"

She nervously tucked a curl behind her ear and took another drink. "I have," she said with hesitation. "I haven't been on a real date in a long time."

"I'm glad."

They settled into a short silence, staring at one another with buzzed smiles. The drink had gone to his head and he could see Antonia's face was flushed as well. Their dessert had gone abandoned while they talked, leaving the ice cream a melted pool of white. After a moment, Antonia reached a hand across the table and wiggled her fingers. Aiden saw that as a sign.

He took her by the hand and stared into her deep brown eyes. "Antonia," he said softly. "I've enjoyed these last few days with you, immensely."

She stroked his knuckles with her thumb, her smile downward cast. "I have too."

There was something that lingered over their table, some unspoken request that they were both too frightened to make. After all, it had been less than a week of talking and laughing and…other things. He wondered if she minded if things were moving swiftly or if she liked rolling with the punches as well. Whatever this was, he didn't want it to end.

Antonia stood outside of the hotel that she'd been unable to check into just last Thursday. Instead of feeling hurt and anger, she now felt trepidation and desire. She stood beside Aiden who dared her to make this reservation. She knew what he was asking of her and was only half-afraid to indulge him. The other half of her was still afraid to indulge herself. "Are you sure this is a good idea?"

He looked down at her. "I think it's a brilliant idea. We can watch a television that has more than seven channels, walk around in robes, maybe order some room service…"

She shot him a sidelong glance. "You know that's not what I meant."

Aiden took her by the hand and led her to the front entrance. "I think I know what you meant, Antonia," he said as he opened the door. "But your 'dare' obligation has been met. You successfully booked a hotel room because I'm too intoxicated to drive us home."

As they entered the lobby, Antonia looked him over. Aiden appeared relaxed, but it didn't seem necessary to take the risk. "And whatever happens up there… happens?"

"Exactly."

Antonia held her breath as they approached the front desk. Breda was there, manning the station. *Oh Jesus…* The young woman looked at the two of them, hands locked, and smiled brightly. "Ms. Harper! How are you?"

"I'm fine, Breda. I'd like to check in."

"It's nice to see you back in Clifden," Breda said, staring at Aiden. "How was Tully Cross?"

Aiden looked at her with a smirk. "I think Tully Cross did her a world of good." He went into his pocket to produce his wallet. "Ms. Harper reserved our room, but I'd like to pay for it."

"Of course," said the receptionist, taking his card. "Mr. Byrnes, is this your first stay in the Atlantic Coast Hotel?"

"Yes, it is."

The young woman looked around them. "And do you need help with your luggage?"

Antonia's face reddened. They had no luggage.

"Won't be necessary," Aiden said with a handsome smile.

"Right, well here are your keys for room 205. The elevator banks are to the left of our lobby." Breda gestured to her right. "Thank you for choosing Atlantic Coast Hotel, again."

They waited for the elevator in silence. Antonia gazed upward at the numbers, while Aiden stared at her. She turned to face him. "What?"

"Would you like to use the shampoo and conditioner in the morning?" he asked.

She laughed. "Why are you like this?"

"I'm concerned about your hair maintenance," he replied. "You know, since we don't have luggage."

"That was so embarrassing," she said in a low voice. "She thinks that we're just here for…"

He nodded. "Yup." He didn't seem very concerned at all.

When the empty elevator bank opened, they stepped inside and watched the doors slide before them. "I hope that she—"

Antonia was interrupted by Aiden's mouth covering her own. His lips were ravenous as his tongue plundered fast and loose. His hands dug into her hair, pulling her close to him as he edged her against the elevator wall. Aiden's lean, hard body pressed against her, making her moan beneath his lips. She raised her hands to his strong chest and gently pushed back. When he got the message, she was able to pull back from his lips. "Aiden," she breathed.

"I'm sorry," he said panting. "I've been waiting to do that all night."

She peered at him from beneath her lashes. "Can you wait just a moment more?"

"Patience has always been a challenge for me," he said, glancing from her to flashing numbers.

When the doors slid open, he grabbed her by the hand and took off down the hallway. Antonia had to run to keep up with him, laughing along the way. Upon reaching their room, she watched Aiden fumble with the key, nearly dropping it before he could slide it in. She stood fidgeting, tucking an errant curl behind her ear and smoothing down her wool sweater. Once he unlocked the door, their actions seemed to slow to an achingly awkward pace. He stepped inside first, turned the light on and swept an arm to gesture, "this is it." She took a tentative step forward and gave an appraising nod.

"Yep, this is what I remember from the website," she said. She closed the door behind her with a soft bump and locked it with an even softer click.

"Would you like anything to drink?" he asked with a hoarse voice. He gave a small cough and wiped his hands on his jeans.

Antonia smiled and shook her head. Complete awareness was what she wanted at that moment. Her eyes traveled from him to the window. Below them, on the streets of Clifden, people were still out roaming the bars. Street vendors and buskers called for customers to try their trad music over at the next drinking establishment. She looked at the door where the bathroom was and wondered if, afterward, they'd shower together. Her gaze finally rested on the bed and a surge went through her body, just below her belly. Everything in her, nerves, anxieties, and nagging insecurities began to pool at her feet. Without looking at Aiden, she heard his strained breathing. He sounded as though he were in agony. Antonia's eyes traveled back to him. He stared at her with a look in his eyes she'd never seen in a man. In the pale light of their room, his eyes shone, burning forest green. They were hungry.

"I've never done this before," she finally said.

He finally exhaled, giving a short laugh. "I was just thinking that same thing myself."

She let her arms hang helplessly. "I don't know how to start," she admitted.

He slowly approached her. "We can start wherever you want."

Antonia smiled. "From the beginning then."

She stood between him and the door, her back resting against the cool wood. She was feverish and dazed as he raised his hands slightly and rested them on her hips. The movement seemed familiar and necessary. Antonia put her hands on his arms, feeling the cords of his muscles beneath her thumbs. His forearms were covered in springy dark hair, the same hair that peppered his chest. "Pretend we're dancing and you're taking the lead."

"I don't know how to dance," she reminded him.

"Yes, but you've done this dance before," Aiden said,

removing his hands from her and placing them on the door on either side of her head. "Today is the day Antonia gets to get powerful."

She gazed into his eyes and waited for him to touch her. "You'll keep your hands to yourself?" she asked.

"As best as I can."

Antonia was grateful for the chance to slowly explore him at her leisure. Aiden tended to overwhelm her senses, making it impossible to catch up with him. The way he stood over her was already incorrect. "No, this won't work," she murmured, switching places with him. She gently pushed him against the door and stood before him.

"That better?"

"Take off your sweater," she said.

His eyes challenged her. "You take it off."

Her hands trembled slightly as she reached for his waistband, dragging his sweater and T-shirt up his torso. As she pulled them over his head, he shook his hair out of his face. "That's easy enough," she said.

"Easy peasy."

She ignored him and fanned her hands against his chest. His sleek hair was smooth and soft beneath her fingers. He stiffened under her touch as she grazed his nipples, watching her with the same stoic expression. Antonia slowly ran her fingers down his taut, rippling abs until she stopped at his belt buckle. She tentatively leaned forward on her tiptoes and planted a light kiss on the side of his neck. Aiden lifted his jaw slightly to receive her kisses.

"You're too tall," she whispered. "Go sit on the bed."

"Yes, ma'am." She took him by the hand and pulled him away from the door. She pushed Aiden onto the bed roughly, where he bounced and landed on his back. "Oof, okay."

Antonia's hands flew to her mouth. "Oh, I'm sorry! Are you okay?"

He drew himself up on his elbow. "A little whiplash, but I want to see where this goes."

She wondered the same thing. Antonia didn't know what she was doing. Sure, she tried to write about this sort of thing in her novel, but she didn't know how to properly seduce a man. Her character Augusta would know what she was doing. She'd take Bryon's belt off with one flick of the wrist. Things were different when she had a real flesh and blood man in her midst. Usually, it was the man who took charge in these kinds of situations. "I'm uh...blanking here."

"Do what feels right."

"I don't know what to do with my hands," she said, laughing. She held them up in defense. "I don't usually do this."

"What do you usually do?" he asked.

"I just let the man...you know, do his thing. You all seem happy to take the reins."

"Darling, you're going to write about this in your book. Does your girl ever just have her way with her guy?"

"Augusta?" She was surprised that Aiden would refer to her. "She would just go for it."

"Confidence, Antonia."

"Confidence," she repeated. *Confidence*. She straightened up and put her hands on her hips. "Okay," she breathed.

"Okay."

"I'm going to straddle you now."

He suppressed his laughter. "Okay."

"Don't laugh at me."

"Not laughing," he said with a gorgeous smile. "Give it to me."

She climbed onto the bed and crawled up his body, her legs on either side of him, pinning him to the bed. "Okay," she breathed. He felt great between her thighs. It was empowering to be in this position. "You feel like a stallion."

"Yes, that's how you make a man happy," Aiden said, bucking his hips against her.

Antonia jumped. "Oh!"

"Would you like a ride?"

"Stop teasing me," she said, slapping his arm.

"See how easy this is? We're just having fun."

"You're right," she said. "This isn't a big deal. We're having fun."

"That's right." He bucked his hips again. "Are you saddled up?"

She hopped again, with a squeal. "I'm not actually saddled up yet," she said in a mischievous voice. She reached into her back pocket and pulled out a little packet, tossing it on his chest. "Not yet."

He looked at the condom and back at her, his brow arched in surprise. "When did you have time to get that?"

"Before we went to the restaurant," she said with pride. "When I ducked into the pharmacy."

"You saucy little minx."

"I wanted to return the favor," she said.

"I think you need to stop talking and saddle up."

Chapter Twenty-Three

Aiden guided Antonia with his eyes.

Her nerves were getting the best of her and he hoped that she was up to the task. He watched her nervously regard his body, with tentative hands and darting eyes. "What do men generally like?"

Aiden did his best to remain serious but she was making it difficult with novice questions. "I liked what you did before," he said. "I liked the way you kissed my neck."

Antonia nodded as she leaned down on top of him. The pressure from her hips against his groin was pleasant, but grew painful the more she moved. She hovered over him, planting slow, luscious kisses down his jaw and neck. Her eyes were still open, she kept glancing to him for approval. Her hands cradled his face as she deepened her kisses, darting her tongue against his neck. He groaned in response. "That feels nice," he murmured.

"Mmh?" Her lips traveled over his Adam's apple, running the tip of her tongue down to the valley where his collarbones met. She scooted down his body, her lips tracing a delicate line at the center of his chest. Her hands followed behind, intent on finding his nipples which were already stiff from the friction of her sweater. Raking her fingernails across one, made Aiden's breath hitch in his throat. He closed his eyes and rested his head against the bed.

"Yes," he breathed.

She paused to measure his response before running her tongue along the small flat disk of his nipple while fanning her fingers across the other one. Antonia switched nipples, giving each its own special attention. In a move that Aiden didn't expect, she blew cold air on one of them, sending a shiver down his spine. He couldn't help himself as he took her by the hips and ground his straining erection against her. Antonia's gaze flew to his face once she felt it.

"Turns out I don't need that much foreplay," he said, pushing into her. "You might want to prepare to mount."

"Okay," she breathed. She raised her hips slightly to pull her own sweater off. When she tossed it to the floor, she quickly unhooked her bra.

Aiden nearly lost control as he watched her full breasts tumble from her undergarment. The gentle slope of her breasts ended in stiff peaks. Like magnets, Aiden's hands went to them. Squeezing and massaging while she unfastened her jeans. She wasn't going fast enough for him, so he flipped her onto her back.

"Oh!" she yelped.

"I can help you with that," he said, unzipping her jeans and pulling them from her waist.

"Thank you," she said. "Can I help you with anything?"

Aiden grinned at her pleasantries. Antonia was a real smart-ass when she wanted to be. He wrenched her pants to her knees and past her feet before tossing them to the floor. He started on his own pants next, his hands shook as he quickly tore apart his belt buckle. "No, I think I can manage from here."

Sliding his pants down was more of a chore than he thought it would be. He nearly tripped over himself as he freed one foot. Aiden hopped out of the other pant leg and kicked them across the room. Finally, he stood triumphantly, in his underwear, fists on his hips and beaming down at Antonia.

Her expression changed from wanton sex goddess to alarm when her eyes traveled to his waist. Her voice caught in her throat and her mouth fell open when she saw his arousal through his gray boxer briefs. He glanced down at himself. "Yep," he said with a satisfied grin.

"Your length…it's rather, lengthy," she said as she absently licked her bottom lip.

"I'll expect to read about it in your book," he said. When he pushed his underwear down, he heard a soft gasp escape her lips. Aiden hung there in all his glory, while Antonia stared at him. She found the small packet near her and absently tossed it at him. Aiden caught it with one hand and ripped it open with his teeth. He watched her as he slid the sheath up along his cock, feeling a jolt of pleasure from her expression. Aiden knelt down and climbed onto the bed beside her. With his head rested against plush pillows he beckoned her with his eyes.

"Now what?" she asked.

"Now you can take a ride," he said with a wink.

Antonia slid her panties down her thighs and kicked them to the floor. She slowly crawled up to the head-board and straddled him again. Her wet softness rested against his thigh as she struggled to figure out her next step. While she waited, he explored her body with his hands. With firm thighs on either side of him, he spread them wider so he could see her even better.

Beautiful.

He ran the back of his fingers up her velvet soft lips and stopped at her belly. He reached around and cupped her bottom with one large hand. Her ass was a perfect fit within his grasp, he wondered what else would be a perfect fit. Antonia's skin was so soft under his fingertips. He was amazed by her movements, the careful rocking of her hips along his length. Antonia's breathing became deeper as his became shallow.

She took his heavy cock in her hand and stroked upward. Aiden swallowed and released a long, ragged breath. She had no idea what she was doing to him. "Antonia, please."

"Please what?" she purred in dulcet tones. Her eyes seemed to grow darker above him. Under the halo of loose curls that framed her face, she looked wild and alive. If he was the devil, she was the temptress who bewitched his body. She handled him like a cat playing with a mouse. *She knows what she's doing.*

The words died in his throat while she rubbed the head of his cock against her opening. "Jaysus…" he groaned. Aiden's eyes fell shut as his back arched away from the bed.

When Antonia eased herself onto him, he thought he would come from that bit of tension. The resistance made him grit his teeth. She was slow and teasing, pulling away from him and slipping on again. He gripped her hips and tried to steady his breathing. He wanted desperately to be inside her, but waited in agony as she played with him.

"Antonia," he rasped, the cords of his neck stretching.

"What, Aiden?" Her smile curled as she gazed at him under hooded lids. She looked positively radiant hovering above him, her breasts pushed together as she gripped him. "What do you want?"

He gave up. "Fuck me," he growled, pushing her hips down roughly. Only after filling her to the hilt did he take a tiny breath.

She rode him expertly, lifting and rolling her hips forward while her hands were planted on his chest. The sensation of her wet walls tightening around him drove him on the edge of madness. As she continued the slow and steady motion, sliding up and down his engorged rod, Aiden took a hold of her bouncing breasts, pulling and pinching her nipples.

Antonia's head tilted back and lolled to the side as she picked up the pace. She sighed to the ceiling as she rocked against him. "Aiden…"

He fell into her rhythm, thrusting his hips to meet hers, while holding her in place. He was breathing fire as he slid in and out of her like a locomotive. He was teetering on the edge when she tensed around him. Antonia threw her head back and cried a long, guttural moan, her grip loosening on his chest. Her face contorted in exaltation as she shuddered. Aiden lost control and sped up his thrusts, running his hands all over her body.

The explosion of pleasure made him see stars. He roared as he pulled her to his chest, squeezing her close. Antonia wrapped her arms around his shoulders and choked back a sob. "Jesus," she whispered against his chest.

"Yes," he breathed. They remained interlocked for a moment, gasping for breath and clutching one another.

When she finally pulled herself from him, settling on her elbow, her grin was goofy. "How was that?"

Aiden looked down at his spent member. "Marvelous, Antonia."

She beamed at him, a thin sheen of sweat covered her brow, her hair disheveled and gorgeous. Aiden thought that he loved her in that moment. "Confidence."

He reached over and cupped her face in his palm. "Yes, m'dear. Confidence."

Chapter Twenty-Four

Bryon closed the distance between them by backing her against the wall of the shower stall and easing a strong thigh between her legs. Augusta could feel the sweet tingling of arousal at the apex of her thighs and heaviness of her breasts as she watched Bryon slowly lather up his hands with soap. He never took his eyes off hers, even while placing his sudsy hands on her neck, his thumbs tracing the lines of her collarbones. They traveled slowly toward her breasts, massaging them gently. Her knees shook under the weight of her desire, as he deliberately pinched and flicked at her constricted nipples.

Blushing heat crept up her neck and settled in her cheeks as he slid his hands down the front of her flat belly. His hands traveled around her back, making tender circles before descending to the curve of her bottom. He cupped her there, applying the same slow ministrations, making her mad with pleasure. Her back arched off the wall, pushing her breasts closer to him. What was he waiting for? Her thoughts screamed for him to ravish her. Surely, he was running out of patience after their last interruption. But he did the opposite of what she demanded. He took his time, caring for each part of her body with the fortitude of a monk.

As he knelt before her, Augusta's world slowed to a point where she could count the individual jets of water spray above his head. Bryon teased her unhurriedly, coursing his hands around the fronts of her thighs and down her legs. He refused to touch her where she wanted him the most. She nearly collapsed when he bent her leg to soap her foot. "Please," she whimpered. Her womb quaked with want. His face was so close to her mound; she could feel his hot breath against her skin.

Antonia paused to release a shaky breath. *My god, this is hot.*

She was living the dream. There was a naked Irishman in her bed and she was writing compelling smut. The morning after exquisite lovemaking had inspired her to leave the bed and retrieve the tablet from her purse. While Aiden slept, she tapped out twelve more pages of Augusta and Bryon's Bangkok tales.

"Are you back to work, Ms. Harper?" Aiden's groggy voice murmured.

His hair was tousled from sleep as he squinted at her screen. "I had an idea," she said, putting her tablet on the nightstand.

"Are they fucking yet?"

Antonia shrugged back under the duvet and faced him. "They're nearly there," she said with a coy smile.

Aiden rubbed his eyes. "You, my dear, are a purveyor

of artistic porn. And I cannot wait for when you have a book signing line out the feckin' door."

"You think I'll have a book signing?" she asked, snuggling against his warm body. Under the covers, he found her leg and sandwiched his powerful thighs around it. He draped an arm over her and pulled her into his chest.

"Of course you will, and I'll be there changing out your ink pens when they die."

Antonia chuckled against his chest. "How thoughtful of you."

"I'll even massage your tired little fingers at the end of the night."

He dropped another hint about their lives outside of this cozy time in West Country. While those hints excited her, she was still unsure of what they were doing. Was this just a vacation fling? People had them all the time, but it didn't always mean real relationships sprang from them. When it came to Aiden, she didn't know if wishful thinking was an appropriate approach.

"I was contemplating our conversation on the boat." he said, interrupting her thoughts. "You said something about coming back to Galway with me. I think you should. You could come to the conference on Thursday and see me in my element: Professor Aiden."

Antonia gazed up at his goofy grin. He was beautiful, nearly perfect, and waiting on her to say something. The answer caught in her throat as she smiled and shook her head. *This is moving too fast.* It was only about a week since she ran away from Chicago to jump in bed with another man. "You want me to go to Galway?"

"If you're worried about my mam, I can run interference. All you'd need to do is be your charming self and have tea with her, thirty minutes tops. I'm not above kicking me own dear mother and niece to a hotel," he said with a chuckle.

"Sure, I'd like that," she said, trying to join in his laughter, but panic seized her heart. *Are we dating? He knows I have to go back to another country, right? How can he be so calm and lighthearted about something that's only going to be lost to citizenship?* Her mind was a flurry of questions that she couldn't answer in that moment and that made her more anxious. Maybe she didn't plan her meals, but Antonia didn't like to be flapping in the wind when it came to other matters in her life. Aiden had a lot on his plate with preparing for the conference and writing book proposals. Clearly he underestimated how much time he'd need to do either of those things properly.

"What's on your mind, little lady?" he asked peering down at her.

"Nothing," Antonia lied. "I'm just thinking about the future."

"About being on a fancy bestselling list?"

She nodded. "Right."

"And perhaps what you'll eat for breakfast?"

Antonia chuckled. "I'm starving."

Aiden shifted to a seated position in bed and pushed his hair out of his face. "Because of all the sex, right?"

"Possibly," she said as she ran her eyes over him.

Antonia enjoyed watching the muscles of his torso flex and ripple with each movement. His body was a treasure trove of many erotic secrets; from the muscular V at his pelvis to the hard-knotted calves slung over the white covers. When she held his hand, he seemed to marvel over her in the same manner. Turning her hand over by the wrist, Aiden kissed her palm and it sent a tremor of arousal through her belly. His emerald eyes flickered to hers, causing her breath to hitch in her throat. *When will this feeling leave me? When will my body stop reacting to his touch like some ninny?* Wordlessly, he ran his lips against her open palm before placing it on the center of his chest. The tuft of black hair brushed against her fingers in a promise of more to come. Antonia was ready to accept anything he had to offer, if it meant more baking experiments or canoe rides, she was game if it meant riding him again.

"Sometimes I can't tell what's on your mind," he said, sliding her hand downward. "Other times, it appears quite evident that you're contemplating filth."

Her hand ran down his abs, his skin hot beneath her touch. With her eyes trained on his, she blushed. *When will I stop blushing like this?* "And right now?"

Her hand stopped at the hot stiff club under the covers.

"Pure filth," he said.

It annoyed her when he was right. He read her thoughts and her body like no other man and it was unnerving how little she could keep from him. Under his intense gaze and soft caress, she came undone and couldn't be put back together until they kissed. She couldn't recall feeling this intensity with Derek. Even in the beginning, she was more nervous of messing up or not being the vixen he expected in bed. Anxiety made her brain tight as she performed pleasure for a man who barely asked if "it was good" for her.

"No, lass, back to filth," he said.

Her mind snapped back to her fingers that encircled

his cock. "How did you know?" she asked with a be-mused grin.

"Your face is an open book that I can read well enough." He cupped her cheek with one large hand. "It's a book I want to lose myself in on a rainy afternoon."

Another glimmer of tenderness that left her arrested yet full of hope. Antonia's words died on her lips as she stared into his smiling eyes. Aiden made her tongue-tied and unable to think. She was clearly in lust, but there was something about him that made her want to stay in his arms, safe from the world and from the hurt Derek had caused. Antonia squeezed her hand in response.

"Oh, there she is," he said with a chuckle.

While Aiden had his nose in his French Revolution ro-mance novel, Antonia tapped her story on her tablet and jotted notes in her notebook. They sat quietly in the cafe where she'd originally planned to visit when she planned her Clifden trip. This was also their second time in a cafe after their fight in Letterfrack. As Antonia paused to drink coffee, she glanced at Aiden and felt they were in a better place. He shifted in his seat while flipping to the next page and furrowed his brow at a passage. She wanted to ask him where he was in the story, but thought against it. No need to pull him away from the pleasure of romance. Instead, Antonia smiled and let her gaze drift around the small cafe.

The eatery's large windows faced the street, giv-ing her a fascinating view of a new world. Tourists oc-casionally stopped in, some with large backpacks or with bored children in tow. An American family walked in with two children under fifteen who were attached to cellphones. The father, who appeared exhausted, asked the boy and girl what they wanted to drink several times before they were able to pry their eyes from their screens. Antonia shook her head, struggling to imagine her mother having had the resources to take her or Octavia abroad. It was impossible, but she knew Diane would've liked a place like Ireland. Her mother had grown up with a desire to be a stewardess, traveling in a cute uniform to far off cities like London and Paris. But like many women of her time, life happened, and she'd been forced to put her dreams on hold. With deferred dreams and a dead husband, Diane pushed Antonia and Octavia to perform what should have been seen as miracles. Leaving the Southside of Chicago and going to school and when finished with that, attending more school. Their mother's pushing and nagging had created as much friction as it produced success.

Antonia felt a pang of guilt, as she remembered her last conversation with her mother. Their phone calls had always been infrequent, but she should have called Diane after she canceled the wedding. Instead, she let her sister handle it. If she was truly going to make changes in her life, Antonia needed to call her mother and have a long talk. Some of the conversation would have to include "you were right and I was wrong," but she also wanted her mother to stop being so critical when it came to most of her decision-making. The work ethic Diane had instilled in them was a double-edged sword. Antonia may have been a workhorse, but she generally made safe bets, taking care not to move too far out of her lane. Even within her lane, she doubted herself at every turn.

And now she was in Ireland. Writing a book. Fucking a handsome professor.

She'd traveled outside her lane for the first time in her life and managed to accomplish something huge. Instead of thinking about what was next on her list, Antonia finally felt like sitting back and basking.

Aiden gave a low whistle. "Claudette is being enlisted to be a feckin' spy."

Pulled from her reverie, Antonia glanced at him before chuckling. "It's a good thing, I promise you."

He dog-eared his page and sighed. "I don't know why she doesn't just live a simple life in the country with Jean-Paul. They could continue making wine and start a family."

Antonia rolled her eyes. "Because no story is without conflict. You have to insert drama somewhere and you can't do better than a war."

Aiden raised a brow. "I know how literature works, love. But I feel something for these two."

"You're attached to Claudette and Jean-Paul?"

"I want them to be happy," he said in an exasperated tone. "She's already lost her da and Jean-Paul might not have status, but they deserve a bleedin' chance, eh?"

She smiled. "They do and they will. The author just wants to put you through the wringer first."

He picked up the book, flipping back to his spot. "Well, they feckin' better."

Fearing she might hurt his feelings, Antonia fought the urge to laugh at him and returned to people watching. Just outside the cafe window, her gaze settled on a tall man in his sixties who stopped for a smoke. She watched him turn his back to the wind and unpocket a small white slip of paper. In it, he tucked a sprinkle of tobacco and, with expert fingers, rolled it until he created a thin cigarette. The older man raised the cigarette to his mouth and sealed the paper with a lick. When he did this, Antonia narrowed her eyes.

Something in his windswept face reminded her of someone. The wrinkles around the corners of his eyes, his square jaw set as he inhaled the smoke. Even the bridge of his bent boxer's nose, seemed familiar. He was handsome for a man his age, he stood solid with broad shoulders and a straight back. As he faced the window, protecting his cigarette from the bay winds, Antonia studied him for a moment. And then she looked to Aiden who was lounging in his chair, his eyes cast down at his book. She frowned as her eyes darted from him to the man outside. The older man was blond, the wind blew his thin hair every which way. *Light hair, but then his brother, Sean, is a blonde as well...*

Back to Aiden's face: his lips were pursed, the bottom one was full and stuck out. As it usually did when he was in deep concentration. The older man's lip did the same while he assembled his cigarette. Surely she was making silly connections. The man outside smoked half the cigarette before stomping it out on the sidewalk. He wiped his hands on his worn black pea coat and walked to the cafe door. When he stepped inside, Antonia held her breath and continued to discreetly spy on him. The man wiped his boots on the mat just inside the door and took his place in line behind the American family that was still ordering coffee. The children whined about being bored, while the parents demanded customized drinks that mimicked a suburban Starbucks order. The man muttered something under his breath as he waited.

The way he stood, the way he ran his meaty hand through his hair in frustration, even his expressions… Antonia's eyes cut back to Aiden who'd sat up in his seat, no doubt from another dramatic turn in his own story. When Aiden ran his hand through his own black hair and sighed at Claudette's misadventures, her heart sped up. *Jesus Christ, Toni, you're being an idiot. What are the odds? What are the damn odds that an estranged father would show up in a coffee shop after twenty years?* After years of being steeped in fiction, Antonia wondered if she was finally losing her mind.

"There's other people in line, boyo," said the older man. He cocked his head to the side as he addressed the father of the American family. "I ain't got all day."

He wasn't loud about it, but his tone was edged with steel and it betrayed his disarmingly thick Irish accent. The father quietly acknowledged him and tried to hurry his family along. When they were out of the way, the man stepped to the counter and towered over the barista.

"What can I get for you?" she asked.

"Aye, since it's too early in the marnin' fer Poitín, I'll a coffee, love. None of that rawny ponce shite, I'll just take it black."

"Of course, sir. Could I have your name?"

"Whatdya need me name for?" he asked, resting his hip against the counter. He crossed his arms and peered down at her.

The young barista appeared flustered as she quickly pulled a cup from the stand. "Helps us keep track of the orders, sir."

His heavy brow raised. "D'ye need me birth certificate as well?" he asked in an imperious tone.

"Just a name," the girl's marker poised at his paper cup.

"Me name's Liam Byrnes, love. That alright fer ya?"

Antonia gasped. "Jesus fuckin' Christ."

She hadn't realized how loud she was. The man's face whipped around and locked eyes on her. "You said it, dearie. Y'need a feckin' form to fill outta form these days."

Antonia couldn't speak. She could only look from one man to the next. Aiden stared daggers at the man whom Antonia assumed he'd called da when he was a boy. Liam, unfazed by them, finished his transaction and joined the American family to wait on his drink.

For a fleeting moment, Aiden's face blanched before it quickly turned to stone. "Jaysus, Mary, and Joseph…"

"Aiden."

His chair scraped against the hardwood floor as he stood. "You eejit son of a bitch."

Chapter Twenty-Five

Twenty-three years blew through him like a freight train, taking him back to the angry little boy he used to be. With blood pounding in his ears, Aiden stared into a face that could have been a mirror. In twenty more years, his father's face would be his own. The unfounded fear his mother had told him to ignore finally found him and grabbed his shirt collar. Aside from the receding hairline and a red face battered from years of salt air and drink, this was indeed the father he remembered.

"Yer gawkin' mighty hard, boyo," Liam said in a familiar grumble hardened by years of tobacco. "Got something on yer mind?"

Aiden couldn't find his voice. To his left, Antonia made a strangled noise and moved to stand. The cashier, a young woman with oversized hipster glasses looked between the two men, wondering what to do.

Liam squinted. "Do I know ya, boyo?"

Anger boiled over and spilled before he could contain it or his mouth. "I don't know why you feckin' wouldn't, *boyo*. You're still legally married to my mam, Clare Hannigan. My brothers Liam, Sean, and Ryan still belong to you as well."

Only the sound of a coffee grinder punctuated the heavy silence of the cafe. The American family had quit their chatter and the kids looked up from their mobile devices with renewed interest. Liam eyes widened in recognition as he stared at Aiden a little closer. "Aiden Donagh Byrnes," the old man muttered. "For all me sins, it's you."

Hearing his father say his name was a jarring experience, but he held on to the rage he'd cultivated. Aiden kept the rage safely stored away in a small box in his heart, nursing it for such an occasion. He promised himself that if he ever crossed paths with the man who fathered him so cavalierly, he'd open the box and salt the earth with his anger. "For all your sins, I'm he."

"Aiden," Antonia said. She stood at his side and touched his arm.

He barely heard or felt her. "Outside."

Liam didn't have to be told twice, the old man forgot about his coffee and exited the cafe without a word. Aiden pulled away from Antonia and followed him.

"Aiden, don't go out there," she said.

He looked over his shoulder, meeting her round and panicky eyes as she watched him move away.

It didn't slow his pace.

Outside in the cold, gray air, Liam waited on him with hands stuffed in his coat pockets. "Listen, son. I know yer probably sore about—"

Aiden didn't let the man finish his sentence before punching him square in the jaw. His mind blank as his fist connected with bone. The follow-through on his jab knocked him off-balance and he stumbled over his feet, falling into Liam.

"—Fer fuck's sake!"

Aiden straightened up and smoothed his sweater down. "I've been wantin' to do that for twenty-three years, you miserable gobshite of an arsehole."

His father held his face and stared at him in awe. "Who taught ya to belt like that?"

"You did," Aiden said, rubbing sore knuckles. "You taught us all how to fight and then you left. I kept fighting."

"Could have been a boxer with a reach like that. Nearly took me head off, y'did."

Aiden was surprised how little attention they attracted on the street. From inside, people had crowded around the window, watching for the next blow. Antonia was there too, wearing an expression of pity and horror. "What the hell are you doing here?"

"You ain't gonna belt me again?" Liam asked with a wary gaze.

Aiden felt strangely empty after the first punch and couldn't muster the energy for another. The adrenaline left his body as quickly as it had guided his reckless actions. It had been ages since he'd gotten into a fistfight and it sickened him to stoop that low. He wasn't a student who could jump in as a barroom brawler anymore. He shook his head and slumped against the cafe's wall. "No."

"Fair play, the first is free fer old times."

"Fuck the old times," Aiden panted. "Where the hell have you been and why the hell do I have to see you now?"

"Here fer the festival with a boatload of oysters. I still fish, y'know."

Aiden looked up. The casual tone his father used, as if his whereabouts for two decades were common knowledge, angered him all over again. "You're trying to wind me up, aren't you?"

"I'm doin' no such thing, boyo," Liam said, holding his hands up. "God's honest truth."

"What do you know about god's honest anything, Liam? You're a feckin' coward if I've ever known one."

"Aye, that I am." His father's pale blue eyes lowered to his feet. "I left yer mam and brothers in tatters."

He hadn't expected honesty from his father. The thousands of times he played this fantasy out, he had pictured an elderly man who had a convincing excuse. He'd also pictured himself dragging the truth out of a faceless man. He never saw this playing out as pitiful and short as it was. Aiden sighed and sank to the sidewalk in exhaustion. The door beside him jangled and Antonia was by his side once again.

"Are you okay?" she asked in a low voice.

Aiden rested his arms on his knees, as he hung his head, and spoke to the ground. "I'll live."

"Are *you* okay?" Antonia asked Liam.

"He'll live too," Aiden said in a harsh voice. "He said the first one was free for old times."

"I'll make out okay," Liam said. "Are you me son's lass?"

"Um… Sure? Listen, they're about to call the police in there."

"I'm sure sorry you had to see that." Liam's tone was contrite, pissing off Aiden even more.

"So long as you're tossing around apologies," he snapped. "You could start with your own son, you know?"

"Aww, you know I'm sorry," Liam said in a tired voice. "Hell, I've been a sorry sod fer donkey's ears."

"Should we go back inside?" Antonia asked Aiden.

"Let me take you fer a jawful, boyo."

Aiden looked between Antonia and his father. Her worried eyes searched his face for any signs of injury, nervous hands fluttering around his arms. Instead of worrying about his own frayed nerves, he needed to see after her. His father would have to wait. "It's noon, Liam. Drinking isn't going to repair the fact that you're a sorry sod."

"Aye, but I could take the lump out m'jaw with a stiff drink," his father said.

"I would advise you against that," Antonia whispered as she knelt close to him. She touched his sweater sleeve, imploring him with her eyes. "You need space to think about this."

Aiden's muscles slowly relaxed under her touch. There weren't many things he could hold on to at his age. His career he currently struggled with, and the stress that accompanied it, gave him an identity and purpose. The absence of Liam Byrnes made him the man he is today. Without the hole in his heart, Aiden wouldn't have the grit to overcome being a poor kid from Limerick. He held on to the hate for a reason: it drove him. Had he never seen his father, he could have easily kept it hidden from Antonia. And now that the box was opened, he went and behaved like a feral animal in front of her.

"Aw, come on then." Liam asked, rubbing his face. "Let me buy you a drink and we'll call it even."

His father's flippant tone made the beast in his heart reemerge. *Even?* The man was out of his whiskey addled mind if he thought one midday drink was going to set right all the wrong he'd saddled him with. Liam shifted his feet like he'd rather be anywhere but there. That part was natural enough. The shifting in his father's feet hasn't stopped since his first son was born. But right now, it was Aiden's turn to leave. He took Antonia's hand and hauled himself from the sidewalk. "Let's get our things and get home," he said as he stared Liam down.

She squeezed his arm and gave a quick nod. "Okay."

"So that's that?" Liam asked, crossing his arms over his barrel chest.

"Can you undo all the damage you did to your family over the last twenty years?" Aiden shot back.

Liam gave a tired shrug. "Y'know it ain't in the cards."

Aiden sighed and turned away. "Then that's that." He and Antonia were about to return to the nosy patrons of the coffee shop when his father said something that gave him pause.

"I'll be holed up here fer a couple days… Stayin' over at the Arch Guesthouse."

With his back to Liam, his hand hovered above the door handle. It was an invitation. To what, Aiden couldn't be certain. A chance to talk to the man? Antonia laid a hand on his back and pressed. "You do whatever you want to do," she said in a low voice. "I'll still be here if you need me."

That was all he needed to hear.

Aiden opened the door and ushered her inside. Shutting Liam out.

Chapter Twenty-Six

While she drove them back to Tully Cross, Antonia struggled to keep her eyes on the road while checking on Aiden. He sat quietly in the passenger's seat, staring out the window, tapping his fingers against his knee. Midway through their drive, Antonia glanced at him again. "Do you want to talk about it?"

Aiden sighed. "I wouldn't even know what to say."

Eyes back on the road, she nodded. When she slowed for a sharp curve, Antonia didn't change gears fast enough and rode the clutch. It made an awful grinding sound that added to her anxiety. "Shit, I'm sorry," she said.

"I can drive if you like," Aiden said in a tired voice.

She shook her head as she maneuvered the gear shaft. "Absolutely not," she said. "You just had the biggest shock of your life. Let me do this for you."

He paused. "I'm fine, darling."

"I'm sure you think you are," Antonia said, checking her speed. Cars passed them as she hugged the rocky shoulder. "But you're in shock right now, Aiden."

"But you don't like driving."

"I'm not about to sit here and argue with you," Antonia said.

Aiden went silent. He was back to watching the scenery and ignoring the elephant in the Volvo. She glanced at him again and found a defeated man who didn't resemble the person she'd met in SuperValu several days ago. This Aiden slumped in his seat with a despondent expression. There was no wit or humor in his eyes and it killed her. If he wouldn't talk about the bomb that had gone off, she'd needle it out of him.

When she and Octavia were girls, Antonia had a terrible time expressing herself. When she was hurting, it felt easier to hold it in. Her sister was there to needle her worries out with a calm voice and probing questions. In this stressful moment, *what would Octavia do?* was more helpful than *what would Augusta do?* If she behaved like her protagonist, Aiden would probably get his feelings hurt with a short-tempered "snap out of it!"

A softer approach was needed.

"One time, when I was in fifth grade, I got a terrible cold," Antonia began. "I was blowing my nose every five minutes on those terrible paper towels from the bathroom and coughing up a storm. I should have stayed home, but I was working on my fifth year of perfect attendance and I didn't want to ruin it. At some point in the day, maybe during reading groups, I was with some girls and I was talking about how important The Baby-Sitters Club was. I had a coughing fit that must have burst a blood vessel in my head because my nose started bleeding while I was going on and on about the merits of preteen labor. Only I didn't notice until this girl, Vanessa Michaels, shouted 'Omigod, ewww! Toni's bleeding all over the place!' Sure enough, I was gushing blood out of my nose."

Antonia peeked at Aiden, whose attention appeared elsewhere.

"Anyway, everyone started screaming like they'd never seen a nosebleed. I mean, Christ, you'd have thought there was a real emergency. The teacher ran over with a huge wad of paper towels and damn near smothered my face as she walked me to the nurse's office. I had to go home that day, which ruined my perfect attendance because full days counted. When I returned to school, I found out I got a new nickname in my absence."

"What?" Aiden asked.

Antonia grinned. "Bloody Mary. Not the most creative, but Vanessa was popular enough to get it off the ground. She even attached the lore to me, claiming that if anyone said Bloody Mary three times in a bathroom mirror, I would show up and bleed on them. Again, it's pretty derivative, but she ruined the rest of school year for me. The only thing that saved me was summer vacation and entering sixth grade where we'd all split up anyway. By the time we all got to the middle school, we had bigger problems to contend with; how to get to classes on time, sorting out our lockers, changing clothes for gym. No one had time to bring up my nickname and I hardly saw Vanessa."

"And the point?"

"We're getting there. I hated Vanessa for the eight months of hell she put me through. But I didn't stop there. Together, we got through seven more years of school and graduated while I quietly hated her. The girl didn't even acknowledge me, she didn't apologize to me. I held a grudge against her for a full decade. Do you know when that ended?"

"When?"

"I was working at Wild Hare for three years, copy-editing shit I didn't care about, and I felt sorry for myself. I got drunk on a cheap bottle of wine, which I'm known to do, and started searching for Vanessa Michaels on social media. She was married with a career in advertising, which made sense. She was basically living her best life in L.A. with some guy who looked like a male model. All of her photos looked professional, her vacations looked expensive, her house had one of those circle driveways...and then it clicked. After all that time, I'd held on to nonsense. Bloody Mary wasn't my battle to fight anymore, but I kept fighting. Vanessa Michaels did the damage and moved on without another thought. I had to understand that I was the furthest thing from her mind while she was in her Pilates class. I wouldn't get an apology and if I met her on the street, she wouldn't even recognize me."

"You drank the poison hoping she'd get sick."

Antonia nodded. That was probably the best way to phrase it. "Yes, and she didn't get sick."

"So you cut the rope?"

As they neared Tully Cross, she felt comfortable enough to go the posted speed limit. She thought about Aiden's question as they passed the town's only church. "I don't think I did," Antonia murmured.

"No?"

She pulled up to the cottages, right behind her rental car and cut the engine. Antonia faced Aiden and shook her head. "I didn't. Because I met Derek about a month later at that sports bar. When he approached me, my brain went to mush. As my mom would say, I didn't use the sense god gave me and I fell for him immediately."

The words tumbled from her mouth before she could stop and properly assess them. These ideas had never occurred to her before now. In her Chicago apartment, Octavia told Antonia that she'd eventually have to ask herself the question, *Why Derek?*

Now she knew.

"I didn't want to be Bloody Mary anymore. I looked at Derek and saw one of Vanessa's valuables. He chose me and I was grateful for it."

Aiden remained silent.

"To use your metaphor, it's a thick rope, Aiden," she explained. "I didn't start hacking at it until I ran from his apartment. Until I came here and met you. You help me cut the last frayed edge when he called me."

He frowned as he reached over and cupped her face in his palm. "Oh, darling."

"And if we really want to mix our metaphors, I grabbed my seal's coat from him. I'm free to do whatever I want on my own timeline. I'm done with stupid things like Vanessa, fifth grade nosebleeds, and men who walk all over me," she said with a sad smile.

"Of course you are, my love." Aiden stroked her cheek with his thumb. "You can be whoever you want to be."

Antonia reached out and laid her hand on his chest. "Believe it or not, you can too. After all these years, you saw your version of Vanessa, only much worse. Your father…" What could she say about a man who was laid out by his own son after a twenty-plus year absence? "You might not find what you need from him. You have to give yourself what he couldn't or wouldn't give you."

He pressed his lips into a thin line. "I don't need anything from him."

She shook her head. "That's not true and you know it." She pointed her finger against his chest. "He took something in there a long time ago and you're hoping he'll give it back."

Aiden exhaled and hung his head. "Antonia…" His hands closed over her finger, pressing it against his beating heart. It thudded through his sweater as her own broke in response.

With her free hand, she took him by the chin and lifted his face. "You had the confidence to punch him in the jaw," she said, biting back a grin. "But you're also going to need confidence for this next step. You'll have to let go of the hurt and give that little boy what he needs now."

He chuckled and tried averting his shining eyes. "You're giving me the confidence lecture now, Ms. Harper?"

Antonia leaned forward and brushed her lips against his. While she searched his gaze, she gave him a tentative kiss, tracing the seam of his lips with her tongue until he allowed her entry. Antonia gripped the back of his neck and pushed forward. When she felt a single tear wet both of their faces, she wiped his cheek with her thumb. Antonia kissed him as if it could erase his pain. It wouldn't, but it was worth trying.

Chapter Twenty-Seven

Exhaustion was etched on Antonia's face.

As she gave herself a cursory glance in her bathroom mirror, it became clear what kind of toll the morning's events took on her body. If someone had told her that she'd be put in the middle of a painful Irish family reunion, she would have laughed. She splashed her face with cold water, hoping it would make a difference. The frigid water gave her a temporary wake up, but her eyes still looked tired.

Antonia walked to her bedroom and flopped onto the mattress where she contemplated sleep. She was in no condition to write anything, but her mind was still abuzz with racing thoughts. She wondered what Aiden was doing and if he was alright. It would probably take him a long time to be "alright," but that didn't stop her from worrying.

Her phone rang in her back pocket, startling her. It was Eddie.

"Hey Ed," she answered.

"Have you checked your emails?"

She sat up from her bed. "No, what's up?"

"Wild Hare has been sold as a subsidiary of Sixpence Publishing," he shouted. "Why aren't you check-ing your emails?"

Antonia tucked the phone between her ear and her shoulder, grabbing for her laptop. "When did you find this out?"

"Last night," he said excitedly. "The board sent out a company-wide email, but there's individual emails asking us to come back."

She held her breath as she checked her email. She found it. "Dear Antonia Harper," she breathed. Anto-nia's eyes scanned the page, picking out the key phrases like "our apologies for a tumultuous change in manage-ment" and "your work has not gone unnoticed." A small gasp escaped her lips as she read, then reread, the last paragraph. "Oh no…" she groaned.

"What is it?"

She couldn't articulate the news until she read it for a third time. It was like passing through some strange reverse in fortune. Just yesterday, she'd finally cut ties with Derek and now she was being offered a job. Hadn't she already gone through enough of these changes? "They can't do this," she moaned.

"Spit it out!"

"They're offering me the position of publisher," she said. "I'd have to apply for it, but they're hiring in-house, and they think I would be a good candidate based on my previous experience. They want me to have Rich-ard's job…"

"Holy shit, forget everything I said. You have to take this job."

Antonia shook her head. "They want me to interview on Thursday, Eddie. Today is Tuesday."

"Okay, so you cut your trip a little short or ask them

to reschedule for next week. This could be the chance to work for a place that will take you seriously. They forced Richard out for you!"

Antonia's head was spinning. "But what about my book? What about Aiden? I thought I was out here trying to find myself."

Eddie went quiet.

"Well?" she said. "What about it? They can't just dog-whistle me back to Chicago to do a job that I might not want to do. I'm still figuring things out." Her eyes filled with tears of frustration.

Her friend sighed. "I know what I said, Toni. I guess I'm just relieved that we might have jobs. I still have those interviews, but wouldn't it be nice to know we've got something to fall back on?"

She couldn't believe Eddie's hypocrisy. "But I thought that all we were doing was 'falling back on' something that was dragging us down."

"I get it, Toni. But I have a lot to consider. I've got debt and I need a job. I can't just run off to Ireland whenever shit hits the fan."

"Baby, you're being rude!" Megan chastised. Antonia didn't want to hear it right now.

"I've gotta go, Ed."

"Look, I'm sorry…"

She hung up on her friend and tossed the phone on her bed. "Fuck everything," she muttered. Where did Eddie get the nerve to talk to her like that? He was totally backtracking on his own advice, making her feel guilty in the process. She hadn't just run away to Ireland when the shit hit the fan.

Antonia sat back against her pillows. *Well, that is exactly what I did.* But Eddie didn't realize how his words shook her foundation. She was reminded, once again, that Ireland wasn't just a vacation from her worries. She had to make critical decisions about her future. Antonia just hadn't counted on Aiden to act as a tornado in her life. Regardless of how she felt about him, the news of another job opportunity couldn't be ignored. She had to go back to Chicago sooner or later, and she needed a job when the time did come. Publishing was safe. She knew the industry inside and out, and Sixpence was a great place to rise in the ranks. Antonia would have more responsibility, people under her, and a large pay raise.

But then there was the promise of creating something that was hers. Her character, Augusta needed her. Antonia was already molding her into something strong and powerful, a better version of herself. The thought of putting Augusta on hold, stagnant on the page, made her heart sink. And then there was Aiden. She was just getting used to the idea of following him to Galway. She truly wanted to see his world, a place where things were hopefully more normal than today's events.

But she had no idea how he was holding up. When she left him, he didn't look any better than when she'd pulled him off the Clifden sidewalk. Since their last kiss, she ached for his touch, some small measure of comfort in his arms that could tell her he was okay. Antonia kept reminding herself that he needed space. He needed time. Time that she was quickly running out of. Tired as she was, she needed him.

Chapter Twenty-Eight

After he left Antonia, Aiden had fallen onto his bed and slept for several hours. His nap was only interrupted by a quick meal of frozen shepherd's pie before guilt tired him out and sent him back to bed. The night had been filled with fitful sleep and an empty space in his bed where Antonia should have been.

When he awoke the following morning, with a throbbing headache and sore fist, the shame of yesterday returned. He'd done a foolish thing. Upon reuniting with his father, he assaulted Liam, a man in his seventies. He was lucky he hadn't seriously harmed him and ended up in the Clifden jail. As he hauled himself out of bed, still dressed in yesterday's clothes, he was careful not to disturb his bruised knuckles. Aiden searched his suitcase for a bottle of aspirin and then his phone.

The loneliness of his Tully Cross cottage was really setting in, but he couldn't bother his mother with this. And as far as he knew, his brothers didn't share the same angst he had regarding their father. Aiden hadn't bothered to broach the topic with any of them in years. He needed to talk to someone who wasn't Antonia. While he appreciated her help, he didn't want to shovel more shit onto her shoulders. She was too good to have to put up with his drama. Aiden was already frightened of the prospect of her leaving him, he didn't need to rush along the process with his dysfunctional relationship with Liam.

He turned his phone over in his sore hand and decided to call the one man who could help him. His boss, Robert, was as steady as they came. Even though he and Penny were on vacation, Aiden figured a phone call could be managed.

After a few rings, Robert answered. "Aiden, what can I do for you?"

"Is this a bad time?" he asked. "I can call back."

"No, no, Penny and I are off to lunch in a bit, but I can speak now. What's on your mind? Did the anthology look like something you could submit to?"

Aiden had already forgot about the anthology. "Oh that, yeah, I'm sure it's something I can manage. But I actually wanted to talk to you about something else."

Sensing something in Aiden's tone, Robert paused before asking, "What's wrong, my boy?"

My boy. Something about the way Robert said it, the hint of urgency and affection, was remarkably different from his father's *boyo.* "I just wanted to tell you... I know I won't replace James, but Robert, you've been more of a father to me than my own. I wanted you to know that."

Silence filled the phone line, making Aiden's face hot with embarrassment. "I appreciate you saying that, Aiden," Robert finally said. "You remind us a lot of James, you know? Had he lived, I believe you two would have been good friends."

Aiden smiled. "I'm sure you're right, Robert."

"You haven't spoken of your father in quite a while. Anything the matter?"

"Well, you're not going to believe this, but I accidentally ran into him yesterday."

Robert inhaled sharply. "Really?"

He chuckled as the ridiculousness of it all. "I saw him in Clifden yesterday morning, punched him in the face, and then left him. That sounds healthy, right?"

Robert joined in his laughter. "I'm not entirely sure," the old man said. "Certainly sounds cathartic. How are you holding up?"

Aiden shook his head. "I don't think I am. He blew through like a hurricane and now I'm picking up the pieces. It's not too different from when I was a kid actually." When Liam had come back from his long hauls, Clare and the boys had rearranged the household to make room for him. Each adjustment grew more and more difficult to manage, which was probably why Clare had finally put her foot down.

"Will you see him again?"

"That's the question, isn't it? After all this time, I don't trust him to be a stable presence in my life. He'll probably leave again and then where will I be?"

"Good point," Robert said. "But I wonder, would words be more effective than a fist?"

"The fist felt mighty effective at the time," Aiden said in a short tone.

"Mmh. But the pen is mightier than the sword," his mentor reminded him. "I'm not telling you what to do, my boy. But a little closure might be the ticket, eh?"

"I'll think about it," Aiden said, rubbing his temple.

"Good."

"Good?" Aiden repeated.

"Opportunities like this aren't afforded to everyone, Aiden. When we get them we have to take them seriously. What will you do with yours?"

The question caught Aiden off guard. He hadn't thought of this as an opportunity in the least. An appearance from Liam was only another wrench in his summer plans. He had actual work to do without the addition of emotional labor. "I haven't a clue."

Robert gave a throaty chuckle. "When I told you to go to the water, I didn't think you'd find your father. After his odyssey, your father is faced with his past and has to atone for his actions. You have to admit there's a certain beauty in that."

"I have yet to find the beauty."

"When you let go, you will, my boy. You will." Robert paused before delivering a stern warning. "Whether you talk to him or not, you will have to let him go. The man who he was; the boy you were. You must leave them behind."

Aiden sniffed. "Yeah."

"This too shall pass, Aiden. And when it does, you'll be a better man for it. Your father isn't the only facet of your full life, nor is your career. I hope I didn't give you the impression that being a professor was all there was in life. Family, love, and passion makes the man. Cling to those things and cut loose the things that can't bring you joy."

Cut the rope.

Aiden's voice was a lump caught in his throat. "Thank you, Robert."

"Of course," his mentor said. "We've got reservations to make, but let's talk this evening."

"Sure, I'd like that."

When he hung up, Aiden stood from his bed and paced the room. The next thing on his mind was Antonia. He wanted to see her, but he was thoroughly embarrassed by how their day unfolded. He wanted to call or text her, but in the convenience of being neighbors, they'd forgotten to exchange phone numbers. Antonia was only on the other side of his wall, possibly sitting on her bed worried about him. Aiden should go over there. He started toward the door and stopped himself.

Realization struck him hard.

Both Robert and Antonia were correct. Yes, he needed closure. He had to see his father again. God knows what they would talk about, but he'd regret not meeting with the man and saying his piece. The bitterness would follow him for the rest of his days if he didn't nip this in the bud. Despite the way their conversation turned out, Aiden had heard Antonia's words from yesterday's ride home. Even if the best case scenario magically unfolded and his father apologized, it still wouldn't change the past. He was still walking around with something missing. He had to give himself the love he'd missed all those years ago. Aiden felt her words ring in his mind as clearly as he felt her warm hand pressed to his chest, over his heart.

Aiden glanced at the time. If he took off now, he could be back to meet with Antonia in the evening. After this whole messy business was finished, he would plan the next leg of the journey with her. The idea of taking her to Galway filled him with energy as he quickly washed up and changed his clothes. When he looked a bit more presentable, he grabbed his keys and left the cottage. He was on his way to Clifden.

Chapter Twenty-Nine

For once, his father was actually true to his word.

He was still in Clifden at the small B&B near the bay. When Aiden asked the front desk to call him down, Liam appeared in the lobby about thirty minutes later looking about as haggard as Aiden remembered. His father had obviously hit the bottle hard with his seafaring earnings, and it showed in his glassy eyes and red face. A handsome man used to be under that battered face, possibly one his mother fell in love with.

Aiden stuffed his hands in his pockets as he gazed at his father. "I wanted to talk if you had time."

Liam ran a hand over his mouth. "Sure, I got time." His eyes darted toward the exit. "Lowry's is just down the street if you want a drink."

Aiden took a deep breath. "It's still morning, Liam. How about we stay here for some tea?" He gestured to the quiet dining room behind them. The breakfast crowd had already dispersed, leaving them with some privacy.

Liam gave a noncommittal shrug and followed him to the empty dining room. Aiden went straight to where the coffee and tea station was and set about preparing two cups of tea. Behind him, a chair scraped against the floor as his father took a seat. Either this was the dumbest thing he'd ever attempted or this would finally release him. Aiden stirred hot water in both cups and tried not to think about the consequences of his decision to return to Clifden. When he carried the tea to the table, Liam was lounging in his seat, tapping his calloused fingers against the table surface. His expression was the same as yesterday's: Anywhere else was a better place to be than here.

Good. Let him sweat.

As he sat across the divide, he pushed a cup toward Liam. "Maybe you could let this warm you up instead of the old morning Bushmills."

Liam regarded the tea with suspicion before his eyes flitted back to Aiden. "Go ahead and say what you need to say, boyo."

Aiden swirled his teabag around his cup. "Where's your next port of call?"

"It's up to me, really," his father replied. "Thinkin' about stayin' here for a while. I ain't come down in the last shower, y'know? Ould codger like me can't sail all his life."

"That's surprising to hear," Aiden said, as he pulled the bag out and set it on his saucer. He picked up his cup, holding the steaming liquid before his face. "I wondered if even you were aware of that."

"How's your mother doing?"

Aiden's grip tightened on his cup. That's what Liam did; took the piss and wound his own children up with mean humor. "Now you're concerned?"

"Still shriekin' mad, is she?" Liam asked with a grin. "I'm only windin' ye up, boyo. If I came 'round Hannigan's house, she'd take a knife to me."

Aiden's lip quirked. "Kinda like my tenth birthday?"

"Jaysus, you remember that?"

He rolled his eyes before taking a sip of tea. "Of course I do. You ruined my birthday, coming home pissed with that damn stray dog."

Liam shook his head as his laughter turned into a raspy cough. "I'd just come back from a long haul in Dublin and remembered it was someone's birthday. Christ, a little old reverend mother couldn't have saved me from the Hannigan wrath that night. Thought she'd pan me head in, but she pulled a knife instead."

"You tried to convince us that you bought the dog from travelers, but the damn thing was so long in the tooth, he limped in the door like he'd just entered the pearly gates," Aiden said, biting back a smile. "This ancient hound found his way to the kitchen and stuck its fuckin' maws into the birthday cake Mam made."

His father doubled over laughing at the story. "She screamed like the bean sídhe when that mutt dragged the cake off the table. Hollerin', 'we'll never get the feckin' fleas out the rugs.' And wee Ryan just sat on the floor and started eatin' cake with the dog."

Liam's coarse laughter shocked Aiden back to reality. He remembered his mother's face in that moment. It hadn't been funny at the time and no matter how much Clare apologized to her children, he never forgot the pain in her face when she understood the end-result of trying to maintain a normal household. Liam would just show up and make a mess of it again. *My god, it feels more like a tragic anecdote from* Angela's Ashes. Perhaps there would be something to smile about if it had only happened once. Unfortunately, destruction was the one thing his father was consistent with. "Are you sorry, Liam? For any of it?"

When his father's laughter receded, he cleared his throat and cut his gaze to a nearby window. "Sure I'm sorry, I said so yesterday."

Aiden shook his head. "You admitted to being a sorry sod and I didn't disagree. But are you sorry for what you did? How you left?"

Liam crossed his beefy arms across his chest and stared his son down with cold blue eyes. "What good's sorry when yer as old as ye are? Hell, boyo, t'was a lifetime ago. Yer mam told me if I didn't stick to land and stop me drinking, she'd put me out. I didn't and so she did. Simple as y'like. Judging by the looks of it, y'turned out alright, yeah?" he asked with a smirk. "Ya hardly sound like a boy from Limerick. Ya sound a bit lace-curtain nowadays."

He stared back at his father, searching for the remorse in his eyes. When he couldn't find it, he fell back on the emotion he knew best: Anger. "Limerick was hard in the '90s. That flat above the washers on William Street was just a small piece of how shitty 'Stab City' was. And you left us for the fish?" Aiden asked, setting down his cup, fearing he'd fling it at a wall. "While Mam taught, she cleaned the hospital. She came home late, feet hurting and hands raw from chemicals, and sat down to write lessons when she should have been sleeping. She fed us every day with no fish and no coin from you, Liam. We begged her to let us get jobs and she wouldn't let us. It tore Junior up to not go work in some factory, but she made him stay in school. He's got two boys of his own, you know that?"

Liam didn't answer.

"Works at a bank in Dublin too. Sean and Ryan run their own businesses and they're happy and you've got grandchildren. That's what's happened while you were off fishing."

"Good on 'em," Liam said, shifting in his seat. "And what of you, boyo?"

Aiden exhaled through his nose. "I'm a university professor in Galway."

Liam finally took a sip of his own tea. "Don't surprise me none that ye went to teaching. Always took after yer mam."

Aiden let out a harsh laugh. "And I got my aimlessness from you. Every time I look out over the ocean, I feel something I want to bury," He ducked his head and ran his hand down his face. When he looked up and met his father's gaze, the fight was gone and replaced with sadness. "It was so much easier when I thought you were dead, Liam."

"That's fair," Liam said. His pale blue eyes stared at his son's sweater, his teacup, the window behind him… But never directly into Aiden's eyes. He cleared his throat and nodded before taking another swallow of tea.

An uncomfortable silence settled over the table as Aiden ran his fingertips over the rim of his cup. He was starting to see the futility of this meeting. The only thing that had changed about Liam was his age.

Liam broke the silence. "What else ye got fer me?"

Aiden ran his hand over his mouth before answering. He was already tired and left empty from this exchange, but if his father wanted it, he'd give it. Best to get all this shite out in the open before he turned the page. "I'm sorry I hit you," he said, "Mam didn't raise me to get on like that. But I've hated you ever since 1995. You can say, all you want, that mam gave you an ultimatum, but it wasn't just her. You had four growing boys to see after. Not one coin came back from Dublin, from England, from Spain, or wherever the fuck you went. Not one phone call on any of our birthdays. The Hannigans came to our graduations and quietly spit on the pauper's grave they hoped you were buried in.

"I defended you the longest, and boyo, I was a fool for that. Everyone else moved on before I got the sense to stop sneaking off and searching for you at every feckin' harbor in Ireland. When that wasn't enough, I taught myself how to sail against mam's wishes. She was cross with me over it. You know why? Because of all my brothers, I was the one she had to worry about. She wrung her hands over if I'd take off on a boat and get a dozen women in trouble. The training must have worked because I'm finally respectable. But when I look into your sorry face, I see my other half and I hate it."

When Aiden finished, he sank against his chair and closed his eyes. Liam sat there and took it, mulling over each word like glass in his mouth. "I can't tell ya anything you want to hear, son," Liam said in a low voice. "Would it make ye feel better if I said yer not me? Not a bone in you, worth something, belongs to me. Yer County Mayo, Hannigan blood, through and though. Yeah, you got them good looks and the craic from me," he said with a mirthless laugh. "But the parts that matter…yer Clare's boy, alright."

Aiden opened his eyes, recognizing this was the first time Liam referred to him as "son" and not boyo. A strange realization settled over him: *This is as good as it is going to get.* This was Liam's admission of guilt and Aiden was likely to never hear it again. "I think it might be time for me to head out."

His father nodded. There were no objections, no arguments. Liam still had that shifty look in his eye. "So where are you and that little lady staying?"

"Her name is Antonia and we're up in Tully Cross," Aiden said, drinking the rest of his tea.

"She a good lass fer ya?"

Aiden pushed his cup and saucer away. "She's probably far better than I deserve."

"Sounds familiar," Liam joked. "Listen, boyo. Can I leave a phone number with ye? Maybe we can catch up another day down the road."

Aiden decided to humor the old man instead of the knee-jerk reaction of denying him. He nodded and watched as his father reached into his jacket for a small spiral notepad and worn down pencil. Liam scribbled down something and ripped out the page. He folded the small scrap of paper and slid it across the table like a business transaction. Aiden picked it up and stuffed it in his pocket before pushing away from the table. Liam rose with him, unsure of what to do with his hands. After more shifty glances around the room, his gaze finally settled on Aiden.

"Well, I guess this is it," he said.

Aiden held out his hand, a peace offering. "Yes, it is."

His father heard the resolute tone in Aiden's voice and it made his brow furrow slightly. He awkwardly took his hand and gave it a single shake. "Right then. You, uh…take care of yerself."

Aiden released his father's strong hand, a grip made for tying ropes and hauling traps, not for hugs or pats on the back. "I'll keep doing that, Liam." He backed away from the old man, feeling a combination of lightness and sadness. With time, he hoped those two feelings could evolve into relief and salvation. Aiden left the dining room and then the guesthouse without looking over his shoulder.

The search for Liam was complete.

It was time to return to Tully Cross.

Chapter Thirty

"Here's the problem with publishing, Danny," Antonia said watching the bartender pour another whiskey. She sat on the edge of her barstool, propped on her elbows. "If I take this job, I'll just be back where I was. No, that's not exactly true. I'll have way more work to do."

Danny passed her glass back to her and whipped his towel back to his shoulder. She'd been talking his ear off for the last hour while she tended to other patrons. Antonia knew she should have been talking to Aiden. But when she started her day, his car was already gone. After yesterday's terrible events, she figured he probably needed to be alone. Antonia didn't want to pester him with her recent reverse of fortune. It was difficult to compete with an existential meltdown, nor did she want to. He needed space and time to think about things. As did she. "How much do you like eating, lass?"

Antonia sipped on her second whiskey and soda before answering. "I love it."

"And you say you've got no job now?"

"Correct."

"Gotcha."

"I wish I could just stay in Tully Cross and work the bar with you," Antonia said with a pout.

Danny scoffed. "You got any experience?"

"I was a bartender in college."

"Were ye now?" he asked, raising a blond brow. "Can you pull a decent pint, love?"

Antonia sat up straight and shot him a defiant glare. "Of course I can."

He raised his hands in defense. "Only asking."

"And I can make a killer dirty martini," she added.

"There ain't really a martini crowd here."

Antonia slumped in her seat. "I suppose there isn't."

"I can't hire you, but I'd like to take a cigarette break and Nellie doesn't come in until seven. You think you can handle the bar while I'm outside?"

Antonia frowned. "Are you serious?"

He swiped the cigarette off his ear and winked at her. "All you need to know is that Michael is working on his fifth Guinness, I've got it written here. You ever use an SPS-2000?" he asked, cocking his head to the register behind him.

"Sure," she said with a startled laugh. "It's not as good as the SPS-3000, but it's a solid machine."

Danny tossed his towel at her. "Well, la-dee-da," he said. "Can you handle about fifteen minutes?"

She turned around to look at the nearly empty pub. Michael sat at the end of the bar, dressed in another stylish three-piece suit. If he picked tonight to fall off his stool, she'd have to let him stay on the floor. "Okay," she said, leaving her perch and walking behind the bar.

"Don't play fast and loose with your pouring either," Danny said over his shoulder as he exited. "I'm still running a business after all."

Antonia hadn't been behind a bar since she was twenty-eight. Back then, she had the energy to work third shift and show up to a nine o'clock lecture. The club she worked at was much busier than the crowd here. With Michael at the bar and a couple sitting near the fireplace, she quickly sized up their orders. The man and wife were a beer and white wine couple. Michael was on his last swallow, so Antonia washed her hands and found a glass. The red-faced gentleman would want his sixth drink.

She tilted the glass at the spout and pulled two thirds of the pint, just as she'd watched Danny do so many times. As she set the glass to rest, Michael announced he was ready for another drink. Antonia smiled to herself. "Coming up."

She watched the light brown foam rise to the top and slowly transition to a dark molasses. There was a certainly calmness and beauty to this wait. When Danny did this, his actions seemed trained and elegant. She continued to watch the drink as the pub's door clattered and footsteps traveled to the bar. "Couldn't trust me for two minutes?" Antonia asked.

"Ms. Harper behind the bar," said a familiar voice. "Not for a minute."

Her gaze shot up to meet Aiden's. "Hey," she breathed.

"You couldn't pay your tab," he said. "And Danny's forcing you to work it off. I've seen it before, but usually in the form of dishwashing."

His eyes were red and tired, but the handsome smile was back and it was contagious. Antonia found herself mirroring it immediately. "He's outside on a smoke break and left the bar in my capable hands," She filled the rest of Michael's beer, driving the foam to the top of the glass. *Only a centimeter of foamy head. Not bad.* "Sometimes trying something new gives you perspective on the life you're already living," she said, setting the glass in front of Michael.

"Thank ye, lass," he muttered.

"Makes sense to me," Aiden said, eyeing Michael. "You're not over-serving him, are you? I don't know if my back can handle another incident."

"It's his sixth one," Antonia said, making a note in Danny's notebook.

"You look adorable back there," Aiden said with a grin. "Although there's very little you can do to not look adorable."

"Danny doesn't want me giving out free drinks," she said, whipping the towel over her shoulder. "So you can keep your compliments to yourself."

Aiden nodded in appreciation. "You got me." He perched a knee on the barstool and leaned over the bar. "Can I have a kiss instead?"

Her face warmed at the suggestion, but she was already on her tiptoes meeting him halfway. "That's on the house."

Aiden took her by the chin and drew her closer. "God, how I've missed these lips," he said, brushing them with his own. She licked the corner of his mouth until her tongue met his. His fingers slowly grazed her throat as he tasted her mouth. Before their kiss could border on improper, she pulled away and let him return to his barstool. His lazy smile warmed her insides faster than any high-proof spirit.

She let out a breath. "What can I get you?"

"I could taste whiskey on you, my dear." He picked up her glass of whiskey. "Is this yours?"

"It was."

Aiden tilted his head and took it all in one gulp. She

watched his Adam's apple bob as he swallowed and felt a fire in her belly. Even in his tired state, Aiden's sexiness shined through. He'd retired his Aran sweater and wore a simple gray T-shirt that revealed the bulge of his biceps as he leaned against the bar. "I'll have another, if you don't mind."

She rolled her eyes as though it was an annoyance, but secretly wanted to show off her skills. She rinsed out a nearby jigger and poured the correct portion into a rocks glass. "Soda?"

"I'm not a child," he chided. "I'll take it neat, thank you."

Antonia smiled. "Fair play."

"Ah, look at you," he said, sitting down. "You're picking up the slang."

"I suppose I am," she said, setting his glass before him.

"You've already developed the lilt and cadence of the accent, you know? You learned the melody without overplaying it. Imagine what you'd sound like if you stayed here."

Antonia froze. She had imagined staying in Ireland and it made her anxious. His plans, no matter how hopeful they were, worried her. Aiden spoke of the future so easily when his past, and her present, were barriers for both of them. "I'm sure it's something all tourists pick up," she said, busying herself with the glasses. She picked up a clean one and began wiping it down for no reason. "How was your day? I didn't see your car this morning."

His mouth twisted as his eyes dropped to his drink. "I drove back to Clifden."

"Could you find him?"

Aiden seemed surprised by the question. He gave a jerky nod and cleared his throat. "Yeah, I did. We had a talk."

Antonia set down her glass and started on the next. Part of her wanted to respect his privacy... But my god, was she going to have to pull the details out of him? He'd driven to another town to get answers from a man who wronged him twenty-years ago and all she could get was *we had a talk*? "How do you feel?"

Aiden propped his chin on his knuckles and stared at her. His forest-green eyes glittered in the pub's low lights. "Exhausted."

She nodded. *Okay then.* His expression shifted from tired to pensive in a flash. He had something else on his mind, she just couldn't decipher the answer in his eyes.

"Darling, I thank you for being with me during an especially low point," he said through a forced smile. "But I don't want to spend any more time on my da when we have other issues."

Antonia averted her gaze, doing a quick scan of the pub patrons. Everyone had nearly full drinks. The patron who sat before her, required her full attention and she couldn't bear to give it to him. She finally understood what was bothering him. It was them.

"We have to talk about it at some point," he said in a soft voice. His fingers grazed the top of his small glass as he stared at her, his expression drawn.

"I liked it much better when we could keep pretending."

"I did too," Aiden admitted. "But I'm finding it hard at the moment."

When she finally met his gaze, she exhaled. "I got an email," she said. "From another publisher."

He only nodded.

"They're buying out my old company and they'd like to interview me for my boss's old job. I would be running an imprint."

Aiden swirled the contents in his glass before taking a sip. "When?"

Antonia waited a beat before answering him. "Thursday."

He looked down at the bar, fiddled with his coaster, and nodded again. What she hadn't told him was that she'd already searched the flights. She found a way to exchange her return flight for a straight shot from Shannon to Chicago and saved it. She'd held off purchasing it because she was frightened of leaving him. "You should go."

Her heart stilled.

"If you've got a job to return to, I think you should take it," he continued. His demeanor shifted into something harder. He regarded her like he had his father. The bar became a giant chasm between them.

"I don't even know if I'll get it. They need to interview me like anyone else."

He shook his head. "In my experience, they do that to complete the necessary paperwork. If they're really in-house hiring for a new division, they're going to take the most qualified person for the position. You're it, love." Aiden tossed back his drink.

Antonia's heart sank as she listened to his matter-of-fact tone. Where was the talk about her book and how important it was? They'd argued about this very thing not but two or three days ago and now he was tossing back liquor and acquiescing all over the place. He wasn't going to stop her, he wasn't even going to throw out a mild objection. "You're probably right."

"You have to go back at some time, darling," he said. "And when you do, you need a job." Aiden held out his glass.

She regarded him and his glass warily. "Would you like some water?"

"No, love," he said, shaking his head. "But who knows, maybe you'll visit?"

Antonia took his glass and filled it with a single shot and handed it back. "I can," she said carefully. "And you can visit me too."

He nodded, forcing a smile. "Sure. We'll just line up our tight schedules, book flights with precision, and spend four days with one another. Easy peasy," he said. "With the time difference, we'll just Skype at odd hours of the day, the rest of the time."

"Aiden…"

"Yes, darling."

"I don't have to go now," she said. "I could stay for the next week like I had planned."

He nodded. "But that was before you found out you had a second chance."

Unsure of what to say, Antonia simply stood there and watched the man she had feelings for wall himself from her. When Danny came back from his smoke break, she was still silent and Aiden had continued drinking.

"Ah, the professor is here," he said, clapping Aiden on the back.

Aiden smiled. "You know I'm a constant presence when I come back to Tully Cross."

Relieved of her bar duties, Antonia returned to the

other side where she belonged. However, she was hesitant to sit with Aiden. His new distant attitude was unsettling after all they went through yesterday. She wasn't expecting any brash proclamations of love, but she certainly needed him to say something more encouraging than "you should go."

Danny flipped his towel over his shoulder. "How'd she do?" he asked Aiden.

"She pours fair and kisses even better," Aiden said, tipping his glass toward the barman. "Beats looking at you while I drink."

"Are ye sayin' I ain't pretty?" Danny asked, fluttering his lashes.

As the men shared a laugh, Antonia's irritation pushed her to snap. "Can we talk outside?"

Aiden set down his glass. "Of course."

He took his time getting off his stool and followed her wordlessly out the door into the cool damp air. Anger made her skin itch and her heart thud in her chest. If he wasn't going to talk about their status, she was prepared to go back to the cottage and purchase her ticket.

He knew she was angry.

Aiden saw it in the way she held her spine erect and clenched her fists. She shoved the door open and let it swing without regard for him as he followed. Antonia paced the sidewalk, looking down at the ground. Even the cool country night couldn't stop her steaming. "What would you like to talk about?" Aiden said, leaning against the side of the building.

She stopped her pacing and faced him with hands planted on her hips. "What do you think?"

"Your departure from Ireland?" The thought of her leaving him was ripping his heart into pieces, but he tried to maintain a passive expression.

"Sure, that's a start," she said. "I'm not going to pretend that I'm excited about it. I'm scared, actually."

"There's nothing to be scared of," he said, pulling away from the wall, drawing her into his arms. The fear in her eyes gutted him as he squeezed her tight. He nuzzled her hair and inhaled deeply. What he wouldn't give for more time to embrace her tenderly... But time was escaping them, surely she understood that. "When you get started, you'll get to show them what you're made of. If anyone can do this job, it's you."

She looked up with a frown. "I'm not... That's not what worries me."

He took a deep breath. What she was asking for was damn near impossible. Aiden tried to ignore how her body shook and focus on reality. People leave, and those who are left behind must move on and make the best of it. Antonia needed someone steady in her life, not a man who was still drifting, barely keeping himself afloat. "Darling, I don't know what else to do but let you go."

She pulled away from his grasp. "What are you saying?"

Aiden didn't know where he was going with this conversation. Talking to his stonewalled father was infinitely easier than this. All he knew was that he cared for her. He cared enough to let her go and let her find her way. "Antonia, you have an interview."

"I do." She folded her arms across her chest. "But I could stay. I said that in the bar and you didn't even sound interested. I'm not trying to beg, Aiden, but I need to know if I *should* stay."

"I'd love for you to stay, but—"

"Then there's no 'but' about it," Antonia said, her voice climbing. "If you wanted me to stick around so we can figure out...us, I would."

Aiden looked up at the night sky and sighed. She spoke from the heart, where he desperately wanted to follow, but he was stuck in his head. Everything she said made sense, he felt it everywhere in his being, and it made his skin itch not to touch her. An invisible rope pulled him to her warmth. The tremble of her bottom lip made his heart fall. *She's not your lighthouse, boyo. She's not here to save you...* "I want you to stay, darling. But it would be temporary, wouldn't it? Holidays have to come to an end eventually, if not today, then two weeks from now. Where will we be then? My life, if you haven't already noticed, is messy. The last thing I want is to drag you down with it."

Antonia shook her head. "Why are you still making this about your father, Aiden?"

"It's not about him," he protested in anger. He wanted her, badly, but that want warred with an insistent message: *People leave, people leave, people leave.* Liam left because Aiden wasn't good enough. Lisa left because he *still* wasn't good enough. Antonia would soon wise up. It was best to stop this now before anyone got hurt. "I'm frightened about my future just like you. If I don't get my shit together and solidify my career, I'm out on my arse. It just wouldn't be good for you, Antonia. At least you have the chance for something stable."

"Then just fucking do it," she said in exasperation. "Stop talking about it and do it. If it helps, pretend you're baking a cake. Confidence, remember?"

Aiden exhaled a mirthless laughed. "A cake? My

dear, this isn't a cute kitchen experiment based on blind luck and whim. This is real life."

"Hypocritical and lacking critical thinking skills," Antonia shot back. "Those are the makings of a pretty terrible teacher."

Aiden was at the end of his rope. "We don't have to do this," he tried. "We don't have to spend our last hours fighting."

"Do you even know what we're fighting about?"

Aiden didn't answer. Instead, his gaze dropped to the pavement.

He shouldn't have been surprised when Antonia walked away from the discussion, but the sound of her hard steps against the gravel kicked him in the gut. Aiden understood what self-preservation looked like; he was currently denying his own feelings to make this easier on them both. He meant only half of what he said. Of course he didn't want her to go back home, but he wasn't living in a dream world. He wouldn't allow her to get attached to a dream world either.

But every step she took, pulled the invisible rope around his heart until it threatened to snap. Aiden left the sidewalk and followed her across the street, his chest tightening the closer he got to her.

"Antonia, please."

"No," she said, breathing hard. "You don't want to fight."

"I don't," he said, half-jogging to catch up with her. "I just want to hold you and kiss you."

She spun around, her eyes blazed with anger. "That's the problem," she said.

Aiden stopped short. "I don't want us to part like this," he said loudly. "I just want you to be happy."

"And I'm telling you what it takes, you're just not listening to me. I'm sick of dealing with men who can't get their shit together. Between the ones who gaslight me and lie to my face and the ones who can't figure out what they want, I'm sitting here looking foolish."

"Don't compare me to your ex-boyfriend," Aiden said. "I've never lied to you and I'd never cheat on you."

Her laugh was humorless. "Derek was enough for me," she said, shaking her head. "I don't need another man wallowing in their pitiful daddy issues while the women in their lives are desperate to just fucking live."

"Jaysus, can you cut me some slack, Antonia?" he asked. "I'm trying my hardest to make sense of my life and you've only been here for a snapshot of it."

"Everyone is trying to make sense of their lives! How do you think I got here? I was escaping a mental breakdown and my only choice was to run to another country for some peace and quiet."

"I'm not going to have a pissing contest with you over who's got it worst, I just want you to give me some credit," Aiden shouted. "I care for you, Antonia. I really do. I just…"

"You just can't fight," she finished. Her shoulders slumped in resignation. "Goodbye, Aiden."

"Goddamn it," he said, taking a step toward her. "Please don't do this."

"I'm not doing anything that you didn't do fifteen minutes ago," Antonia said as she walked away. "You told me how you felt and I should have listened."

"Antonia!" She unlocked her cottage door and disappeared inside. He stood speechless, an inert spectator of his own life. A life that was quickly spiraling toward a lonesome status quo. It was alarming how his inability to do anything had propelled her out of his life. His idiotic plan to push her away was a success. She may have closed the door on him, but, brick by brick, he'd built the first wall. One excuse after another fell from his lips and killed any possibility for a dream world. He'd helped her make her decision. Antonia was going home and it was possibly the easiest thing he'd fucked up in a long while.

If that was the case, Aiden couldn't be there when she took off. If he heard her car door slam shut in the morning, he'd lose it. If it was over, he had to quickly move forward. In a state of numbness, he entered his own cottage and began gathering his things. He turned his brain off and worked on autopilot as he put dishes back into cupboards and tossed the contents of the refrigerator into garbage bags. Outside, the lights of Antonia's cottage were on and music was playing. When Aiden moved back inside, toward his bedroom, he glanced at the wall separating their homes and tried not to imagine what she was doing.

Booking her plane ticket. *Because people leave.*

He walked to the wall and stood there for a moment, pressing his ear to the smooth surface, and listened for signs of life. Muffled sounds of slow R&B leeched through, hitting his heart with an overwhelming sadness. Yesterday morning, they had shared a bed. Tonight, they were parting ways. It was his fault and the only solution he had was to leave. He would rather leave like a coward in the night, than go over there and tell her the first lie of their relationship: It doesn't matter, Antonia. We'll find a way to make it work.

Aiden forced himself to move away from the wall and go back to packing. In less than an hour, he loaded up his car. He turned one last time to Antonia's cottage. The lights were still on, but he sensed no movement. His feet were frozen as he stood outside in the cold dark. Part of him had just enough energy to bang on her door and tell her to stay, if only for just a week more. He wanted to gather her into his arms and kiss her passionately, hoping he could show her what he couldn't articulate. The other part of him was the fool who'd ran out of options and had already told her as much. He fell in line with the latter. Aiden left his house key inside the lock and got into his car. Soon, Tully Cross and Antonia were in his rearview mirror.

Chapter Thirty-One

The next morning, Aiden was awoken by his doorbell. The sound traveled upstairs and jarred him from fitful sleep. He rolled over in bed and cracked his eyes against the morning light. He was back in his own bed. In Claddagh. He struggled to remember the night before, but it came back in foggy patches. The pain in his hand was a helpful reminder that he'd done something foolish. The doorbell rang again, pushing him from his bed.

"I'm coming!" he bellowed. He put on a shirt and loped down the stairs. From the stairwell, he could see his mother and niece peering into his living room window. "Fuck me," he muttered under his breath. *What day was it?* Aiden was certain that it was only Thursday and he didn't have to see them until tomorrow. He was also in a state that he didn't want on display in front of his mother and a twelve-year-old.

He opened the door to a worried-looking Clare. "What are you doing here?" he asked, squinting against the sun.

His mother pursed her lips. "Is that anyway to greet your own mother, Aiden Donagh Byrnes?" She grabbed Soircha by the hand and pushed her way past him. "You smell like a distillery."

Aiden closed the door behind them and rested his head against it. "I had a rough night," he said.

"Well you're about to have a rough morning if you don't adjust your attitude," Clare said in a huff.

"Are you drunk, Uncle Aiden?" Soircha asked. There was concern in her voice.

"Only slightly, love," he admitted as he carried himself to the couch and plopped down. Soircha sat beside him and laid her head on his chest. Her fluffy blonde curls tickled his nose and obscured the vision of his mother whose fists were planted on her hips.

"Really, Aiden," Clare admonished.

He reached a weak hand up and ruffled Soircha's hair. "I'm sorry," he said. "What are you doing here?"

"I tried calling you last night," Clare said, drifting to the kitchen. Plates clattered and water ran as she put the kettle on the stove. "Of course, you didn't answer. Too busy to take a phone call. I thought we'd show up early since you have your conference today."

He wasn't going to be distracted by his mother's passive aggressive tone. "What are you *really* doing here?" he whispered to his niece.

"Nana wanted to meet your girlfriend," she said softly.

Aiden closed his eyes. "I don't have a girlfriend."

"How did you scare this one off?" Clare asked, breezing back into the living room. She sat on the chair across from him and eyed him suspiciously.

He cracked one eye open and saw that she wasn't joking. "Mother, don't."

"I'm just concerned that one of my sons is incapable of bending to the will of any woman because he's so bullheaded. What was it this time?"

"What does it matter?" he asked. "It's not like you were a fan of Lisa "Lace-Curtains" Brennan. How did you get so invested in a woman you've never met?"

"Where is your bottle of Jameson?"

He lifted his head from the couch and stared at his mother head-on. She met his gaze with her stern teacher's glare. "It's upstairs."

"Grand place for it to be," she said stiffly. "It's like seeing your father wake up in the morning."

"You have no idea," he muttered. His mind flashed back to Antonia and what she said about his father. As soon as he got back into town, he'd gone to the same pub that he used to get over Lisa. After he walked home, he'd raided the cabinets for any spare alcohol to get to sleep. He closed his eyes. *I've got to walk to the pub for my car.*

"You're a bit too young to depend on a bottle to get you through a rough patch."

"Antonia already gave me a dressing down," he said annoyed. "I don't need it from you too."

"What was your fight about?"

He paused, unsure of how much to tell his mother. "I didn't fight enough," he said. "That was the problem."

Clare narrowed her eyes. "I'm not sure I'm following you, dear."

Aiden leaned forward, resting his elbows on his knees. "Mam, the long and short of it is that I acted like a coward and I left her at Tully Cross."

His mother leaned back in her seat. "Drinking yourself to death over a woman *does* seem like your style, but I have a feeling you're leaving something out. I think you'd better get to the long of it."

He rubbed the back of his neck and looked from his

mother to his niece. He didn't want to spring the news on either of them. Part of him believed that even speaking to his father was a betrayal to his mother. "A couple days ago, while we were in Clifden, we ran into Liam."

Clare's silver brows knitted in confusion. "What business does Liam have in Clifden?" she asked. "Were Mary Catherine and the boys with him?"

Aiden shook his head. "We ran into Da."

He couldn't read the expression on his mother's face. Her head tilted to the side as she thoughtfully stared down at the coffee table separating them. Clare's eyes slowly closed as she let out a sigh. "How is my husband?" she asked with a sad smile.

"Bit of the same."

She nodded. "I see. And how are you?"

Aiden couldn't answer her question without holding his head in his hands and focusing on the rug beneath his feet. "Not good, Mam."

"Nana's husband?" Soircha asked, baffled by the conversation taking place over her head.

"Yes," Clare said with pursed lips. "Your da's father, your grandfather."

"What's he like?" she asked excitedly. "I've never met him."

"And there's good reason for that, m'dear," Clare replied in a dry tone. "No one can ever find him. Goodness, I can't imagine how upsetting it was for Antonia to be in the middle of that chance meeting. Is that why she's not talking to you?"

"Not exactly. It's a bit more complicated than that," Aiden said. "I talked to Liam, not before giving him a pop in the mouth."

Soircha's blue eyes grew round behind her glasses. "You punched your own da?"

Aiden looked down at her amazed expression. "Yes, but it's not good to use your fists when you can use your words."

"Whoa…"

Aiden glanced back at her and frowned. "Could you be a dear and check on the tea?"

Soircha rolled her eyes. "It hasn't whistled."

He kept his impatience in check as he spoke. "But it will very soon."

She hauled herself off his couch and slouched to the kitchen, muttering under her breath about not being a baby.

Clare crossed herself and let out another heavy sigh. "Lord help us."

"After the incident with Liam, she drove us home," Aiden explained. "I went back to Clifden to talk to him and I don't know what I got out of that. When I returned to Antonia, she told me about her job interview back home. Jaysus… I left her, Mam."

"She has an interview?"

Aiden did his best to explain everything he could about the woman whom his mother only met through a phone app. Once Clare had an investment in one of the boys' lady friends, she became incredibly attentive. When he finished, his mother was sitting on the edge of her seat with worried eyes.

"Dear god, Aiden. Are you daft?"

That wasn't exactly the response he imagined. "Maybe?" he said.

"Am I to understand that you saw your da and then did exactly what he did to us? Can't you tell that the girl cares for you? She wanted you to tell her to stay and you ran off in the night?" Clare shot up from her seat and began pacing his living room. "I thought I raised you better than that, young man. My god, you've gone mucked it up, haven't ye?"

Aiden frowned. He hadn't heard that kind of anger in his mother's voice since he failed Statistics at university. She'd raved at him for a full week after grades were released, convinced that she didn't raise a lazy academic. "I wanted to spare her the trouble, Mam. I loved our time together, but she's too good of a woman to fool around with my shite."

Clare spun on her heel and glared at him. "And did it ever occur to you that she cares enough to see you through your shite? There aren't very many women like her and when you meet them, you don't turn tail like a coward."

His mother's words hit him in the gut, knocking him speechless.

Her expression softened when she saw his face. "Aiden, I was one of those women. When Liam was around, I put up with his long list of ailments because I loved him. You're nothing like the man, but somehow you got it into your head that you are. Antonia wasn't going to run away at the sight of a deadbeat like your da."

"She doesn't love me," he said. "Mam, she's an American on holiday who has to go back home sometime. Better to cut the rope now rather than delay the inevitable."

His mother scoffed as Soircha brought the tea tray from the kitchen and quietly set it on the coffee table. "You're in love with her, right?" asked the child. His niece settled beside him and helped herself to a biscuit. "This is just like the movies."

"This is not something I want to talk about with a twelve-year-old in the room," Aiden said, ignoring Soircha.

"From the mouths of babes," Clare murmured, staring at the child. "She's right, you know that? You're in love with the girl and you mucked it up on purpose. I can't think of a better reason why you'd behave so irresponsibly."

"Mam…"

"Well it's true. I saw the two of you together in your little boat. She was a delightful girl and you were just as bashful as you were going on your first grade-school date."

"I don't have the time to romance when I'm trying to get tenure," Aiden said. When he heard himself say the words, even he didn't believe them.

"You didn't have time for romance when you weren't working toward tenure," Clare said, sitting down. "If you are to cut a rope, Aiden, it should be the one attached to Liam."

God, I hate it when she's right.

More often than not, Clare Hannigan was right on the money. This proved to be no different. "What do you love about her?" Soircha asked as she munched on her biscuit.

Aiden looked down at his niece, who was much more mature than he, and sighed. "So many things, I suppose. I love her sense of humor. She's good for a craic and she's very witty. I love her smile and her laugh. She's smart, sometimes much smarter than I am. Antonia's infuriating and passionate and…beautiful…"

He trailed off when he remembered waking up beside her. She was furiously plugging away on her novel, radiant from the glow of good sleep and a good romp. He wanted to tell her in that moment that he loved her, but something held him back. Even before he knew Liam would blow into their lives, Aiden had been convinced that a relationship with her was too good to be true. No one could ever be that lucky.

"She sounds lovely," Soircha said.

A sharp stab of anguish pierced his heart as he hung his head in despair. "Christ, what've I done?"

Soircha patted his back. "You can still call her."

"You can still call her," Clare repeated in a softer tone.

Aiden was a fool. He'd done the very thing that he hated his father for: run away. He ran in the black of night and drove until he came back to his lonely house. "I can't," he said.

"Why not?" Clare said.

"I don't have her bleeding phone number, Mam. We lived right next door to one another and I didn't think to ask her for it."

"Oh dear," his mother said, setting her teacup on the table. "Well then the ball is in her court, isn't it?"

Aiden was afraid that his mother was correct again. How could he be so stupid? If he knew Antonia like he thought he did, she was already on her way to the airport in an effort to solidify her future.

"I might have an idea," his niece said in a small voice.

He lifted his head. Soircha wore an impish smile on her face. "You do?"

Chapter Thirty-Two

When Antonia woke up the next morning, she didn't feel like writing. The words didn't come to her as swiftly as she was used to. She wandered the cottage thinking about Aiden instead. She hadn't purchased her plane ticket the previous night. She held off on it, convinced that she could still salvage her trip. The original plan did not include Aiden. Antonia was here for an entirely different purpose and Aiden's interruption was a minor distraction.

As she stood at the kitchen sink, she stared into the meadow past her clothesline and realized that wasn't true. Aiden wasn't a minor distraction. He'd showed up like a freight train and she enjoyed his presence. The thought made her tear up. She sniffed and raked the back of her arm over her eyes. She wasn't going to cry over a man who couldn't be bothered to be strong enough to tell her how he felt.

Antonia drew a deep breath and moved away from the kitchen sink. She tried to remember the details of her night with Aiden; it was a blur of tears and raised voices. The things she'd shouted at him replayed in her mind. She couldn't believe how she spoke to him and chalked it up to her newfound confidence. Once she was able to cuss out Derek, everyone else seemed easy. But she hurled insults at a man who only wanted to talk to her, to hold and kiss her. The things she said were honest, but she shouted them in embarrassment. Antonia had been close to telling Aiden how she really felt about him when she felt him retreat.

When he'd told her to take the job in Chicago, she was reminded of Derek who always assumed he knew what was best for her. But perhaps some of that was her fault. She was as aimless as Aiden and constantly called upon friends and family to direct her life. She called Octavia for advice on her love life, Eddie for advice on her career, and her mother popped up every once in a while to offer unsolicited advice. The only voice in her head that belonged to her was the one she created for her character, Augusta. Oddly enough, she found herself asking "What would Augusta do?" far less while in Ireland.

With Aiden, she felt liberated.

Maybe it was vacation freedom, maybe it was him. While he preached confidence, without practicing it, much of what he said rubbed off on her. Until she met him, she had been faking it to make it. Antonia knew for certain there was something she couldn't fake with Aiden. The raw passion she felt for him was quite real. Being around him, in his arms, in his bed, were the best physical experiences she'd had in her life. Being with Aiden was like living in hyperbole. He was "the most" in every way she could think of.

And that's how Antonia knew she couldn't leave.

"Oh god, I've made a mistake," she whispered to an empty cottage. Deep in her heart, she needed to run next door and tell Aiden she loved him. He pushed her away last night, but she wasn't going out like that. If she were Augusta, she would say the words first, before Bryon could have looked at her with those sad green eyes. Aiden could take it or leave it, but if she left Ireland without saying the words, she'd regret it until she found another man like him. *Who knows when that will happen?*

Before she could contemplate becoming an old spinster, Antonia grabbed her keys and ran to Aiden's cottage. When she got to his door, she was puzzled to see his keys in the lock. A bag of garbage leaned against his stoop. Her heart dropped in her chest. "Oh no…"

She let herself inside his cottage. "Aiden," she called out.

The space was empty. Antonia ran from room to room shouting his name, but his clothes and suitcase were gone. Even the refrigerator was empty. *Oh no, oh no…* This was the mess she was afraid of. If she hadn't tap danced around the real issue, she could have said her piece last night. Antonia exited the cottage and ran straight to Mr. Creely's rental office. She hoped he was there and didn't believe in customer confidentiality. She needed Aiden's information as soon as possible. She banged on his door and prayed for a miracle. "Please be home," she whispered.

"I'm a'coming, hold on now." She heard his muffled voice from behind the door.

"Mr. Creely, it's Antonia Harper," she yelled. "I need your help."

The old man opened the door, drawing his robe closer to his small frame. "Ms. Harper? What's wrong?"

"Aiden left," she said in a hurried voice. "He's gone."

Creely peered at her. "Well that happens from time

to time," he said easily. "Visitors can leave early, but they have to pay for the full stay."

She shook her head. "No, you don't understand," she said. "We had a fight, I said some stupid things. Actually, he said some stupid things too. But I didn't know he'd leave."

In the proper context, Creely nodded. "Nothing a little cake can't take care of?"

Antonia tried to ignore his meaning. "No, and I need your help."

"What can I do for you?"

"I need you to give me his contact information," she breathed. "A phone number or something. Anything would be helpful."

The old man hesitated for a moment. "I don't know…"

"Please," she begged. "I have to find him and tell him something."

"You really like him, huh?" he said with a sly grin.

She nodded. "I think I do, but I need to talk to him."

He gave her a good long look in the eye before shaking his head. "Aye, come inside and I'll see what I can find for ye."

"Exit Connemara Loop. Stay in right lane for N59," Vera's mechanical voice intoned.

Antonia carefully switched lanes and let out a breath when the highway widened. She had white-knuckled most of the drive and wanted to get off the road as soon as possible. She swiped at the GPS screen and was relieved to know that the rest of the long stretch would lead straight to Galway. She remembered that Aiden said his neighborhood was in a small township called

Claddagh. Hopefully, that wouldn't involve driving in a busy tourist city. It didn't matter, though. She was on a mission.

Her phone rang while she drove. Antonia groaned. That was the last thing she needed to deal with while making these dangerous curves. She pulled it out of her purse and swiped without looking down. "Yeah?"

"Yes," her mother corrected.

Dammit.

"Hey Mom," Antonia said putting her on speaker. "I'm in the car."

"Your sister shared some information with me," Diane said. She imagined her mother's mouth set like Octavia's, the quiet judgmental pursing of the lips.

"I'm sure she did," Antonia replied. "That's all you guys seem to do these days."

"I'm just calling to tell you not to take that fool back."

She kept her eyes on the road. "You don't have to worry about that, Mom. I gave Derek a good cussing out already."

"Good. I know I raised you with some self-respect." Even though she couldn't help but jab at her daughter, Diane did sound relieved. *Perhaps even proud?* "And I don't want you to come back until you've found what you were looking for."

Antonia didn't know what to say to that. Her mother didn't get sentimental with her daughters. Ever. It was foreign to her ears. "What are you talking about, Mom?"

"I'm just saying." Diane paused. "Don't always settle for what's easier. I didn't work as hard as I did for you girls to settle for any old thing."

It only took thousands of miles of distance for her

mother to have a moment with her. She smiled to herself as she drove. "I won't."

"Your sister shared something else."

Antonia's smile dropped as she decreased her speed. "Oh yeah?"

"She said that you were back to writing. If I remember correctly, it's been awhile."

She breathed a sigh of relief, thankful that her sister was thoughtful enough to keep information about Aiden to herself. "It has, Mom. I'm writing a novel." Saying the words aloud to her biggest critic was a relief. "I'm…a writer," she added.

"I know you're a writer," Diane said with a smart tone. "I just wondered when you'd get back to it. I only wanted to say I'm glad to hear it."

She swallowed the lump in her throat before replying, "Thank you."

"Okay," Diane was already running out of things to say. "Charlie and I are about to sit down to some coffee, I'll get at you later."

"Of course, Mom."

"We're proud of you for doing the right thing, baby."

Antonia drew a shaky breath. She didn't want to start crying while she was on the phone with her mother. "Thanks, Mama. I love you," she said with a sniff. "I'll talk to you later?"

"Yep, stay safe, baby."

She waited until she'd hung up before she started crying. Only Diane Harper, in her own strange confusing way, could say the right thing when she needed it the most. Antonia wiped her eyes with the back of her hand and breathed in deeply. Today, Antonia would not settle.

Chapter Thirty-Three

"Do your parents know you have a Facebook account?" Aiden asked as he hovered over Soircha and her laptop.

"Everyone has Facebook."

"I don't have one," he replied in a dry tone. "Or a Twitter."

Soircha laughed openly as she typed. "That's because you're old."

Aiden straightened up and looked at his niece. She had certainly become feistier since he last saw her. "Mother, could you tell this child that thirty-eight is not old?"

"Well, even I have a Facebook account, dear," Clare called from the kitchen.

"That hardly proves anything," he said. "Are you sure you can find her?"

"Already did," Soircha said after pointing and clicking. "Antonia 'Toni' Harper from Chicago."

Aiden leaned back over the computer. The profile picture was of her sitting in a city park. She wasn't looking at the camera lens, instead her gaze was directed behind the photographer. Her face was frozen in laughter, her brown eyes squinted against the sun. Her beautiful seemed so effortless, so easy and true.

"She so pretty," Soircha said, resting her chin against her fist. "I love her curly hair."

"I do too," he said. "Scroll through her stuff."

"This is it," she said. "I have to send her a friend request to look at any more."

"Go ahead then," he urged.

Soircha looked up, her tone teasing. "Are you sure?"

"Do as he says," Clare called from the kitchen.

Aiden watched her click a button and type a message. "What are you doing now?"

"Well, it looks weird that a kid is friending her," she said pointedly. "I'm sending her a message from you."

"Okay, tell her that I need to speak to her and give her my phone number." Aiden worried a hangnail on his thumb as he watched his niece play messenger. "Do you think this will work?"

When Soircha was finished she sat back in her chair. "There's no guarantee," she said with a serious face. "But it's worth a try. *Ádh mór.*"

Good luck indeed. "Thanks, love."

There were no guarantees, but it was better than nothing. All these years, he told himself that he was different from Liam, obsessing over the past in an effort not to repeat it. Yet, the obvious mistakes were under his nose the whole time. If he had sat still long enough to think about it, he'd done the same thing to Lisa. He hadn't physically left her, but his heart had drifted away without explanation. That was the only way a woman could have found a job in another country without him knowing. Aiden was in the wrong. Of course Antonia couldn't help but be torn between him and her job and home. She needed him to tell her that he loved her. She needed to know that he'd do anything in his power to make it work. Even though it felt impossible last night, he now had the push to try. Antonia Harper wasn't the kind of woman to be left and he could kick himself for doing just that.

"Don't worry," Clare said, emerging from the kitchen. She wiped her wet hands on a dish towel and flung it over her shoulder. "If it's meant to happen, she'll find you."

Aiden sat leaning against his couch. "What if she doesn't want to?"

"Well then you've learned the lesson you should have learned before you left to Tully Cross," she said with a raised brow. "You may not remember it, but I distinctly told you not to forget about Lisa, but to learn from her. I get tired of my advice fallin' on deaf ears."

Aiden sighed.

"But you don't need an 'I told you so,'" she said. "My boy probably needs a good hug. Come on, Soircha, give your uncle Aiden a hug."

He was enclosed by his mother and niece, as they stood in his living room. Aiden squeezed them against him and gazed over their heads, at the missing parts of his home. He was alone again and it was more painful than he could have ever imagined.

Chapter Thirty-Four

Here goes nothing.

Every grand adventure or humiliating disaster started with those words. Antonia steeled herself against the latter and boldly knocked on Aiden's front door. While she waited, she took another look at his house number, just to make certain she was at the right place. She also examined his small front yard. The grass was green and the space was bricked off from the neighbors on either side of him. Several small bushes of salmon-hued roses were planted near his front window. It was a cute enough little house that she could see herself living in. But one step at a time. She needed to talk to the man first.

The door opened just as she raised her hand to knock again.

A young girl peered up at her. *Soircha.* Her glasses were perched on the end of her small pert nose, her eyes widened at the sight of Antonia. "Whoa," she murmured. "It's you."

This wasn't what Antonia expected. "Hi, Soircha?"

The girl's freckled face broke into a grin. "You remember me?"

"Of course I do. How could I forget those beautiful curls?"

Soircha blushed deeply and attempted to hide behind the front door. "I don't like my hair," she said. "I keep asking my mom to straighten it, but she won't."

Antonia's heart was still pounding, hoping that Aiden was there, but she felt for the girl. She wore a T-shirt that said read: "Fungi the Dolphin" and jean shorts that were cut off at the knees. At twelve, she was already tall and gangly. "You have your whole life to play around with your hair," Antonia said. "Um, also, is your uncle Aiden home?"

"So you got my Facebook message?" The girl asked with excitement.

Antonia was confused. Facebook? She hadn't checked it in nearly a week since she broke up with Derek and started writing her novel. She didn't want the distractions that social media offered. "I don't—"

"Who's at the door, Soircha?" an older woman's voice called from beyond the vestibule.

Antonia cringed.

"It's Uncle Aiden's girlfriend, Nana," Soircha shouted.

"What?" Clare said a little too loudly. The older woman came swiftly to the front door with a worried expression. But when she saw Antonia her, she lit up. "Oh my goodness, it's Antonia."

Soircha rolled her eyes. "I know, Nana."

"Hi," Antonia said, giving a weak wave.

"Dear me, let her in for heaven's sake," Clare pulled open the door and rushed Antonia inside.

"I'm sorry for intruding like this," Antonia replied.

"Goodness no! It's no intrusion; this is a delightful

surprise," Aiden's mother took her by the shoulders, ushered her straight to the living room, and pushed her onto Aiden's gray sofa. "Can I make you some tea?"

"Um, that's not—"

"—Soircha, be a dear and fire up your uncle's kettle."

Antonia was overwhelmed. She was sitting in Aiden's quaint home; it was exactly the kind of place that she would love to live. His eclectic décor mirrored her apartment back home with its interesting wall art and mismatched furniture pieces.

"It's so lovely to meet you in person," Clare said, seating herself across from Antonia. A large round coffee table separated them. Aiden's mother was a very attractive woman. Her kelly green eyes sparkled as she looked Antonia over. A knowing smile spread over her face. "I can see why he's so depressed."

Antonia's mouth fell open. "I'm sorry?"

Clare let out a hearty chuckle. "You're involved with my most dramatic child, you know that? The row in the country must have been a banger because he came back in the foulest of moods."

Antonia bowed her head in embarrassment, her body slumped in despair. "Oh, I'm an idiot…"

"My dear, you're in love!" Clare said with glee.

She looked up. "What?"

"And he is too."

"Excuse me?"

Soircha appeared at her side with a plate of cookies. "My uncle is in love with you," she said in a serious voice. She pushed her glasses up the bridge of her nose and held out the plate. "Biscuit?"

Antonia shook her head. She was too scared to believe it. "How do you know?"

"He sounded insistent when he described it to us, right Soircha?" Clare asked.

Soircha nodded. "Oh yes, that's why I sent you a Facebook message. He wanted to find you. He wanted to see you before you caught your plane. Like the movies!"

"But…" Antonia trailed off in a daze. *He loves me?* What about all that nonsense he threw at her last night?

"You should tell us what happened," Soircha said, sitting beside her, starting on the cookies herself.

"The girl's right," Clare said with a nod. "We can't work our magic until we know the full story."

Antonia sat back against the couch, experiencing a gamut of perplexing emotions. As she stared at the coffee table, she tried her best to recount what happened in Tully Cross. "I told him about my job interview and how I had to leave soon," she said in a dull voice. "When he didn't respond the way I wanted him to, I threw his issues with his father in his face."

"Oh dear," Clare said, crossing her legs and leaning in closer. "Soircha, you better check on the tea."

"I didn't hear anything," the girl replied.

"Check on it."

"Fine." Soircha reluctantly pulled herself off the couch and slumped back into the kitchen.

She felt weird discussing Clare's estranged husband with her, but in an effort of fully disclosing all the drama, Antonia went ahead. "I understand that he's stressed out with the idea of his father back in his life. And then there's the stuff about his tenure review. I get it. I just wanted him to say…"

"That he loves you," Clare finished. She didn't appear to be upset about the news regarding Liam. "Even with all his degrees, the boy still can't manage three little words."

"At the very least, I needed him to tell me to stay," she said with a shrug. "Also, I want to say that I'm sorry that we're talking about your husband in this context."

Aiden's mother waved away her concern. "Oh dear me, if I worried about that man, I'd be in a constant state, wouldn't I? I've not worried for Liam Byrnes since he left in 1995. Now, what's this about your job?"

Antonia looked up to the ceiling. She swallowed hard and bit back the tears. "I told him that I might go back to the job that fired me. At one point, he told me that I should focus on the thing that made me happy; being a writer. Last night, he told me to go take the job."

"And what do you want?"

She shrugged helplessly. "My interview was today," she said. "And here I am, trying for a shot at love."

"Of course," Clare said. From where Antonia sat, she could tell the woman was trying to contain her excitement. "A woman's career is important, but you've already done publishing. You're probably meant to write a book, don't you think?"

"I'm not taking the job," Antonia said, finally bursting into tears. "I *do* want to write my book. I want to finish the damn thing and be happy with myself for once."

She heard the whistle of the teakettle and Soircha banging around the cabinets. "The tea is ready."

There was silence in the living room. The only sound was Antonia's quiet sniffling. It felt good to confess what was weighing heavy on her heart. Although she didn't know Aiden's mother from Adam, her calm presence made it easier to cry and talk. They waited for

Soircha to bring in the tea tray. Only then, did Antonia feel comfortable enough to take a cookie and eat through her tears. "Thank you both for listening to me. I feel so stupid."

"Oh no, dear," Clare said, getting up from her chair and coming around the coffee table. She edged Antonia and Soircha down the couch and sat down. "You mustn't feel like that."

Antonia sat between Aiden's mother and niece, crying and eating a soggy cookie. She still felt like a prize idiot. "What will I do?" she asked.

Soircha poured them all tea. "You should wear a fancy dress and go to him," she said excitedly. "That's how they do it in the movies."

Antonia and Clare both looked at Soircha, who pushed her glasses back up the bridge of her nose. "That's not a bad idea," the older woman mused. She picked up her cup of tea and stared at it thoughtfully. "That's not a bad idea at all."

"I don't even know where he is," Antonia said.

"He's getting ready for the conference," Soircha said, wrinkling her nose.

"That's right, he is," Clare said.

Antonia's breathing was unsteady. "I don't know if I can do that."

"You're already here in Galway," Clara said. "You don't know what you can do until you try. You have to have a little confidence, dear."

"Do you think he'll want to see me?"

"Definitely," they said in unison.

Antonia thought about it for a moment. It was a crazy plan, much like this whole trip. But she was finally free of the restraints from back home. Derek was firmly stuck in the past and her job now was to work on her novel. And to find love. "Can I tell you guys something?" she said to the both of them. She paused. "I think I might love Aiden."

They both clapped in delight. "That's what I said," Clare cried.

Soircha swooned from the excitement. "This *is* just like a movie!"

Sure, Antonia thought. *Just like the movies.*

Chapter Thirty-Five

"I trust you found what you needed in the country?" Robert asked, taking his seat next to Aiden. The large conference table they sat at was on a raised stage facing an audience that was still streaming in. Robert and Aiden were only half of the panel that was to present; they were waiting on Lisa and Donald Maguire from the philosophy department.

Aiden shuffled his papers before answering. "I may have, but I did a poor job of holding on to it." Robert may have been referring to his father, but Aiden had Antonia on his mind. He hadn't counted on missing her so intensely. For the last few days, he had grown used to opening his cottage door to find her. The hole in his heart came from a twelve-hour absence. "I finished the paper in a day like you said I would," he added.

Robert chuckled as he clapped Aiden on the back. "Of course you did. I finished my paper this morning."

"I'm winging my introduction though," Aiden said. "I was struck with inspiration during my Tully Cross visit."

"In the form of a woman?" Robert asked.

He nodded and looked down at his papers. Antonia was a large part of his inspiration. Talking to her about her own writing kicked him into gear and energized his scholarship. While he was able to plow through the main points of his paper, the introduction had evaded him until he made it to the university. On his drive over, Aiden thought about his father and asked himself why he wanted to be a professor. Why would he devote his time to this path if he couldn't give it his full attention and passion? The answer could no longer be: *I just don't want to end up like him.* Whether he was ready to reconcile with the fact or not, his parents were right. They could see what he'd been blind to all these years. Aiden Donagh Byrnes was his father's son *and* he was his own man. Antonia had been able to see it as well.

"Behind every great man…" Robert murmured as he opened his portfolio. He placed his papers and note cards neatly before him. "Speaking of women, I hope seeing Professor Brennan won't be too awkward?"

Lisa was the least of his worries. Aiden knew how to be cordial with another professional if it meant getting on with the day. He'd had plenty of practice. "Not at all."

"That's my boy." Robert stood, clapping him on the back. "I'm going to see about my projector slides." Aiden smiled as he watched the old man wander off in search of the graduate student who was running the panel. Robert was so old-school that he still didn't understand someone, possibly a graduate assistant, had already turned his presentation into a PowerPoint.

Out in the audience, the seats were steadily filling with scholars from all over the country. It was going to be a packed house tonight. The crowd didn't bother Aiden, he had presented and attended enough of these conferences to know how to work a crowd. Inevitably, there would be questions from scholars who only stood to talk about their own research. They would no doubt take away the focus from the speaker with droll observations and long explanations about how wrong he was. *No, Aiden. You're not going to be a nihilist about this.* It was still an honor to be accepted into the conference and he promised himself to attend the other panels after his.

"Dr. Byrnes," said a familiar female voice behind him.

Aiden turned in his seat. "Dr. Brennan."

She sat beside him, wearing her most professional black pantsuit. Her black bob was pinned to the side. "It appears that we'll have a good turnout today," she said in a light voice.

"Looks like it," he said. "Could you find parking alright?"

She chuckled. "Barely. Now that I don't work here anymore, parking privileges are a thing of the past. And the kids going to Spiddal are already getting bussed out."

"Yeah, my niece is heading out on Friday."

"Hell might be trying to navigate a sea of preteen girls to get to school," she said. "I felt like I was transported to grade school again and got triggered."

Aiden smiled. "There's been a lot of that going around."

Donald Maguire eventually showed up, greeted the panel, and commenced with setting up the podium microphone. He would be presenting a paper and chairing the panel. His presence meant that they were finally getting started. Aiden smoothed down his neck tie and straightened his blazer. He decided to take a formal approach to his conference attire, wearing the suit that he bought for last year's commencement ceremony. When

Lisa dragged him to the tailor to purchase it, she insisted on the European cut, which made him uncomfortable. He at least chose the color, a gun-metal gray that worked well with his eyes according to the saleswoman.

The auditorium was filled to capacity just as Donald cleared his throat. "I think it's time we got started," he said to the shuffling audience. People took their seats and chatter died down. "I'd like to introduce this panel of scholars who have set aside time to share their valuable research in cultural studies. These men and women will discuss the importance of Irish Literature and its role in the global community. I will contribute through the lens of philosophy, so I offer my apologies now."

The audience chuckled at Donald's self-deprecating humor. Robert came back to the stage and sat beside Aiden. "He tells that joke every year," he said in a low voice.

"I would like to start us off with Dr. Aiden Byrnes, our own senior lecturer from the English Department. His paper, 'Roll the Old Chariot Home: The Parallel History of African American and Irish Homecomings' will surely set the tone for this evening's education. Please help me welcome Dr. Aiden Byrnes to the podium."

Aiden stood as the audience clapped for him, and walked to the podium. As he settled his papers and adjusted the microphone for his height, he looked over the crowd that sat waiting. He imagined them as his students, only happier to be there. A smile came to his lips.

"My father," he started. "Was a Limerick man in search of a home. He was a restless sort who took to the water when the itch caught him. And when he did return to his family, it was only in fleeting appearances punctuated with his bombastic voice singing a tune that still sticks with me. 'Roll the Old Chariot' was not his song, but he adopted it in a way that folks have adopted narratives for centuries. Raise your hand if you've ever heard the song,"

Aiden waited and a few audience members raised their hands. He was surprised to find a good few of them did know the song. He continued. "Now this isn't part of my timed talk, but if you'll indulge me, I'd like to sing just a couple of lines from the song. Will you allow that? I promise that I'm a better singer than my father."

There was a collective laugh from the audience with a few people clapping their encouragement.

"Excellent, follow along with me if you're brave enough," Aiden said, clearing his throat. "Oh we'd be alright, if the wind were in our sails, we'd be alright if the wind were in our sails…" He was surprised yet again, when a few brave souls fell in sync with him. Their voices rising in trepidation and good humor. Aiden sang with a comical bravado that got people to laugh, but the majority of the audience was actually singing by the time he wrapped it up. The crowd applauded him and themselves for their participation. Scholars were a stuffy bunch, but Aiden had the ability to shake them loose from their solemn protocol. Perhaps this was the charm Robert talked about.

"Alright, alright," he said, holding his hands up. "I still have to get to my paper," he said with a smile. "That song was easy enough to follow because it's what's known as 'call and response.' You can find rhetorical device in many work songs but a great deal of its roots are found in the African American church and ultimately on the old plantations of the South. This song especially. What my father failed to recognize, as an Irishman, was that he wasn't the only one trying to get home or even find a home for his restless spirit. There was an entire people that he could relate to, a people who were forcibly wrenched from a homeland and aching to return. Today I want to talk to you about this call and response between the black experience and the Irish Experience. We'll focus on my observations on homecoming narratives."

Now that he had their attention with a stirring introduction, Aiden went through his paper at a steady speed, pausing at the right spots to interject an anecdote or joke. He had the crowd wrapped around his finger. When he finished, he realized that this moment was the most excited he'd ever been about his own work. His ideas and delivery had the power to entertain and educate people. At the podium, he created an intimacy with people that rivaled a man holding court in a local pub. Looking over his audience, he seemed to see them for the first time, not as a hurdle to cross, but as fellow intellects. Aiden belonged beside them.

That was when a flash of yellow caught his eye.

Aiden's mouth went dry and the pounding in his head drowned out the sound of applause. Antonia stood in the back of the auditorium wearing the yellow dress from Tully Cross. She looked just as beautiful today as she did on that day. A surge of excitement shot through his body, as he watched her tucked a curl behind her ear. The only thing missing was a soggy cake in her hands.

Aiden gripped the sides of the podium as he locked gazes with her. *She came to me.* He barely heard Donald approach the podium. It was time for a quick Q&A and for the first time, Aiden was nervous. *She came to me...*

"We're going to make time for a couple of quick questions for each speaker," Donald announced. "And after all the speakers have presented, we'll have a larger rolling dialogue."

Aiden nodded, still shaken by his lover's appearance. "Yes," he breathed. "If anyone has a question..." Dozens of hands went up, but Aiden kept his eyes trained on Antonia, who raised her hand with hesitance. "Right, you in the yellow?"

A grad student ran toward her with a microphone, when she took it she thanked him with a shaky voice. "Hello," she started. "I'm very interested in the link you've made between black and Irish work songs. Can you speak on the intersection of the two folklores and the music they've produced?"

Aiden leaned toward the microphone. "Could you give me an example of what you mean?"

Antonia paused where she stood and held the microphone close. "Well... I've only just learned about the Celtic folklore of the selkie and it reminds me of the Nina Simone song 'Sealion Woman.' I just wondered if there were any connections."

Aiden could have walked off stage and kissed her. "Yes, my selkie... I mean the selkie folklore," he said, quickly covering his misstep. "Uhh, for those of you who might not be familiar: The selkie is a seal maiden who becomes a woman and falls in love with a hapless fisherman, but her true home is the sea. If the fisherman can successfully hide the selkie's fur coat, she can stay with him forever. But it rarely works out.

"The Nina Simone song is an adaptation from a folk song from Mississippi," he continued. "While its origins are probably sea-related, the woman in question may not be a selkie… She's most likely a prostitute, who tricked sailors out of their money. We're still unclear on the actual title of the song. It could be See-lyin' Woman or Sea-line Woman, which would suggest a more sexual nature."

"Thank you," she replied. Her voice now on solid footing. "Perhaps I could ask you more about seafaring folklore after the talk."

Aiden cleared his throat as he stared at her. *Cheeky little…* "Yes," he said in a husky voice. "I can, uh, clarify that with you. Afterward. I mean, later. Sure." Before he could stumble over himself anymore, he stepped away from the podium. Aiden returned to his seat at the table without taking another question, prompting Donald to quickly introduce the next presenter. He glanced at Lisa, who raised a black brow in his direction. She looked from him to Antonia, who'd receded back against the doors, and back to him. Lisa Brennan actually smirked while she gathered her papers, causing Aiden to blush.

Antonia didn't stay for long. She exited the auditorium after her question, leaving Aiden to wonder why she came. What did it mean? And would she stay for just a little while longer to talk things out? While Donald introduced Lisa to the podium, he felt a buzz in his breast pocket. Aiden quietly slipped his phone out and laid it on the table. The text that lit his screen answered his questions.

I thought I'd try this again. That's if you want to talk.

Aiden exhaled. They never exchanged phone numbers, but she was texting him. He figured that he had his mother to thank for that. Glancing over at Lisa, who was starting her paper, he carefully typed his reply. Of course I do. I have a fight to continue.

He set his phone to silent and waited for her reply.

I was hoping you'd say that. Fight after your panel?

Please meet me at the banquet for drinks. Thank you for wearing yellow xxx.

I will. Now put away your phone. You don't want to look like a student.

Aiden did as he was told, slipping the phone back into his jacket. He fought to keep a smile from his face as his ex-girlfriend presented on Bram Stoker. His lover was nearby, waiting for him.

Chapter Thirty-Six

Antonia held a long-stemmed champagne glass tightly as she spoke to the kindly old gentleman whom she recognized from Aiden's panel. He introduced himself as Robert and refused to leave her side as she waited for Aiden.

"You made a very apt observation about Dr. Byrnes's work. Tell me, do you teach in the States?"

She blushed and shook her head. "Oh no, I'm afraid I haven't taught since grad school," she replied. "I'm actually in publishing."

Robert's owlish brows raised. "Publishing? How wonderful. How long?"

Antonia managed a smile. "About five years," she said. "But I'm currently transitioning to the other side of the desk. I'm working on a novel of my own."

"Impressive," he said with a nod.

She tried to keep up her conversation with him while seeking out Aiden. She wondered where he was and if he was serious about meeting with her. Showing up in a lemon-colored summer dress to apologize to a man was not exactly her style, but his mother and niece seemed dead-set on the theatrics. As a result, Antonia stuck out like a sore thumb amongst all these academics. People stared at her as they drifted by, making her feel even more self-conscious.

"Well, I thought it was time to try something new," she said, trying to sound engaged. She was actually grateful that the elderly man stopped to chat. It was definitely better than standing around by herself.

"I can understand that," he said. "I'm in my eighties and wondering what retirement will look like."

"I wouldn't look at it that way," Antonia said, taking a sip. "I think we're all capable of exciting change at any time."

"I hope so," said a deep voice from behind her.

Robert looked over her shoulder. "Aiden, come and meet this enchanting woman. My dear, tell me your name again."

A warm glow flowed through her body and she was certain that it wasn't the champagne. "Antonia," she said, turning to face Aiden. He stood over her flashing a beautiful smile. It had only been less than a day since they last saw one another, but his expression was that of a starved man.

"Yes, Antonia Harper. She's a publisher," Robert said. "She's come all the way from America for this conference."

Antonia kept up the act, holding her hand out for him to shake. "Dr. Byrnes," she breathed.

Aiden took her hand and brought it to his lips. She shivered as his kiss brushed the back of her fingers. "I've had the pleasure of bumping into Ms. Harper more than once."

"You know, Aiden," Robert continued. "With Professor Brennan gone, we still have a vacant position in our department. I'm currently talking to Doyle about setting up a publishing track for our students. What do you think?"

Aiden didn't take his eyes off her. His hands still gripped hers, sending a wave of heat throughout her body. "I think it would be a perfect addition to the English major."

Antonia swallowed as she pulled her hand back. "It could give your English students more options on the job market," she said, trying to direct her attention back to Robert.

The old man nodded. "My thoughts exactly! Our Vice-Chancellor is just as interested in increasing enrollment as I am in expanding the department."

"You know, Robert, if you're thinking of offering Ms. Harper a job, you'd better be quick about it." Aiden's voice was low and silky. "She's very close to accepting a position as a head editor with another publisher."

Antonia's gaze flew to his. *What is he saying?*

The old man looked alarmed. "Is that true?" he asked.

"Uh…it's possible," she said, searching Aiden's twinkling green eyes. "I haven't quite decided. My book has taken up a lot of my time these days."

"Oh my," Robert said, patting his jacket. "If I may, let me put my bid in right now." He retrieved a business card from one of his pockets and held it out to her.

Antonia's mouth fell open in shock. She looked from the card, to Robert, to Aiden. "Are you sure?"

"We'll have to do the traditional job search, of course. But I'd love to have someone from the industry at the top of the pile. If you have a current CV, please consider sending it."

Antonia took his card and smiled. "I'll definitely consider it."

"You should," Aiden insisted. "It will give you a chance to attend more of these functions. Academics in Ireland know how to throw a party."

Robert chuckled. "They certainly do," he said, quickly swiping another glass of champagne from a passing waiter. "Doyle has hired a string quartet for a simple conference banquet. You don't see that sort of thing often."

As if on cue, the musicians started. Antonia was still in disbelief, holding Robert's card in her hands. Had she managed to land a job position while avoiding another? She quickly tucked the card into her purse with trembling hands. "That would be lovely," she murmured.

"I hate to steal Antonia away, Robert," Aiden said, placing a hand on the small of her back. "But I was hoping to continue our conversation on the dance floor."

"I'm not a good dancer," she said, looking at the open area where couples were already gathered.

"I might be good enough for the both of us," he said.

"You two go on," Robert said. "They've laid out more salmon at the buffet. I've got to get there before Maguire." He left them before Antonia could protest any further.

She looked up at him. "What have you done?"

"I've created another excuse to hold on to your coat," he said, taking her hand.

Antonia was in a daze as she let him lead her to the dance floor. He took her empty glass and set it on a nearby table before resting her hand on his shoulder. He held her other hand aloft and moved slowly against her. "This could end badly for the both of us," she whispered, keeping her eyes on their feet. "I'm wearing high heels this time."

"I'm sorry, Antonia," he said.

She looked up. "What?"

"I want you to be happy...but I'd rather it be with me," he said solemnly. "I'm so sorry I didn't say that when it mattered."

A hot tear spilled down her cheek as she stared up at him. His eyes were earnest and warm with regret. She didn't know what to say so she went back to watching their feet. She was amazed that she hadn't managed to step on his toes yet. Her mind wasn't on their movements, but on how she was going to say her piece without crying.

"Antonia," he softly urged her to speak. "Please let me fight for you still. If you want me, I'll do whatever it takes. Only a coward would let a woman like you leave him without a fight. I don't want to be that man."

She let out an exasperated laugh. "You're right," she said. "Only a coward doesn't reach out and take what they want. I don't want to be that woman either." Antonia looked up, tears brimming her eyes. "I love you, but I can't tolerate being with someone who can't express themselves. If you're hurting, you have to let people in. And dammit, you have to listen to them."

Aiden froze. "Did you say you love me?"

She gave him a tremulous smile. "I did and I do."

He stopped in his tracks, still holding her hand aloft. "I love you too, Antonia."

"Then it's settled," she said, wiping her eyes with the back of her hand. "Now we just figure out how the next step goes." She promptly stepped on his foot and stumbled into his chest.

He pulled her closer and tried to contain his laughter. "Would you allow me to give you dance lessons, darling? I'd like our future to include dancing."

Antonia's heart sang in delight. Even though she was incredibly clumsy on her feet, she felt buoyant in his arms. "Can you say it again?"

He wrapped her arms around his shoulders and held her by the waist. "I will say it every day for the rest of my life," Aiden whispered in her ear. "I love you, Antonia. My selkie from Chicago."

"In America."

He grinned down at her. "I want to get out of here."

She looked around at the crowded banquet hall. "Don't you have to stay?"

"My obligation ended as soon as I presented that paper. A paper I couldn't have finished without your help, by the way. You complement me, Antonia."

"You want to leave now?"

"I want to love you somewhere private," he whispered before stepping away to lead her off the dance floor. Her face grew flush as she followed him toward the exit. She gripped his hand tightly. *Where is he taking me?* Her mind was a flurry of excitement as they wove through the crowd. Before she knew it they were outside in the crisp cool air of a quiet garden. The sound of crickets and distant Galway traffic was their only company as they wandered through the tall rose bushes.

Aiden found a stone bench that was out of view from the conference attendees. He sat down and pulled her onto his lap. A shiver ran through her body as he wrapped his arms around her waist. "This is lovely," she said as she bathed in the floral scent of their surroundings. "You have a beautiful university."

Aiden took her by the face and held her gently. "It pales in comparison to you."

The touch of his hand was almost unbearable in its tenderness. She relaxed, sinking into his embrace. She wanted the warmth of his arms, fearful that she'd almost lost him for good. She tilted her head back, eagerly waiting to receive his kiss. Reclaiming her lips, he crushed her to him in a kiss that reminded her of their past intimacy. Antonia relived the velvet warmth of his tongue as it coaxed its way past her parted lips. When he released her, her head swam with a heady desire that only increased under his piercing gaze.

"My love," he whispered. "You came back to me."

"I had to be the brave one," she said with a shaky laugh. "I hope that's not going to be a habit."

Aiden ran his fingers up and down her arm and planted a soft kiss on her shoulder. "The next time we part, it'll be so you can bring your things from Chicago to my home. I want you to clack away on several books, pausing only to make love to me." He looked up with smiling eyes. "Hell, we can go all over Europe for your writing."

"You'll massage my tired fingers," she teased.

"I swear to Jaysus and all his carpenter friends, I will massage more than your tired fingers."

She almost believed she was dreaming; that this man's hand wasn't cradling her face. But that wasn't true in the least. This man wasn't some character she had dreamt up for her novel. He was as real as the salt air that blew in from the Atlantic. He was real and he belonged to her.

What would Augusta do?

Antonia reached up with a tentative hand, making

contact with the stubble along his strong jaw. The heat of his skin felt real enough. She'd have to return his kiss to make certain. *That's what Augusta would probably do.*

Epilogue

"Professor Harper, how long would you like our cover letter?"

Antonia pursed her lips before answering her star pupil, Abby. The girl had barely let her pass out the assignment prompt before assaulting her with a series of questions. She liked the young woman's fervor, but wondered if this was going to be a trend for the rest of the semester. "Well, your query letter should not be more than a page," she announced to the entire class. "Any more and your editor will chuck the whole thing."

She watched in amazement as the students took notes while she spoke. She wondered if that would be a lasting trend as well. "We've only got a few more minutes before I let you go, so I want you to look over the parameters of this assignment before you ask any more questions."

Antonia waited for them to read the handout. This was almost surreal. It was her first semester in front of the classroom since she was in her twenties. The only difference between this experience and graduate school was that she now had a published book under her belt.

True to his word, Eddie had pushed her manuscript,

The Bangkok Assignment, to the front of the line. She finally let him read the finished product when he settled into his new position at Holloway Press, a more prestigious post than Wild Hare. After her decision to turn down Sixpence, Eddie took a gamble and shot for something more ambitious. Although she was finished with the industry, she was forever grateful for her friend's confidence in her ability. Making the edits himself, he had made her complete two rewrites, before giving her the green light.

Abby's hand shot up again. "Professor Harper."

Antonia trained her smile at the girl. "Yes, Abby."

"If we already have a book project in mind, could we pretend to market that one?" The young woman's question was so earnest, it made Antonia smile.

"Of course you can. This will make for a great experiment when you're ready to shop a book."

"Cool."

"Does anyone else have questions?"

Students shook their heads and started packing up. She had to remember she didn't necessarily dismiss them. Apparently students had an internal clock for when a class was dying down.

"Great, when we meet again, we're going to look at real cover letter examples," Antonia said loudly over the shuffle of papers.

As they filtered out of the room, some running to their next class, Antonia exhaled and sat down at her desk. As she sank into her chair, she rested her head against the old wooden surface. She had an actual first day under her belt.

"Has the herd finished stampeding?" asked a masculine voice from the doorway.

Antonia's head shot up. Aiden leaned against the doorframe with his hands in his pockets. The late afternoon sun shone on the planes of his face, brightening his green eyes. He wore a pleasant smile as he gazed at her. "Hey."

"How was your first day, my love?"

"Have you ever had a student named Abby Connors?"

Aiden gave a throaty laugh. "Oh Jaysus, you're in for a hell of a semester." He entered the room and sat in one of the student chairs. "She's a brilliant student; just a little…intense."

"Overall, I think it went really well," she said. "I can't wait to get home, though."

"Ah yes, but before we go home, we have to talk." He looked a little silly sitting in the small desk, but he wore a serious expression on his face. "I have to ask you something."

Antonia frowned in confusion. After living with him for a year, he still had tricks up his sleeve. Moving her life to Ireland had its challenges, but living with him was easier than she thought it would be. She fit into his life without losing herself. She enjoyed waking up next to him and having breakfast together, before taking off by herself to walk along the banks of the River Corrib. Her quiet time was usually spent near the Spanish Arch, people watching and writing notes for her next novel. With Aiden, she finally had the freedom to create and the love she needed. She already felt like she was the luckiest woman in the world.

That was until he reached into his pocket.

"Aiden," she breathed.

"Just so you know, my mother is on her way from Limerick. She's already angry that I'm doing this without an audience."

Antonia rigidly held her tears in check as she watched him pull out a small box. He stood up from his seat and walked to the front of her desk. "Oh my god…" Her voice sounded distant to her own ears.

He opened the box, displaying a gold Claddagh ring with a diamond set between two hands. "Professor Harper," he started in a calm voice. "Will you roll the old chariot with me?"

Antonia froze, then a cry of relief broke from her lips. "Yes," she whispered.

Her reaction seemed to amuse him. Aiden's smile turned into a chuckle as he took the ring from the box. "Will you continue to inspire me?"

She lifted her hand to meet him. As he slipped the ring on her finger, he leaned down to kiss the back of her hand. "Yes," she said through shallow breaths.

"And will you plan another wedding?"

Antonia threw her head back and laughed in sheer joy. "Sure."

She had no problem trying it again. The life that she wanted to live was with Aiden. Writing, laughing, and loving with Aiden Byrnes.

* * * * *

Reviews are an invaluable tool when it comes to spreading the word about great reads. Please consider leaving an honest review for this or any of Carina Press's other titles that you've read on your favorite retailer or review site.

To purchase and read more books by Charish Reid please visit Charish's website at:
https://charishreid.com/

Acknowledgements

To my husband, Noah. All you've given me, for the last ten years, is unconditional love. Thank you for rolling the old chariot along with me. To my writing-buddy, Sandra, our time on the red couch wasn't just about writing books. The book writing was a result of a friendship. I reckon we'll have plenty more books to write in the future.

Thank you to the friends who knew I was a writer well before I had the courage to admit it aloud. Melissa, Evan, Drew, Ricia, Lily, Angela and Courtney, your confidence in my ability has made more of an impact than you'll ever know.

To my aunt Carolyn and sister Ronnie: You have taught me that black girls *do* get their "Happily-Ever-Afters"... We just have to forge the path ourselves and walk with purpose.

Thank you to my editors, Kate and Stephanie, of Carina Press. You took a chance on an idea and helped me mold Antonia and Aiden into people I'd want to know. To my agent, Saritza Hernandez, thank you for representing me and my ideas. You took a chance as well.

To the beautiful nation of Ireland and the village of Tully Cross: Thank you for the craic. This is my love letter to you.

About the Author

Charish Reid currently lives in Sweden with her professor husband, who enjoys walking and biking way more than she does. While he walks and bikes, she writes contemporary romance featuring sexy academics, who are trying to find love and adventure from under stacks of student papers. While she was born in Little Rock, Arkansas, she has lived all over the United States observing people and taking notes for poetry, essays, and novels.

After earning her Masters in Literature, she went on to teach English and Rhetoric at several universities before penning her first book. Cashiering at a major discount retailer, being a menswear salesperson, and bartending were fairly easy compared to class prep, performing for students, and grading. When she's not writing or teaching, Charish enjoys watching movies and talking to folks in other countries. Travels to Thailand, Latvia, Estonia, Finland, Ireland and Sweden will probably find their way into future books.

You can catch up with Charish here:
Website: https://charishreid.com/
Twitter: https://twitter.com/AuthorCharish
Facebook: https://www.facebook.com/CharishReidAuthor/

Chapter One

Even as her face burned with embarrassment, Victoria managed to read the email twice before staring out the window of her office. Three p.m. on Pembroke's campus was cloudy with a stiff wind blowing the scarves and jackets of students who hurried to their next class. The middle of October was colder than folks had anticipated, since Illinois had experienced a scorching summer. But the town of Farmingdale was dealing with a cold snap that forced Pembroke University students to change out their flip-flops for UGG boots. The chill that burrowed its way into Victoria's meager office was replaced with a furnace in her chest. She glanced back at the email and read it once more. Her eyes settled on the book title and narrowed.

For the Duke's Convenience.

"I returned that," she whispered to her computer screen. As she calculated the length of time it had been since her last visit to the Farmingdale library, she clicked on their website. Her account was flagged with a fine. Victoria's eyes went round. $27.10. "Jesus, effin' Christ."

Perspiration pricked her scalp and under her arms while she searched for answers. The account information didn't tell her much, but the amount was alarming enough. She clicked back to John Donovan's email and tried to read his tone. Joking, laid-back, and late. He would be tardy to their first meeting, which was just as annoying as the overdue book comment. Her time was precious and getting more scarce by the day. After their meeting, she would have to gather the graduate students for an emergency meeting regarding the writing center. Later that evening, she'd have to start on the first wave of grading. She'd made the mistake of assigning papers to two classes only two days apart. On top of all that, she'd stolen a library book.

Victoria needed some air.

She gathered herself and shook out her arms in a desperate attempt to cool her armpits. A dull headache joined the itchy sensation of her too-tight braids. She resisted the urge to scratch, since she'd only gotten them done yesterday and still wanted them to have that fresh look. Oh, but she could have used an ibuprofen. Victoria swung her glossy black braids, some decorated with cowrie shells and gold cuffs, behind her shoulder and smoothed down her skirt before leaving her office.

In the hallway, she glanced at the open doors and spotted Paula's office. Paula Michaels was an adjunct who shared workspace with two other part-time lecturers. When she wasn't lesson-planning, the rest of her time was spent writing romance novels that made women flush and swoon. She admired her friend's passion to create and grade papers at the same time. She peeked in Paula's workstation and saw her friend with her feet on her desk, balancing a pencil between her lip and nose.

"Workin' hard or hardly workin'," Victoria asked, wiggling her eyebrows.

Paula glanced up, letting the pencil fall from her face. "A bit of both," she said with a grin.

Paula was alone with a small measure of privacy, so Victoria invited herself in and sat at her desk. "What are you working hard on and what are you slacking on?"

Her friend put her sneakered feet on the floor and straightened up in her chair. After she stuck the pencil in her short afro, she swung her computer monitor around to face Victoria. "Read that," she said, pointing a bubblegum-pink fingernail at the screen.

Victoria squinted and leaned forward. "Billy yanked her panties down her thighs…"

"To yourself," Paula said.

"Is this your new book?"

"Mm-hmm."

Victoria skimmed the page before resting her chin on her knuckles. "Mmh."

"Is that a good 'mmh' or a bad 'mmh'?"

"Do you have to say the p-word so much?"

Paula let out an exaggerated sigh and rolled her eyes. "My readers love the p-word. What else am I going to call it?"

Victoria shrugged her shoulders, her hair ornaments clattering. "I don't know," she said. "The books I read have more subtle words like mound and womanhood."

"Too much hedging. A lot of women like to get straight to the point, girl. If I labored over the millions of different ways to say pussy, I wouldn't have time to write what Billy does to it." She pointed to the second page, forcing Victoria to continue reading.

Victoria raised a brow as her face burned. "Jeez, Paula. Do guys even do that?"

Paula raised her own brow in response. "Ooh, baby, what is you doing?"

"Not that," she said nodding to the screen. Although, Victoria did have to do some mental calculation to remember the last time any man had shared her bed. Thirty-three and now thirty-four were particularly dry years since her break up with Kevin. Not that he did anything mind-blowing when they did share a bed. Lights off, missionary, and quick was Kevin's style. His brand of lovemaking wasn't even long enough for her to think of a theme for the next day's lecture.

"Well we need to fix that," Paula said, turning the monitor back. "Any prospects?"

"You sound like my mom."

"Don't tell me that," her friend said with a barking laugh. "Your mom is a piece of work and I don't want to be associated with her."

Victoria debated whether to tell Paula about the strange email she received from John Donovan. Since Paula signed on for the fall semester, it felt easier to face

the stressful culture of Pembroke University. Victoria
didn't have very many people to talk to in the English
department even though she'd worked there for four
years herself. But because of the exclusive air of the
private institution, a fear of judgement made it difficult
to share one's ideas or problems with equally competi-
tive professors. But this was Paula, her former graduate school buddy and the third member of The Write
Bitches Gang. If there was anyone on Pembroke's campus she could trust it was her girl. "Can I talk to you
about administration?" Victoria asked, casting a nervous glance over shoulder.

Paula typed something before pressing backspace
several times. "Girl, yes. Who's being messy today?"

"Did you get a chance to go to that all-campus meeting last Thursday?"

"Adjuncts don't have to go," her friend said with a
smile.

Victoria nodded. "Right. So the new president cor-
ralled us in an auditorium like Stalin would and told us
that the university is basically broke."

Paula looked up from her work. "What?"

"The last president had been playing the stocks with
university money and they lost big," Victoria said in a
low voice.

"Did they tell you this?" Paula asked. She folded her
arms over her ample bosom, obscuring the Free Angela
graphic on her T-shirt with her brown arms.

"They didn't have to," Victoria said with a sigh. "We
all knew they had a ton of investments. But that's not
quite the problem. President Kowalski wants faculty
and staff to make up the enrollment numbers. I mean,
they're already increasing tuition for next year, but we

need to put our heads down and push for higher numbers."

Paula frowned. "How?"

"Well, I'll say this about the president, she's business savvy—"

"Is she?"

"—she's starting a new open door policy that might work," Victoria finished.

Her friend remained unimpressed. "Open-door policies are bullshit."

"Be that as it may, the Three-Week Initiative might work. Kowalski is giving us three weeks to come up with innovative programs to attract incoming freshmen. They have to be low-cost of course, but also something that generates excitement."

Paula fixed her mouth and sighed. "What have you come up with, Vicki?"

Victoria grew excited. "Okay, so I'm thinking of a library internship for the English department students. We'll partner with the Farmingdale Public Library to give students a real-world learning experience that can carry over to graduate school or outside of academia. What do you think?"

There was a pregnant pause that made her tense. Victoria needed to know that someone liked her idea before she busted down President Kowalski's door. When Paula finally spoke, she gave a pitying smile. "Girl, I think that's a great idea. A library internship is going to help students get a leg up in any discipline they choose."

Eyeing her smile, Victoria leaned forward. "But?"

Paula's shoulders slumped. "But I worry that you think you always have to save someone. It's like graduate school all over again. Reggi and I had to talk you off a ledge every time you piled too much on your plate. The president's problems aren't your problems and you don't have to work yourself into a lather over mismanaged funds."

Victoria frowned. "I'm not working myself into a lather."

"You don't see it until your elaborate plans are near the end. Afterward, you tell us that you'll never work that hard on bullshit projects. This is not your problem."

She shook her head. "That's where you're wrong, Paula. Pembroke's problems *are* my problems. I chose this path because I wanted to teach and research. If my school goes under, how am I supposed to do either?"

"I get it, girl. I have the luxury of not needing this job, so I take it for granted. But you're going to work yourself into an early grave if you keep this up. Being the mule that Zora wrote about is not sustainable."

Victoria swallowed. Whenever Paula made literary references during debates, she meant business. Throwing Zora Neale Hurston into the conversation made her both irritated and hesitant to defend her school. Sure, Victoria liked pulling her weight, sometimes even a couple extra pounds, if it meant tasks got done and boxes got checked. But if history was any indication of how this project would turn out, she might want to pace herself. "I hear you loud and clear," she said. "But I'm going to try my best anyway."

Paula reached out and took her hand. "And that's what I love about you," she said in a softer tone. "Your work ethic is something I'd like to bottle up and take twice daily. But I just wish you'd rest."

Victoria squeezed her friend's hand. "I'll rest when I reach my goals," she said with a chuckle.

"Bitch, please."

Victoria pulled away. "We'll see if any of this actually gets off the ground. Today, I'm supposed to have a meeting with a librarian and he's already going to be late. I don't know how that can bode well."

"Aww, he's probably an elderly dude who's just trying to make his way across town," her friend said with a grin.

Victoria didn't get the sense that John Donovan was a doddering old man. The tone of his email suggested that he might be closer to her age. Originally, she addressed her email to the library's aging director, Howard Wegman. She was surprised that it was Donovan who replied to her. He was terribly informal and familiar with his message, making her nervous. *What if he doesn't take the project seriously? What if he is incompetent?* "He also informed me of an overdue library book," she said.

"Stealing books, are we?"

"No, I definitely returned it," Victoria said absently. She wondered what she had been doing several months ago that would warrant a missing book. "I just find it weird that he would put that in an email regarding our meeting today."

"Did he sound mad?"

"No," Victoria said slowly. "He wrote it with a wink face emoji."

"Hmm."

"Is that a good 'hmm' or a bad 'hmm'?" Victoria asked.

Paula shrugged. "Depends on what the book was."

She sighed and averted her gaze. "*For the Duke's Convenience.*"

Paula burst into laughter. "Goddamn, Vicki…"

"I definitely returned it."

Her laughter had not yet abated as she wiped tears from her eyes. "Oh my god… You are still reading that shit? That's why the p-word is foreign to your virgin ears!"

"It's titillating without the vulgarity."

Paula doubled over. "Oh man, I needed that," she said, taking a breath. "It feels so good to laugh."

"You're welcome," she said in a dry voice.

"Girl, you were always averse to 'vulgarity,' as you like to call it. I'd hate to think that the prim, rule-abiding girl inside you doesn't want to get her back broke with some great dick. Also, did it ever occur to you that John Donovan might be flirting with you?"

Victoria frowned. The idea had *not* occurred to her. "That's not professional at all."

"People get by all the time without being professional. How do you think I got here?"

Victoria sat back in her chair. Comparatively, the two friends had always stood on opposite sides of what one would deem "professional." Paula and her cute afro, jeans, and sneakers attracted others with her charm and humor. Things seemed to come easily to the one member of The Write Bitches who always remained herself. Even through grad school. Regina and Victoria stayed in line, choosing fields that required giving up a piece of their personality. Reggi had gone for a career in banking, even though she was an editor for the university newspaper, while Victoria was aiming to make it in academia. Her four years at Pembroke had been devoted to making tenure and she was determined to fight tooth and nail for it. "I'm not here for that, Paula," she said. "I plan to stay the course. I've got an outline and everything."

Paula gave her a knowing smile. "She's got an outline and everything… Baby, it might be time to let your hair down."

"My hair is fine right where it is."

"True," Paula said, narrowing her eyes. "Did Reggi do those braids? Because they look hella cute."

Victoria rolled her eyes. Her head was still aching. "Forty dollars and you have to bring the bundles."

"Okay, that's what's up."

She smiled. No matter how she disagreed with her friends, they could always switch it up and make light of most situations. "I'm going to wait for Donovan in my office. I'll talk to you later?"

"Sure," Paula said, returning to her screen. "Let me know if I need to bail you out of book jail."

Don't miss
the next book from Charish Reid,
available wherever
Carina Press ebooks are sold.
www.CarinaPress.com